AWAKENING OF SHADOWS

RJD Ferguson

ISBN: 978-0-9997910-4-2

Published in 2026

Printed in the United States of America

To my siblings—
Even with miles between us, we've stayed close.
I'm not always the one who shows up, but you've never loved me any less.
I'm blessed to have been given such a loving—and wonderfully insane—group of people.
This book is for you.

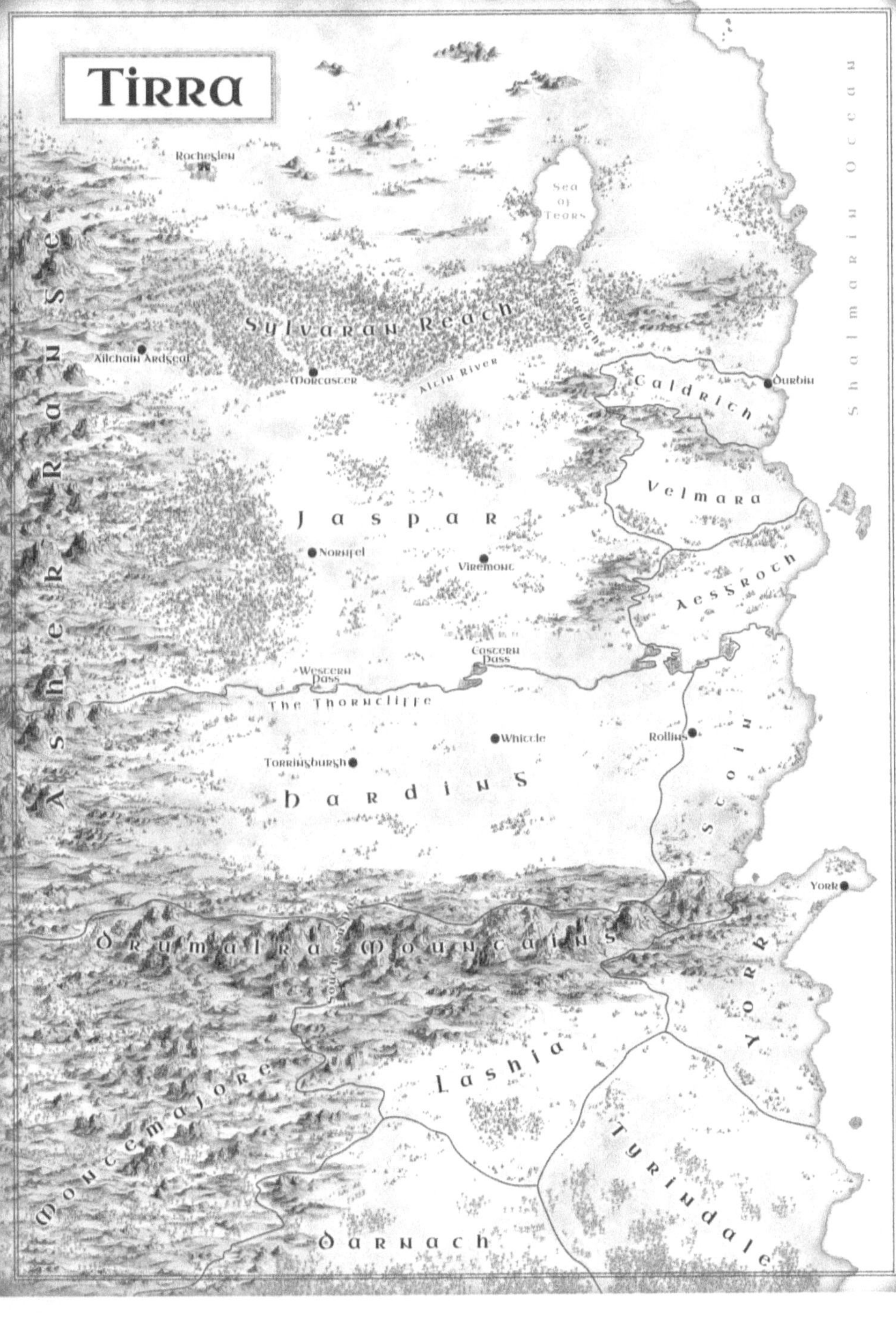

Tirra
Rochesley
Sea of Tears
Sylvaran Reach
Ailchain Ardscal
Morcaster
Ailin River
Caldrich
Durbin
Velmara
Jaspar
Nornfel
Viremont
Aes Sroch
Eastern Pass
Western Pass
The Thorncliffe
Whittle
Rollins
Scoin
Torringburgh
Hardins
Drumalra Mountains
York
York
Moncemajore
Lashia
Turindale
Darnach
Ashen Range
Shalmarin Ocean

Contents

TYR

Tyr blinked as he emerged from below decks, the thick, tangy scent of the harbor assaulting his senses. Most days, he worked below—at the forge, doing joinery, or mending sails—but he often came topside in the waning hours. He liked the fresh, salty air of the open sea.

The harbor was a different matter.

It was a cacophony of odors—some pleasant, like meats grilling on open fires; others less so, like the rank stench of sewage. Still, he smiled. *Who am I kidding? I love it—smells and all. There's nothing like the feel of solid earth beneath my feet.*

He shrugged his broad shoulders and adjusted his pack, gauging its weight. Space aboard a merchant vessel was tight, and he'd been forced to leave all but the essentials back in Morcaster. He nodded, mentally ticking off the items inside. *That should be all of it.*

He scanned the deck. The crew was busy: topsmen furling sails, deckhands securing lines and mopping planks, others rigging cargo to be swung ashore. Near the rail, the quartermaster argued with someone out of sight. Too busy for goodbyes—arrival always brought chaos.

Normally, he'd be in the thick of it.

Not this time.

This was his last stop.

A pang of sadness struck him. He'd traveled with the *Majonolle* crew for just over two months. *Feels like a lifetime ago,* he thought, remembering Morcaster.

His hand drifted to the coin pouch at his side—his wages, plus a little extra gifted by the captain. *It's not much, but if I'm careful, it should last until I find a smithy willing to take me on.*

The ship swayed gently beneath him. He barely noticed. With a final glance around the deck, he made his way down the gangplank toward the city.

He stepped onto the dock and moved easily through the bustling crew. He wasn't tall—barely five and a half feet—but his build compensated. Stocky and powerful, he carried himself with quiet confidence. Even the roughest dockhands gave him space. Though, to be fair, Tyr did his best not to be in anyone's way.

Once clear of the chaos, he found a quiet spot and took in the view.

The docks were familiar—grimy, crowded—but older than most he'd seen. His gaze drifted to the tall stone walls separating harbor from city. He knelt, running a calloused hand over the cobbled street.

These are old… expertly laid. This place must've been something when it was first built.

He stood and inhaled deeply. Bread. Grilled meat. Seaweed. Tar. Grease. The distant reek of a slaughterhouse. Beneath the familiar scents were others—rich, foreign spices and the acrid bite of some unfamiliar industry.

The moment passed.

With his eyes closed, he still felt the ship's gentle rocking. He staggered slightly, then chuckled as he found his balance.

He turned his back on the ship that had carried him—out from Morcaster, down the Altin River, along the coast, through inlets and ports—until they reached their destination: York.

The journey had been slow, with many stops, but he didn't mind. Work aboard the *Majonolle* had earned him food, lodging, and the chance to hone his craft. He wasn't a master—couldn't be paid—but the captain valued his skill. That had been enough.

Now the *Majonolle* was behind him. York lay ahead.

Even the docks were alive. Compared to Morcaster, York was a giant—louder, dirtier, more crowded… but somehow more vital.

He grinned, watching the chaos: errand boys dodging wagons, vendors shouting over one another, urchins, beggars, and whores loitering nearby. The smell of spiced meat and fresh fish filled the air. His stomach growled. Weeks of dried beans and hard tack had dulled his appetite, but now it returned with a vengeance.

A hard slap on the back and a familiar laugh broke his thoughts.

"Tyr! Where you be going in such a rush? Not trying to give your shipmates the slip, I hope?"

It was Tunny—one of the topsmen. About Tyr's height, but lean and always in motion, the man never lacked for words.

Tyr grinned as other crewmates disembarked behind him, laughing. "Couldn't slip away if I tried," he said, clapping Tunny on the shoulder. "Just wanted to feel solid ground again."

"And besides," he added with a smirk, "the captain'll have your hide if he finds out you left the ship before she's unloaded."

"Ptah!" Tunny spat with a wave. "Solid ground's overrated. Give me a ship's roll any day. And don't worry about the captain—he's the one who sent us after you."

His face turned half-serious—though the corners of his mouth twitched, refusing solemnity. "You thought about his offer? Staying with your jolly mates?"

Tyr hesitated. The offer pulled at him. But the forge called louder.

He'd been lucky to earn a spot on the *Majonolle*—a temporary smith, working for passage. But he'd proven himself. Last night, the captain offered him a regular crew position. Half share. Skilled rate.

His smile faded to a thoughtful frown.

"I wish I could," he said. "But like I told him—I'm not a master yet. If I take a spot reserved for one, the guild might blacklist me. They'd never let me test. I've got to finish my journeyman years first."

Tunny nodded. "Well, lad, you'll be missed. We've grown used to your annoying racket during the day." His grin widened. "But enough of that. The wind takes each man where it will, and only fools fight it. So tonight—let it take us to a rowdy farewell for our little smith!"

The crew, now joined by the captain, gave a cheer and swept Tyr toward one of the dockside taverns.

They walked in a tight, laughing pack until they reached a small but bustling tavern. Inside, it took a moment for Tyr's eyes to adjust.

The place was dimly lit, with low-hanging lanterns casting warm, flickering light over worn wooden tables and benches. The scent of stale ale and spilled liquor mingled with the mouthwatering aroma of roasted meat and thick stews drifting in from the kitchen. The floor was uneven—thick wooden planks, scuffed by years of heavy boots. The walls were lined with nautical décor: old ship wheels, rusted anchors, and faded maps. It was the kind of place meant for sailors and dockworkers.

The atmosphere buzzed with rowdy energy—boisterous laughter, clinking tankards, and the occasional off-key shanty. Sailors huddled at tables, swapping exaggerated tales of storms, sea beasts, and near-death escapes. In one corner, dice rattled, and coins clinked as bets were made. The barkeep—a grizzled man with a thick beard—moved quickly behind the bar, barely keeping pace with the thirsty crowd. The place had a rough-edged camaraderie, but to those who knew the life of the sea, it was warm and familiar.

Tyr and the crew found a corner table where they could spread out. As the first round of ale arrived and food was ordered, Tyr reached for his purse and winced. He had little coin to spare—he'd have to nurse his drinks. Sensing the hesitation, the captain gave him a reassuring pat on the shoulder and leaned in.

"Relax, lad. Drink freely. It's my treat tonight. Call it a down payment—so when you make master, you'll reconsider my offer," he said with a grin.

As the night wore on, the stories grew more absurd and the laughter louder. Tyr overheard one of the crew cackling, "—and then this giant of a man grabs Tunny by the scruff, ready to toss him through the window, when Tyr grabs the bastard's wrist in that meat mitt of his and just starts tightening. The giant drops Tunny, falls to his knees, and starts begging our tiny blacksmith to let go! I thought he was gonna piss himself!"

The table roared with laughter. Tyr smiled, a little embarrassed. He didn't like getting physical—but if it meant protecting one of his own, he would.

As the revelry ebbed and night settled in, the crew began staggering back to the ship—some on their own, others half-carried. Tyr smiled as the usual suspects slurred their goodbyes. He hugged each in turn. In the end, only he, Tunny, and the captain remained.

The captain ordered three shots of brandy.

Raising his glass, he said, "Tyr, I've known a lot of sailors in my time, and I can confidently say—you're probably the worst one I've ever met."

The three of them burst into laughter.

"Wait, wait—let me finish," the captain added, grinning. "You're the worst sailor, but the best damn blacksmith I've ever seen. And more than that, you're one of the kindest, truest shipmates I've had the pleasure to serve with." He lifted his glass a little higher. "To your good health, and may fortune follow you."

Tunny raised his glass. "Hear, hear!"

They clinked glasses and downed the brandy.

"Thank you—both of you," Tyr said, setting his empty glass down. "You honor me, truly. I wouldn't trade my time on the *Majonolle*

for anything. You're family now. And it pains me to know she'll sail
without me. But I'll be watching for her return—every day."

He looked at the captain. "Next time we share a drink, the night's
on me."

They sat a while longer, then walked together back to the ship.
Once they boarded, Tyr turned and made his way back toward the
tavern.

Thanks to the captain's recommendation, he'd arranged a cheap
room upstairs in exchange for doing a few repairs the next day.

By the time he returned, the tavern had quieted. He sat on the
steps out front and lit his pipe. As he looked up at the stars, his
thoughts drifted—as they often did—to Al and Steven.

Suddenly, a barmaid sat beside him and handed him a hot cup of
tea with a smile.

"Thank you…" he began, trailing off.

"Cindy," she said.

"Thank you, Cindy." He took a sip.

"It'll help you sleep. Too much ale's no good for you." She was
pretty—but too tall for him.

"Are you always this kind to strays?" he asked, offering a tired
smile.

She laughed. "Hardly. My husband would throw a fit if I were.
But you seem to have a good heart. And—truthfully—it was his idea
to bring you the tea."

She paused, then added, "He's a member of the city guard. Heard
you were in Morcaster before… everything. He wondered if you knew
anything."

Tyr lowered the cup, his expression darkening. He shook his head
slowly.

"No. We must've been one of the last ships out before it
happened. We didn't hear a thing until a month later, when we made
port. But even then, it was all rumors. No one knew anything for sure.
I tried to find out more every chance I got, but we always seemed to
stay ahead of the news. I was hoping to learn more here."

Cindy's voice grew quiet. "We don't know much either. Just…
something terrible happened. Something that killed everyone in the
city." She lowered her voice further. "Everyone."

"I'm sorry," Tyr said. "I wish I could tell you more."

She shrugged. "It was a long shot. The truth will reach us eventually." She gave him a soft smile. "Then we'll both know."

She stood. "When you're ready to turn in, come find me. I'll show you to your room."

"Thank you, Cindy," he said. "I'll be along shortly."

Alone again, Tyr stared into his tea.

Al… you better not have been in Morcaster when it happened. You better be alive. You and I still need to thrash Steven for being such a pain—and laugh about how stupid we were.

He took another sip, then ran a hand over his face and through his beard, now thick again.

Master Fenwil… I hope you're at peace. You and the missus never did leave, but I pray your end came swiftly—without pain.

His eyes grew wet as faces from Morcaster crowded his mind. He closed his eyes and forced himself to steady his breathing.

Not now, he told himself. *This isn't the time to mourn. First—I need to know what happened.*

Tyr finished his tea, stamped out his pipe, and returned inside. He stayed to help Cindy, her husband, and the other workers clean up the tavern. It didn't feel right to head off to bed without lending a hand.

While mopping the floor, he asked, "Where can I find the blacksmiths in the city? Are they all in one place, or scattered around?"

"You'll find them in the Craftsman District—plenty of them," someone replied.

"Aye," said another. "No shortage of smithies here. Always demand for weapons and armor."

"Are you a master smith?" someone else asked. "If so, why are you mopping floors?"

Tyr smiled. "Nothing wrong with mopping. A clean shop is the sign of an organized craftsman. I usually start and end my day cleaning. But no, I'm not a master—just a journeyman, looking for one."

"Lots of shops," said Trent, Cindy's husband. "Not many good ones. Choose wisely. Some care more about quantity than quality— little better than sweatshops."

"I've heard of places like that," Tyr said with a nod. "Any recommendations?"

Trent shook his head. "Can't say. I rarely make it to the Craftsman District. I patrol the docks by day, and old Mittle lets me earn a few coins at night keeping things calm here—on account of Cindy working the bar."

Tyr thanked them all. After the last dish was washed and the shutters latched, Cindy led him to his room.

"It's not much," she said as she opened the door, "but it's warm and dry."

He smiled. "Thank you. It'll be most welcome. And thank you—and your husband—for your kindness."

She returned the smile. "Breakfast for the crew is at sunup. If you're late, you'll have to eat with the customers—and pay like one. So don't be late."

He nodded. "I'll be there."

Tyr woke the next morning to the smell of coffee and bacon. He dressed quickly, made his bed, and packed his gear before heading downstairs, worried he had overslept. Relief washed over him when he saw it was only the cook beginning her morning routine. She smiled as he entered.

"Ooo, look at you—up bright and early, you are," she said, flashing him a wide, toothless grin.

She was old—very old—but hale. Tyr guessed the wrinkles on her face had been carved more by laughter than hardship. He liked her instantly.

"Good morning, Mistress of the Kitchen. How could I sleep with the sweet aroma of coffee and that oh-so-tantalizing scent of bacon?" He returned her grin. "I was afraid I'd overslept. I promised to work for my room and a bit of breakfast," he added, eyeing the bacon hungrily.

"Ha! Typical man—wants food before the work's done," she teased. "No one eats until the whole team's seated. And no one sits until the morning chores are finished." She gave a conspiratorial wink and nodded toward the coffee pot. "Help yourself to some coffee, though."

Gratefully, he poured himself a mug. After a sip, he asked, "Since I'm up and waiting, what can I do to help?"

She turned and looked him up and down. "You're a short bastard, aren't you? Half the height, but twice the width. You'd make a hell of a wrestler."

She wiped her hands on her apron. "Name's Phelli. And if you're not afraid of doing 'women's work,' grab a knife and start peeling those potatoes." She pointed to a large mound piled on the table.

Tyr tied on an apron, grabbed a knife, and sat down. "Never heard of women's work or men's work—just work. If something needs doing, it's everyone's job to see it done right."

He paused, then stood and gave a small bow. "And my apologies—Tyr, at your service."

"Pleasure to meet you, Tyr. But careful with that kind of talk. I don't know where you're from, but here, everyone has a station. Women, men, rich, poor—we're meant to remember our place, unless you're looking for trouble."

Tyr shrugged. "No trouble. Just not the type to sit around while others do the work. Doesn't sit right with me."

She laughed. "If only more folks felt that way. So what are you, anyway? I've never seen anyone quite like you."

He blinked. "I'm not sure I follow."

"I've seen men from all over pass through this tavern. You look like a man, sure enough, and I doubt most would notice anything strange—but there's something different about you. Where are your people from?"

Tyr was quiet for a moment. He'd never really thought about it. Sure, he was short—so were his parents. Both had the same stocky build.

Phelli spoke again. "Sorry, lad. I didn't mean to upset you. Just old Phelli rambling again."

Tyr looked up from the potato he was peeling. "Not at all. I just… never really gave it much thought. My folks came from western Harding, near the mountains, I think. Place had an old name… Tarnivault, I believe."

She shook her head. "Never heard of it. But things get strange out west." She smiled and shrugged. "That's probably it, then. The people from Tarnivault must just be short and broad. But if they're half as polite as you, it must be a wonderful place to live."

By the time the potatoes were peeled, the rest of the morning crew had arrived. Tyr smiled at Cindy and gave her a friendly nod. She walked over and glanced at the pile of peeled potatoes.

"Phelli, what'd you do—wake him up early to help you?"

"Not at all, child," Phelli replied. "This one came down about an hour ago, looking for coffee and work. I obliged him on both counts."

Cindy chuckled. "Now I feel bad about giving you the chores Mittle left for you."

Tyr removed his apron and smiled. "Not at all. Just show me what you need."

She led him around the tavern, pointing out small carpentry repairs that needed a skilled hand, and showed him the workbench and tools. Tyr set to it with enthusiasm, the promise of breakfast quickly forgotten as he lost himself in the work.

He was just finishing up when Cindy returned, carrying a large plate piled high with bacon, eggs, fresh buttered bread, and a bowl of oatmeal.

"What's this?" he asked.

She laughed. "You worked right through breakfast. Phelli was beside herself and insisted on making you a plate. And you've more than earned it—you finished everything Mittle wanted done and a few things he didn't even know needed fixing."

Tyr took the tray and sat down at one of the tables. "It was my pleasure. I appreciate the room—and with my coin running low, I'll need to be frugal until I find a smithy that'll take me on."

Cindy considered that for a moment. "Come back tonight. Let me talk to Mittle. Maybe we can work something out—room and board in exchange for help around the place, like today." She glanced around the tavern and added under her breath, "Goodness knows it needs it."

The morning was well underway when Tyr stepped out of the tavern. He was grateful to leave his pack upstairs—it meant he didn't have to lug it through the city.

The docks were already buzzing with activity. He glanced toward the berth where the *Majonolle* was moored. She sat low in the water—clearly reloaded overnight. For a moment, he considered stopping by, but the crew had said they'd be in York for a couple of days. Best to swing by later, when they'd be less busy.

He turned down the main thoroughfare and soon found himself standing before the city's towering stone wall. The grand archway loomed ahead, its two massive wooden doors standing wide open. Tyr marveled again at the craftsmanship. Flanking the arch were two large, weathered banners bearing the crest of York—a nautical compass set inside a ship's wheel, with a tentacled sea monster looming behind it.

Steeling himself, Tyr stepped through the gate and into the city proper.

The main avenue stretched out before him, lined with carts and stalls. Vendors were still setting up, but already the scent of sizzling meats drifted through the air.

Good thing I had a big breakfast, he thought with a grin. *Or my money wouldn't have lasted long.*

All right, he told himself. *Big city. First things first—I need to get a feel for the layout, then check out the smithies. Tomorrow I'll start speaking to the masters. That's the plan.*

He knew he should head straight to the Craftsman District.

But the chance to explore—free of obligation for one day—was too tempting to ignore, even for him.

The main avenue was at least a hundred feet wide, paved with the same expertly laid cobblestones he'd seen at the docks. Slightly elevated walkways flanked both sides of the street, where vendors were already arranging their goods. A low brick wall separated the adjoining districts from the thoroughfare, though most people still walked along the main road itself.

The street ran east from the docks and west into the countryside. Tyr looked down at the cobbles beneath his feet and smiled, thinking:

The dirt path outside my father's house leads to the village road, which leads to the road to Torringburgh, which leads to the great southern market road… and that road leads over the mountains… and eventually to York. So, if I walk far enough, this road will take me home.

The thought comforted him in an unexpected way.

He spent the next two hours slowly walking westward along the northern side of the avenue. Two main roads branched north: the first led to the Craftsman District—where he planned to spend tomorrow seeking out a smithy; the second led to the Market District. A third, farther along, veered toward what looked like a working-class residential area.

At last, he reached the western gates. The outer walls were as imposing as those by the docks, but even thicker. He spotted members of the watch patrolling the top—relaxed, but alert. *Enough of such thoughts,* he told himself. *The sun is out, the weather is warm—let's see what the south side of the avenue has to show.*

The first road east of the gate felt different—more like a park than a city street. Curious, he turned south and followed the avenue past row upon row of pleasant homes. Better than the ones he'd seen earlier, though nothing extravagant. At the far end, he saw an old man seated in front of a closed iron gate, reading a thick book.

As Tyr approached, the man looked up and gave him a quick once-over. Though he hadn't spoken a word, Tyr had the distinct impression the man had already sized him up completely.

"I daresay," the old man said, clearly surprised. "You shouldn't be here."

He said it more to himself than to Tyr.

"I'm sorry," Tyr replied. "I didn't realize this was private property. I'll leave right away."

"What? No, no—not like that." The man waved a hand. "This is a public road. I didn't mean it that way. I meant you shouldn't be here. Or anywhere, really."

Tyr blinked. "I… I don't understand."

"Where are you from?" the man asked, still studying him.

"I'm Tyr. From Southold, in Harding."

The old man frowned. "No, no, that's not right. Your kind never lived in Harding—not that I know of—and certainly not so far east."

"My kind?" Tyr asked, raising an eyebrow. "You mean blacksmiths?"

The man stared at him for a long moment—then burst into laughter.

"Blacksmith! Oh, that's rich. A dwarf… shoeing horses!"

Tyr scowled. "A dwarf? Look, I know I'm short, but that doesn't make me a dwarf. I've heard they haven't been seen in over five hundred years."

The man tilted his head, studying him. "Maybe. Maybe not. Maybe you just look like the stories say. Or maybe you're more than you know. The ancient dwarven homes were sealed off five centuries ago—who's to say some didn't get left out when the gates closed?"

He shrugged. "Either way, I'm curious. Are you?"

"Me? I know who I am," Tyr said firmly. "I'm my father's son. I hope to be a master blacksmith someday, with my own little shop in a quiet hamlet and a family of my own. That's who I am—and all I need to be."

The old man nodded slowly. "Hard to argue with a man who's content. But if you ever change your mind—or get bored and feel like humoring an old scholar—come back and speak with me. If I'm not at the gate, just tell them you're here to see Preceptor Winslow. They'll know where to find me."

Tyr glanced at the iron gate. "Before I go… what is this place?"

The old man smiled. "This is the Academy of Knowledge. Within these walls is the collected wisdom of the ages—or at least as much of it as we've been able to gather. It's the largest repository of its kind… at least on this side of the ocean."

Tyr's brow lifted. "What sort of knowledge?"

"A bit of everything. Blacksmithing, military history, engineering, natural sciences… even magic."

"Magic?" Tyr repeated, skeptical.

Winslow chuckled. "Yes, even that. It hasn't worked in five hundred years, they say—but the tomes are preserved. Every scholar tries it at least once. Nothing ever happens. My guess? Just ancient superstition. But who am I to say?"

Tyr said his goodbyes and headed back toward the main avenue—curious, and more than a little confused.

Why would he think I'm a dwarf? he wondered. *Surely they've met short men before—even here in the south. Tunny's not exactly tall.*

Shaking his head, he continued eastward.

The next avenue he passed led to a much wealthier residential section—nearly as large as the first, but with fewer, larger homes and sprawling grounds. Clearly, this was where the city's elite lived.

Almost back to the docks, Tyr came to one final avenue heading south. It was nearly as broad as the main thoroughfare and lined with the Kingdom's pennants, flying proudly from poles every fifty feet. In the distance, he could just make out the high stone walls of the royal palace.

Think I'll avoid walking down that one, he thought with a wry smile. *Just to be safe.*

The day was nearly spent, and his stomach rumbled in protest.

"I hear you," he said aloud. "Let's get back to the tavern—see if any of the crew stopped by for a drink."

CRAFTSMAN DISTRICT

The following morning, Tyr was up early. He dressed, poured himself a cup of coffee, and received his initial marching orders from Phelli. He considered himself lucky—Cindy and Trent had convinced Mittle to let him stay on until he could find a smithy, earning his keep with work, lodging, and food.

Pausing for a moment, coffee in hand, he looked at Phelli and smiled. "What do you have for me today?"

"Ha! You don't scare me, little man. Today we've got parsnips and turnips that need peeling. Watch yourself—if you keep helping me like this, I'm going to think you've got a thing for me," she cackled, flashing her toothless grin.

"Oh no, mistress of the kitchen. I don't think I'm man enough to handle you," he said with a chuckle.

"You got that right, little man. Now start peeling!" she barked, still laughing.

By the time he finished, the rest of the team had arrived, and Cindy set him to his chores. As usual, he went above and beyond, tackling a few extra tasks he noticed along the way as a show of thanks.

After breakfast, he wandered down to the docks, surprised to see that the *Majonolle* was no longer in her berth. He'd had a few drinks with some of the crew the night before, and no one had mentioned her departure. Curious, he made his way to the harbor master's office.

The man inside was tall, heavyset, and balding—still broad in the shoulders, but now equally wide at the waist. He glanced up from a stack of shipping documents as Tyr entered.

"How can I help you, lad?" he asked, already turning his attention back to the paperwork.

"I'm just curious. I thought the *Majonolle* wasn't slated to sail for another three days. Did something happen?"

"One of the crew owe you money or something?" the harbor master asked without looking up.

"No, I crewed on her on my way south. Just curious, is all," Tyr said.

The man shrugged. "Ain't no secret. Word came in the storms were starting to blow in from the south, and the captain figured he'd best get ahead of them while he could. Should be back in port in a month or two, depending on the weather."

It made sense. Tyr hadn't faced any serious storms during his time aboard, but the crew had told plenty of horror stories about what they'd endured. *Be safe, my friends,* he thought.

He thanked the harbor master, who absently waved him away—already buried back in his papers.

On his way back into the city, Tyr cast one last glance at the now-empty berth. A small pang of unease twisted in his stomach.

Okay, he thought. *First, I'll locate all the smithies I can, get a sense of what each one specializes in, and form a general impression of the shops. Then I'll visit the ones that focus on weapons and seem well-maintained.*

Unfortunately, that plan unraveled quickly. The sheer number of smithies in York was overwhelming. He soon discovered that most specialized in only one or two areas—a rule strictly enforced by the guild. The largest and most respected among them were the weaponsmiths. York was famous for its blades, and the kingdom maintained a strong export trade in arms forged here.

It took time to sort through the shops. Many displayed a wide selection—armor, weapons, farm tools, farrier gear, and general goods—but not all of it was made on-site. Some simply bought display pieces to give the appearance of being more versatile than they were.

By day's end, Tyr estimated he had visited maybe a third of the smithies in the district—and to be honest, he wasn't all that impressed. Most were focused on volume, not craftsmanship. Sitting on a bench along the avenue, he pulled out his pipe and a dwindling pouch of tobacco.

I'll need to find more soon—or go without for a while, he thought as he packed the pipe. *A problem for another day.*

He lit the pipe and watched the vendors and townsfolk go about their business. Everyone seemed to have a place—a purpose. Everyone but him. *What if I can't find a master here? Maybe I should've stayed in Morcaster...* His thought trailed off. *No. If I had stayed, I'd be dead. You better have gotten out, Al.*

He stood, brushing tobacco flakes from his lap. *Nothing's ever been solved by feeling sorry for yourself. Tomorrow, I'll find a master. Or maybe the next day,* he added with a sigh.

His days soon settled into a routine: wake early, help at the tavern, explore the Craftsman District, visit smithies, return to assist with evening tasks at the inn, and then sit outside before bed. By week's end, he'd seen every shop, watched the ones he liked, and made his decision. Only one stood out—it was the only one that made sense to him.

Sitting on the edge of his bed, staring at his worn leather boots, he inhaled the scent of coffee and sausages drifting up from the kitchen. He wanted to run to the smithy and speak to the master immediately, but today was Sathairn—the last day of the week and considered a day of rest. All the shops were closed, with only taverns, inns, and street vendors allowed to operate.

Tomorrow was Luain, the first day of the workweek. He'd have to wait, and try to be at the smithy before it opened—hoping to catch the master before the bustle began. Other than his morning chores, he had no obligations today. A blessing—and a curse.

He smiled. *This was usually the day Al, Steven, and I would get ourselves into trouble—usually in Whittle.*

He pulled on his boots and headed downstairs. After finishing his tasks, he stepped out front and sat down. It wasn't long before Cindy joined him, quietly settling beside him.

After a moment, Tyr gave her a questioning look.

"You seem sad," she said. "It's not like you. I don't like seeing you like this."

He offered a soft smile. "I'm okay. Just thinking about home. And friends."

She brightened. "You're homesick. Why didn't you say so? Some of the others and I are off today—other than the morning routine. We could take you into town, go exploring, maybe have a picnic in the country?"

He smiled again. "No, no, I promise—I'm okay. Work helps. It keeps the mind off things."

She paused. "When was the last time you wrote home?"

He blinked, genuinely surprised. "Never."

"Never?" She stared at him. "No wonder you're homesick. You haven't had any contact with your family or friends this whole time? They must be worried sick." She stood, suddenly determined. "Go to your room. I'll bring you a quill, ink, and paper—and don't come back down until you've written your parents a letter. Then I'll walk you to the Postal Office so you can send it."

He hesitated, then nodded, a smile spreading across his face. "Thank you. That's exactly what I'll do."

It took him most of the morning. He'd never been good at writing letters—never knew how to begin or end them, or what to say in between. But he started at the beginning: his departure, his time in Morcaster, and his narrow escape from the tragedy there. He wrote about his journey aboard the *Majonolle*, his arrival in York, and, at Cindy's urging, included the Drunken Donkey as a return address so they could reach him.

He closed with warm wishes to his parents and siblings. Before sealing the letter, he added a short postscript:

P.S. – A strange old man here mistook me for a dwarf. Has anything like that ever happened to either of you?

The next morning, Tyr finished his chores as quickly as he could, making sure everything was still done to his satisfaction. Then he hurried—fast as he dared—toward the shop he had set his heart on. He smiled as he approached. He was early; the sun hadn't yet risen, but the shop was already lit, and he could hear the rhythmic sound of hammering from within.

As he drew closer, a gruff voice reached him from inside. "Easy, lad. Keep the bellows at a constant rate. You don't want the coals too hot—but don't ignore them either. Keep them just right while the metal heats."

The barn doors stood open, letting the cool morning air circulate through the shop. Tyr paused just outside, watching. The old master smith was instructing one of his apprentices. Tyr nodded with approval. He always appreciated when a master took time for personal instruction. The boy was probably just as grateful.

The old smith glanced up and spotted Tyr. "Keep working, lad. I'll be back in a moment."

He grabbed a rag and wiped his hands as he walked over. He stood a head taller than Tyr—strong, though not as broad. His bald head gleamed in the early light, and his long salt-and-pepper beard rested atop a large belly.

He gave Tyr a long look, then turned back to the forge.

"Come to gloat?" he asked quietly.

"Nope," Tyr replied.

"You don't have the look of a collector. Though, by the size of you, you'd make a terrifying one."

"Don't even know what a collector is," Tyr said.

The smith turned toward him again. "If you're not here to collect on a debt or mock me, then what brings you here?"

"My name is Tyr," he said, extending a hand. "I'm a journeyman blacksmith. My last shop was in Morcaster—mostly tools for mining and lumber, and parts for shipwrights. I worked off my passage as a ship's smith aboard the *Majonolle*. She made port on Ceada of last week." He scratched the back of his neck, glancing around the shop. "And if you don't mind my saying so, it looks like you could use a little help."

The older smith laughed. "Pleased to meet you, Tyr. I'm Master Crowin, and this"—he swept a hand toward the forge—"is my shop. Morcaster, you say? Nothing but foul news coming out of that city lately. Though your accent's more Harding than Jaspar, I'd wager." He sighed, looking back over the workspace. "And aye, I could use help— that's true. But unless you're looking to work for free, I'm not sure how much I can offer."

Tyr shook his head. "No, I wouldn't ask that. I'd want enough to cover my room and board, and permission to make and sell one item a month—something I'd keep all the profit from."

The smith blinked, giving him a baffled look. "You're serious? I'm not sure if you noticed, but I'm not exactly thriving here. You'd be better off across the street."

Tyr shook his head again. "That kind of shop isn't for me. I've still got a couple of years left on my journeyman path, and I want to learn from a master who's both skilled and careful with the details. I can see both in your work."

"Room, board, and one item a month, huh?" Crowin repeated, considering. "Not that I'm one to look a gift horse in the mouth… but I should take a look at your letters before I say yes. Guild requirements and all."

Tyr was ready. He pulled a few folded pages from inside his tunic and handed them over. They included a letter of introduction from his father outlining his apprenticeship, a recommendation from Master

Fenwil in Morcaster, and a certification from the Morcaster Guild verifying his standing and eligibility for journeyman placement.

Crowin opened them and read carefully. "Ranfel?" he muttered, eyeing the signature. "I knew a smith by that name back when I was an apprentice. He was a journeyman at the same forge. Best damn weaponsmith I'd ever seen. Could've opened his own shop the day he made master—but instead, he left and went back to Harding."

He looked up at Tyr with renewed curiosity. "I suppose Ranfel's a common enough name in Harding, but still…" He gave Tyr another once-over. "You do resemble him. Where did your father serve his journeymanship?"

"Here in York," Tyr replied. "That's one of the reasons I came south—to follow in his footsteps."

The old smith rubbed his chin, his eyes distant. "What are the odds? You look like him, you know. Short, strong, and very serious."

Tyr was about to argue that he wasn't the brooding type, but Crowin chuckled.

"I'm just teasing you. Your father's an incredible smith. I'd bet he's only gotten better over the years. If you learned weaponsmithing from him, I doubt there's much I could teach you. Probably no one in this city could."

"Well… that's the thing. My pa isn't a weaponsmith. He's just a local blacksmith in the same village I grew up in. Says that's all he ever wanted."

The older smith laughed—deep and genuine. "That sounds like him, all right. Every smith in this city's chasing big contracts and serious coin. But not your pa. He made master and walked away from it all. Good for him. A man's not a man if he doesn't follow his heart now and then."

He handed the papers back. "Take the rest of the day to get settled in—and tomorrow too, if you need it. If not, be here half an hour before first light. I'll put you through your paces and see whether I need to send your pa a nasty letter."

He smiled. "Tell Madaline to start a tab for your room and board and to send me the bill every fortnight."

Tyr nodded and was about to leave when Crowin added, "By the way—we've been hearing rumors. Something terrible up in Morcaster.

I assume you left before it happened… but have you heard anything on your way south?"

Tyr frowned and shook his head. "Very little. We first heard about it maybe a month after it happened. We sailed out of Morcaster, hitting towns and cities along the Altin until we reached the open sea. That alone was an experience for a landlocked boy like me."

He smiled briefly before continuing. "From there, we went north, then upriver to the Bay of Tears to trade with the northern nomads, and finally turned back south. It wasn't until we landed at Durbin, just south of the Altin Delta, that we heard rumors—something about a strange fog that killed everyone in the city."

He looked down. "We didn't believe it at first. But at every port we stopped at, the stories kept coming. I still don't know what happened, or how many people died—but every version agrees something awful occurred. I'm still hoping the friends I made there— and the one I traveled with—managed to survive."

Crowin nodded solemnly and placed a hand on Tyr's shoulder. "Rumors. That's about all we've had as well. Keep your hopes up— rumors are rarely accurate. Go on. Get settled in. There'll be plenty of time to talk in the days to come. The truth—or what they decide is the truth   we'll learn eventually."

Before Tyr left, Crowin gave him a quick tour of the smithy and formally introduced him to the other masters and the apprentice, Jym.

"This is the parlor," Mistress Madaline said, gesturing around the front room, which took up most of the entryway. Several comfortable-looking chairs—upholstered in worn but inviting fabrics—were arranged around a low table, with a few end tables tucked near the walls. Morning light poured through tall windows, casting long golden shafts across the hardwood floor. A couple of old landscape paintings hung on the walls—nothing fancy, but enough to make the place feel lived-in.

"If you ever have guests, this is as far as they go. There are other people staying here, and everyone likes their privacy." Tyr nodded, noting how the space—though modest—had a certain warmth to it.

Across from the front door, the parlor had two exits. A broad archway in the center led into a hallway, while a wide staircase to the right curved upward toward the second floor, where the guest rooms were located. She nodded toward a smaller door to the left of the stairs.

"Through there is the kitchen. I don't mind if you're in and out, but keep it tidy. I make the meals here, and we're on a schedule."

A faint smell of baking bread and something savory drifted from that direction, and Tyr's stomach growled in response.

They moved through the archway into the hallway, where she pointed toward two small rooms.

"These are offices—if you ever need them. Just quiet spaces with a desk to write letters or go over business."

Each room held a modest writing desk, a simple chair, and a few shelves with scattered papers and quills.

At the end of the hall, the space opened into a common dining room with a large wooden table at its center—enough to seat a dozen. The furniture was simple but sturdy, and the place settings were neatly arranged. Candles stood ready in the center for evening meals.

"You'll take your meals here," she said. "Breakfast is at sunrise, lunch for those in the house, and dinner just after sunset."

Across from the dining room was a small bathroom. Its fixtures were plain but clean. A washbasin stood in one corner, with neatly folded towels stacked on a nearby shelf.

"Nothing fancy, but it's clean," she said, clearly proud of the space.

They ascended the broad staircase. The wooden steps creaked softly underfoot. Upstairs, the hall was quiet, with six small doors lining either side.

"These are the guest rooms—six in all," she said, stopping at one of the doors and opening it. "This is room four."

The room was simple, like the rest of the house. A small bed with a worn but clean quilt sat against the far wall, with a wooden trunk at its foot for storage. A writing desk and chair stood near the window, letting in a modest stream of sunlight. A dresser rested along the opposite wall.

"Not much," she said, "but enough to keep your things in order."

Tyr nodded. It wasn't much, but it felt comfortable—a place to rest after long days at the forge. "Thank you, Mistress Madaline," he said sincerely.

She gave a slight nod, then turned back toward the hallway. "Well, if you need anything, just give a holler. Otherwise, I'll let you get settled."

She handed him two keys—one for the house, the other for his room.

"I'll be back later," Tyr said. "I need to check out of the tavern and grab my pack."

She nodded as she started back down the stairs. "There's a larger bathroom at the end of the hall," she called over her shoulder. "There's a bath in there and a small woodstove. You'll have to fetch and heat the water yourself."

Tyr locked the room and headed back to the tavern, his step lighter than it had been since he arrived.

It was midday by the time he returned. Trent, now in the uniform of York's guard, was sitting at a table with another soldier. He smiled as Tyr entered.

"Tyr! Come join us. We're just about to eat. It'll help keep us on our feet while we patrol the docks."

His companion pulled out a chair beside him.

"I wish I could," Tyr said. "I'm on a mission. I just secured a position with a smith, and I need to move my few belongings over to the boarding house."

There was a touch of excitement in his voice.

"That's fantastic," Trent said. "A good smith, I hope? Not one of those mills that just churn out junk."

Tyr thought for a moment. "No. I think it's a good smithy—not the biggest or the shiniest, but the master's a true craftsman. Someone I'd be honored to learn from."

Trent nodded solemnly. "That's high praise coming from you. He must be a good man indeed. Will we be seeing you again?"

Tyr smiled broadly. "Count on it. I'll try to stop by nightly when I can. A man has to eat, and I've grown fond of the company. Besides, Mittle always has something that needs tending to."

Tyr left them as their food arrived. He headed upstairs to his room, stuffed his few belongings into his pack, and made his bed. After checking for Phelli or Cindy—neither of whom were around— he said his goodbyes to those present and promised to return soon.

The sun was just beginning to set when he returned to the boarding house. Madaline heard him come in and poked her head out of the kitchen.

"Dinner's just about ready. Go get washed up and join us."

"Yes, ma'am," he replied—the words so much like his mother's that he nearly laughed.

He tossed his pack onto the bed and went to the washroom at the end of the hall. After a quick wash, he joined the small group gathering at the table.

All eyes turned toward him as he entered.

Three people were already seated: two men and one woman. One man, tall and fair-skinned, looked to be about Tyr's age, with long blond hair. The other was older—not as tall, but broader in the middle. The woman was as young as the first man but opposite in appearance. Her skin was a rich, deep brown, her hair jet black, and her eyes dark and intelligent.

Tyr smiled and offered a small bow. "Evening. My name is Tyr."

The young woman smiled brightly. Her accent was thick but melodic.

"A pleasure, Master Tyr. I am Saphira Aluna."

"Delighted to meet you," Tyr said, feeling slightly awkward.

The older man spoke next, with an air of superiority. "Bastian Viremont, from Montemajore."

The younger man hesitated, glancing around shyly before adding, "Lyricen Farrow."

Tyr thought the boy seemed almost uncertain of his own name. Odd, he mused.

Just then, the kitchen door opened and Madaline entered, carrying a large platter of roasted, stuffed pork loin. Root vegetables, mashed turnips, and a thick, aromatic gravy accompanied it.

After everyone had filled their plates, Saphira turned to Tyr. "I hope I'm not being rude—the customs of this land are still new to me—but I've never seen anyone quite like you."

She giggled softly. "I'm sorry—that didn't come out right," she added quickly. "I mean, we have men taller or shorter than others, but always in proportion. You seem unnaturally large for your height. Why, I dare say you could best a bakira in a bare-knuckle fight. May I ask what your profession is?"

Tyr smiled, a bit embarrassed by the question. Before coming to York, no one had ever given his stature a second thought. Here, it seemed to be a topic of endless fascination. He wiped his mouth with a napkin. "No offense taken. I'm a blacksmith."

"Oh!" she said with delight. "That must be it. The men who work the forge are powerful indeed. And what a coincidence—I've just finished negotiations with your guild. Are you a master with your own shop?"

Shaking his head, he replied, "Goodness, no. I still have a few years before I can even hope to stand before the guild and be deemed worthy of that title. I'm just a simple journeyman, newly arrived to finish my studies." He paused. "If I may ask, what were you negotiating with the guild for?"

She smiled politely. "It's no secret. I represent a powerful faction in my homeland and have come to arrange a large weapons shipment. If I'd known you a few days earlier, I might have insisted your shop be included."

"You're too kind. But to be honest, I haven't even started at the shop yet, so I wouldn't have been in any position to agree or disagree." He took another bite. "Might I ask where you hail from?"

"Oh, no place special," she said evasively. "Just a small land far from here."

"She is from the land of Zamoya," said Lyricen with a toothy grin, clearly enjoying Saphira's surprise. "It must be a marvelous place if the women are even half as lovely as you." He nearly sang the words.

"You surprise me, young troubadour. I didn't expect anyone here to have heard of Zamoya. It lies far to the south and east, and seldom do my people venture to Tirra." She eyed him with a newfound caution.

Tyr raised an eyebrow. "And where are you from?" he asked, turning to Lyricen.

"Harbinger's Cove," he replied with a shrug. "Well, most recently, that is. Really, just from here and there. I move around a lot—seeking my fortune on the road and in whatever city or town I find myself." His smile was sickly sweet.

"Harbinger's Cove? Nasty place, I hear. When we sailed south, our captain stayed well clear of it," Tyr said quietly.

He looked the man over. Harbinger's Cove was, by all accounts, a seedy little port along the coast of Velmara, said to be home to pirates and privateers. Tyr looked Lyricen over once more—he doubted the man had ever worked a day in his life, but he seemed to have some money. Tyr decided to let it lie, but reminded himself to keep his door locked.

Instead, he turned to the heavier man. "And what about you, Master Viremont? Montemajore—that's high in the mountains south of the Drumalra, isn't it?"

The other man, who had been quietly stuffing himself while the others talked, sighed heavily at the interruption. He swallowed, wiped his mouth, and gave Tyr a forced smile.

"You are quite correct, young journeyman. Like the fair Saphira, I am here on business. But instead of weapons, I'm overseeing a shipment of tobacco."

He was about to return to his meal when Tyr added, "Oh, then I'm in luck. I'm nearly out of pipeweed. Would you happen to have some I could purchase?"

Bastian huffed. "Young man, I do not carry the shipment on me. It's delivered by caravan to the wholesalers in the Market District— and I do not smoke the foul stuff." He paused, then added with a touch of civility, "But if you are truly in need, visit Pentiglass Emporium. You'll find it near the entrance to the Market District. Tell him you know me, and he may give you a discount."

Tyr smiled. "I will. And thank you."

"Now, if you don't mind," Bastian said, already picking up his fork, "I'd like to get back to this incredible meal."

The rest of dinner passed quietly. Each guest seemed lost in their own thoughts. One by one, they excused themselves until only Tyr remained.

He rose, gathered the dishes, and carried them—along with the leftovers—into the kitchen. Madaline was there, washing pots and pans. She gave him an odd look as he set the platter and dishes down.

Grabbing an apron, he said, "Tell me what needs doing."

Together, they washed and dried everything in companionable silence. When the work was done, Tyr stepped out onto the front porch and lit his pipe. He made a mental note to visit Pentiglass soon—he was almost out of tobacco.

He leaned back and looked up at the sky, a bit saddened. The stars didn't shine nearly as brightly here in the city—not like they did back home. And nothing compared to what he'd seen at sea.

Before turning in, he sat at the small desk in his room and penned a letter to his parents.

JOURNEYMAN

Tyr rose early, pulled on his work clothes, and headed to the shop, determined to arrive before Master Crowin. He was only partially successful. As he approached the forge, he spotted the smith turning the corner.

Crowin smiled as he recognized him. "Ah, my new journeyman—right on time. Good, very good. Come, let's get the heart of the beast warmed up," he said.

He unlocked the door. "Go light the forges. I'll make a pot of coffee."

Tyr nodded and went to work. It felt good to be back in a proper shop. This was where he felt at home—not in the city, not at sea, not riding across open plains under endless sky—but here, in the glow of a sweltering forge, with heat and metal for company.

As he lit the forges, Jym joined him, sleep still in his eyes. The two hit it off immediately. The boy was short and skinny now, but like most men in York, he'd grow tall—and with a few years at the forge, he'd be a powerhouse. Tyr was pleased to see that when asked to do something, Jym jumped to it—and, more importantly, asked questions if he didn't understand. Too many men never asked and suffered for it in the long run.

With the forges roaring to life, Tyr asked Jym to grab a couple of brooms. Together, they began sweeping out the shop just as the masters filed in and headed to their stations.

Crowin approached and handed Tyr a steaming cup of coffee.

"If you don't like it, you can make it yourself when you get in," he said with a smirk.

Tyr took a cautious sip and winced. "No, no—it's good," he replied through clenched teeth.

Crowin grinned. "Good. That's what I like to hear. Follow me."

He led Tyr to an unused forge. "This'll be yours. It's a bit older, but still functional, and the anvil's as big as they come. If you need tools, let me know and I'll see what we can scrounge up."

Tyr smiled. His own forge.

"Get settled in, get it cleaned and fired up, then come find me. I'll give you some of the routine orders that have been sitting around too long. Also, I'd like you to take Jym under your wing—help him learn the trade. You know the drill. Anyway, get squared away, and we'll talk soon."

Jym stood at his side. "Where do we start?"

Tyr, still smiling, scanned the area. "Bring me that small table," he said, pointing to an unused bench off to one side.

Jym slid it over, and Tyr quickly began laying out everything that had been piled around the forge over the years. The two of them cleaned the hearth inside and out, making sure it was free of ash.

"Good. Check the bellows—if there's any tears, we'll lose pressure and won't be able hold heat in the forge."

As Jym inspected the bellows, Tyr turned his attention to the tools they'd unearthed, sorting them by type. "Clean and oil these," he instructed.

Jym nodded and set to work.

Tyr moved on to the anvil, checking it for rust and imperfections. "I know you know how to light a forge and keep the temperature steady," he said. Jym nodded again, already working. "Good. I'm going to find the Master and see what he's got for us."

It wasn't long before Tyr returned with a stack of straight stock and a few order sheets.

"Okay, this looks pretty straightforward."

Before long, he had fallen back into rhythm—into the heartbeat of the forge. He worked like a machine, pausing only to show Jym new techniques, correct his form, or offer advice. The day passed quickly.

He finally set down the last dagger—a petite, overly ornate thing. Too delicate for his tastes, but probably meant as a gift for a child or a ceremonial piece. As he laid it aside, he realized Crowin was standing behind him.

The master picked up the dagger, turning it in his hand. Then he moved on to the other pieces Tyr had finished, inspecting them one by one.

"Why are you here, boy?" he asked quietly.

Tyr froze, startled. "I'm sorry—what did I do? I'll fix it," he said anxiously.

Crowin blinked at him, surprised. "Fix it? Boy, these are works of art. And you cleared out half the backlog in a single day. I've no idea how you managed it."

Tyr exhaled in relief. "Well, to be fair, I had Jym helping. He'll make a fine smith one day—he listens well and takes correction without fuss."

Crowin gave him a long look. "And you took time to train Jym, too."

Tyr glanced out the window. The sun had fully set. The other smiths were gone, and so was Jym.

"How long was I working?"

"The sun went down about two hours ago," Crowin said. "You seemed on a mission, so I let you be. I even grabbed some dinner from Madaline's."

He gestured to a covered plate sitting on the table Jym had dragged over.

"She insisted I bring you something."

Tyr sat down and dug in, suddenly realizing how hungry he was.

"I guess I missed the work more than I realized. What do you have for me tomorrow?"

"A little more of the same—but without Jym. I'm sending him out with the work you finished today, see if we can get some coin flowing in. Once you wrap up the smaller stuff, I'll have you start on some of the larger pieces I've been putting off. And once those are done…" He smiled. "We'll go over the basics of sword-making."

Tyr looked up and grinned. "Thank you for taking me on."

Crowin chuckled. "I honestly think I got the better end of the deal."

The streetlamps were lit now, though in the craftsmen's district they cast little true light—just enough to find your way. Tyr looked down the road toward the main avenue and considered walking to the Donkey for a pint and some company.

No, he thought. *Morning comes early. Time enough for that on Sathairn Eve.*

He turned and headed back to the boarding house.

The next couple of days flew by. Tyr fully immersed himself in life at the forge, quickly working through the backlog of orders and absorbing everything he could from Master Crowin. Crowin was amazed—not just at how naturally Tyr picked up even the most complex techniques, but at how instinctively he seemed to understand why they worked.

As was tradition at Crowin's forge, they closed early on Sathairn Eve—a small way of saying thanks for the team's hard work. It was also payday. While Tyr swept the floors, the other masters and Jym lined up to receive their weekly wages.

Unlike apprentices, journeymen weren't paid a set wage. Instead, they were allowed—at minimum—to craft and sell one item per month, with the proceeds going entirely to them. More could be permitted at the discretion of the master. It was a way of encouraging them to build a future through their own skill and enterprise.

Since Tyr had only just started, he hadn't yet had the chance to make, let alone sell, anything. Still, he had room and board—and with the few coins he had left, plus the tip from Bastian, he'd managed to refill his pipeweed at a fair price and still had enough for a pint or two at the Donkey.

Crowin approached, wiping his hands on a rag.

"You can put the broom down, lad. Shop's closed—go relax." He handed Tyr a small leather pouch that jingled as it changed hands. "It's not much, but with all the work you did this week, we were able to bring in some much-needed coin. I think you more than earned it."

He smiled warmly.

Tyr moved to hand the pouch back. "I couldn't. You're already covering my room and board, and you said yourself when we first met that the debtors were close to coming. Please, keep this for that."

Crowin gently closed Tyr's hand around the pouch. "You're a very skilled smith—and very humble. But like your father, a little thickheaded at times." He raised an eyebrow. "Am I not your master?"

Tyr nodded.

"Then do as I say—take the coin, thank me for being the benevolent soul that I am, and go have a pint or two on me," he said with mock grandeur.

Tyr was about to protest, but swallowed his pride and gave a sheepish, grateful grin. "Thank you. And yes, you are truly benevolent. However, I won't put the broom down until this floor has been swept to my satisfaction."

Crowin laughed. "As you wish. Just lock up when you leave. I'll see you on Luain."

It was another hour before Tyr was satisfied with the shop's condition. He locked up and headed straight to the docks, arriving just before sunset—disappointed to find that the *Majonolle* had not yet returned.

He made his way to the Donkey and spotted Trent sitting by the door, keeping an eye on things. Cindy bustled from table to table, taking orders, and Tyr had no doubt that Phelli was busy working her magic in the kitchen.

"There he is!" Trent shouted when he spotted him. "We thought you'd all but forgotten about us poor slobs down at the docks!"

He stood and reached out with a firm handshake, which Tyr returned in kind. Trent immediately winced and shook out his hand.

"That'll teach me to be a smart-ass," he laughed. "A little time back at the forge and your grip's gone deadly."

Tyr smirked. "Are you sure you're not just a wee bit soft?"

Trent glanced at his hand. "I didn't think so, but now you've got me questioning myself."

Just then, a couple of sailors started getting rowdy. "Sorry—duty calls," Trent said, already moving to calm the ruckus before it got out of hand.

Tyr made his way to the bar and hopped onto a stool.

"Ooo, this is my lucky day!" came a familiar voice behind him.

He turned to see Cindy beaming as she wrapped him in a hug.

"Did you say hi to Trent when you came in? He's been keeping an eye out for you."

Tyr nodded.

"No sign of your ship yet," she added, "but it's only been a week—that's to be expected."

She hopped up on the stool beside him. "So, tell me about the shop. Is it all you hoped for? Is the master treating you well? Have you been eating? You look like you've lost a little weight."

Tyr smiled again. "Everything's been wonderful. I would've come back sooner, but the days are long and exhausting. At least for now, once a week is probably the best I can do."

"Once a week is perfect—and better than most of our regulars. We only see them when their ships come into port." She stood. "Let me get you a pint, and I'll tell Phelli you're here. She'd never forgive us if we didn't."

With that, Cindy disappeared into the back.

Tyr turned to look around the tavern. He had enjoyed his time here and cherished the friendships he'd made, but now he felt slightly out of place. He couldn't explain why, but the realization brought a subtle pang of sadness.

Cindy soon returned with a pint and a big bowl of chowder.

"On the house," she said. "Old man Mittle insisted. Phelli would've come out herself, but"—she gestured to the crowded room—"she's a bit busy. Be sure to say hi to her before you leave. And make sure you see me too—I've got something for you. Remind me if I forget!"

With a wink, she vanished again, weaving through the crowd.

Tyr stayed at the Donkey until closing and helped his friends clean up. It was after midnight when he finally made his way back to the boarding house.

Two months had passed since Tyr had first stepped into Master Crowin's forge. Winter had given way to spring. The older smith was as kindhearted as he was skilled, but a quiet sadness always lingered behind his eyes. Jym had confided that Crowin was still mourning the loss of his wife, though she'd passed several years ago. Since her death, he'd never quite been the same.

After she died, the shop began to slip. Most of the smiths had been hired away by other forges, and Crowin made no effort to stop them. Jym stayed on—being Crowin's nephew—and a handful of other smiths remained out of loyalty or because they lacked the experience to be taken elsewhere.

Tyr was standing near the front of the forge when Master Crowin came walking up, a huge grin on his face.

"We did it, my friend—we really did it!"

Tyr smiled back, though puzzled.

Crowin laughed, eyes shining. "I just paid off the last of the creditors. From now on, the shop can run without having to hand over most of our profits."

"Congratulations!" Tyr said, genuinely excited.

"That means I can even start giving you an actual salary," Crowin added.

Tyr raised a hand. "No—I'm just a journeyman. I can only take a small stipend, and you've already been more than fair. I'm content with what I have."

Crowin shook his head. "Please. You're more of a master than anyone working here—including myself. It's not right that the others are lining their pockets off the work you've been doing."

"That's the way it always is—at least until I'm made a master and open my own shop," Tyr said. "Until then, I'm content with my stipend. Besides, the others have all done their time as journeymen and stood before the guild. I haven't."

Crowin made a dismissive noise. "That bunch has learned more by watching you than they probably did in all their years as smiths—and you can ask any one of them; they'd tell you the same."

Tyr smiled but folded his arms. "I'm flattered, truly. But I'll do my time like everyone else. There are no shortcuts in life."

The older smith shook his head but grinned. "Well, there's nothing against me giving you the occasional bonus, now is there?"

Tyr thought a moment, then conceded. "No, there's not."

"Damn right," Crowin said, satisfied.

At that moment, four sailors came rambling up to the forge. The apparent leader eyed them both with a broad, easy smile.

"Gentlemen," he said with a slight slur. "We've been sent on an urgent mission—straight from our ship. We're looking for a smith by the name of Tyr. Any idea where we might find him?"

Tyr stifled a smirk. *Straight from the ship... via the tavern*, he guessed.

"You're in luck," he said. "You found me on your first try."

"Must be me lucky day," the sailor replied, still grinning.

"Well, now that you've found me, how can I help?"

The sailor pulled a parchment from his tunic and handed it to Tyr. "This here's an order for some weapons. We had a bit of a row with a pirate ship on our way in, and the captain decided it was high time for some new sabers and the like."

Tyr opened the parchment and gave it a quick glance—thirty sabers, forty belt knives, and fifteen boat spears. He raised an eyebrow but said nothing.

Crowin asked, "You said you were looking for Tyr—mind if I ask how you heard about him?"

"Our captain's drinking buddies with the captain of the *Majonolle*. From what I heard, he spoke real highly of him—good enough to impress our own captain, anyway."

"Really?" Tyr perked up. "Do you know if the *Majonolle* is in port? I'd love to see my old shipmates."

"No, she was still plying the waters to the south when we last saw her—maybe two weeks ago. She should be back this way in a month or so, weather permitting. And the weather's fickle this time of year."

Tyr nodded. He still visited the docks whenever he could, hoping to see her return—and to stop by the *Drunken Donkey*.

"How soon do you need the order filled?" he asked, returning to the matter at hand.

"No real rush. We're heading out again on the morning tide and won't be back for at least a month—so let's say, a month."

Tyr considered it. "That's doable. How many of the sabers are for officers or anyone of rank?"

"Let's see… one's for the captain, then there's the lieutenant, and two midshipmen."

"And one for the first mate as well," Tyr added to himself. Then he looked up. "I'll need a deposit before you leave."

He handed the parchment to Crowin. "Master Crowin will handle the costs with you. It's his shop, after all."

Crowin smiled but pushed the parchment back toward Tyr. "No. This one's all you. It was a special request for you. All I ask is that you cover the materials, pay for any help from the other smiths, and give the customary five percent back to the forge. The rest is yours to keep."

Tyr blinked, stunned. This would be his first real sale—and a lucrative one at that.

"If you're sure…" he began.

"I am," Crowin said simply.

"Okay then. If you'll follow me," Tyr said, leading the men to the forge's small office.

The following month seemed to fly by. With help from the other smiths, Tyr completed the order ahead of schedule. He forged the five sabers for the officers and first mate himself, taking extra care. Each blade was personalized with the bearer's rank, and the ship's pennant was etched into the steel of every weapon.

He could only hope they'd appreciate the work.

"Ahoy, forge!" boomed a familiar voice from the street.

"Ahoy!" Tyr shouted back as he stepped outside, spotting the sailor from before with two crewmates and a small wagon.

"I've come for the goods," the sailor grinned.

"Then you'd better have some coin," Tyr replied with a smirk.

"How about an ale instead?" the sailor offered.

Tyr laughed. "More like an ale in addition."

"Ha! That's the spirit. Let me see the goods, and I'll give you the coin."

Tyr had the apprentices—now three in number—begin loading the weapons onto the wagon. He handed the sailor one of the officer's sabers, guessing correctly that this man was the first mate. No captain would entrust a task like this to anyone else.

The man let out a low whistle as he unsheathed the blade. His expression went blank as he turned it over in his hands, examining every inch with reverent focus.

"Lad," he said softly, "you've underpriced these—by a lot."

Tyr nearly beamed. "I hope you never have to use it," he said, "but if you do, I hope it serves you well."

The sailor shook his head. "The captain's going to be overjoyed when he sees these. Come to the *Rusty Bucket* tonight—I'm sure he'll want to thank you properly."

Tyr was about to decline, but he missed his own shipmates—and hoped he might hear some word of them if he went.

"I will. What time?"

"Eight bells of the last dog watch," the man said, still admiring the blade.

"I'll be there."

To Tyr's disappointment, he learned nothing about the *Majonolle* that night—but the first mate hadn't been wrong: the captain gave him a generous bonus for the order. Tyr tried to split it with Master Crowin, and though Crowin protested, Tyr insisted.

From that night on, Tyr made a habit of walking the docks, always watching for the *Majonolle*. But weeks passed, and she still hadn't returned. No ships had news of her.

Word of Tyr's craftsmanship spread quickly among the sailors and captains who frequented York. The quality of the sabers made an impression, and new orders began coming in steadily.

Tyr, however, insisted that Crowin take the jobs under the shop's name and use his own mark on the blades. They agreed not to expand the team further. Instead, they'd take only one order at a time. It meant customers had to wait, but it ensured the quality remained high—up to Tyr's exacting standards.

One afternoon, Tyr was working on a captain's sword. He insisted on crafting every officer's blade in each order himself, but the captain's sword was always the capstone—the piece he took the most pride in. He especially enjoyed working subtle details into each weapon, small touches that told a story or honored the bearer.

CUTTER

Steven slowed his horse to a walk as he turned onto the final stretch of dirt road. He had pushed hard over the past two weeks, ever since leaving the black-robed bag of bones known as Cygnus. The nightmare in the north was, for now, behind him. It hadn't ended the way the Order had wanted, but the result was good enough that—with the right spin and the right ears—he might still come out looking like a hero. If he played it right, there could be a promotion—or, if fortune truly smiled, even a commission.

At what cost? The thought returned, unbidden, twisting his stomach with a pang of regret. He tightened his grip on the reins. *Am I willing to pay this price?* He shook the thought away. *No cost is too high.*

He had made a pact with himself the day he betrayed Al: to walk this path no matter where it led.

Al had nearly died in the battle. The thought surfaced again, and his stomach turned.

It's his own fault, Steven countered. *What was he thinking, taking on an ogre army with a few nomads? If it weren't for me, he'd probably be dead. I actually saved his life. And probably most of those obnoxious nomads, too.*

His stomach twisted again at the lie. He grimaced at the betrayal of his own body, then spat into the dust, as if to clear the sour taste from his mouth.

No sense second-guessing now. What's done is done. *You can't uncut the cloth,* as his father used to say.

By the time the Chapter House came into view, Steven had fully composed himself. This was his opportunity. He knew it.

First, he thought, *I need to get the ear of the General Superior—privately.* Not easy for a mere sergeant, especially one only recently promoted. *But I need to capitalize on this hand. Hand?* He smirked. *It's a hand of my own making. I stacked the deck. Now I just need to reel them in and take what I deserve.*

All thoughts of Al faded. Only the next move mattered.

As he entered the Chapter House, he was met by the Door Warden.

"Welcome back, brother," the aging sentry said in the usual monotone, gesturing to the logbook. Everyone was required to sign in and out.

Steven complied, noting the man's disapproving glance as he reached for a sealed letter from a nearby pile.

"You are to report to Captain Gregor immediately upon your arrival," the warden said flatly, his tone as dull as ever.

Steven opened the letter, as required. It said nothing beyond what the warden had told him—he was to report to Captain Gregor without delay.

His mind raced. *I should go straight to his office… but I'm filthy after a month on the road.*

He studied the letter again. *They knew I was coming. For how long? Were they watching for me? Could be good… or very bad. Depends what they've heard.*

He forced a smile and nodded. "Of course. Right away."

As he turned to leave, he paused. "Warden, what day is it? I've been in the wilds for so long I've lost track."

"It's Aoine, the twenty-ninth of Earus."

"Earus, hmm. Days will be getting warmer soon," Steven murmured, then turned away.

He didn't head for the captain's office.

Instead, he made for his quarters. After over a month on the road, he needed to drop his gear and clean up. A quick stop at the barracks for a fresh uniform wouldn't go amiss either. *The captain should thank me if he knew how bad I smell.*

His room was just as immaculate as he'd left it. He opened his wardrobe and looked over the perfectly pressed uniforms. Most sergeants had two or three issue sets. Steven had eight—all tailored by his own hand to fit perfectly.

Well… they did, he thought. *I'll need to take these in. Months on the road have thinned me out.*

He quickly changed and headed to the captain's office.

The adjutant was waiting outside, looking sour. He had clearly been notified of Steven's arrival and had expected him to report immediately.

"Wait here," he said curtly before stepping into the office. A moment later, he returned.

"The captain is expecting you."

Captain Gregor was writing when Steven entered. He neither looked up nor acknowledged him. Steven stood at attention, knowing the delay was deliberate—retribution for not reporting immediately.

After several long minutes, the captain set his quill down and finally looked up.

"Sergeant Waistwain. Welcome back. I trust the events in the north have been satisfactorily handled?"

"I believe they have, sir."

"Oh, do you?" the captain replied coolly. "And how exactly am I to know that? We sent you north with your own squad, and the moment you met the enemy, you dismissed them. You return without prisoners, without wounds, and now claim the matter has been resolved. On what basis should I believe you?"

Steven opened his mouth to respond, but the captain raised a hand.

"Don't." His voice was sharp. "You've been begging for a promotion since the day you arrived. We took a risk—and by 'we,' I mean *I* took a risk—giving you one. I thought I saw potential in you."

He gave Steven a long, disapproving look.

Steven clenched his jaw. He had to force his teeth not to grind. It took every ounce of control not to shout back. *He has no idea the game I'm playing...*

"I don't want to hear anything from you right now. Nothing you say will appease me, and nothing I say will be good for you."

The captain took a breath, composing himself.

"Go to your quarters and write your report—including your rationale for dismissing the squad. I'll review it when I have time. Until then, you are confined to the Chapter House."

He paused.

"For the record, I was the vote that got you promoted to sergeant. Most of the others thought it was too soon—that you lacked the experience. But my family name still carries some weight, and I got my way."

He sighed.

"Maybe I misjudged you. Maybe not. Either way, until I've read your report and made my decision, you have no active role in this Order. Do you understand?"

Steven burned with fury but kept it buried. "Yes, sir."

"Good. You're dismissed."

Steven turned to go, but the captain called after him.

"Sergeant—just so you know, I'm not against you. But in this Order, when you're promoted, you're entrusted with the lives of others. It's a sacred obligation—and it only gets heavier as you rise."

He leaned forward, voice low and direct.

"Those who rise too fast don't feel that weight the same way. They don't understand what's been given to them. I hope I haven't made a mistake. Do you understand?"

Steven considered lying. Just say what the man wanted to hear. But his anger wouldn't let him.

"No, sir. I do not."

The captain sighed. "At least you're honest. Hopefully, in time, you will. Dismissed."

For the next week, Steven was forced to cool his heels at the Chapter House while his fate was debated by the senior officers. Try as he might, he was unable to secure a meeting with the General Superior and had all but given up hope—until, quite by accident, he literally bumped into the man while rounding a corner, knocking him to the floor.

Steven froze for a split second before realizing who it was. His instincts kicked in. He quickly helped the general to his feet, apologizing profusely.

"My deepest apologies, sir," he said. "I wasn't watching where I was going."

The general chuckled, brushing himself off. "Quite all right, young man. My own fault—I had my head buried in these daily reports and wasn't paying attention."

He looked up at Steven, and recognition flickered in his eyes.

"You're that young sergeant who had Captain Gregor all in a twist a while back, aren't you?"

Steven nodded. "Yes, sir. I'm afraid I am," he replied, feigning embarrassment.

"Not to worry, lad. I read your report. I understand what you were thinking when you dismissed the squad. But the captain is also right—it's not something you should ever do. The Order made you their head, and you chose to handicap yourself by cutting off your own body."

He paused, watching Steven's expression.

"Consider how things might have turned out differently had you kept your squad with you."

Steven lowered his gaze. A somber expression crossed his face, and he nodded quietly.

The general gave a faint smile. "Cheer up. You'll get a slap on the wrist, learn your lesson, and be back in full standing in no time. As for me, I'm late for a meeting with my senior officers."

He turned to leave.

"Sir," Steven said quickly. "May I have one more moment of your time?"

The general stopped, clearly annoyed. "Is there something you wish to add, Sergeant?"

"Yes, sir. Something I had to leave out of the official report."

"Oh? And what exactly did you feel the need to withhold from my officers?"

Steven glanced around and lowered his voice. He paused, considering what he was about to say—there would be no going back.

"I met with Cygnus," he said simply, then waited for the general's reaction.

He knew it might get him thrown in chains. *The only path is forward,* he thought.

The general became very still, his posture stiffening.

"You did, did you? And why do you think that name should mean anything to me?"

"Forgive me, sir. It's not my place to question the policies of the Order," Steven began carefully. Now was not the time for boldness. "Cygnus told me he had entered into an agreement with the Order— and that I was to report what he told me directly to you, and no one else. If I was mistaken, I apologize."

The general's face was unreadable.

"He did, did he? Do you make a habit of listening to the enemy?"

Steven gave a shrug, his impish grin returning. "I listen to everyone—even when I'm not supposed to. Information is valuable, no matter the source."

The general studied him for a long moment. "I'll play along for the moment. What did this Cygnus tell you about our so-called agreement?"

"Only that there was an understanding. That you were working toward similar goals. He asked me to help him achieve those ends—and, in doing so, help the Order as well."

"And did you?" the general asked.

"Yes, sir. What I left out of the report is that—"

He stopped. The next part could get him executed.

He closed his eyes, took a slow breath, and whispered, "Is it safe to speak of these matters in the hallway, sir?"

The general hesitated, looked around, then handed Steven his stack of papers. "Follow me. And keep your mouth shut."

Steven obeyed, trailing the general down the corridor into the War Room. Inside, the senior officers were already gathered. As the general entered, they all stood at attention.

"As you were," he said. The officers relaxed slightly.

He pointed to a spot behind his chair. "Stand there," he said to Steven, who moved quickly to comply.

The general called the meeting to order. Steven couldn't believe he was actually present at a senior staff meeting. He scanned the room, spotting Captain Gregor, who looked both puzzled and deeply displeased—much like the other officers.

As the meeting began, one of the majors gestured toward Steven and asked, "Sir, if I may—"

"You may not," the general cut in coldly.

The others got the message and let the matter drop.

Steven listened intently. The Order had spies everywhere and seemed to be monitoring affairs in both the north and the south. No mention was made of Cygnus or the events in the northern wilds, other than that the Order had completed clearing out Morcaster and was in the process of capping the main conduits before allowing resettlement. They had claimed the largest residence in the Noble District for use as a Chapter House.

The meeting then shifted to finances and other tedious matters that Steven found difficult to follow.

After nearly two hours, the general dismissed the gathering. As the last officer left the room, he turned to Steven.

"Close the doors."

Steven did as instructed.

"All right, Sergeant. What were you afraid to mention earlier?"

"I released the citadel's gate and allowed the enemy to enter."

The general leaned back in his chair. "Did you now. That took some guts. They would've killed you if they'd caught you."

"Two tried," Steven said with a thin smile. "Once the enemy was inside, I followed after Al to be there when Cygnus arrived."

"What can you tell me of Cygnus? What kind of man is he?"

"You've never met him?" Steven asked, surprised.

The general shook his head. "No. He had a minor functionary act as his intermediary. Why? Would it have made a difference?"

"That brings me to something else I left out of the report," Steven said.

The general sighed, clearly growing annoyed. "Oh?"

Steven rubbed his face. "It's about the force that took the citadel—and why they did."

"Explain," the general said.

"Let me start by saying this: if I hadn't seen it with my own eyes, I wouldn't believe it myself. But I swear to you it's true."

"Go on. What about the troops?"

"They were ogres, sir."

The general blinked. "Ogres?"

"Yes, sir. Real ones. In the flesh. Each stood nearly nine feet tall and twice as wide as a man. Their skin is so thick a sword slash barely hurts them. The nomads use a short spear with a long, razor-edged blade to pierce their bellies—but it's dangerous. They say the ogres kill three for every one they lose."

The general sat back, studying Steven closely.

"Ogres?" he repeated, incredulous.

"Yes, sir."

"An army of them?"

"About five thousand strong. Plus an unknown number of Klav."

The general frowned. "I'm almost afraid to ask… what in the world is a Klav?"

"A nasty creature—only stands about this high," Steven said, raising his hand to mid-chest. "When they're on two legs, that is. They seem like a cross between a dog and a man, though I'd say they're more beast than human. They attack in packs and use their teeth as much as their blades. I saw more than one man literally ripped apart by them."

He closed his eyes and shuddered, trying to drive the memory from his mind.

The general was silent for a moment, weighing the description. "If this is true," he said slowly, "why would such an army follow a human?"

"According to the nomads… Cygnus isn't human," Steven replied.

The general gave him a sharp look, prompting him to elaborate.

"They claim he's one of the Alkier."

At the sound of the word, the general stiffened. He stood abruptly, fists clenched, and walked to the window. He stared out at the courtyard below where soldiers drilled in formation.

"What do you know of the Alkier?" he asked quietly, almost in a whisper.

"Only what they told me. That they're the servants of the Dokkalfar."

The general's voice dropped further. "Did they say why they thought he was one of them?"

Steven nodded. "Al described him to them… and they saw his pendant. It was black—"

"With a golden winged serpent," the general finished.

Steven blinked in surprise. "Yes, sir. They said it was—"

"The Serpent of Trigon," the general said grimly.

"Yes, sir."

"Damn," the general muttered. He turned from the window and looked at Steven. "We're heading into dark days, Sergeant. If the nomads knew who they were facing, why would they try to stop him? Surely they understood he was a foe beyond their ability to defeat."

"Because of Al, sir," Steven answered without hesitation.

"The friend you brought false charges against to join the Order?" the general asked pointedly.

Steven opened his mouth in protest, but closed it again—caught off guard.

"Relax. You're hardly the first," the general continued. "I know it was Captain Tuttle who put the idea in your head—he included it in his report. Don't worry. It's not held against you. In fact, it's useful to know how far a man is willing to go for the Order."

He stepped closer, lowering his voice.

"But tell me… why would the nomads face not just any Alkier, but the most notorious of them all—an army of ogres and whatever these Klav are—for the sake of a disowned former farmer? A boy barely come to manhood?"

Steven's hands clenched at his sides.

"Because they believe he's one of the Alfarbani."

The general sniffed in disbelief. "Impossible. The Alfarbani were destroyed by the Dokkalfar. That was his final and greatest betrayal. And even if one had survived, they'd be ancient by now—not some boy you grew up with. And if the old tales are true, like the elves, they couldn't reproduce."

Steven nodded as if agreeing with every point. "They said the same thing. But still… they were convinced. And so am I."

"Oh? And why's that?" the general asked.

"The things he can do. The way he fights. His eyes…"

"What about his eyes?" the general interrupted sharply.

"They change in the dark," Steven said. "They turn red—and the iris splits into three, or at least that's what it looks like. And then there's the sword."

The general's voice dropped to a whisper. "That's how the Alfarbani's eyes were described in the ancient texts… but that's not possible."

He looked hard at Steven. "What's this about a sword?"

"Supposedly, it was given to him by one of Cygnus's servants while he was in Morcaster. It's said to be one of the Alfarbani blades of old."

"And you believe that?"

Steven shrugged. "I don't know. I'd never heard of the Alfarbani, or the Alkier, or magic swords. But I've seen this one in action. A normal man, with a normal blade, wouldn't stand a chance against a fully armored ogre. But I watched Al—singlehandedly—cut down at least six of them during our first engagement."

He paused, jaw tightening.

"And when he let the sword 'feed' on them…"

Steven went quiet for a moment. He closed his eyes and shuddered.

"I'm not a squeamish man, sir. But the sound they made—it was like their very essence was being ripped from their bodies. And afterward… Al's strength, his speed, everything increased. His wounds would mend. He wasn't tired anymore. It was as if the sword had… nourished and healed him using the lives it had taken."

The general sank slowly into his chair, clearly shaken.

"Damn," he muttered.

He looked up at Steven. "Thank you, Sergeant. You've given me a great deal to think about."

Steven didn't move. "Sir… if I may offer one last thought?"

The general nodded.

"I heard you ask about Harding during the meeting," Steven said. "I may know why you haven't heard anything."

The general gestured for him to continue.

"Cygnus is heading for the Five Kingdoms. He told me Harding is already being… harassed by his agents. He knows we'll have to stabilize the region eventually. He gave me a contact in Whittle— someone we can coordinate with before making our move."

Steven stepped forward slightly.

"And I know Al. He'll go after Cygnus as fast as he can—with as many of the clans as he can convince to join him. He won't leave Harding at the mercy of an occupying force—not if he thinks he can help them. Which means, when he gets there, he'll try to clear it out before continuing."

He held the general's gaze.

"We need to get there first. Or we risk losing a golden opportunity."

The general eyed him carefully. "Go on."

"Sir, give me command of a legion. I'll go to Harding, meet the contact in Whittle, and have the country cleared before Al ever gets there."

The general raised an eyebrow. "Command of a legion?" he asked, a trace of amusement in his voice. "Boy, only a full colonel or higher can command a legion. You're still technically confined to the Chapter House. And when we gave you a squad, you dismissed them the first chance you got. What makes you think I'd give you command of anything?"

Steven paused.

Time to roll the dice.

"Permission to speak freely, sir?"

The general nodded.

"Sir, we're on the verge of a war unlike any fought in living memory. No one else in the Order has seen this enemy—let alone fought them. I have. I know them."

He squared his shoulders.

"I may be the son of a tailor, and a lowly sergeant—but I'm no fool. I know the Order is playing both sides to capitalize on the chaos and expand our influence in the south. I also know Cygnus—and he knows me. He trusts me—at least more than anyone else in the Order. He gave me the contact in Harding."

He stepped forward, voice low and intense.

"Give me the legion. Give me the promotion. And I'll give the Order new holdings in Harding—and influence in each of the Five Kingdoms."

TENEBRIS

Steven rubbed his eyes. When the general had said it would take "some time," he hadn't realized that meant nearly two weeks of sitting around the Chapter House.

He'd spent his days poring over maps of Harding and the surrounding nations. He'd also tailored the new uniforms issued to him—and made a few more himself. The other officers weren't subtle about their disdain for his promotion. Their stares, their murmurs—they didn't bother hiding it.

He ignored them. He had a plan. And if this was the path that would take him there, then he'd walk it—no matter where it led.

As for the cohort they'd given him... Each captain had been asked to transfer a few soldiers from their own units to his. Naturally, most had used it as an opportunity to offload their troublemakers and layabouts. There were a few exceptions—some promising recruits mixed in—but the bulk of the unit was made up of fresh conscripts or unattached veterans no other officer had claimed.

Steven had avoided spending much time with them during the buildup. But now they were on the march—and he was with them constantly. He was beginning to feel the strain of command, unsure at times how to carry himself in front of them.

"Captain, if I may have a moment of your time?" came a woman's voice from behind.

He cringed. People usually wanted to speak with him only to complain.

"Now's not really a good time," he began.

"It will only take a moment," she said smoothly, "and you may find what I have to say... beneficial."

That got his attention. He turned to find a hard-looking woman—not unattractive, about his age, and only slightly smaller. She looked like she was made of muscle and grit, though he suspected there was more beneath the uniform than met the eye.

She smiled knowingly. "Like what you see?" she asked quietly.

Steven returned her smile. "Maybe," he said, his voice dropping. "Maybe. What is it you want to discuss?"

She stepped a little closer and whispered, "Can we speak in private? I promise it'll be worth your time."

His eyes widened slightly. *Is she coming on to me?* he wondered, hopeful. Only one way to find out.

"My tent's just ahead," he said with a grin. "We can talk there."

He turned and walked on, and she followed close behind.

Inside, Steven dropped into his chair and waited. The woman glanced around outside before closing the tent flap and stepping forward.

"Sir, I'm Corporal Tenebris. One of your scouts."

Steven raised an eyebrow. "Which captain sent you? Or were you one of the unattached?"

"Captain Gregor, sir. But he didn't send me. I volunteered."

He leaned forward slightly. "Really? Why?"

"Because I believe I can be of service to you. And I think you can help me as well."

"Go on," he said, intrigued.

"I don't fit within the Order," she said, shrugging. "Or maybe I should say the Order doesn't yet fit me. I think it needs to be… reformed. And I think you're the man to do it."

Steven studied her. "And why would I want to reform the Order?"

"May I speak plainly, sir?"

Steven smirked. "Not sure I could stop you if I tried."

She gave him a wicked little grin in return. "First, let me tell you a little story—about my very sad life," she said lightly.

"When I was four, my parents sold me to a Lyashian noble."

Steven's face twisted in disgust, but she waved it away.

"Where I come from, Lyashia, selling children—especially by the poor—isn't frowned upon. It's even seen as an act of mercy if it means a better household. Unfortunately, this man didn't want a daughter. He made his money buying children, raising them to be either assassins or consorts—depending on their talents."

She smiled darkly. "Lucky for me, I turned out to be a natural. Assassin, that is. So at the age of four, my training began—and my childhood ended."

Steven shook his head. "That's… horrible. How could your parents do something like that?"

She shrugged. "I don't know. I barely remember them. Maybe they needed the money, or maybe I was just one mouth too many. I'm not angry. Selling me to that little monster put me on a path of rigorous, brutal training—which I loved.”

Her eyes gleamed.

“Normally, kids aren’t sent into the field until twelve. That’s when they start practicing with ‘live subjects.’”

Steven looked confused.

She grinned. “I told you—this life came naturally to me. I never liked being held back. If I see something I want, I take it. I begged my teachers to let me advance early. They refused. So I took matters into my own hands.”

Steven leaned forward slightly. “What did you do?”

“I was barely ten. Still had at least two years of fundamentals left. But I was done waiting. One night, I slipped out of my cell—well, it was technically my room, but we were locked in at night, so we all called them cells. I got dressed, grabbed my training gear, picked the lock, and went looking for the headmistress.”

“She was practicing with a sword. When she saw me, she knew exactly why I was there. She came at me—to teach me some humility.”

Tenebris smiled again. “She didn’t know I wasn’t planning to fight fair.”

Steven raised an eyebrow. “What happened?”

“I feigned panic. Curled up on the ground, trembling like a terrified child. She couldn’t kill me if I didn’t strike first. I gambled she’d try to scare me straight. And she did.”

Her voice lowered. “When she came close—too close—I flipped and threw a dagger I’d hidden. My aim was perfect. She was furious, and I knew she might still kill me… if not for the poison I’d coated the blade with. Fast-acting. I’d stolen it from one of the labs earlier that day.”

A distant look crossed her face. “She dropped to the floor, twitching. Couldn’t even scream—paralyzed, including her vocal cords. I sat beside her. Watched her die. I was calm. Focused. The poison is said to be excruciating.”

Steven stared. “Then what?”

“I stayed there until someone found us. They took me to the noble. He asked why I’d done it. I told him I was ready. That she was holding me back.”

She shrugged again. “He didn’t punish me. He promoted me.”

Steven was quiet for a long moment, entranced by this strange, dangerous woman.

"If you loved the life so much... why did you leave?"

"When I was twelve, the noble decided he would take me as a lover," she said with a broad smile. "Not the smartest decision. I had been trained very well. He was dead before his hand ever touched me."

She paused, studying his reaction. "I knew if I stayed, I'd be killed—or sold into slavery—so I took as much coin as I could find in his quarters, slipped out of the estate, stole a horse, and fled for the border as fast as I could. I didn't breathe easy until I crossed the border. I kept going north until I entered Jaspar."

Steven said nothing, letting her continue.

"There wasn't exactly work for a twelve-year-old assassin, so I found the nearest Order Chapter House and convinced them to take me in as a scout. Scouting was part of my training, after all."

"Does the Order know about your past?" Steven asked.

She shook her head. "No. You're the first person I've ever told."

"Why me?"

"Like I said—because I think you can help me. And I can help you."

"How, exactly?"

She smiled and knelt down between his legs, leaning in to whisper in his ear.

"Let's be honest. You want power and respect. Don't bother denying it. I've been trained to read people—and you're not a complicated book."

She let the words hang, then continued in a lower voice. "But you don't want the mundane responsibilities that come with those things. Day-to-day administration. Petty logistics. Disciplining soldiers. Writing reports. Running a cohort—"

She arched a brow. "—or a legion."

Standing, she moved behind him, resting her hands on his shoulders. Her voice shifted to his other ear. "I can handle those things for you. I know how the Order works—its politics, its personalities. I can keep the troops in line and deal with the officers. Name me your second. Let me smooth the path while you climb the ranks."

Steven turned his head to meet her gaze. Her eyes were deep brown, with a hint of gold. "Name you my second?" he asked.

She laughed—not mockingly, but with playful amusement—and moved back around in front of him.

"Oh, my. You really do need me," she said with a teasing smile. "Every captain in command of a cohort or larger can name a second. It would make me your executive officer—technically a lieutenant. The Order's been dragging its feet on promoting me. This would force their hand."

Steven gave her a long look. He liked her. She was dangerous, driven, and pragmatic—like him. She didn't accept the hand life had dealt her and was willing to do whatever it took to change her fate.

"I think you overestimate my authority," he said cautiously. "I'm only an acting captain. The General Superior said he'd formalize the rank if I complete the mission successfully."

She gave him a sweet, knowing smile. "Silly boy. Acting or permanent, you have the full rights of the position while you hold it. If I'm only an acting lieutenant for the duration of the mission, I'll survive. But that's all the more reason to have me at your side. The other captains won't help you. As far as they're concerned, you're a pretender."

Steven's expression darkened. Anger flared in his gut. "I figured as much," he muttered. "I'll show them before this is over."

"We'll show them," she corrected. "Though that might require a few of them being... retired."

Steven blinked, confused.

Bris leaned in close, settling herself in his lap and pressing her lips near his ear. "I may have to eliminate a few officers," she whispered, so softly he could barely hear her. "If they can't be turned to our side. Will that be a problem?"

Steven thought for a moment. Then he wrapped his arm around her waist and grinned. "Not in the least. In fact, if you get bored, I already have a list of potential candidates."

She giggled. "Oh, we're going to get along very well. Do give me your list. I've been dreadfully bored."

Things started running more smoothly after Steven appointed Bris—her preferred name—as his second. She took to the position like she was born for it. First, she reviewed the squads and reorganized them, dispersing negative influences and tightening discipline. She met with every squad leader, making sure they knew what she expected—not just of their men, but of themselves.

She also began handling all requests and issues from the two allied cohorts traveling with them, shielding Steven from petty distractions. Within a week, her influence showed in the increased discipline and efficiency across the ranks.

She's good, Steven thought, watching her from a distance. *Relatively speaking. But how much can I trust her?*

He smirked. *Probably about as much as she can trust me. For now, the arrangement benefits us both. What happens after? Time will tell. Might as well enjoy the ride while I can.*

Steven, meanwhile, focused on his upcoming meeting with Uso—Cygnus's contact in Whittle. First, he had to figure out how to slip away from the cohort for a couple of days. Technically, they weren't supposed to enter Harding until all forces unified on the eastern border. The road would soon split: the cohort heading east along the Jaspar side of the escarpment, while the path south led directly into Harding.

Captain Gregor and his forces were traveling a day behind them.

No mistaking the reason for that, Steven thought bitterly. *The Order—and the General Superior—don't trust me.* He had no doubt Gregor had spies within his ranks, reporting back regularly. If he abandoned the cohort, Gregor would know almost immediately.

Bris. He needed her input. But could he trust her?

I have to, he told himself.

That night, after the camp had been set, Steven invited Bris to dine with him in his tent.

He kept the conversation light at first—asking about her work with the squads, any issues, what she expected ahead. She had traveled these lands more than he had and knew the terrain well.

But as dinner wore on, he kept delaying the real question. When the attendant cleared the last of the plates, he worried he'd missed his chance.

Bris leaned back and smiled. "So," she said, "what aren't you asking me?"

Steven blinked. "What makes you think I'm not asking something?" he said innocently.

She laughed—a soft, velvet laugh. "My captain," she said playfully, "I'm a trained assassin. I can read a man from a mile away. You've been dancing around something all evening. I told you—I want you to succeed. *Need* you to succeed. It's the only path forward for me. So whatever it is... just ask. I doubt either of us will be shocked."

Steven poured them each a glass of wine, then leaned back, watching her carefully. His mind raced.

Damn it. I'm too far in to back out now. Time to roll the dice.

"How much do you know about what happened in Morcaster?" he asked. "I mean... what *really* happened?"

"Morcaster?" she echoed with a shrug. "About what everyone else knows, I guess. Some sort of attack—poisonous gas released through an old ventilation system no one knew existed. Last I heard, no one knows who did it or why."

Steven nodded. "That's true... to a point. Except—we *do* know who did it. And why."

She raised an eyebrow. "Then why haven't we gone after them? Unless... it was one of the Five Kingdoms?"

Steven shook his head. "No. Not them. It was a foreign power. From across the ocean."

She blinked. "Across the ocean? I thought only slavers and smugglers were mad enough to cross it."

He stood, took a sip of wine, and began pacing. "This is where it starts getting... strange."

She tilted her head, intrigued.

"What do you know about the last great war?" he asked. "The one that ended the reign of the Dokkalfar?"

"Not much," she admitted. "And most of what I do know is probably more myth than truth. Tales of ogres, dwarves, the dreaded Alkier... the sort of stories kids love. Why?"

He met her gaze.

"Because it's all true. The ogres. The Alkier. The Alfarbani. Even the monsters. All of it."

She laughed softly. "Now you're just having fun at my expense."

But her smile faded when she saw the look in his eyes.

"No... you're serious. What did you see?"

"Too much," he said. "Not enough. I don't know." He poured more wine. "I've fought against—and with—an ogre army led by one of the Alkier. Not just any Alkier, either. Cygnus of Trigon."

Bris stilled, her eyes narrowing.

"He's here," Steven continued, "and he's trying to break the seals on the Dokkalfar's prison. Gods know how many others have already joined him."

"You said you fought *against* and *with*?" she asked carefully.

He nodded. "Yes. Twice now, I've betrayed my best friend. The only person who might actually have a chance of stopping Cygnus."

He paused, locking eyes with her.

"And why, you ask? Because I want more than what society says I'm entitled to. And if that means sacrificing my best friend—" he held her gaze "—or anyone else, to achieve that goal… I will."

Bris studied him for a moment, her expression unreadable. Then she smiled.

"Good. You finally said it out loud." She nodded, almost approvingly. "Now we understand each other. There are no limits we won't cross."

She paused, then added, "If the legends are true, though, no man can defeat an Alkier."

"He's not a man," Steven said. "He's an Alfarbani."

"I thought they were wiped out at the end of the last war?"

Steven shrugged. "Apparently not. Honestly, I hadn't even heard of them before I went north. But he is one—no doubt about it. He even carries one of their mythic swords. Damned thing feeds on its victims."

He shuddered, eyes distant.

"You can hear it. The screaming. It rips their life force out—it's the stuff of nightmares."

"An Alfarbani?" she repeated, stunned. "No way."

"You said it yourself—no human can beat an Alkier. He fought one. Killed it. He thought it was Cygnus, but it wasn't. There was a second Alkier, one Al didn't know about."

Bris's voice dropped to a whisper. "He *killed* an Alkier…"

She shook her head in awe. "So… why betray him?"

"There's more," Steven said. "Turns out, the Order is in league with Cygnus. He showed me the seal of the General Superior."

Bris's eyebrows shot up.

Steven shrugged. "What was I supposed to do? If the Order's crawling into bed with Trigon, I figured I might as well advance the Order's goals… and my own."

He gave her a wicked grin.

Bris chuckled. "That was a golden opportunity. Nicely played. Is that how you convinced them to give you this command?"

"Partly. The other part is that Cygnus gave me a contact in Harding. He knows we'll eventually move in, and he wants coordination through that contact. We look like we're taking action, while he keeps his forces mostly intact."

"His forces—are they ogres?" she asked, almost breathlessly.

Steven nodded. "At least in the north they were. They came south with him. But I doubt he'll unleash them in Harding. Too conspicuous. More likely, we'll be dealing with the klav."

"Klav?" she echoed.

Steven grimaced. "Nasty things. Part dog, part man—more dog than man, I think. They wear armor, carry short swords, but they can also run on all fours. Their claws and fangs are just as deadly. They attack in packs, like wild animals. And they eat their victims. Sometimes before they're dead."

Bris went pale. "Charming. No wonder they didn't make it into the bedtime stories."

She took a long drink from her glass.

"So… we're working with the enemy."

Steven shrugged. "Partly. For now, our interests align. That could change at any moment."

She refilled her glass. "Then we're walking a tightrope."

"There's one more thing," Steven said, hesitating. He gave her a long look. Then, nodding to himself, he continued.

"Cygnus wants me to work for him directly. So… you should know. My loyalties are—at the moment—divided."

He waited.

She raised her glass in salute. "That's all right. My loyalties aren't divided. I'm not loyal to the Order, or to Cygnus—just to you."

Steven grinned, flashing a broad, toothy smile. "Until you aren't," he teased. "Keep saying things like that and I'm going to fall for you."

She giggled. "Oh, please—you already have. At least until you don't."

He laughed, still smiling.

"When and where do you need to meet your contact?" she asked, shifting back to business.

"I need to reach Whittle in Harding before the cohorts hit the eastern border," he said. "But I'm convinced Gregor has spies in our camp."

"He does," she replied without hesitation. "And I know exactly who they are."

Steven blinked.

"Don't worry," she added casually, like she was discussing inventory. "I'll take care of them before morning. No one will find the bodies."

He raised an eyebrow. "If we do that, won't it raise suspicion?"

Bris shook her head. "No. They only report if they have something to report. If nothing happens, they go the entire journey without sending a word. Less risk of being discovered that way," she added, noting his doubtful expression. "Trust me."

He nodded. "Then I just need a way to sneak out of camp before the road splits east. I trust you have no problem taking command while I'm away?"

She smiled. "I thought I took command a few days ago."

"Ow," he said with a mock wince. "That one hurt."

"I'll pick a few men to go with you," she said, lifting a hand before he could protest. "Hand-picked. Discreet. Loyal. Good with a sword."

She thought for a moment.

"We should reach the turn the day after tomorrow. A few hours before sunrise, you and your little band should ride out ahead of the column. From there, it should only be about two days' ride to the border."

"Sounds like a plan," he agreed. "Just do me a favor—try not to kill everyone while I'm gone."

She shrugged, grinning. "I make no such promise. Your best bet is to finish your business quickly and return before I get bored."

"You do like killing, don't you?"

She sighed. "Not the killing part—not exactly. I enjoy the challenge of doing it well, without getting caught. It's often the quickest way to solve a problem. And I'll admit—there's a thrill in watching the life drain from someone's eyes."

She paused, then gave a small smile.

"Okay… I guess I do like killing. Does that bother you?"

Steven met her gaze and smiled. "Not in the slightest."

He set his glass down. "I should turn in."

Bris put her own glass aside, then took his hand gently. "I was just thinking the same thing."

A few hours before dawn—two days after he and Bris began sharing a bed—Steven rose in silence, dressing quickly in the dark. He leaned down and kissed her softly on the cheek, then slipped out of the tent.

The camp was still asleep as he made his way toward the southern edge. His horse was already saddled, and five hand-picked soldiers stood waiting. He gave one last glance back toward the tent where Bris still slept, and for a brief moment, he wished he could crawl back into bed beside her.

Instead, he mounted his horse, turned south, and rode into the darkness with his small band—toward the border, and whatever came next.

USO

It took Steven four days of hard riding to reach the walls of Whittle. At the border between Harding and Jaspar, he and his men were stopped by a group of well-armored soldiers bearing a symbol unfamiliar to him. They were clearly under strict orders—not allowing anyone to enter or leave Harding. Only after Steven revealed the symbol of Trigon were they reluctantly permitted passage.

The hard ride, at least for the moment, was over. The six of them sat slumped on their horses, weary and coated in dust, watching the town walls glow in the pale light of early morning. Unlike the last time he'd visited, the gates were closed and guarded. Armed men stood along the ramparts, and the arrival of a small detachment of Odio soldiers caused a noticeable stir.

"Harding asked the Odio for help months ago," called down one of the guards, squinting. "Better late than never, I guess. How far behind are the rest of your troops?"

Steven didn't bother hiding his annoyance. "I'd prefer not to discuss troop movements from the back of my horse with someone I don't know."

"Sorry, sorry," the guard stammered. Then he turned and shouted down: "Open the gates!"

He looked back at Steven. "Please report to the commander, you'll find him at Town Hall. He'll want to hear whatever news you bring. I can send one of my men to guide you—"

"That won't be necessary," Steven cut him off. "I grew up not far from here. I know the town well enough."

He turned to Mathers, the soldier nearest him—a competent blade, if not the brightest. "So much for a quiet in and out," Steven muttered. "Now we have to go play nice with the locals."

Mathers said nothing, only nodded.

Once they passed through the gates and were out of earshot of the guards, Steven slowed his horse and gestured for Mathers to ride beside him.

"I'm going to deal with the local commander. Take the men to the Plow and Lantern and get us rooms. I'll meet you there as soon as I can."

Mathers frowned. "Just one question—where is this inn? I'm not from around here, remember?"

Steven chuckled. "Fair enough."

He turned in the saddle and pointed ahead.

"This road runs north-south. Another main road cuts east-west through the center of town. Right up ahead is the magistrate's office—that's where I expect I'll find the commander. You'll want to keep going north for a bit. First major road on your right leads into the residential district. The inn is just down that road."

He looked at the group and added, "I know the men probably want to let off steam, but try to keep them in line. The people around here don't like the Order—and we want them to trust us, not fear us. Stay low profile."

Mathers nodded again. "Understood."

By the time Steven rode up to Town Hall, word of their arrival had already spread. The local commander and the mayor were standing on the stone steps with several others gathered behind them.

The commander looked down the road behind Steven, as if searching for more troops. Then he turned his attention to Steven.

"Is your commander far behind?"

Steven's face hardened. "Very far. My commander is the General Superior of the Order. If you'd like to speak with him, I suggest you start riding immediately—he's at the Chapter House in Jaspar."

The commander gave Steven a long look, as if trying to size him up. He opened his mouth to speak but paused, collecting his thoughts.

"My apologies," he said at last. "No insult intended. You're just… quite young to wear a commander's badge. That's… an accomplishment."

The lack of sincerity wasn't lost on Steven.

The mayor said nothing but kept shifting his weight uncomfortably. Steven guessed he was itching to speak.

Steven offered a stiff smile. "Perfectly understandable. And I apologize for being curt—it's been a long ride, and I didn't expect to be summoned the moment I arrived."

The magistrate and commander exchanged a look.

"Surprised?" the mayor asked. "Aren't you here in response to our call for help? Riders were dispatched from Torringburgh weeks ago. Surely they've reached the Chapter House by now?"

Steven shook his head. "Not to my knowledge. When I departed, there had been no official request—or at least, none I was aware of."

"Then why are you here?" the commander asked, suddenly wary. "And how did you get past the border?"

Steven glanced at the crowd of onlookers. "Perhaps we should continue this conversation somewhere more private?"

The magistrate nodded quickly. "Yes, yes, of course. Follow me."

He led them through the hall and down a few corridors to a modest but well-appointed study. Morning sunlight streamed in through large windows, casting a warm glow across the room.

The magistrate moved behind the desk and slumped into a large chair with an exhausted sigh.

"All right, Commander," he said, "please explain—why isn't the Order sending help?"

Steven smiled politely. "Just to clarify—I am a captain, not a commander. But that's beside the point."

He moved to the window and looked out over the rooftops.

"As for your question—I don't know that they aren't sending help. All I can say is that, when I left, I hadn't heard anything about it."

"Then why are you in Whittle?" the commander repeated.

"I'm here on Odio business," Steven replied evenly. "And, before you ask, I'm not at liberty to discuss the details."

He let their frustration build for a beat, then lowered his voice and leaned slightly toward them.

"But," he added, "and you didn't hear this from me…"

Both men instinctively leaned in.

"…it's possible my presence here means the Order is aware of your situation—and is preparing to act."

The magistrate's face lit up with hope. He rose from his chair.

"Why didn't you say so sooner? That changes everything—"

Steven raised a hand. "Quietly. And your discretion is critical. I'm only here for tonight—maybe tomorrow. I'll be gone as soon as my business is finished. No one must know why I came, or where I go next."

He turned back to the window, eyes scanning the town.

"You'll need to hold out just a little longer. But I give you my word—the next time you see me, I'll be at the head of several thousand soldiers."

The magistrate was nearly giddy, struggling to contain his excitement. The commander, though more reserved and clearly confused, wasn't about to dismiss the possibility of aid.

"Is there anything we can do to assist you?" he offered.

Steven shook his head. "For now, the best help you can provide is discretion. I'll try to send runners ahead of our approach so your people can prepare."

The commander and magistrate nodded, seemingly satisfied. Steven turned to leave, then paused without looking back.

"Can you describe the enemy to me?" he asked.

"I doubt you'd believe me if I did," the commander replied.

"Try me," Steven said over his shoulder.

"Some kind of feral beast. Part animal, part human. They run in packs. Vicious bastards."

Steven nodded. "As I thought. The Klav. Keep your doors locked. Don't let anyone travel alone."

"You've seen them before?" the commander asked, surprised.

"Oh yeah. See them. Fought them. Killed them. And it looks like I'll be doing it again." Without another word, he left.

Steven took the long way back to the inn, wandering through streets he once thought he'd never see again. The sun had long since set by the time he reached the Plow and Lantern.

As he approached, a wave of memory washed over him. The building stood just as he remembered—sturdy, welcoming, nestled in the heart of the rural town. Built of thick timber and stone, its earthy brown paint and thatched roof blended perfectly into the agrarian surroundings. Lanterns glowed warmly beneath the eaves of the wide wooden porch, where patrons lounged, laughed, and smoked. A swinging sign carved with a plow and lantern creaked gently above the entrance.

Steven stopped, gazing at it with an unexpected ache. He could almost see himself, Tyr, and Al sitting on that porch, joking about things that had once seemed so important.

Why did I pick this inn? he muttered to himself.

Stepping inside, he was greeted by a cozy, familiar warmth. The rustic interior was unchanged—exposed beams, stone walls adorned with old tools and local paintings. Lanterns flickered, and a fireplace crackled with soft light. Wooden tables draped in checkered cloths were scattered about, vases of fresh flowers providing bursts of color. A fiddler played a cheerful tune in the corner while farmers, traders, and townsfolk drank and laughed, their voices weaving a sense of community.

He spotted his men at a table near the center. As he approached, they made room for him.

"Everything all right?" Mathers asked.

Steven nodded. "No trouble from the local guard," he said, glancing around. "Last time I was here was the day I left to join the Order."

"You almost sound sad when you say that, sir," Mathers noted.

Steven scoffed. "Hardly. Best decision I ever made—walking away from this backwater and its backward ways." But the knot in his stomach betrayed the lie.

"Sergeant said you grew up near here?" asked the youngest of the group—Will, Steven recalled.

"I did. About a day's walk west of here."

"Do you miss them, sir? Your folks, I mean?" Will asked, almost shyly.

Steven took a long pull from his ale before answering. "The Order is my family now, boy." Another knot twisted inside.

Mathers leaned in and lowered his voice. "We've been listening to the locals. There's unrest—more than just fear of monsters."

Steven raised an eyebrow.

"The townsfolk are angry the farmers aren't protecting them. The farmers want refuge behind the walls. The merchants and tradesmen are talking—saying maybe they should have a voice on Harding's council."

Steven leaned back, rubbing his chin. "Are they now..."

Harding's a republic run by landowners. Without a standing army, the farmlands are defenseless. Normally, threats from nations wouldn't matter— treaties would force allies to intervene. But Cygnus has closed the borders. No one outside even knows what's happening. This... this could be useful.

"Did you hear anything else?" he asked quietly.

"Just whispers. Tensions are rising, but nothing's happened yet. Still, they're worried what happens when the food runs low."

Steven scratched his head. *A food shortage? In Harding? That's not something I ever thought I'd hear.* He nodded to Mathers. "Good work. Keep listening. Let me know if anything changes."

Mathers looked around the room. "Any idea who you're supposed to be meeting?"

Steven waved a server over. "No clue. I showed the coin to the innkeeper when I arrived. He didn't say anything—just waved me into the common room. I figure someone's watching. They'll send word when it's time."

He glanced at Riff, one of the younger men, who was counting his coins under the table.

"The Order really doesn't pay us what we're worth, do they?"

Mathers picked up on the cue. "No, they most certainly do not."

Steven reached into his pouch and pulled out two silver coins—part of what Cygnus had given him. He let them jingle in his palm.

"My second tells me I can trust you five. Says you're good in a fight, that I can count on you when it matters. Is she right?"

The table erupted in a resounding, "Heck yeah!"

Steven grinned and tossed the coins onto the table. "Good. Then tonight, the beer's on me. Drink up—but remember, we may be leaving early. So make sure you can stay in a saddle, conscious or otherwise."

The cheer that followed was as loud as it was genuine. Steven sat back, savoring the moment. *This*—this was what he wanted. Men who saw him not as a tailor's son, but as a leader.

As the night wore on, the tavern grew louder and more crowded. Steven, though tempted, kept his head clear. It was nearing midnight, the noise at its peak, when a small boy tugged on his sleeve.

Steven instinctively raised a hand, about to cuff the child for the interruption—but the boy cringed and blurted out, "Uso is waiting for you. Follow me."

Steven paused, then dropped his hand and stood.

"Wait here," he told his men. "This shouldn't take long."

He followed the boy through the bustling crowd and into the dimmer recesses of the inn.

Uso sat alone in the far corner of the common room, where the light barely reached. He was bundled in heavy robes with a deep hood pulled low over his head, thick leather gloves covering his hands. At first glance, he looked like a vagrant. But his posture—still, composed—betrayed a military discipline.

"You have something for me? Something to prove you come from my Lord Cygnus?" His voice was deep and raspy.

Steven had expected something like this. He pulled one of the strange tokens Cygnus had given him and tossed it toward Uso. With startling speed, Uso snatched it from the air. For a split second, Steven glimpsed the skin of his right arm—leathery, almost scaled, with a faint greenish hue. He blinked. *Must be the dim light playing tricks.*

Uso examined the token, then handed it to a nearby man, who silently affixed it to a long metal rod and walked toward the nearest fireplace. He inserted it into the flames.

Steven frowned but said nothing.

"My Lord knew you would come. He knows what you want. The answer is yes—but only as far as Whittle. No farther."

Steven arched an eyebrow. "I doubt he *knew* I'd come. More likely, he gambled I would. And what, exactly, does he think I want?"

Uso leaned forward. In the shadows, Steven caught a glimpse of his eyes—reptilian, slitted like a snake's. Again, he told himself it was just the light.

"You want to chase the Klav from Harding. You want to be its hero," Uso whispered.

Steven shrugged. "Hardly a surprise. He told me that much himself. But I need more than Whittle. I need to go all the way to Torringburgh. Otherwise, the job's only half done."

Uso hissed softly. "Whittle. No farther. That is what our Lord commands."

"Your Lord. Not mine," Steven replied, his voice sharpening. "And I don't think you fully understand the situation. I'll be arriving with a large military force. It'll raise suspicion if we stop in Whittle and go no farther."

Uso coughed violently. "Apologies," he rasped, "your food takes some getting used to." He composed himself. "What you ask is… difficult. Our Lord needs time to withdraw his forces. The southern pass is not yet ready to be surrendered. It leads directly to Torringburgh."

Steven nodded slowly. "Then tell him this: I'll occupy Torringburgh—but I won't move against the pass. Let him withdraw on his own timeline."

Uso paused, then fell into another coughing fit before replying. "I will pass your message along. But understand—our Lord does not take kindly to having his commands questioned."

Steven didn't flinch. "Again. *Your* Lord. Not mine."

"You keep saying that," Uso said. "Yet you took his gold. He spared your life. He aids you now. Do you deny these things?"

"I don't. But what I did—and what he did—was for mutual benefit. That's all."

Uso leaned in again, voice dropping to a whisper. "I told you. Our Lord knows what you truly want. You say you want to be a hero. But what you *truly* want... is respect. Power. Fear. Obedience. He can give you all of that."

Steven shifted slightly. He knew he should walk away—but something about Uso's words compelled him.

"Why would he help me?"

"Our Lord watches for those willing to do what others won't. For those unshackled by the moral constraints of lesser men. He sees that in you. He wants to fan the spark and see how brightly your flame might burn."

Steven's eyes narrowed. "And what would I have to do to earn his trust?"

Uso gestured toward the fireplace, where the token now glowed red-hot. "Simply accept his mark."

Steven stared at the glowing symbol. "And then what?"

"He will aid you in gaining what you desire. But make no mistake—once marked, you serve him. Or you suffer."

"Why would I agree to that?" Steven asked.

In response, Uso pushed back his hood and leaned into the flickering light.

His face was leathery, green-hued, unmistakably inhuman. His eyes—yellow, slit-pupiled—locked on Steven's like a predator sizing up prey.

Steven recoiled slightly. "What are you?"

"I am a goblin. Attached to a force far larger than the one you faced in the north. Much larger. Stronger. Better equipped."

He paused.

"Your Order is outmatched. Cygnus is willing to let you claim a victory here in Harding. A ruse—one that places you at the forefront, giving him influence without drawing suspicion. He will rule from the shadows, while the people see you as their savior."

He pulled his hood back up and melted into the darkness.

"Or," he continued, "you can cast your lot with your precious Order. But once my Lord finishes with the Five Kingdoms, he will turn his gaze on Harding. And those who did not help him… will be dealt with."

Steven stood still, weighing his options. He glanced at the token in the fireplace, its metal glowing red-hot. *I hate this land,* he thought. *But if I play this right, I could rule it. And if I defy Cygnus…* He didn't finish the thought. Not aloud. Not even to himself. Somewhere in the back of his mind, he thought of his parents… and of Al.

Finally, he looked back at Uso and gave a single, deliberate nod.

"Splendid," Uso said as he stood. With a motion of his hand, he signaled to the man by the fire, who removed the iron from the pit and brought it over. Turning to Steven, he instructed, "Remove your shirt."

Steven obeyed. The other man gripped his shoulder to steady him as Uso pressed the glowing brand against the left side of his chest— just over his heart.

The searing pain was blinding. Steven clenched his jaw, every muscle trembling with the effort of silence. He longed to scream but refused to give Uso the satisfaction. When the iron was finally lifted, the scent of scorched flesh filled the room.

"Not bad," Uso said, with something almost like approval. "You held your tongue well."

He placed his hand over the brand and whispered a few words in a language Steven didn't recognize. Whatever the spell was, it drove the mark deeper into his flesh—searing not just his skin, but something deeper. His very essence.

Then, Uso reached into his robes and produced a small jar of dark ointment. "Apply this. It will dull the pain and speed the healing."

Steven shot him a venomous look but took the jar and rubbed the salve over the fresh wound. The relief was minimal—but enough. He redressed in silence, pulling his shirt gingerly over the raw skin.

As he turned to go, Uso spoke again. "One more thing."

Steven paused. "Yes?"

"Make sure anyone among your troops who might oppose you doesn't live long enough to return here."

Steven turned back with a cold glare. "Cygnus may be my lord now, but you don't command how I run my men. That said—on this matter, we are of like mind. Cleaning house is already high on my list of priorities."

Uso chuckled—low and gravelly. "You do have some steel in you. I see now why our Lord has accepted your service."

When Steven returned to the tavern's common room, his men were deep in their cups, singing bawdy songs and banging their mugs together in drunken celebration. But the moment Mathers saw the look on Steven's face, he sobered immediately.

"Problems?" he asked. The others fell quiet, watching Steven expectantly.

Steven shook his head. "No. Just a very disagreeable fellow. But the meeting was a success."

He reached into his pouch and tossed a few more silver coins onto the table. "I'm going to get a few hours of sleep. You lot can stay up all night if you want—just be ready to ride after breakfast."

"Breakfast?" Mathers asked, surprised. "I thought you wanted to be gone before sunup."

"I did," Steven admitted. "But I'm tired. And in pain. And I've got a lot to think about." He looked over the group, his voice dropping slightly. "Try to keep them out of trouble."

He nodded to Mathers, then turned toward the stairs. "I'll see you in the morning."

HAYSEED

The winter in the north had been brutal. The month of *Earus* was when spring typically returned—a time of warming and rebirth. But Al sat on a small rock outcrop just outside the camp, Talionis stretched out at his feet, and saw no sign of either. He stared across the frozen plain, trying to picture Harding in spring. People were always happier then, their moods lighter. But try as he might, he couldn't recall the smell of new grass—or even the scent of his mother's honey bread, which she loved to bake when the thaw came.

He sighed. Talionis looked up at him with curious eyes. Al reached down and scratched the wolf behind his ears—he had grown large over the past month. *Nearly as big as his mother was*, Al thought. As he rubbed, Talionis rolled onto his back, eager for more. Al smiled despite his mood.

"You always want your belly rubbed, don't you?" he said aloud.

"You do realize how crazy that looks?" came a familiar voice that never failed to make him smile.

"Rubbing a dog's belly isn't crazy, is it, boy?" he replied.

"Except this isn't a dog. It's a timber wolf the size of a small horse," Ryanna laughed.

She sat down beside him and joined in rubbing Talionis's belly. The wolf only let the two of them near him—anyone else got a warning growl.

"How can you sit out here in just a light shirt?" she asked. "Even this rock is freezing. Come back to the camp and sit by the fire. You haven't fully healed yet."

"I'm all right," Al replied. "The cold doesn't affect me anymore— just like the darkness stopped bothering me back in Morcaster."

"You shouldn't be using your powers—not while you're still healing. You'll overexert yourself."

He gave a mirthless smile. "I'm not doing anything. Like my eyes, my body's changed again. My skin's gotten harder since the fight with Cygnus." He pressed a finger into his forearm. "Probably tough enough to stop an arrow without me focusing any energy into it."

She touched his arm gently. "Isn't that a good thing?"

Al looked out over the snow-covered plains. "I used to think so. Now I'm not so sure. It feels like the more I use this power, the more it changes me—into something else."

"You're still you. You're my warrior. *Our Takeshi*," she said with a teasing jab to his ribs. She knew he hated the title and used it whenever she wanted to get a rise out of him.

"Am I?" he asked.

She frowned, and he continued. "Ever since the fight with Cygnus, I've felt… off. I worry that if I keep using this power, I'll lose my humanity. And then I'll be no better than those we're fighting. No better than Cygnus."

She looped her arm around his and leaned her head on his shoulder. "You could never be like Cygnus."

"How can you be so sure?"

"Because he's a man buried in his own darkness. If the stories are true, he's lived for centuries and slaughtered innocents for his own amusement. You, my love, fight to protect. You heal. You resist. And you stand against a greater darkness. Your heart is noble—and a noble heart doesn't turn so easily."

He gave a small smile. "I hope you're right. But I don't think Cygnus was always evil. And I don't think he sees himself that way. What if the more I use this power, the colder I become?"

"Then I'll stop you," she said simply. "We'll stop you—me, the clans, Talionis." She reached down and scratched the wolf again. "Right, boy?"

Talionis sat up and licked Al's face. Al and Ryanna burst into laughter.

"That's better," she said, though the smile faded too quickly from his face. "Something else is bothering you."

He looked at her for a moment. "You truly are something special," he said softly.

"I know," she replied with a grin.

"It's the clans," he said at last.

She sat up straighter. "What about them?"

"It saddens me that they're all leaving the north. I was hoping some of the families might stay. They could've been an anchor— something to return to when this is all over."

She looked at him seriously. "Al, look around. This is a hard land. The clans stayed because of the seal—because it was their duty. That duty has ended. The seal failed. There's nothing binding us here anymore. Now the clans feel it's their duty to stop Cygnus before he destroys the remaining seals. They believe it's their fault the Dokkalfar might be released. So yes, we're leaving the north. And we'll never return. We plan to defeat Cygnus—or die trying."

"I know," Al said softly. "I don't disagree. It just makes me sad."

"You have a gentle heart for such a dangerous man," she said sweetly. Then she stood and offered him her hand. "But I don't have your resistance to the cold. I'm going back to the fire."

He looked at her hand, then down at Talionis. "What do you say, boy? Should we go find something to eat?"

Talionis's tail thumped eagerly. Al laughed and took Ryanna's hand. "I'll take that as a yes."

The three of them walked back to camp together.

Later that night, a messenger came to their tent and reported that the pass to the south had cleared enough for the clans to move through. Rogan had given word—they would leave at first light.

"So, I'll finally get to see these famous Southlands," Ryanna said lightly as she sat on the rugs across from Al. "What should I expect?"

Al shrugged. "In my experience, people are pretty much the same wherever you go. Some good, some bad. Most just trying to get by."

She studied him for a moment. He had risen and now stood near the wall of the tent, staring at the sword Gutamino had given him— the Alfarbani blade, the one that could make him nearly invincible.

"Don't worry, Al. We'll catch up to him. And this time, you'll have the clans at your side when you face him," she said, her voice calm and reassuring.

He smiled faintly. "I know. I'm just trying to decide..." He paused, eyes still on the weapon. "...if I can face him without this."

"Would that be wise? I thought that was the only way to stop him."

But at what cost? Al asked himself, but only smiled at Ryanna and said, "You're right, of course."

It had taken Al nearly five weeks to travel alone from the southern edge of the forest to its northern rim, where he met Kylindo, Glyn, and Ryanna. Now, with the entirety of the northern clans behind him, it had taken less than three weeks to return south.

To be fair, I had no idea where I was going the first time, he consoled himself. *And I spent half of it wandering east instead of north.* Not to mention, the ogres had carved a rather wide path south—one that was now easy to follow.

He slowed his horse a bit to fall in beside Tyfin, who rarely strayed far from his side.

"Takeshi," the Talpon chieftain greeted him with respectful warmth.

Al groaned inwardly at the title but made no comment. "Could you send a runner back to Glyn and ask him to ride up? I'd like a word." He never gave orders to the chieftains—the role the clans had unofficially bestowed on him still sat uneasily on his shoulders.

Tyfin smiled broadly. "I'll go myself, Takeshi. I've a matter to discuss with him as well." Before Al could thank him, he'd already wheeled his horse around and trotted back into the column.

About half an hour later, Tyfin returned with both Glyn and Rogan. Judging by the expressions on their faces, Tyfin and Glyn had been arguing again. Al raised a questioning brow at Rogan, who simply rolled his eyes and shook his head. Al decided not to pry.

"Glyn, thanks for coming. Rogan," he added with a respectful nod, "you honor me."

"The honor is mine, Takeshi," Rogan replied. "I would speak with you after, if you'll permit it."

"I am at your service, as always," Al said.

"So, if the formalities are out of the way," Glyn cut in, "how can I help you, Al?"

Glyn had matured since they'd first met, but he still brimmed with energy and a thirst for adventure.

"I have an idea that might be perfect for you—if you're up for a little excitement."

"Hmmm. Will it get me away from this maddeningly slow march?"

"As a matter of fact, yes," Al said with a smile.

"Then I don't care what it is. I'm your guy."

"I was hoping you'd say that." Al leaned slightly in his saddle. "I'd like you to meet with each of the Clan Chiefs—since Rogan and Tyfin are here, you'll only need to visit the other three. I want each of them to choose twenty of their hunters or warriors. They don't have to be the best at either, but they do need to be agile, quick on horseback, and have excellent eyesight and hearing."

The three exchanged confused glances.

"All right," Glyn said cautiously. "But for what purpose?"

"I want to form a scouting unit," Al explained. "And I want you to train and lead them—assuming the Council of Elders agrees," he added, glancing at Rogan.

"A scouting unit," Glyn repeated, the gears already turning in his head.

"With this many people and mouths to feed, we'll need them riding ahead to find good campsites, fresh water, grazing for the herds—and places to trade or barter for supplies if we need them."

All three nodded in agreement.

"We should reach the edge of the forest by tomorrow afternoon. Once we do, I think the clans should separate a bit. It'll ease the strain on the land and make travel easier for everyone."

Tyfin spoke up. "I'll talk with the other chieftains tonight and put the idea before them."

"Thanks," Al said.

Glyn grinned. "Well, I suppose I'd better get started on this little mission of yours."

"If you're not opposed," Tyfin added with a sly grin, "I'll join you. It sounds exciting."

Glyn groaned theatrically. "I can never tell if he's being serious or making fun of me. Ah well, come on then. Could use the company— and it'll give us a chance to finish our earlier conversation."

The two rode off together, already immersed in animated conversation.

As they disappeared into the column, Rogan rode up beside Al. "Those two are like brothers—half the time at each other's throats, the other half inseparable."

Al chuckled. "Quite the pair."

"So, how can I help the mighty Rogan today?" he asked playfully.

"Two things. First, when we make camp tomorrow on the open fields, I suggest we remain there for a day."

Al tilted his head. "Why? Once we're out of the woods, we'll make better time."

"I know," Rogan said. "But the day after tomorrow we are going to celebrate the spring equinox. It's a day honored by all the clans. Once we leave these woods, we leave our old lives behind. This would be a good time to honor that life—before we move on."

"The equinox was more than a month ago. It was before we attacked Citadel," Al said quietly.

Rogan nodded. "I know," he said, glancing around at the clans. "We all know. But things were too chaotic then—and have been ever since. Now, we're about to leave our homes behind, and the people need something to mark the transition."

Al looked south. They needed to make up time if they had any hope of catching Cygnus. He looked back at the clans and nodded with a sigh. *Spring is a time of renewal,* he thought. *This is a good chance for the clans to celebrate their own emergence from the cold into a new life in the sun.*

"Agreed. They deserve their day," he said aloud.

"Good. The other issue is a little more personal."

Al raised an eyebrow. "Go on."

"Ryanna spoke to me about your fears."

Before Al could say anything, Rogan raised a hand. "Don't be cross with her. She came to me both as the Rogan and as her father. She's worried about you—and since you're now part of our family, so am I."

"I appreciate that," Al said quietly. "I really do. It's nice to belong again. I just fear that using that blade will keep changing me—and not for the better."

Rogan nodded in understanding. "Then I'd suggest you only use it when you're in the most need. Your skills and abilities already make you one of the most fearsome warriors alive—even without that blade feeding you its unnatural strength. So minimize its use. That way, when you do need it, it will be there—and you'll still be yourself."

Al sighed. "Basically, you're telling me to grow up and carry the sword with me?"

"Well, I think I said it a little nicer than that—but yes, basically."

"What if it changes me?" he asked.

"Do you follow the Dokkalfar? Do you follow his tenets?"

"What? No, of course not. I don't even know what his tenets are," Al said, a little taken aback.

"Then what are you worried about? Al, you're at least half Alfarbani. How, I don't know—but you are. You fear this change, but I have to imagine that the Alfarbani, like humans, are born neither good nor evil—they choose their own path. You still have that choice. You always have the choice to do good—or not. Regardless of what your eyes do in the dark, or how fast, strong, or durable you become."

"I hope you're right," he murmured. But deep inside, he feared he wasn't. Rogan couldn't know the rush that came when the blade fed him—the way it made him crave more. The strength. The clarity. The hunger. He was afraid he wouldn't be strong enough to stop if he kept using it.

The clans had emerged from the woods and made camp on the open fields. Al had pitched his tent near the edge of the forest so Talionis could venture out if he wished. He sat by the fire with Talionis at his feet, watching as dozens of small fires lit up the plains. The mood among the clans had lifted the moment they cleared the forest.

Except for Talionis, Al thought, glancing down. The wolf, sensing the thought, looked up at him and then back toward the woods.

Al ran a hand through the wolf's thick fur. "I know, boy. I know," he said quietly. "We have to leave for a while—and I don't know when we'll be back." Talionis dropped his head between his paws.

Ryanna walked up and sat beside them. "How are my two favorite boys doing tonight?" she asked with a smile.

Al smiled back; Talionis, predictably, just looked toward the forest again.

She gave Al a questioning look.

"It's his home," he explained. "He knows we're leaving it—and I don't think he wants to go."

"He'll be alright once we're moving again," she said, ever the optimist.

"Maybe," Al replied, unconvinced. "How are the elders doing?"

"They're grumpy as always," she laughed, "but they're grateful you agreed to let the clans rest tomorrow for the equinox celebration. It means a lot to them."

Al shrugged. "What's one more day? It's tough to say goodbye to the only life you've ever known," he said, his eyes drifting toward the edge of the woods—and the silent wolf beside him.

"They're committed to the mission," she agreed. "But they do appreciate the gesture."

She looked at Talionis and smiled. "Perhaps they all do."

Just then, Glyn and Tyfin arrived and sat across the fire from them.

"Takeshi. Deadly woman of the Takeshi," Glyn quipped before Tyfin could speak. Unbothered, Tyfin simply nodded to both and took his seat.

"Any luck getting the people you need for the scouts?" Al asked.

Glyn nodded. "The clans love the idea. We've been swamped with volunteers. It hasn't been easy keeping it to twenty per clan."

"Good. Better than I'd hoped," Al said. "I've no doubt we'll find a use for anyone who wants to help."

They sat for a moment, watching the flames dance.

"Tyfin," Al asked, "how far do you think the clans can travel in a day?"

Tyfin thought for a moment. "Ten, maybe fifteen miles. It'll depend on the terrain, the weather, the herds... Why? How far do we have to go?"

It was Al's turn to think. "If I remember my maps correctly, Jaspar is roughly three hundred miles north to south. So that would take us between twenty and thirty days to reach the border."

"Unless the warriors ride ahead," Glyn chimed in. "Then we could reach the border in ten to fifteen days—maybe even catch up to Cygnus. He can't be moving much faster than us."

"That's a lot of mouths to feed, and we'd be leaving our supply chain behind," Tyfin interjected.

"We can hunt, forage, and buy what we need," Glyn began.

"Hunting and foraging take time, which would slow us down. And without the rest of the clan, we'd have nothing to barter with to purchase the volume of food and feed we'll require," Tyfin countered.

Al looked at Ryanna. She shrugged. "I don't see that we have a choice, at least not yet. Besides, we don't even know how far ahead Cygnus is at this point."

Al nodded. "Good point." He stared into the fire. He hated making these kinds of decisions. Just a year ago, all he had to worry about was getting the fields turned over and planted. Large-scale troop movements were far beyond anything he'd ever imagined. As much as he tried to push these logistical matters back to the Elder Council, they always seemed to circle back to him.

Fortunately, he'd anticipated this conversation and had already spoken with Rogan the night before.

"Tyfin, when you speak with the Elders tomorrow, let them know that when we break camp, I want the clans to separate. Let's try to keep the distance to less than an hour between each group. That way, we won't overtax the land as we pass through it. Also, let's try to avoid having entire clans enter towns when possible. If you come upon a town or village and need supplies, send in a small company to trade. Tell them I'd like to make as many miles per day as possible, but no one clan should outpace the others. We'll need runners assigned to keep everyone coordinated."

Tyfin nodded in understanding.

"Maybe we can use some of those volunteers you mentioned," Ryanna offered.

Glyn nodded. "Good idea. I'll handle that tomorrow."

"While you're at it, Glyn, I want the first scouts out at daybreak. I know it means they'll miss the day of rest, but I want eyes ahead of us as soon as possible."

Glyn nodded again. "I'll put it to them. Some of the younger ones are more interested in adventure than ceremony."

"We need information," Al said. "Please coordinate with the Elder Council to determine what they need most, then send groups out to investigate. I want at least two teams tracking Cygnus's trail— or at least identifying when and where he passed through."

"Tyfin," he continued, "all your years running your city have made you a master of logistics. I need you to handle all major trade between the clans and local villages—supplies, food, anything significant. I'll also need your advice. You've got a good head and a sharp mind, and I fear I'll need both in the days ahead."

"It will be my honor," Tyfin said, bowing his head.

"And what about me?" Ryanna asked, her voice playful. "Any special mission for me?"

He smiled. "Always."

She slapped his arm with a laugh. "You're horrible."

His smile faded. Looking out over the southern fields, where the moon was rising above the mountains, he dropped his voice to a whisper. "I need you at my side. I need your strength and your vision. I can't do this alone."

She giggled but answered in a matching whisper, "Al, you have the strength to match an ogre and the vision of a hawk."

He shook his head. "No—I need your strength of conviction. You know what's right and what's wrong, and you never waver. You see things clearly—people too. You seem to sense if someone's being truthful or not." He looked at her. "The clans are pushing me more and more into a role I've never been prepared for. I need people I can trust—people I can rely on. Otherwise, I won't be able to do this."

She nudged his shoulder with hers. "Love, you know I'll stand by you—come what may."

He exhaled slowly, relief washing over him. "Then I can face whatever Cygnus—or the world—throws at us," he said with a smile.

Al sat quietly, watching as the clans moved about the camp. Songs rose and fell on the breeze, laughter carried across the fields, and for the first time in a long while, the air felt lighter. It was good to be out of the forest, he thought. The oppressive weight of the woods, with its long shadows and unspoken memories, had finally lifted.

At his feet, a soft whimper broke the calm.

He looked down and saw Talionis resting with his head between his paws, eyes turned toward the distant line of trees.

Al reached down and scratched him gently behind the ears. "Not for everyone, I guess," he murmured.

The great wolf gave a low sigh but leaned into the touch.

Al looked back out across the firelit plains, the warmth of the gathering clans, and the open sky above them.

Tomorrow, they would begin again.

JASPAR

It was a brisk morning, with a light snow falling as the clans broke camp. They had enjoyed their day of rest and celebrated the equinox—a time to honor the past, mourn the fallen, and embrace their commitment to the future. Now, as the sun rose in the east, it was time to move again.

Al sat mounted on his mare, scanning the edge of the clearing for Talionis. Not seeing him, he reached out with his mind. He felt the wolf sitting at the forest's edge, watching the clans prepare to depart. *Let's go, boy. Time to leave*, he thought.

All that came back were images of the hunt.

Al smiled faintly. *I wish we could, boy, but we need to go.* No images followed this time—just a lingering sense of sadness.

He rode to the edge of the woods. Talionis was there, unmoving.

Ryanna joined him moments later, sensing something was wrong. "He's afraid," she said softly.

"Afraid? He's not afraid of anything," Al replied.

"Except leaving everything he knows. This is his land—more than it ever was the clans'. His kind have always roamed these forests. And now we're asking him to leave it." She placed a hand on Al's shoulder. "He may not be able to."

Tears welled in Al's eyes at the thought of leaving Talionis behind. He dismounted and knelt before the large wolf. "Is that it, boy? You want to stay?" Talionis whined and buried his muzzle in Al's open cloak.

"I can't stay," Al whispered, "but I can't ask you to leave, either." He took Talionis's face in his hands. "You are my family. I love you. I want you to come with me. But if this is where you need to be… then I understand. I promise, when I finish in the south, I'll come back for you."

Talionis, as always, seemed to understand. He curled up at Al's feet, resting his head on Al's thigh.

"Ryanna," Al said quietly.

"Yes, Al?"

"Lead the clans south for now. I'll catch up in a day or two. I think Talionis and I need to hunt one more time."

At the word *hunt*, Talionis leapt to his feet and dashed into the woods.

Ryanna, blinking away a few tears of her own, nodded. "Catch up when you can, my love."

Al spent the rest of the day and night with Talionis—just the two of them—hunting, running through the trees, and sleeping under the stars. At first light, he gave his friend one last, long hug, then looked him in the eyes, his reflection mirrored in the wolf's gaze.

I love you, my friend… my brother. I'll come back as soon as I can.

He grabbed Talionis by the scruff and pressed his forehead to the wolf's. "I promise," he said aloud.

Then he stood, turned, and mounted his mare. He did not look back. As he rode away, Talionis howled—long and mournfully—at the new day. With every step south, Al felt a little more of his heart break.

The ride through Jaspar began uneventfully. The days alternated between snow and clear skies. At night, campfires flickered with laughter and song.

For now, the land was sparsely populated, and with help from Glyn and the scouts, they steered clear of farms and settlements. Al knew it would grow harder the farther south they traveled.

It didn't take the scouts long to pick up Cygnus's trail. An army of ogres was hard to miss—they left a lasting impression on both the land and its people. Unlike the clans, Cygnus's army made no attempt to avoid settlements. Every report told the same tale: prisoners taken, holdings burned.

Al cringed at the thought of what awaited those captured. Even if the ogres didn't eat humans, the Klav certainly had no such qualms. And like Al, Cygnus's power was fueled by life essence.

On the sixth day—an overcast, sunless one—Glyn rode up beside Al but said nothing.

Al raised an eyebrow. "Something bothering you?"

Glyn smiled. "Not at all. You just looked deep in thought, so I figured I'd wait until you were ready."

Al shrugged. "Sorry. My mind's a jumble lately. How can I help you? Hopefully, it's something to take my mind off everything else," he added, without much conviction.

Glyn chuckled. "Nope. None of that from your number-one scout. I bring word of Cygnus's location."

Al's attention snapped into focus. "How far ahead?"

"At least three weeks. They don't appear to be making better time than we are."

"That would put them near Harding's northern border," Al said, a knot forming in his stomach. His thoughts turned to his parents and siblings. He had already lost so much since the night he left home. He didn't want to imagine his family at the mercy of Cygnus.

No, he reassured himself. *They're more than a week to the east. He would have no reason to head there—even if he knew where the hamlet was. If he's heading for the mountain pass into the Five Kingdoms, that would take him southwest of their location.*

Not for the first time, Al looked back north, his enhanced vision scanning the empty horizon for any sign of a large ball of fur. *At least you're safe, my friend.* He sighed and turned back to the south.

"That's our estimate as well," Glyn confirmed.

Al nodded. "Understood. Keep me informed."

Glyn looked like he was about to make a quip but thought better of it. Instead, he gave a short nod and rode off.

That night, as he did every night after camp was set up, Al walked away from the tents until he was far enough that no ordinary ears would hear the camp's noise. The day's overcast skies had finally cleared, the moon wouldn't rise for a few hours yet, leaving a deep, starlit darkness.

The stars were magnificent—scattered like diamonds across a black sea. He scanned the nearby field where they had stopped. Though most would find it pitch black, for him it was nearly as bright as dusk. The colors were muted, but his vision was sharp.

He found a bare patch of earth, sat cross-legged, and focused on his breathing. He emptied his mind of the day's noise and thoughts. He was tempted to enter the Elsewhere, but ever since his fight with Cygnus, he had avoided it—avoided the old building. Tonight, like most nights, he remained grounded.

Once centered, he began testing the limits of his Alfarbani gifts— this time focusing on hearing. He didn't care what he heard in the camp; he wasn't eavesdropping. This was training. He pushed his hearing farther and farther, trying to make it instinctual—like his reflexes, his vision, and now his hardened skin. The less he relied on the sword, the better.

When he could hear even the faintest murmurs, he promised himself he'd walk farther tomorrow.

Then, amid the noise, he heard a whisper—Ryanna's voice, clear and intimate in his mind:

Al. If you can hear me, the elders would like to speak with you. Nothing urgent, but if you have time tonight, they would be glad for it.

He smiled. She always knew what he was doing and often whispered a simple *I love you* for him to catch. He stood, gave the starlit field one last glance, and made his way back to the firelight of camp.

Al entered the elders' tent and paused to let his eyes adjust. The central fire crackled, casting warm shadows across the canvas walls. The tent was crowded—each clan was represented. The Chief Elders sat in the center, the chieftains to their right, and the remaining elders to their left. Others lined the tent's length, flanking the fire.

Conversation and laughter filled the room. Somewhere behind the Chief Elders, musicians played soft tunes.

Al looked around. Rogan raised his mug in greeting. Tyfin gave a nod. Martin was deep in one of his rambling stories, with Corvus laughing at the punchline. Wilna smiled as an attendant refilled her ale.

But Al's gaze sought only one person.

Ryanna.

The moment he saw her, the rest of the tent blurred into the background. His pulse quickened. She had already risen and was weaving through the crowd toward him.

She smiled and gave him a quick kiss. "You heard me, didn't you?" she asked.

His smile widened. "I may have."

She shook her head in mock disbelief. "I still can't believe you could hear a single whisper over all this noise."

"Yours is the one voice I always listen for," he said.

She placed a hand on his chest. "Come. The Chief Elders wish to speak with you."

"Now?" he asked, glancing around at the revelry.

"It's nothing urgent. Sounds more like logistics than anything," she said with a wink.

"Then I'm the last person they should be talking to," Al whispered as Ryanna led him up the center aisle, around the fire, and to the Chief Elders. With a raise of his hand, the Hugga Chief Elder silenced the musicians. Once the music stopped, so did all conversation in the tent. What had been a cheerful cacophony a moment earlier was now dead silent. Al shifted on his feet, suddenly self-conscious, but said nothing.

"Evening, Takeshi," the Hugga Elder said in a kindly tone.

Al bowed slightly. "I am honored to be invited before you tonight."

The elders all smiled. "I think at this point we can dispense with the formalities. Al, we are all pleased you came. We've missed you at our gatherings. Rogan says you spend your evenings away from camp, alone in meditation," he added with a hint of curiosity.

Al nodded. "I apologize. It's not that I wouldn't prefer to be here, but my fight against the Alkier taught me how little I understand my own abilities—their potentials and their limits. I'd rather figure that out now, when lives don't hang in the balance, than discover those limits mid-battle. Whenever I lost a practice dual, Gutamino would say - *Victory teaches little, Al. But loss—loss lays you bare. If you know your enemy and know yourself, you will win often. But when you lose, and still choose to learn, you become dangerous in ways victory never could teach.*"

The elders and chieftains nodded in approval.

"Wisely said," offered the Jinto Elder. "If you can learn something from a battle—even in defeat—then that battle wasn't truly lost."

Al had never heard any of the Chief Elders' actual names. Ryanna once explained that when someone joined the Council, their given name was never spoken in public again. From that day forward, they were known only as Elder.

"How may I serve the Council?" Al asked, knowing the others wouldn't return to the festivities until this business was resolved.

The Hugga Elder motioned to Corvus, who stood and gave the elders a slight bow before turning to Al.

"We have an interesting situation developing as we travel south," Corvus said. "It seems that with every mile, more and more locals approach us, asking to join."

Al raised an eyebrow.

Corvus continued, "When we ask why, they all tell us the same thing: they want revenge."

"Revenge?" Al repeated, confused.

Corvus nodded. "According to them—and Glyn's scouts back this up—Cygnus's army was brutal on its march south. Those who survived are convinced he's also responsible for what befell Morcaster."

At the mention of the ruined city, Al's stomach tightened. A familiar guilt crept in—the same guilt that whispered *you could have done more,* even though he knew he had done everything he could. It was the same guilt that lingered over the death of his friend.

"Seeing us—marching after Cygnus, thousands strong—gives them hope. They want to help. They want to pay him back."

"How many are we talking about?" Al asked. They were still in northern Jaspar, a region he didn't think was heavily populated.

"So far, a couple hundred. But word is spreading, and we suspect that number will grow as we continue south."

Al glanced around at the elders. "I'm not sure how I can help with this," he said honestly.

The Hugga Elder motioned for Corvus to sit. "We're trying to decide whether we should allow them to join us or send them home. On one hand, they would add to our numbers—and we will likely be sorely outnumbered when we reach Cygnus. On the other, most of them are farmers, merchants, or tradesmen. Only a handful have real combat experience. They could become more of a burden than a boon. We're still debating it, but we wanted to hear your thoughts."

Al was quiet for a moment. "My thoughts?" he repeated, a trace of sorrow in his voice. "Lately, I've begun to question my past decisions. Most seem to have led to pain—mine or someone else's. I don't know how much weight my opinion should carry anymore."

The elder nodded slowly. "There is value in reflection. We must all look back from time to time and ask, 'What if I had chosen differently?' It's how we gain wisdom. But reflection should not rob you of your voice in future matters. If it does, that isn't wisdom—it's paralysis."

Al sighed. They wouldn't let him slip away without answering.

"No matter how you look at it, we could use the extra forces," Al said at last.

Corvus frowned. "An untrained army may be more of a liability than an asset."

Al responded without hesitation. "With proper guidance, even the most unlikely recruit can become effective. With time, effort, and the right discipline, they can learn to fight as one. If you send them into battle without discipline, you don't lead warriors—you throw lives away. Teach first. Then ask if they still wish to follow."

The others nodded in agreement. Al continued, lost in memories of lessons drilled into him by Gutamino: "In battle, flexibility—adapting to the situation at hand—is of utmost importance."

"What's that?" asked the Chief Elder.

"We cannot always choose the warriors we desire, but we can shape those we have."

Martin rapped Corvus on the shoulder and made a hand gesture, clearly indicating that a point had just been proven. Apparently, this was the very argument the two of them had been debating earlier. Ripples of quiet conversation rolled through the tent until the Hugga Chief Elder raised his hand to restore silence.

"Thank you, Al. Rest assured your voice will be added to our discussion. For now, please stay, eat, and drink a little. We'll have another long day in the saddle tomorrow."

Al bowed slightly, and Ryanna led him back to where she had been sitting. As he took his seat, those gathered accepted that the formalities were over and the lively energy returned. Music resumed, voices rose, and laughter again filled the tent.

It had been three weeks since the council decided to allow the volunteers to remain with the clans. To avoid overburdening any single group, they had organized the new recruits into five distinct categories: hand-to-hand combatants, ranged fighters, cavalry, logistics and supply, and medical units. The first three made immediate sense to Al. The latter two, however—logistics and medical—he had never really considered before.

But as he was learning, without supply lines, they would not have made it this far. And without healers, they would be unprepared when the real fighting began. Thankfully, the clans—seasoned in the coordination of large migrations—were already well-versed in these disciplines. Al, for his part, found the complexity fascinating.

The Hugga Clan, under Ryanna's leadership, had been entrusted with the training of the ranged fighters.

That evening, as he often did, Al left the camp. There was still some daylight remaining, so he wandered toward the area where Ryanna had been training her archers. He found them a short distance from the main camp. Rather than intrude, he quietly settled on the grass off to one side.

No need to get in the way, he thought, smiling as he watched her.

She turned, as if sensing his presence, and smiled back. *Did I ever know happiness before I met you?* he wondered. *If I did, I don't recall.*

He looked up toward the western sky. The sun had dipped low, painting the clouds in streaks of gold and crimson. She should have at least another hour of light, he figured.

Al studied the group. Most of the recruits appeared to have never held a bow or sling before. There were a few exceptions—likely former shepherds, judging by their natural comfort with a sling. He watched as Ryanna moved among them, correcting postures, adjusting grips, encouraging those who needed it.

He sat in silence, simply observing her in motion. The last of the light finally vanished, replaced by the twinkling of stars. His eyes adjusted seamlessly. He no longer even noticed the transition—it was as natural as breathing now.

Eventually, Ryanna dismissed the weary recruits. Their tired cheers followed her as she made her way over to him. He stood as she approached and opened his arms, embracing her warmly.

"So, what do you think?" she asked after a light kiss.

"There are a few with some talent," he said honestly. "But by and large, you've got a long road ahead of you."

Ryanna nodded. Neither of them ever sugar-coated things.

"Luckily, we have some time. I doubt we'll catch him before he reaches the Five Kingdoms—and I'm sure they'll have an army, or five, waiting for him."

"That would be ideal," Al replied, though his tone held little conviction.

She narrowed her eyes slightly. "You don't think so?"

He shrugged. "I don't know. Cygnus is many things—most of which I hope to never learn—but rash isn't one of them. I can't see him moving an army into the Five Kingdoms without a plan. It would be doomed to fail."

"So, what do you think he's planning? Any ideas?"

He shook his head. "I wish I did. I think we need to prepare for another fight with just us, and hope we can find a way to turn the advantage to our side for a change."

The two of them started walking back toward camp.

"You miss him, don't you?" she asked quietly. It was the first time she had spoken about Talionis since Al had returned without him.

Al nodded. "Yeah. Every night when I sit out in the field, I can't help but tune my hearing to every wolf howl I hear, hoping he changed his mind and is coming after us."

"After you," she corrected with a soft smile.

"Don't kid yourself—I was beginning to think he liked you more than me," he said with a faint laugh.

"When this is done, we'll go find him. Together," she reassured him.

Al stopped abruptly.

"Something wrong?" she asked.

He pointed into the darkness. "Rider coming toward us."

She squinted into the black. "Any idea who it is?"

Al shook his head. "No, but if I had to guess, I'd say it's one of Glyn's scouts. They carry full packs—this one does. A rider from camp wouldn't be so heavily loaded. Must be important if he didn't wait for us to return."

"Takeshi?" the rider called out as he drew close.

"That's me," Al replied.

"I bring word from Scout Master Glyn," the rider said, pulling out a rolled and sealed parchment and handing it to Al.

"Scout Master," Al said quietly to Ryanna.

She smiled. "He felt the new position deserved an equally new title. If you'd prefer something else, I can speak to him."

Al shook his head, a faint grin on his face. "Not at all. I actually like the sound of it."

He unrolled the parchment. Reading at night was still one of the few things that challenged even his Alfarbani-enhanced vision. But the moon was up, and its glow was just enough to make out the contents. His smile quickly faded.

He handed the letter to Ryanna and turned to the rider. "Get back to camp. Grab a bite to eat and get what rest you can. I'll need you to ride back to Glyn at first light. I'll have your orders ready."

The rider struck his chest with a closed fist. "Yes, sir," he said, then wheeled his horse around and galloped back toward camp.

"I don't have your eyes," Ryanna said. "What does Glyn say?"

"He and a few of his scouts were attacked at the border pass into Harding. Outnumbered, they had to fall back. I need to speak with the Elders as soon as we return to camp." He turned to her. "While I'm doing that, can you find me about fifty spears willing to ride at first light?"

"Of course. I'll be one of them," she said without hesitation.

He shook his head. "Not this time, my love."

She was about to protest, but he held up a hand.

"The clans placed the recruits in your care. You can't leave them now. We need them trained and ready—more than ever. Glyn thinks it's just a small force holding the pass. I plan to scout it myself. If possible, we'll take control of it. If not, we'll wait for the clans to catch up."

He smiled, trying to ease her concern. "Don't worry. I won't do anything stupid before you arrive."

She huffed in disapproval. "You'd better not," she said.

HARDING PASS

It took a week of hard riding to reach the border. One of Glyn's scouts found them along the way and led them to the scout camp.

Glyn's face lit up when he saw Al and the others arrive, but it quickly shifted to mock disappointment. "What? No Ryanna?" he asked in a wounded tone.

Al smiled, recognizing the joke. "Please, don't start. If the Elders hadn't given her a task, nothing would've stopped her from coming along."

Glyn's grin returned. "Oh, that's different, then. As long as she has a good excuse." He laughed and embraced Al as he dismounted. "I figured you'd come to take a look," he said, glancing past him at the mounted spears. "And I'm glad for the extra company."

Al shrugged. "Needed to stretch the legs a bit. The clans don't move fast."

"That's for sure," Glyn agreed. "Come on, let's get your tent set up before it gets too dark for us mere humans to see."

Later that night, Al walked the perimeter of the camp with Glyn.

"How far from the border are we?" Al asked.

"Little less than an hour's ride. I wanted enough distance so they wouldn't spot us easily, but close enough to return quickly if we had to."

Al nodded. It made sense. Looking up, he noted the moon already beginning to dip below the horizon. The next week would bring darker nights—an advantage for him, at least.

"What can you tell me about their numbers? You were a little vague in your message."

"Not on purpose," Glyn replied. "Truth is, it's hard to say. Have you been to the pass before?"

Al shook his head. "No. When I came north, we crossed at the eastern pass—hundreds of miles away. I was unconscious at the time, so I know nothing of it."

Glyn frowned. "First, there's the Escarpment. Damn thing must be at least a hundred feet high, and in most places it's a sheer cliff. That makes the pass the only way in or out."

Al nodded. "The Thorncliffe. Supposedly it runs from the ocean in the east to the Ashek Range in the west. They say it's low enough near the ocean that a simple bridge suffices for the crossing."

Glyn glanced eastward. "No such luck here. We've got the pass. It starts in a small town—probably an old customs post. A little settlement grew up around it. At one end, a long, gradual bridge rises toward the Escarpment. It climbs a little more than halfway before ending at a narrow trail cut into the cliff face. From there, it winds upward in a series of switchbacks until it reaches the top."

He paused, then added, "At least, that's what I believe. The summit is cloaked in thick fog—like what we saw at the Citadel," he hesitated, "but not quite the same."

"How so?" Al asked. Could this be Cygnus? If so, that meant he was nearby—maybe they had caught up to him.

He took a steadying breath. *Don't get ahead of yourself. The chances of Cygnus still being here are slim... but...*

"In the north, the fog—though conjured—was still just fog. This... this is something else. When you get close to it, there's this feeling... in the pit of your stomach. Like sudden dread. All you want to do is run. It's not natural. I know it sounds crazy."

Al shrugged. "Everything's been crazy since my eighteenth birthday," he said with a half-laugh. "The world hasn't felt right in nearly two years."

"True," Glyn replied, unusually somber. "But fog? Fog shouldn't make you feel like that."

"It can't," Al said simply. "So, it isn't fog or at least, it isn't just fog. Which means someone—or something—is making it. And that means we need to find them."

"Sounds simple enough," Glyn said with a faint grin—his melancholy never lasted long.

"Any idea who attacked you? Ogres? Klav?"

Glyn shook his head. "No, nothing so obvious. They looked... human. A little short, maybe, but broad. And—" he hesitated. "No, never mind."

"What? Any detail could be important."

"They seemed to have a greenish tint," Glyn admitted, wincing. "But it might've just been the fog messing with my head."

"Green?" Al echoed.

Glyn shrugged again. "Could've been the fog. Which, I might add, they don't seem affected by. That's why I couldn't get a good count. They stay hidden inside it and only come out when we get too close."

"Did you engage them?"

He shook his head. "No. You told me not to. When they charged, we fell back. As soon as we did, they returned to the fog. We tried finding a way around the pass, but the fog stretches for miles, and once it finally thins out, the escarpment is too steep for horses."

He continued, "We tried probing the fog near the edges, but the horses refused to enter it. And honestly? None of us wanted to traipse blindly through that haze any longer than we had to. So we fell back here, set up camp, and I've been sending scouts every morning to observe from a safe distance."

"What about the town? I thought there were settlements on both sides of the pass?"

"I don't know about Harding's side, but the town on this side is gone. Completely destroyed. Not a single building left standing. I'm guessing the ogres razed it when they passed through. I have no idea what happened to the people. But I'm sure some escaped—word must have gotten out. No one's come looking to use the pass since."

Al looked south. It was probably safe to assume the town on the other side had fared just as badly. He turned to Glyn. "I think we should get some sleep. I want to head to the border before sunup and see what we can."

As Al lay waiting for sleep, he thought—just for a moment—that he heard the distant cry of a wolf. But when he strained to hear it again, the sound was gone.

Must be my imagination. Damn you, Cygnus.

He missed his friends deeply. He clung to the hope that Tyr had somehow made it out of Morcaster before the disaster. Talionis— playful, fierce, and loyal—had stayed behind in the northern wilds he called home. And Steven... whether he was dead or being kept alive as bait, Al couldn't be sure. Cygnus might have fed on him already.

One more reason for Cygnus to die.

Sleep finally took him, but he shifted uneasily beneath his blanket. In his dream, he found himself standing ankle-deep in blood. All around him lay bodies—ogres, Klav, and green-skinned humans. He had killed them. The sword in his hand practically sang with the life force it had drawn.

As his gaze passed over the fallen, he saw Talionis lying dead among them.

He dropped the sword and fell to his knees. The ground beneath him trembled, and claws made of fog and shadow rose to grasp at his limbs. A voice whispered in his mind:

You were too slow… too late… too proud…

He sat up with a gasp, drenched in cold sweat, his heart pounding in his chest.

Dawn was still a ways off. He sighed.

Dressing quickly, he stepped outside, only to find a bleary-eyed Glyn waiting for him.

"Did I ever tell you how thrilled I am when you stop by?" Glyn muttered with a grin.

Al returned a mirthless smile. "Oh, come now. This should be nothing for the Master of Scouts."

"The Master of Scouts would like a cup of coffee before riding out into pitch black. Just remember—we, unlike you, can't see in the dark."

Al mounted his horse. "Just stay to the road. There's enough light to do that. But we'll need to dismount before we're within hearing distance, or they'll know we're coming."

Even in the dark, it didn't take long before they reached a small bluff overlooking the road into the pass.

"What do you see?" Glyn whispered.

Al focused his vision, tapping into his growing control of his Alfarbani gifts. His sight sharpened like a drawn lens—his latest trick. It drained energy quickly, but while it lasted, he could see every detail below.

Glyn hadn't exaggerated. The customs houses had been completely destroyed. Al could picture the ogres storming through with axes and hammers, smashing the settlement apart.

He turned his gaze toward the pass, but no matter how much focus he applied, the mist remained impenetrable. *Clever,* he thought.

They waited until the first rays of sunlight crept over the horizon.

"Let's see if anyone's home," Al said aloud.

Glyn raised a hand, signaling the spears to form up.

"Where do you want me and my scouts?" he asked.

Al gave him a steady look, then smiled. "Right at my side, Scout Master Glyn." Glyn smiled at the title.

"I need you to take charge of the spears—but I don't want anyone to engage unless I give the word."

"What if they put an arrow in you?" Glyn asked lightly.

Al smirked. "Then assume the word is given."

He started forward at a slow canter, Glyn at his side. Behind them, five riders across and eleven deep moved into formation.

"Kind of a cocky pace," Glyn observed.

"That's the point. I'm glad you noticed."

As they approached a large mound of rubble, Glyn motioned with his chin. "That pile? That's where they come from every time."

Al raised his hand, bringing the group to a halt. Glyn said nothing, and the spears remained still, hands at the ready.

Sure enough, a group of about twenty figures emerged from the mist.

Al focused his vision again and immediately recognized they weren't human—but he had no idea what they were. Their skin was thick, almost leathery, with a greenish hue. They were squat but powerful, with short black hair and heavily muscled limbs. They wore light armor—mostly hardened leather with the occasional glint of chainmail.

Unlike previous encounters, they didn't charge. Instead, they marched out in tight formation, mirroring Al's own.

When they were roughly a hundred yards apart, one stepped forward.

Al dismounted and handed his reins to Glyn. "Back in a few."

"You want to take that?" Glyn asked, nodding toward Al's Alfarbani sword.

Al shook his head, last nights dream still fresh in his mind. "No. I do not," he said, a note of loathing in his voice.

He walked forward to meet the lone figure, stopping just outside of striking distance.

"The border is closed," the creature said in a deep, raspy voice. His eyes gleamed—serpentine and cold. "Go back, and no harm will befall you."

"Closed? By whom?" Al asked, feigning innocence.

The creature gave a mirthless grin. "By order of the Lord of Trigon. Now go. My patience is already wearing thin."

Al laughed. "Lord of Trigon? I have fought and killed your lord's brother Alkier in single combat. Do you think the likes of you scare me? I hail from this land, and you will not prevent me from entering."

The creature's demeanor shifted instantly. "You? You fought one of the Alkier? You're the one they call... Ornfel," he said, stumbling over Al's former surname.

"DisOrnfel," Al corrected absently.

"My lord left a message for you, should you dare come this way." He reached into a pouch at his side and pulled out a rolled piece of parchment, sealed with the symbol of Trigon. He tossed it to Al.

Al caught it as though it were a venomous serpent. He broke the seal and read:

Albert,

If you are reading this, it would seem you have recovered from your ill-conceived feeding on poor Broderick's life force. Impressive. Perhaps you are made of sturdier metal than I had initially given you credit for. Now, let us test if you have an intellect to match your resilience.

I offer you a choice, though I suspect you already understand the seriousness of the situation. You may come, alone, to the Five Kingdoms and bend the knee to me. Do so, and I will guarantee no harm will befall you or your friends—provided the clans remain north of Harding. If you prefer, you may remain with them, and again I promise that neither I nor any of my servants will seek you out.

But—should you be foolish enough to cross the border into Harding in arms, then my forces will tear you, your friends, and all of Harding to shreds as punishment for your lack of judgment.

Make no mistake, Albert. While I am a patient man, I am not without my limits. You should think carefully before pushing me to them.

—Cygnus,

Lord of Trigon

Al read it twice, then rolled it up and tucked it into his tunic. He looked at the creature. "You know the contents of this letter?"

"I know enough. You may pass—alone—or you may leave. Otherwise, you will die. And those that follow you will die."

Al studied him for a long moment. "What are you?" he asked.

The creature blinked, then let out a low, cruel laugh. "You people of the West are so ignorant. We are goblins. We are the forces of the Dokkalfar. Upon his return, all nations will know and fear us again."

"Goblin," Al repeated, committing the word to memory. "And who are you?"

"We do not give our names to strangers, only our titles. I am Sato. These are my forces. What is your answer, human?"

Al's eyes narrowed. "Before I answer, tell me this: is Harding untouched by Cygnus's forces? What of the residents of this town, and the one on the other side? And all the captives he took as he traveled south?"

Sato's expression shifted to confusion. "There are always casualties in war. An army must eat. We take what we need—or want. It has always been so."

Al sighed. "I thought as much."

He looked past Sato at the ranks of troops. He strained to listen beyond the fog—he could hear others, but couldn't determine their numbers.

Finally, he answered.

"No."

Sato blinked. "No?"

"No, I will not enter alone. No, I will not stay on this side of the border. Cygnus has waged an unprovoked war upon these lands, and he—and all who follow him—must pay for it. The very earth, soaked with the blood of innocents, cries out for justice."

He drew a breath, then continued, "But I will, in fairness, give you a choice. Lay down your weapons and surrender. I give you my word that no harm will come to you, but until Cygnus is defeated, you will remain our prisoners."

Sato let out a cold, mirthless laugh. "Brave," he sneered. "Or perhaps foolish. But I'll give you the benefit of the doubt and call it brave."

His eyes narrowed. "But what I say doesn't matter. My master commanded me to give you the offer—and deal with you should you refuse."

He looked briefly back at his soldiers, then forward again.

"You do have the numbers in your favor. Normally, I would retreat, regroup, and wait for the right time." He sighed.

Then, with a speed that defied his thick frame, he drew a wicked-looking dagger and lunged at Al, shouting:

"But that option has been denied me this day by my master! So die quickly, little human!"

As quick as Sato was, he was no match for Al's speed.

Al snatched the dagger from Sato's hand, spun him around with a firm grip on his wrist, and drove him to his knees in one fluid motion. Pressing the dagger to the stunned goblin's throat, Al said coldly, "I am no human, Sato. I told you—I bested an Alkeir in single combat. I am Alfarbani."

Sato's eyes widened in shock and disbelief.

"Tell your men to drop their weapons," Al ordered, "or die."

The air grew thick as Al waited. He could smell Sato's rage and surprise—but not fear. The goblin's mind churned behind his cold eyes. He'd been hasty, but Al suspected he'd had little choice.

Sato glanced at his soldiers and screamed, "Kill the humans! Kill them a—!"

His command was cut short. Blood filled his mouth as Al, without hesitation, slit his throat. The goblin's body dropped to the dirt.

Gutamino had taught Al that in battle, one must be as fluid as a stream—but also as resolute as stone. There was no path out of this that didn't lead through blood.

The goblins charged.

Al barely had time to ready himself. All he had was the dagger he had taken from Sato. It will be enough, he thought, as he let himself slip into the Warrior's Mind.

The battle was fast and brutal. Al's men had the advantage of numbers, formation, and horses. The goblins didn't go down without a fight, though. Two of Al's soldiers were killed, and another five were wounded—including Al himself.

Near the end of the skirmish, as Al was engaged with a final goblin, another—who had been playing dead—sprang up behind him and drove a dagger into his back. The blade slipped between his shoulder and ribs, puncturing the outer layer of his hardened skin. Al howled in pain and fury, whirling around and slashing the goblin's throat so deeply it nearly decapitated him.

Once the fight was over, Al's unit fell back to a safe distance where they could take cover but still observe the fog-choked road.

Al sat heavily on a rock and pulled off his shirt. Glyn crouched in front of him to examine the wound.

"He got you good," Glyn said, wincing. "But you're lucky—it could've been worse." One of the spears brought water, and Glyn began cleaning the wound before stitching it closed.

"Aaagh! Where in the Nine Hells did you learn to do this?" Al barked.

"Stop squirming," Glyn replied. "And for the record, this would go faster if your skin wasn't tougher than boiled leather." He grinned. "You know, for someone with skin like a rhino, you sure complain a lot."

Al shot him a glare. "Not tough enough," he muttered. He winced again as Glyn tightened the next stitch. *Note to self: even the thickest skin won't stop a determined blade.* He sighed. "I have no one to blame but myself. Even ogres fall to sharp spears."

Glyn, still focused on his work, nodded. "Tough skin's useful—but it's still skin. Still flesh. It bleeds like the rest of us."

Al looked toward the fog. "I want to scout the mist before more of those things show up—probably in greater numbers. I need to know what we're up against before we bring the clans through."

Glyn frowned. "You're in no shape for that. Not for another day or two—unless you want to use that sword of yours. That seems to do the trick."

Al glanced at the Alfarbani blade still hanging from his saddle. He shook his head. "No. Not unless I have to."

"Didn't think so." Glyn sat back on his heels. "Lucky for you, you've got Scout Master Glyn on your side. I'll take a handful of men and go check it out."

Al opened his mouth to protest, but a sharp stab of pain from his side silenced him.

"Alright," he conceded. "But take only a few of the spears—not the scouts. The fewer the better. I didn't hear any more inside when we fought, so a small group might get in and out without being noticed."

He paused. "Stay on the road. Try to find out what's generating that fog—or at least how far back it goes. But don't go too far. Get in, get what you can, and come right back."

"Yes, Dad," Glyn said with mock seriousness.

"Glyn," Al said, narrowing his eyes.

"Relax, Al." Glyn held up a hand. "I'll be careful. I promise. No unnecessary risks."

Satisfied—*mostly*—Al gave Glyn a final nod. "Alright. Go."

While Glyn and the spears prepared, Al and the others built a large fire. They wrapped their fallen in cloth, honoring the dead. The goblin corpses were piled separately.

"We'll burn them," Al said. "After you return safely."

Al walked to the edge of the fog with Glyn and the others, using his Alfarbani sword as a cane. The horses refused to go any farther, so they continued on foot.

Glyn shuddered but kept his voice firm. "Steady, boys. It's only a mist. Ignore that feeling—it's trying to make you afraid. But it's *us* this damn fog should fear."

The others forced nervous laughs, steeling themselves as they stepped into the swirling vapor.

Al tried to pierce the fog with his vision, but even his enhanced eyes saw nothing. So he shifted focus to his hearing. Glyn, aware of how sharp Al's senses had become, kept whispering back to report what they were seeing.

The first hundred feet revealed nothing but damp silence. Then the mist thinned slightly—just enough to make out the pass: a long, wide avenue descending from the Jaspar escarpment into the lowland fields of Harding. Thick woods loomed on either side.

"The fog seems to be emanating from the forest," Glyn whispered. "We haven't seen or heard anything yet. We'll go a little deeper—try to find the source."

Be careful, Glyn. Something doesn't feel right, Al thought.

They had been in the woods nearly thirty minutes when Al heard the first scream—high, raw, and too close. It was followed quickly by others. His blood ran cold.

Glyn's voice came through clearly, frantic and panicked. "Klav! We walked into a trap—they're everywhere! Everyone run! Back to the border! *Run!*"

Al surged forward but staggered, clutching his side in agony. The spears, already wary, rushed to his aid.

"They're under attack!" Al gasped. "Give me a moment!"

He steadied himself, strapped the Alfarbani sword to his hip, and drew a long breath. He would need every drop of stored energy—every reserve—to compensate for the wound and push his body beyond its limits.

Behind him, the spears were forming up.

He turned, eyes blazing. "*Stay here!* Hold this position. Kill anything that comes out of that mist that isn't one of ours. If none of us return—fall back to the camp. The clans should arrive in a day or two. Tell them everything."

"Takeshi, let us go with you!" one of them pleaded.

Al shook his head. *I can't take them. I could use their blades, but not in this fog. Not against the Klav—who hunt by scent as much as sight.*

He clenched his jaw. Too many would die. Sending them in would be selfish—cowardly.

"No," he said grimly. "This is my fault. I should never have let Glyn enter that fog. My curiosity has put them all at risk."

His voice dropped, charged with purpose. "I don't know the full extent of the power in my blood. But if it can help me reach them—then I'll pay that price. The Klav will shed no more clan blood today."

Grim and resolved, Al stepped into the mist alone, the screams of his allies and the feral howls of the Klav echoing through the darkness ahead.

With each stride, his pace quickened. Pain was ignored; his body responded to sheer will.

He drew his Alfarbani blade, feeling its unnatural pulse in his hand. He knew what it would cost him.

So be it, he thought, eyes hard as steel. *My humanity be damned.*

OLD FRIENDS NEW OPPORTUNITIES

As Tyr worked on a captain's blade, he heard a voice behind him. "Well, I'll be damned."

He turned to see a small, young noble—maybe twelve or thirteen years old—perched on one of the workbenches, eating an apple. Sandy-colored hair, overdressed, and just a little too cocky. *Definitely a noble*, Tyr thought, hiding a smile.

"Afternoon, young squire. How can I be of service?"

The boy laughed. "You don't recognize me, do you? Oh, this is grand. Must be all the heat from the forge—" he tapped the side of his head "—messes with the brain, I think." He smiled broadly, hopped off the bench, opened his arms, and spun around. "Come on now, you're not *that* old."

Tyr squinted. *Why does he think I should know him?* He spent most of his days at the forge or The Donkey. But if it weren't for the fine clothes...

"No," Tyr said tentatively, "Gillian?"

The boy grinned. "'Tis I," he replied with a flourishing bow. "I'm very glad to see you alive. I feared the worst when I heard about Morcaster."

Tyr nodded. "Me too. How did you get here?" he asked, checking the billet.

"I came with Gutamino. We must've left just before the incident occurred."

"Is Al with you?" Tyr asked, half-expecting to see him waiting in the street.

"No." Seeing the frown forming on Tyr's face, Gillian quickly added, "But he wasn't in Morcaster either. Gutamino sent him on a mission up north before the end-of-year celebrations. I've been waiting for him to arrive. He was supposed to come by ship once he finished, but he hasn't come yet. So... I don't know where he is."

Gillian's voice sounded both sad and concerned.

"North?" Tyr repeated aloud. "Nothing but slavers and nomads up there. What in the world would Gutamino need him to do up there?"

Gillian shrugged. "Boss doesn't tell me things like that. But don't go worrying about big brother—he's downright scary with a sword, or even without one. He'll come when he's ready, I guess. In the meantime, I suppose it's up to the two of us to keep the place from falling apart until he gets here."

Tyr smirked. "I hadn't noticed that York was in any immediate danger of falling apart," he said, turning the metal over in the coals. "Easy on the bellows—keep the coals at a consistent temperature," he added to Jym, who was working beside him.

"No? You're a lot like Al in that regard—too focused on what you're doing and not paying enough attention to what's going on around you," Gillian said, almost to himself.

"What's that supposed to mean?" Tyr asked.

Gillian just smiled. "Only that I grew up on the streets and you didn't, that's all."

He glanced out to the street, and something seemed to catch his attention. "While this has been fun and all, I've got some errands to run. But before I go, I have an invitation for you."

"An invitation?" Tyr asked, raising a brow.

"Don't sound so surprised. The docks are all abuzz with word of this incredible blacksmith. How long did you think it would take before the stuffed shirts at court caught wind of it?"

"You have an invitation for me to the royal court?" Tyr asked, stunned.

Gillian laughed. "Sorry, nothing so grand. Your name has made it there, though. But that's not who sent me. Gutamino would like a word with you. Privately."

Tyr's fingers tightened on the haft of the hammer. His face twisted into a grimace. "Gutamino," was all he said.

Gillian watched him for a moment, ready to toss off something snarky, but changed his mind. "He's not that bad, Tyr. Al liked and trusted him. Don't get me wrong—I'm not sure I understand a third of the things he's up to—but I *do* know he's honorable."

Tyr pointed the hammer at Gillian. "He works for that Cygnus fellow Al was always going on about. The one Al said was a threat to all of us. So how can he be any better?"

Gillian shrugged. "I've never met Cygnus. Gutamino rarely talks about him, and when he does, I get the impression he doesn't really like him all that much."

Tyr let out a huff of disbelief. "Then why does he serve him?"

"I think their relationship is more... master and servant. I think he serves because he must." Gillian shrugged again. "These people aren't like you and me, Tyr. I can read a street or a dingy tavern with my eyes closed and know what everyone's about—but those people at court?" He shook his head. "Anyway, come or don't. I was just told to deliver the message."

He made to leave but turned back around. "It's good to see you again. If you don't mind, I may stop by once in a while. So do me a favor and come—if for no other reason than to buy your old friend a meal."

"You are always welcome here, Gillian," Tyr replied with a nod.

Gillian smiled and started to leave.

"What would you do?" Tyr asked.

Gillian stopped but didn't turn around. "I'm always curious. If a person is a potential friend—or even more so, a potential foe—I'd go. Because you learn nothing by staying away."

Tyr didn't respond, so Gillian continued out of the shop.

Tyr pulled at his new waistcoat and ran a thick finger around the collar of his new shirt. He hated new clothes—especially ones he couldn't work in.

Nothing but a waste of coin, he thought grimly.

He stood sullenly near the gate, facing two guards. The three of them waited for the runner to return. Despite Tyr's best efforts, Crowin had insisted he meet with Gutamino—and that he dress "appropriately" for the visit.

The guards had sent the runner off to confirm Tyr was expected, but it was taking time, and he was already considering heading back to the shop.

Crowin may have insisted, Tyr thought, *but he doesn't know what I know about the man. Though in fairness, all I know is what Al has told me... and most of that came from a dream.*

He sighed and resigned himself to the meeting. As he looked up, the runner arrived back at the gate and spoke briefly with the guards.

One of the guards motioned toward Tyr. "Alright, lad. You can enter. Just follow Timothy here," he said, nodding toward the runner. "He'll take you to Lord Gutamino."

"Thank you, sir," Tyr replied as he passed.

The guard chuckled. "*Sir?* Boy, I'm many things, but I ain't no 'sir.' 'Sirs' don't stand guard."

Tyr smiled. "My apologies. I'm just a lowly blacksmith—most folks are 'sir' to me."

The second guard dropped his grin. "Hey, are you the blacksmith they're all talking about down at the docks?"

Tyr shrugged. "Maybe. I've been getting some good business from the sailors lately. Mostly word of mouth. I think they feel sorry for me—I sailed with a few of them on my way here."

"Sorry for you? Ha!" the guard said. "The way I hear it, you're putting out good steel at a fair price."

Tyr laughed. "Everyone keeps telling me the price is 'good.' I'm starting to think about raising it."

"Not so fast," said the first guard. "Wait till I come by and put an order in first. Then you can charge *him* whatever you like."

"Hey!" the second guard protested.

"I'll tell you what," Tyr said with a grin, "I'll hold my price for the two of you—and anyone in your company—for the next month."

The two guards beamed and thanked him repeatedly as Tyr followed Timothy into the palace grounds. Timothy said nothing, simply motioning for Tyr to follow. They moved quickly through the gardens, past the main palace.

Tyr paused, admiring the view. He had only ever seen the palace from the street, but up close, it was even more impressive. The vast structure looked to be made of white marble, with bronze accents gleaming in the afternoon sun.

As he stood there, a young woman appeared beside him.

"Something, isn't it?" she said.

Tyr turned to look at her. She was slightly shorter than him and about his age, with long blonde hair braided neatly down her back and the deepest blue eyes he had ever seen.

"Beautiful," Tyr replied.

She blushed and looked back toward the palace.

Before Tyr could say more, Timothy tugged at his sleeve, motioning for him to continue. "My apologies…" Tyr began.

She stopped him with a smile. "No need. I'm sure we'll meet again." With a quick curtsey, she turned and continued toward the palace.

"Come. Lord Gutamino is expecting you," said Timothy.

"Who is she?" Tyr asked, watching her retreating figure.

Timothy looked but shook his head. "I've no idea. She only arrived recently—some noble's daughter, like as not. Now come on, we must hurry."

Reluctantly, Tyr turned away and followed Timothy to a brick building on the palace's flank. They wound through a maze of corridors until they reached a large set of wooden doors. Timothy pointed, and Tyr nodded before knocking with a heavy fist.

After a moment, the doors opened. An older butler gestured for him to enter. He was led into a spacious parlor, where a finely dressed man stood accompanied by two barely dressed young women. The butler motioned for Tyr to wait near the entrance, then approached the trio to announce him.

All three turned toward Tyr. He suddenly felt very self-conscious. The women giggled and whispered to each other, shooting glances his way that drew more laughter. Tyr tugged at his waistcoat, feeling grossly underdressed.

After a moment, Gutamino waved the women away. Still giggling, they left the room, casting lingering looks back at Tyr.

"Pay my companions no mind," Gutamino said with a smile. "They mean no insult." He extended a hand. "My name is Gutamino."

Tyr studied the man. He stood a little taller than Tyr, olive-skinned with short, straight black hair. But it was his eyes that caught Tyr's attention: deep brown, but with an unusual fold in the upper lid— something distinctly foreign. Something Al hadn't mentioned.

"Is something wrong?" Gutamino asked, hand still extended.

Tyr blinked. He hadn't taken the hand. "Sorry—no. My apologies." He shook the man's hand. "My name is Tyr."

Gutamino smiled. "No need to apologize. My people come from a very distant land. Our features tend to stand out here. Though, I must say—you're not exactly local yourself. Shorter of stature, broader of shoulder... if you know what I mean," he added with a wink.

Tyr smiled awkwardly.

"But you seem uncomfortable," Gutamino continued. "Is something troubling you?"

Tyr cast a glance toward the door the women had exited through. "I fear I may be a bit underdressed for the palace."

Gutamino chuckled. "Ah—the girls. It wasn't your clothing they were giggling about." He dropped his voice. "It was you. They think you're cute."

Tyr's eyes widened. "Cute?" he repeated, baffled. He stammered, "I'm sorry—I didn't mean—I would never... not with another man's—"

Gutamino poured two glasses of wine and handed one to Tyr, motioning for him to sit. Still flustered, Tyr took the seat opposite him.

"Don't worry," Gutamino said. "They're not 'with' me—not in that way. My position demands I be surrounded by... aesthetically pleasing company. They're the daughters of a minor noble from my homeland, traveling with me for show. Lovely girls, but I'm old enough to be their father." He leaned forward and added, "Besides, I don't think they have an original thought between them."

He smiled and sipped his wine.

"Gillian tells me you're a friend of Al's," he said, more statement than question.

Tyr nodded and took a cautious sip of the wine. "I am."

"I take it he told you about me," Gutamino said, his tone shifting slightly, "and about my master?"

Tyr set his wine down, suddenly more alert. He wasn't sure he liked where the conversation was going, but he nodded. "He did."

Gutamino took another sip and leaned back in his chair. Noticing Tyr's pensiveness, he said, "Please, relax. I assumed as much long before inviting you—I simply wanted confirmation. If you don't mind my asking, how much did Al tell you? I ask only so I know where to fill in the gaps."

In for an ounce, in for a pound, Tyr thought. "Only that you and your master were up to something. Something Al believed to be dangerous. He wasn't sure what, but he felt you both needed to be stopped."

Gutamino nodded. "That does sound like Al. And he was correct—to a point. We *are* up to something, that much is true. Whether it is good or bad..." He shrugged. "Such questions are not for me to ask. I am bound to Cygnus as a slave is bound to a master. He sends orders, and I carry them out without question."

He leaned forward, his tone softening. "However, that is not what I am asking of you. I'm not going to ask you to support his efforts.

Rather, what I ask is that you help the military forces of this kingdom—along with its allies—and, ultimately, yourself."

Tyr's voice hardened. "Where did you send him?"

"Al?" Gutamino confirmed. Tyr nodded.

"Into the northern wilds, to deliver a message—and to make a choice."

"A choice?" Tyr asked, brows furrowing.

Gutamino took another sip. "Al is not like you or me, and I mean that in more ways than you might guess. As a result, he is of interest to my superiors."

"You mean Cygnus?" Tyr asked.

Gutamino shook his head. "No. Cygnus would just as soon see Al dead. I mean the Lord Commander—Dadius."

"Dadius? We met an old man by that name on our way to Morcaster. He's the one who gave Al your name."

Gutamino nodded. "The same. He wanted me to train Al. Normally, I don't train anyone outside the Brotherhood, but one doesn't question an order from the Lord Commander. Even Cygnus wouldn't casually cross that line."

He leaned back again, gesturing as he spoke. "So, I trained him. And to my surprise, he learned. Everything I threw at him—forms, techniques—he picked up in less than a year. Don't get me wrong, he still needs years of practice to develop the muscle memory required to become a true master. But when he left, he had already far surpassed most warriors in this land."

Gutamino paused, then added, "When he left, I gave him his choice."

"What choice?" Tyr asked again.

"To join us… or to try and stop us. If he had chosen to join, he would have come south as soon as he finished. He didn't. Instead, he chose to try and stop Cygnus—which nearly cost him his life."

He watched Tyr closely.

"I figured that might interest you."

"Do you know what happened to him? Where is he now?" Tyr asked, concern edging his voice.

Gutamino considered the question. "I'll tell you what little I know—which, unfortunately, isn't much. I sent Al to deliver a message to Cygnus and retrieve my next instructions. But when Al met

Cygnus's messenger, he chose to act on his own. I assume he fought and killed the messenger, then headed north to confront Cygnus himself."

He took another sip of wine, his tone growing reflective.

"Apparently, his presence was like a spark among the clans. He managed to undo all the work my counterpart had spent a year constructing. Then... he did the unthinkable: he unified the northern clans."

Tyr raised his eyebrows, impressed.

Gutamino smiled. "Even I have to admit, that was impressive. Alavek—my counterpart in the north—had spent a year sowing discord among them. He even managed to capture Al at one point. Details get fuzzy after that, but apparently Al escaped—and killed Alavek in the process."

He chuckled. "That must have infuriated Cygnus. Alavek was one of his favored servants."

He paused, briefly lost in thought, then went on.

"After that, it seems Al convinced the clans to march south against Cygnus. The rest is vague. Cygnus claimed to have fought him shortly before the Vernal Equinox and said he won—that Al was nearly killed. But apparently... he survived. Last I heard, he was still with the clans in the north, preparing to pursue Cygnus."

He leaned forward, setting his wineglass down. "But to be fair, my information is already out of date."

Tyr exhaled slowly. "After all that, he lost—and nearly died. So, what was it all for?"

Gutamino chuckled softly. "He never had much hope of winning. Not against Cygnus. Al still has much to learn, and even if he learns it, Cygnus is not easily killed. He's far beyond Al's reach." He paused, then added, "Then again, Al *did* survive the fight—which is remarkable in and of itself. Cygnus doesn't spare people. He has no love for Al or what he represents. So perhaps Al is more formidable than even I gave him credit for.

"As for what it was all for?" Gutamino shrugged. "Sometimes, the journey matters more than the destination. Al needed to walk that path to understand who he truly is."

He sat back, folding his hands. "But enough of Al. Let me explain why you're here, and you can tell me if you're interested."

Tyr nodded, though his thoughts were still a storm. He was deeply worried about Al, but he knew this wasn't the moment to press further.

"Excellent," Gutamino continued. "Lord Dadius has tasked me with finding a skilled craftsman capable of unlocking ancient forging techniques. If performed properly, they could produce weapons far stronger and lighter than anything we make today. I need someone trusted and talented—someone who can read an ancient codex and reconstruct the methods. Some parts will be vague, so instinct and interpretation will be vital. Of course, you'd be allowed to select a few smiths to assist under your supervision."

Tyr raised a hand, shaking his head. "I'm afraid you should be speaking with Master Crowin or even the guild. I'm not a master. I'm not allowed to take a position like that."

Gutamino smiled knowingly. "Master Crowin said that would be your response. As for the guild, well leave them to me—and to Crowin. He agrees: you're the right man for this job."

Tyr blinked. "Handle the guild?" he asked, clearly skeptical.

"You're young," Gutamino said, swirling his wine. "The guilds have their rules—they are designed to regulate the trade, maintain quality, and limit the number of masters in a region. This helps control pricing and reputation. But, as with most institutions, their rules aren't quite as rigid as they'd like you to believe."

Tyr narrowed his eyes. "Who would the weapons be for?"

Gutamino refilled his glass and gave a soft laugh. "Good question. But don't worry—they won't be for Cygnus or his army. They'll go to the military here in York, and perhaps a few trusted allies. We're fulfilling a promise to York to provide a few of their selected officers with superior arms."

Just then, the butler entered and made a discreet hand signal that Tyr didn't recognize—but it wiped the smile from Gutamino's face.

"Sadly," Gutamino said, rising, "we'll have to end our discussion here. Take some time. Think it over. It's an honest offer—and you wouldn't be doing anything but aiding the military of York." He gave a slight bow. "My servant will escort you to Gillian, who'll see you safely off the palace grounds."

He paused at the door. "One more thing—another reason I want *you*, specifically. I believe there is more to you than you know. Take the position, and you may uncover truths about yourself you've never imagined."

With another short bow, he disappeared through the doorway, leaving Tyr in thoughtful silence.

Before long, Tyr found himself walking back to the smithy with Gillian at his side. The younger man didn't say a word until they were beyond sight of the palace walls.

"So?" Gillian asked, nearly bouncing with excitement. "How'd it go? Did he say anything about Al?"

Tyr walked several paces in silence before replying. "Hmm. Well... he offered me a job—sort of. And as for Al..."

He paused, then sighed. "He didn't say much, but I'll tell you what he did say."

As they walked, Tyr recounted everything Gutamino had told him about Al—and, to a lesser extent, about the opportunity to forge weapons for the crown.

"When do you start?" Gillian asked, grinning.

Tyr gave a dry chuckle. "No. I can't accept it. I'm still a journeyman. If I take that position, the guild would ban me from practicing for life."

"But what if the Guild said you could? Would you take the position then?" Gillian pressed.

Tyr rubbed his face with one large hand, thinking it over. He did love the idea of having his own shop—and learning a lost, ancient technique no one else knew was a dream come true. And if he took the position, it might lead to more information about Al and his whereabouts. But...

"Then there's Master Crowin," Tyr said at last. "I have obligations to him and the shop. We've only just gotten it back on its feet. What kind of ingrate would I be if I left the first chance I got?"

Gillian smiled up at him. "Oh, I don't know. He seems more than capable of running his own forge. And it looked like he had a full crew working—do you really think he'd miss one guy?"

Tyr wanted to tell him it wasn't that simple, but instead just shrugged. "Gutamino gave me a few days to think it over, so that's what I'll do. I'll speak with Master Crowin, and then with the Guild. I won't do anything behind their backs."

KRYSTAL

The day was already getting warm. Tyr plunged a rag into a barrel of water and squeezed it over his head, letting the cool stream run down his face and shoulders. As hot as the forge was, stepping outside usually brought some relief—at least back in Morcaster. But York was warmer than Morcaster, or even Harding. He ran the wet rag over his face and frowned. Now that spring had arrived, the days would only grow hotter. He plunged the rag back into the barrel, closed his eyes, and let the second soaking wash over him.

He had a lot to do, but Gutamino's offer weighed heavily on his mind. A once-in-a-lifetime opportunity, no doubt—but he was still a journeyman, with several more years of service owed to the Guild. He opened his eyes and blinked. Standing just outside the forge were the two girls from Gutamino's chambers… and with them, the blonde-haired, blue-eyed woman from the palace grounds.

The two girls giggled behind gloved hands, while the blonde simply smiled.

Tyr, suddenly aware of his appearance—shirtless, his forge apron loose around his waist, his hair dripping—felt a surge of self-consciousness. He looked around quickly for his shirt, yanked it on, and did his best to compose himself.

"My ladies," he said with a small bow, unsure of the proper etiquette. "Forgive my appearance. I don't normally receive visitors this early in the day."

The blonde smiled. "It's quite all right, Master Blacksmith. My friends and I fancied a little morning walk." The two girls continued to giggle and whisper, one apparently saying something that made the blonde grin. Noticing Tyr's confusion, she added, "My friend says we should be the ones apologizing, since we came unannounced. And, given how dreadfully hot your forge must be, she also suggests you needn't have bothered putting your shirt back on—at least not on our account."

This sparked a fresh wave of laughter from the other two.

"That's very kind of her," Tyr replied, "but I should be wearing it anyway."

"Pity," the blonde said lightly.

Tyr had the distinct sense he was the target of some inside joke, though he couldn't puzzle out what it was. He opted to change the subject.

"Is there anything I can help you with? I'm afraid I'm not an artisan smith, so I doubt I'd have much to interest ladies of your station."

"Oh, don't be so sure of that," she said with a smirk. "Truthfully, I came to see the great master smith everyone's talking about. Gutamino and Gillian sing your praises endlessly. Even the palace guards speak of your work."

Tyr flushed. "I'm flattered, truly, but I'm no master—not yet. I've still got years before I can even stand before the Guild. For now, I'm content learning what I can—and passing along what little I know to others."

"Oh?" She tilted her head, her eyes twinkling. "And what would you teach me?"

Tyr blinked. His mouth opened and closed a few times before he could speak—but she smiled again, that same soft, mischievous smile.

"I'm just teasing," she said, then added more seriously, "But I do have a small request, if you'd grant me a courtesy."

Still caught in her smile, Tyr replied without hesitation, "If it's something I can do, I'd be honored."

"Good. Very good. We'll speak again soon." She turned, her voice light and carefree. "Come, ladies. Let's stop bothering the Master Smith—we've much to do and little time."

"You didn't tell me what you want me to do!" Tyr called after her.

"Don't worry," she replied over her shoulder. "You'll find out soon enough."

Tyr stood watching her walk away down the street and bellowed, "Damn!"

One of the apprentices ran up. "Everything all right?"

"No," Tyr muttered. "I still don't know her name."

The apprentice laughed and went back to work.

Three days later, Tyr still found himself watching the street each morning. Every day, he stood out front, scanning the flow of pedestrians, hoping to catch sight of the mysterious blonde girl. And every day, after a long sigh, he'd return to the forge, check in on the other smiths, and set about his own work. But he kept glancing toward the street.

Damn me for a fool, he thought. *I'm acting like a child.*

He shook his head and stood tall. *That's it.* He drew a deep breath. *I'm getting too full of myself. She's a noble's daughter, and I'm a journeyman blacksmith. Enough is enough.*

He turned his back to the street and resolved not to look toward it again until day's end. He had just found his rhythm and was drawing out a billet when he heard a familiar voice behind him.

"Damn, it's as hot as a smokehouse in here—only it smells much, much worse."

Tyr turned around to see Gillian eating an apple. Tyr smiled. "Good afternoon, Master Gillian. If you're here for my answer, you're too early. I still have a few days left to consider."

Gillian smiled in return. "Can't an old friend stop by just to say hello?"

"Old friend?" Tyr raised a brow. "Of course you could, but you didn't, did you? You never do anything on impulse."

Gillian looked wounded. "That's not true. I befriended you and Al on impulse."

"Maybe," Tyr conceded. "So then, did you just stop by to say hello?"

Gillian laughed. "Of course not."

Tyr rolled his eyes.

"But I'm not here on Gutamino's behalf either," he added.

"Oh? Then what brings you out this way?"

"Our good Lady Krystal said you owe her a courtesy, and she's ready to collect."

"Krystal…" Tyr whispered. The name sounded musical in his ears. "So that's her name."

Gillian gave him a funny look. "Seriously? You agreed to go to a royal ball with a complete stranger, and you didn't even know her name?"

"A what?" Tyr asked, suddenly concerned.

Gillian roared with laughter. "Oh my, you are so in over your head."

"This isn't funny," Tyr muttered.

"Oh yes, it is," said Master Crowin from behind his desk, never looking up from his paperwork.

"Damn straight it is," Gillian added, still laughing.

"I thought she wanted me to make her something. Or move furniture. Or—I don't know—something reasonable. Why would she want me to go to a ball? I'll be a laughingstock among all those nobles."

"Technically, only a few of them are nobles. Fewer still are actual royalty. Most are minor dignitaries, functionaries, and a few wealthy merchants. They live for this sort of thing."

"See?" Tyr said, pointing at Gillian as he looked at Crowin. "I don't even know that much." He shook his head. "I guess I'll have to wear that damn outfit I bought the other day to go see Gutamino."

Gillian patted him on the shoulder. "No, you must not wear that outfit again. You've already worn it, and it's really not appropriate for a royal ball."

"Then what am I going to wear?" Tyr asked, flustered.

"That's why I'm here. Lady Krystal has informed me what she'll be wearing, and I'm to take you to a tailor to get you outfitted properly—to match."

"Match?" Tyr echoed, appalled. Crowin laughed aloud.

"Never mind him," Gillian said. "Just come with me for now."

"I can't leave. I have work to do."

"Yes, you can," said Crowin. "This is my shop, and there's nothing on your bench that the others can't handle. So off with you."

Tyr opened his mouth to protest, but the look Crowin gave him ended it before it began. With a resigned sigh and lowered head, he followed Gillian to a tailor's shop in the Merchant District. There, he was quickly measured, briefly examined, and just as quickly dismissed with instructions to return by noon the next day.

"They weren't very friendly," Tyr remarked as they stepped back onto the street.

Gillian shrugged. "Tailors tend to be stuffy and not especially chatty. At least, the ones I've met."

"That's not been my experience," Tyr replied. "One of my best friends was a tailor. He loved to talk—and drink, and gamble, and fight. I wonder what he'd think of them?" His voice softened. "I wonder where he is now?"

Before Gillian could reply, Tyr asked, "What is Lady Krystal like?"

Gillian thought for a moment. "Funny. Nice. Scary."

"Scary?" Tyr asked, surprised.

He nodded. "She has this way about her. It's hard to explain. But I've got a feeling that if she did get mad, she could do some serious damage."

He laughed lightly. "In an odd way, she reminds me a lot of Al. All kind and thoughtful most of the time—but when needed, a pure terror in a fight."

"You've seen her fight?"

"No, no. Like I said—it's just a feeling."

"Who is she?" Tyr asked.

"She didn't tell you?" Gillian looked surprised.

Tyr shook his head. "She barely said anything at all."

Gillian smiled knowingly. "You really like her, don't you?"

Tyr blushed. "I—I hardly know her. I mean, I don't not like her, it's just—I don't know what I'm saying."

"Me either, but it's something I've noticed in guys and girls your age—you all get weird in the head around each other." He stopped. "This is where we part for now. I've got more errands to run. Just make sure you get back to that shop tomorrow, or you might get to see Krystal upset for real," he said with a grin, then darted off down one of the blocks.

The day finally arrived. Krystal had sent a carriage to the shop, and it promptly delivered Tyr to her residence on the palace grounds. Attendants opened the carriage door, and Tyr stepped out before a lavish estate—not the largest on the grounds, but to Tyr's eyes, far larger than anyone could ever need.

One of the servants led him up marble steps and through two grand wooden doors into a massive entryway with a ceiling at least forty feet high. Two ornate staircases curved upward on either side. At the first landing, his eyes came to rest upon the loveliest woman he had ever seen. Her long blonde hair was pulled back and braided, and she wore a flowing red dress with silver beading along the waist and sleeves. He began fidgeting with the collar of his fancy doublet, but the servant who had escorted him quickly slapped his hand, as one might chide a child. Tyr shot the man a glare, but the servant returned it with equal firmness. Tyr stopped fussing and turned his full attention to Krystal as she descended the stairs.

"Master Blacksmith, you are well, I hope," she said in the sweetest of voices.

Tyr stood silent a moment, then remembered himself. "Yes, milady. Thank you. You—you…" he stammered.

She smiled. "I what?" she teased.

"Look amazing, milady," he finished.

Her smile beamed, and she blushed slightly. "Why, thank you, Master Blacksmith. And if I do say so myself, you clean up rather nicely as well."

It was Tyr's turn to blush, but before he could respond, a deep voice came from behind him.

"Well now, who might this be calling on my granddaughter?"

"Oh Grandpa, you know full well who it is—and why he's here," Krystal giggled.

Tyr turned and froze. His greeting stuck in his throat. The man before him stood tall, an elderly gentleman still in the prime of his life, wearing a full dress uniform adorned with ribbons. Behind them—Tyr blinked—the man's face was unmistakable. It was the same old man who had helped him and Al across the border into Jaspar.

"Dadius?" was all Tyr could manage.

The old man smiled. "Around here most people call me Lord Dadius, but yes—it is I. It's been some time since we last spoke. How have you been, Tyr? And how is your friend?"

Krystal looked puzzled. "Wait—how do you two know each other?" she asked.

Lord Dadius smiled. "I met Tyr and a friend of his on their way from Harding into Jaspar. His friend was in rough shape, so I stopped and gave them a hand."

Tyr glanced back and forth between Lord Dadius and Krystal. "I'm sorry, this is all so confusing. I've been fine, Lord Dadius—though I think you may know more about how my friend is doing than I do."

"Relax, Tyr," said Lord Dadius. "You have nothing to fear from me—nor does your friend. I've never wanted anything but the best for both of you. From what Gutamino tells me, you're one of the most talented weaponsmiths he's ever seen—and coming from him, that's very high praise. As for your friend, I don't have anything newer than what Gutamino already told you, but I'll be sure to pass on anything I hear."

He patted Tyr on the shoulder and kissed Krystal on the forehead. "I'll see you two at the palace," he said, and exited toward a waiting carriage.

"Harding? I didn't know you were from Harding. Where from?" Krystal asked.

"Oh, a little smidge of a village about a day's walk west of the town of Whittle," Tyr replied, still reeling from the realization that Krystal was Lord Dadius's granddaughter—and by extension, someone he might be expected to consider an enemy.

An enemy to whom? he asked himself. Gutamino? Dadius? Neither has done me or Al any harm. So why am I so cautious with them?

"A day's walk from Whittle," she mused. "Are you from Southold?" she asked.

Tyr blinked. "How in the world could you have known that?" he asked.

Krystal smiled, one of her mischievous smiles. "Oh no, that answer is not going to come so easily. That one you'll have to work for," she said playfully.

"Oh? And what must I do to earn that answer?" he asked, enjoying the game.

"Milady," said the servant. "Your carriage awaits."

She looked at Tyr and let out a small, pouty sigh. "It'll have to wait, I guess. We must make our appearance at court, after all."

Tyr's face fell. He was not looking forward to the ball. Krystal wrapped her arm around his and led him out to the carriage.

"Relax. You'll do fine. The people at these things don't actually hear a word you say—they're too busy waiting to hear themselves talk. All you need to do is listen to me, make me laugh from time to time, and dance with me."

They sat down in the carriage, and it slowly made its way down a few tree-lined streets leading to the palace.

"Well, that doesn't sound so bad," Tyr replied. "I should warn you, though—I'm not the best dancer."

She looked horrified. "If I had known that, I wouldn't have brought you. Now I'll be the laughingstock of the palace!"

The color drained from Tyr's face, and Krystal burst into laughter.

"I'm sorry, Tyr, I couldn't help myself," she said, giggling for a few moments more. Tyr looked as if he might be upset, but then started laughing too, shaking his head.

She leaned in against him, resting her head on his shoulder. "Just hold me tight and we'll sway together—and I'll be happy."

Tyr smiled and put his arm around her. All too soon, the carriage came to a halt and the door swung open. They had arrived.

Krystal quickly composed herself and exited the carriage with all the grace and elegance one would expect of a lady. Tyr, less comfortably and with much less grace, followed. He looked around, momentarily like an animal caught in a trap, until he felt her arm slide through his. He glanced at her—her head was high, chin up, walking as if she glided on air—and she was with him. His heart skipped a beat, and emotion caught in his throat. If she's not ashamed to be seen with me, then I need to do my best not to embarrass her, he thought.

So he squared his shoulders, straightened his back, and walked with confidence he didn't feel—but confidence drawn from her. Krystal noticed the change immediately and looked up at him with a soft smile. He couldn't help but smile back as he led her into the foyer.

They stopped at the entrance to the ballroom and waited as one of the attendants announced them in a loud, regal voice: "The Lady Krystal Blackthorne and Tyr."

Following her lead, they descended the grand staircase arm in arm, slowly and elegantly, into the ballroom.

"Now what do we do?" he whispered.

"Now we mingle," she replied. "I'll go this way, you go the other. We'll meet back by the musicians."

He blinked. "We're mingling separately?" he asked nervously.

She smiled up at him. "You'll do fine. Everyone's going to love you." She paused. "If you prefer, all you really need to do is be willing to listen. These people love to talk—especially about themselves. Give them a willing ear and they'll love you even more." And then she drifted off into the crowd, leaving him with a reassuring smile.

With a barely contained sigh, Tyr moved off in the opposite direction and tried not to make eye contact—an easy task, since most guests were taller than him and gathered in small clusters, chattering away. From what Tyr overheard, it all seemed like petty gossip.

On the rare occasion someone pulled him into conversation, it always followed the same pattern: they asked about him, didn't really listen to his reply, then launched into complaints about something or other. Tyr quickly realized his opinions weren't sought—nor his advice. Krystal had been right all along. So he did his best to appear interested in everything they had to say.

He was surprised how long it took just to make it halfway around the room. While no one seemed particularly invested in him, they were all eager for a turn chatting with the mysterious new guest.

Then he spotted Krystal toward the back of the room. She was speaking with a young nobleman, and by the look on her face, she was on the verge of getting angry.

Tyr studied the noble. He was tall, with long, shoulder-length hair, primped and polished more than most of the women in the room—which was saying something, as the women had clearly spared no expense on their appearance. Tyr frowned. *Man?* he thought. *He looks to be my age. Maybe even younger. And skinny—more suited to riding horses than doing an honest day's work.*

As Tyr approached, the two didn't notice him. The noble appeared to have a few companions nearby. Tyr's frown deepened.

"Come on, Krystal, let's go for a walk on the grounds," the noble said. "We can grab a bottle or two and let loose."

"Give it a rest, Jahn. I'm not going anywhere with you or your lackeys. Not now, not ever," she replied, her voice tired, as if she'd said it countless times before.

"Don't make me pull rank on you, Krystal. I *am* the son of a Count, after all. And you are what, exactly? The granddaughter of a foreign diplomat's foot soldier?"

Krystal looked him in the eyes and flashed a smile that held no warmth. "Jahn, you are the lesser son of an even lesser noble." She stepped closer and casually straightened his collar. "You try to sound tough, like a real man—but your threats are as impotent," her eyes flicked downward to his groin and back up to his face, "as I imagine the rest of you is."

With that, she turned and began to walk away, his friends snickering behind him.

Enraged, Jahn shot out a hand to grab Krystal by the shoulder—but it never made it. Without thinking, Tyr's hand moved faster, snatching Jahn's wrist in a firm, vice-like grip.

Jahn blinked in surprise and tried to yank his arm back, but he couldn't break Tyr's hold.

Wild-eyed, he turned on Tyr. "How *dare* you touch me, peasant! I'll have you clapped in chains and thrown into the darkest cell we have. Unhand me at once!"

His friends stopped laughing, uncertain what to do.

Krystal turned back at the high-pitched strain in Jahn's voice, doing her best not to smile too broadly.

Tyr released his grip and replied coolly, "My apologies, *milord*, but as Lady Krystal's escort, it would have been remiss of me not to intervene. And technically, I'm a craftsman, not a peasant."

Jahn's face flushed crimson—part humiliation, part rage—as the realization set in that Tyr was Krystal's chosen companion at the event.

He turned to his friends. "Find the captain of my father's guard. He's around here somewhere. Tell him I have someone I want arrested."

Before they could leave, Krystal's voice rang out, sharp and commanding.

"You will do no such thing," she said, her expression suddenly stone-hard.

"And why is that?" Jahn asked mockingly.

"Because the craftsman standing before you has the favor not only of my grandfather, but also of Duchess Emrite—under whom, if I recall correctly, your father serves." Her voice was like ice now. "He is working on a special, time-sensitive project for the Duchess. So, tell me, Jahn—how do you think she will react when she learns that her commission was delayed because the Count's idiot son made a fool of himself and overreacted at a ball? Do you think that will reflect well on the Count? Or on you?"

Jahn's face contorted in rage, fists clenching and unclenching at his sides. After a few deep breaths, he seemed to regain some control.

"Fine," he spat. He glared at Tyr. "I'll forgive you this once. But cross me again—get between me and my quarry, or even look at me the wrong way—and I'll personally see to it that you regret it, little man."

He turned on his heel and stormed off, his friends scrambling after him.

Krystal threw her arms around Tyr's neck with a laugh. "My hero!"

Tyr turned from watching Jahn's retreat to meet her smiling face. He smiled in return. "I think that should be my line. You just saved me from a prison cell."

"It was all a bluff," she said with a shrug. "His father's men know to ignore his petty little tantrums. And his father wouldn't dare cross the Duchess."

"About that," Tyr said cautiously. "You do realize I haven't actually agreed to take the project yet?"

She smirked. "Well, now you'll have to—otherwise you'll make me a liar."

Then, without warning, she kissed him gently and whispered, "Now shut up and dance with me, will you? I've been waiting all night."

STANDING BEFORE THE MASTERS

The following couple of days, Tyr found himself unable to concentrate on any project for more than an hour. He kept glancing toward the front of the forge or finding excuses to step out onto the street. Try as he might, his thoughts kept drifting to Krystal.

Master Cowin finally had enough.

"Boy!" he barked, loud and stern, catching Tyr off guard. Cowin had never raised his voice before.

"Go home," he said.

Tyr blinked. "What?"

"You heard me. This is a place of business. Either get your head back into your work or go home until you can."

Tyr blushed. "I'm sorry, Master Cowin. You're right, of course. I just don't know what's come over me—I mean, I think I do, but I don't know—but—"

"Tyr," Cowin interrupted, his voice gentler now. He gestured to a chair beside his desk. "Sit."

Tyr obeyed.

Cowin studied him for a moment. "You didn't date much back home, did you?"

"Date? I hardly had time for anything. You know the life of an apprentice. I went out a couple of times, but nothing serious—"

"Tyr," Cowin interrupted again, this time with a knowing smile. "Boy, that girl's gotten into your head, and there's not much you can do about it except ask her to dinner—or for a ride, or something."

Tyr shook his head and sighed. "No. She's a nobleman's granddaughter. I'm a journeyman blacksmith. I can't ask her anything. You're right, though—this is a business, and I need to get my head back in the game."

Determined, he tied his apron back on, grabbed his favorite hammer, and turned toward his work—just as the all-too-familiar sound of giggling echoed from the shop entrance.

He looked up to see the two young women always in Krystal's company. His face lit up, but Krystal wasn't with them. Trying to hide his disappointment, he smiled and gave a slight bow.

"My ladies. How may I be of service today?"

The two giggled again. Then the one on the left said, "Our lady Krystal would like to know if you would care to accompany her for a ride outside the city this afternoon?"

Tyr realized with a start that he'd never actually spoken to either of them before and didn't even know their names. "I would be honored," he said, "but I don't have a mount."

They giggled again, and Tyr wondered how they got through the day doing anything besides giggling.

"Don't be silly," said the one on the right. "Our lady has already taken that into account. You just need to meet her at the Palace's craftsman gate by noon."

Tyr glanced at Master Cowin, seeking permission. The old smith gave a small smile and nodded.

"Then please tell my lady I will see her presently," Tyr replied.

The two women curtsied and headed down the street, still giggling.

Cowin shook his head. "Nobles," he muttered, a hint of disdain in his voice, before returning to his paperwork.

Tyr had hurried to wash, change, and reach the gate just in time. As he arrived, Krystal was walking through the Palace gates with two horses in tow. Sheas was dressed in a fashionable riding outfit. His heart seemed to skip a step and then beat faster at the sight of her.

"Master Blacksmith," Krystal said in greeting.

Tyr bowed slightly. "My lady."

She laughed softly. "Fair enough. How about I call you Tyr and you just call me Krystal."

He looked ready to object, but her expression made it clear the matter wasn't up for debate. He bowed in defeat, and she smiled broadly, handing him the reins of a small but sturdy black mare.

"You do know how to ride?" she asked, suddenly unsure.

He smiled. "I can manage without falling off—most of the time," he added with a wink as he smoothly mounted the horse.

Krystal leapt lightly into her saddle atop a silvery white mare that looked bred for speed and grace.

Tyr reached out and stroked the mare's neck. "She's beautiful."

Krystal smiled. "She was a gift from my grandfather when he brought me here. Supposedly, she came over the Shalmarin with

Gutamino. She's got fire in her blood, don't you, girl?" The mare whinnied in response.

They rode north into the countryside, past small farms and grazing fields. At first, their conversation was light and casual. But when they reached a grassy hillock far from the city, Krystal dismounted and let the mare graze. Tyr followed suit and sat beside her on the hillside.

She looked out over the city in the distance, then asked quietly, "Why did you go to the Spring Ball with me?"

Tyr grinned. "If I recall correctly, you tricked me into agreeing to do you a favor."

She smiled but didn't laugh this time. "So it was just out of obligation? Duty?"

Tyr fidgeted. "No, not entirely."

"Then why?" she pressed. "And why come riding with me now? You have no obligation to humor me."

Tyr sat up straighter, thinking for a moment before answering. "I'm not sure. From the moment I saw you on the palace grounds, I've been a jumble of mixed emotions," he said softly. "I suppose I…" He hesitated—he knew he shouldn't say it, but—"I like you," he said finally, barely above a whisper.

"But you're a craftsman. Not even a master. Where do you think this will go?" she asked, her tone blunt but not unkind.

His expression grew grim as he braced for the blow he knew must follow. "I know," he said quietly. "I know I'm stepping out of my class. Trust me—I know, and I struggle with it. It's just…"

"Just what?" she asked, her tone now sharper. "Am I a trophy to be won? Someone you can brag about to your mates down at the Donkey?"

"No!" he said, genuinely shocked. "I would never—"

"Then what?" she demanded again.

He looked her in the eyes, steadied himself, and said firmly, "I like you. I really like you. You're unlike any woman I've ever known. And since the moment I first saw you, my mind hasn't been my own. You've taken control of it. But you're right. And I do apologize. I'm just a blacksmith, and you are noble-born. When we get back to the city, I'll bother you no more."

She placed a hand on his arm, her voice softening. "No. That's not good enough. Not by a long shot."

He blinked. "What more would you have of me?"

"Accept Gutamino's offer."

"What?"

She smiled, though it was tinged with vulnerability. "My dearest Tyr, you know so very little about me—and I of you—but like you, my heart hasn't been my own since we met. I've never needed anyone. I fought my own battles—by wit or by steel. But the moment I saw you, I knew I'd never have to fight them alone again. I don't care that you're a craftsman. But we must play by the rules of this city. And for me to keep being seen with you, you must be of station. Which means, if you are a craftsman, you must be a master."

"I can't—" he started.

"Why not?" she interrupted.

"I haven't been judged."

"Then be judged."

"It's not that easy."

"Then make it that easy. Tyr, I've never met anyone like you, and I think you feel the same about me. We can change our stations—it's all about perception. What do you see when you look at me?"

"A high-born lady," he replied.

She laughed. "High-born? I was born to a merchant in Rollins. Yes, we had money, but we weren't nobles. Not even close. You asked how I knew about Southold—my parents arranged a marriage for me to the son of a farmer from that sleepy little hamlet. If he hadn't gotten himself in a world of trouble, we might have met there one day."

Tyr stared at her in disbelief. "Al," he said quietly.

"Al?" she asked, confused.

"The farmer you were supposed to marry… was his name Al?"

She thought for a moment. "I believe it was. You know him?"

Tyr's mind reeled. He was falling in love with the woman Al had once been intended to marry.

Seeing the look on his face, she giggled and nudged him. "Come on, tell me—was he ugly? Or cruel? Or was he the dreamiest of men?"

Tyr exhaled. "Krystal… he's my best friend. The only reason I'm here is because when he got into trouble, we left Southold together."

Suddenly very interested, she sat upright, eyes wide. "Tell me everything. I want to know all about you and Al—how you came to be here in York and what happened to him."

Tyr crossed his legs and sat facing her, then recounted the story—from that fateful day Al, Steven, and he traveled to Whittle to buy a betrothal gift, to Steven's betrayal, their flight from Southold, and their time together in Morcaster.

As he spoke, Krystal's expressions shifted—widened in wonder, narrowed in anger. When he finished, she sat in silence, eyes fixed on the drifting clouds.

Finally, she spoke. "He knew. All this time, he knew—and said nothing."

"Who?" Tyr asked, frowning.

"Grandfather," she replied. "He was the one who arranged the marriage. He was the one who helped you across the border and ordered Gutamino to train Al. And I have no doubt he tipped off Gillian to your presence here in the city…" She trailed off, lost in thought.

"Then maybe I shouldn't consider the position," Tyr said cautiously.

She snapped out of her thoughts at that. "No. Quite the opposite," she replied.

Tyr gave her a puzzled look, so she continued. "That old billy goat is always up to something, so I wouldn't read too much into it." Tyr wondered how much she was reading into it. "Never mind him—think of us. The only way this will work—whatever this is—is if you take the position." She batted her eyes at him for emphasis. "At least tell me you'll consider it."

He nodded, though he knew such a decision wasn't his to make lightly, even for the prettiest girl he had ever known.

"Good," she said, satisfied.

Tyr looked at her for a moment and then asked, "Why?"

It was her turn to look confused. "Why what?"

"Why me? Even if you weren't born at court, you've taken to it like you were. So why risk so much to be seen with a blacksmith?"

"You're more than a blacksmith, Tyr. It's hard for me to explain, but I know things—things I shouldn't have any reason to know, but I do. I'm not sure how I know them…" She shook her head. "Now I'm starting to ramble. Let me just say that when I see you, I see more than a blacksmith. I see—" She stopped herself. "No, I won't say. Other than that I see great things for you. And I see myself at your side. And if I'm not next to you, both of our fates get very dark."

The next day, Tyr was quietly working at the forge, his rhythm and concentration restored. He was doing his best to keep his mind on his work—and off the offer. He nearly made it to midday when a young boy in the livery of the Guild entered the shop. Tyr tried not to look up. Sometimes the Guild sent runners to collect monthly dues—this could be that.

After a moment, Master Cowin stood and motioned Tyr to join them. His expression was serious.

Tyr put the piece he was working on back in the fire and handed his hammer to the apprentice beside him. "Put the metal in the sand to cool. I'll finish when I return," he told him.

Tyr walked up to Cowin and the boy. "Journeyman Tyr?" the boy asked. Tyr nodded. "The Guild Masters have summoned you to appear before them to answer charges," he said solemnly.

Tyr swallowed hard. "What charges?" he asked, trying to keep his voice steady as his hands started to tremble.

The boy shrugged. "I don't know. They just tell me what to say, and I say it."

"When am I to appear?" Tyr asked.

"Right now. They're already assembled in the Grand Hall. You are to follow me at once."

Tyr looked to Master Cowin. The old smith said nothing, only nodded and motioned him to go. For a brief moment, Tyr considered making a run for the docks and hopping on the next ship out—but he sighed. He would face the masters. Technically, he hadn't accepted the offer, so he had broken no Guild rules.

Technically, he thought grimly. Just like Al hadn't technically broken any laws... at least not until after they found him guilty and exiled him.

The Guild Hall was only a few blocks from the shop, but it felt like a walk to his own execution. Inside, he followed the boy down a long corridor into a large antechamber.

"Wait here," the boy said. "I'll let them know you're present. They'll summon you when they're ready."

The boy opened one of the large double doors—Tyr assumed the Guild Masters were beyond them—and stepped through. The antechamber was empty except for a long wooden bench that ran along the wall. Tyr sat down, wishing he'd had time to clean up or at least change his shirt. He sniffed at it and winced.

This day just keeps getting better, he thought.

The hours dragged on. People came and went from the inner chamber, but no one spoke to him. No one even acknowledged his presence. The sunlight shifted slowly across the floor. Evening was fast approaching. His stomach rumbled, reminding him he'd had eaten neither lunch nor supper.

Just when he had nearly given up hope, the small boy finally reappeared and motioned for him to enter.

Tyr stood, rubbing life back into his stiff legs. He stepped into the inner chamber—not as large as the antechamber, but large enough. The Guild Masters sat high upon a U-shaped dais behind a heavy wooden table, looking down on him.

Tyr stood alone at the center of the floor. He swallowed hard. He wasn't easily intimidated, but even he had to admit—this was intimidating.

He looked at the Masters—five of them, all past their prime, each wearing the same expressionless look. Tyr wondered if they practiced that expression together. A smirk threatened to creep onto his face, but he pushed it down. This wasn't the time.

The master seated at the center spoke first. "You are the journeyman known as Tyr Ranfel, currently working under the guidance of Master Cowin at his shop on Cooper Street in the city and kingdom of York. Is this correct?" His tone was firm and matter-of-fact.

Each master had a nameplate set before them so Tyr would know how to address them. "That is correct, Master Quinn," Tyr replied.

"According to our records, you previously worked under Master Fenwil at his shop in the craftsman district of Morcaster, in the nation of Jaspar," Quinn said, glancing down at his notes before looking back at Tyr.

"Yes, Master Quinn."

Quinn nodded slightly and continued, "Before that, you were apprenticed under your father, Master Ranfel, in the hamlet of Southold, in the Republic of Harding."

"Yes, Master Quinn," Tyr confirmed once more.

"How long was your apprenticeship?" asked the master immediately to Quinn's right. His clothing and demeanor set him slightly apart from the others.

"I was formally admitted to the Guild on my eighth birthday and completed my apprenticeship shortly after my eighteenth. So, just over ten years, Master Anders."

"You could've started your journeyman years at fifteen. Why wait an extra three years?"

"I felt I still had more to learn. And the thought of leaving home at such a young age—away from my family and friends..." He trailed off.

"Was what?" pressed Anders.

"Lay off, Anders. Not everyone bolts the first chance they get. Some people actually value family," interjected Master Wilhelm, seated to Anders's right. In front of Wilhelm sat a small mound covered by a cloth.

Anders sniffed derisively but continued, "You spent ten years in your father's forge, learning everything you could, yet you left your first master in under a year. And now, in York, you've worked at Master Crowin's for just under two months. I have to ask—what's the sudden rush?"

"That's a pretty unfair question," said Master Follen gently. "If I'm reading this correctly, had he stayed any longer in Morcaster, he would've been one of the countless victims—and not standing before us now. And I'm not sure we've even established that he is seeking to leave Master Cowin's employ yet, unless I missed something."

"You haven't," rumbled Master Lund, his voice deep and commanding. "And I think we should establish that fact first. Boy, do you know why you've been summoned before us?"

Tyr straightened. "I believe it is in response to an offer I received from Lord Gutamino, Master Lund."

"Have you responded to this offer?" asked Master Quinn.

"Yes, sir. I told him I could not accept unless I were made a master."

The panel of masters exchanged quiet words among themselves for a moment before Quinn spoke again. "Is it true that this Gutamino—a foreigner, I might add—told you that such matters could be arranged?"

"He did," Tyr answered.

"And what was your response?" asked Master Lund.

"I honestly do not recall, Master Lund. I know I've been consistent in telling him and others that there are no shortcuts in our craft. I love what I do, and I hope to keep doing it for years to come."

"Boy," said Wilhelm, pulling back the cloth to reveal a small pile of swords. "Do you recognize these? You may examine them if you wish."

Tyr stepped forward and glanced at them, then shook his head. "No need. I do. They're some of my practice pieces."

"Explain," said Anders.

Tyr flushed slightly. "It's no secret that I'm still a journeyman. At my last shop, I mostly worked on parts for sailing vessels. When I arrived at Master Cowin's forge and received my first weapons commission, I bought some spare stock to practice crafting and design. I've kept the habit ever since with each new style."

"Why?" asked Master Quinn. "It's money out of your pocket. Do you add the cost into the customer's price?"

"No, sir. I can't and won't hand over an inferior product. And I don't believe my clients should pay for my education. I consider it the dues I must pay to advance in my—our—craft."

Lund motioned for one of the swords to be passed down. Each of the masters took a moment to examine the blade. It was one of Tyr's latest pieces, a sword commissioned as a gift for a general—intricately worked, with fine inlays and detailed scrolling, and a double fuller running down its length to strengthen and lighten the blade. When the blade reached Lund, he held it with the ease of one accustomed to such weapons. He tested its balance, judged its weight, and felt its edge before finally setting it down.

"We understand that this Lord Gutamino has promised to give you access to weapon-crafting techniques long forgotten here in the West—and presumably in the East as well. Is this true?"

Tyr nodded. "He made that promise, sir. But since I haven't accepted, I've seen nothing yet."

"You know the guild law—that such knowledge, after five years, must be shared with the Guild."

Though it was more of a statement than a question, Tyr answered all the same. "Yes, Master Lund. But again, I have not been shown anything."

"Is it true that you knew this Gutamino in Morcaster?" asked Master Anders.

"No, sir. I knew of him, but I only came to know one of his servants—a young man named Gillian."

"And what do you think he is doing here in York?" asked Master Quinn.

"Enough," interrupted Master Wilhelm. "We stray from the matter at hand. I believe we have the information we need. I say we put it to a vote and call it a day."

"I second the motion," said Master Lund.

"As do I," added Master Follen.

Quinn, clearly annoyed that his question had been cut short, composed himself and said, "You will wait in the antechamber while this body discusses and votes."

The young boy appeared again at Tyr's side and motioned for him to follow.

Tyr sat once more in the now-darkened antechamber, the only light coming from a few small, flickering candles set in wall sconces. He stared into the shadows, anxiety twisting in his gut. What if they barred him from smithing altogether? He couldn't return home. He couldn't face his father with such a verdict. The best he could hope for would be work as a ship's smith—technically not covered by the Guild, but hardly a career.

The door creaked open. The boy returned and gave a slight nod, motioning Tyr back into the chamber.

The masters appeared somewhat agitated with one another, but Master Quinn—calm and composed as always—spoke first.

"Tyr Ranfel, your character, your work, and your ethos have been tested today. I am pleased to say, in the matter of all three, you have passed." He handed Tyr a rolled piece of vellum, sealed with the insignia of the Guild. "This body grants you the title of Master Smith."

Tyr's jaw dropped. He blinked up at the masters, stunned into silence.

The five of them laughed.

"Boy," said Wilhelm, grinning, "you came to our attention the moment Master Cowin's forge started turning a profit. And none of us could escape the buzz about the craftsman crafting weapons for merchant ships and palace guards. When we heard about the offer from Gutamino, we were excited for you. But since you never made a petition to be judged, we figured we'd have to take matters into our own hands."

"Thank you. Thank you all. I don't know what to say," Tyr stammered.

"Thank us by keeping your quality as high as it's been," said Master Anders.

"And your prices as fair," added Master Follen.

"But not so low that you undercut your brothers and sisters in the craft," finished Master Lund.

"One last thing," said Quinn. "We do have a selfish reason for advancing you. Make no mistake—you earned this. But we're also keen to reclaim knowledge long lost to our craft. Such opportunities are rare, and we do not intend to waste it."

Wilhelm tossed Tyr a silver coin. "Go. Grab your friends and get drunk. First round's on us."

The five masters laughed again—and this time, Tyr laughed with them.

ACTING FIELD COMMANDER

Steven slowed his horse as Tenebris came riding up. She had gone ahead to the rally point to assess the situation on the ground. She smiled as she said, "Commander."

Steven returned a steady gaze, his expression unreadable. The weight of the moment was settling on him. Command was within reach—he only had to take it. He kicked his mount forward, urging it ahead of the column and out of earshot of the troops. Tenebris fell in beside him.

"What awaits us?" he asked quietly.

She shrugged. "About what I expected," she replied in a low voice. "Most of the commanders are uneasy with your appointment. They don't understand how you pulled it off, which has them thinking all sorts of things." She smiled. "We can use that to our advantage."

"What about the common soldiers?" he asked.

"Do you really care?" she teased.

"Of course not. But I need to know they'll follow," he said, tension in his voice.

"They're soldiers. They don't think for themselves. If they did, they wouldn't be soldiers," she said. "They'll follow their commanders' lead. So we'll need to deal with them. And by them, I mean Commander Varak Torvessen. He's a seasoned colonel and the highest-ranking officer present. He's also pitched his tent on the central hill," she added, a note of irritation in her voice.

"What do I care where he puts his tent?" Steven asked, frowning.

"You should care, love," she replied. "You're not just a soldier anymore. At this level, everything is about respect—who has it, who deserves it, and who can take it. By setting his tent on that hill, Torvessen's told the entire camp, without saying a word, that he's the true leader. You'll need to deal with him—first, and hard enough that he won't ever consider crossing you again."

Steven began to understand. He looked back at the troops to ensure no one was within earshot, then lowered his voice.

"Is this something that could be... handled... with your unique skill set?"

She grinned. "Oh, I do love it when you flirt like that." Then her smile faded. "Sadly, no. It wouldn't help your position and would raise too many questions—at least for now. Once the troops are in the field…” She shrugged. “Well, things can happen.”

They rode the rest of the way in silence, stopping atop a small crest where Steven could look down at the camp sprawling below.

“Well. That’s something you don’t see every day,” he said. A legion was supposed to include around five thousand soldiers, plus another fifteen hundred in support. Seeing it all—the expanse of tents, the distant clang of forges, the shouts of officers, and the churn of drills—gave him a new appreciation for the magnitude of what he was about to command.

“Something, isn’t it?” Tenebris said beside him. “And it’s about to be all yours.” She glanced at him. “Nervous?”

He looked back at her and broke into a slow smile. “I’ll get over it.” In a lower voice, he added, “It’s time we embraced our destiny. But first—we deal with Commander Torvessen.”

“Have you decided how?” she asked.

“Not yet. But it’ll be hard. And it’ll be swift.”

She smiled. “Good. I have an idea—or at least the start of one.” And as they rode toward the camp, she filled him in.

By the time they reached the outer perimeter, Steven had the rough shape of a plan. Two guards raised their hands to issue the standard challenge—but Tenebris cut them off.

“As you were. This is Legion Commander Waistwain. Going forward, I expect you to be at attention when addressing him, his staff, or any of his field commanders,” she snapped. “Is that clear?”

The guards, startled, snapped to attention. “Yes, ma’am!”

“Good. Now send runners to each cohort. The Legion Commander will conduct a camp inspection. Each cohort commander and their adjuncts are to accompany him—so any, and I do mean any, infractions can be addressed immediately.” She paused, then narrowed her eyes. “What are you waiting for?”

“Yes, ma’am!” the guards replied, turning to issue orders to nearby soldiers.

Tenebris shared a small, satisfied smile with Steven as they waited.

Before long, the officers began arriving. Judging by their expressions, they were confused—and none too pleased—by the abrupt summons. Steven remained mounted until the last of them had assembled. Then, in perfect unison, he and Tenebris dismounted.

Steven handed the reins of his horse—and hers—to Major Ardan, Colonel Torvessen's adjutant.

"Please see to the horses, Major," he said calmly.

The major looked furious, but a subtle shake of the head from Colonel Torvessen held him in check. Wordlessly, Ardan led the horses toward the paddocks.

Steven scanned the assembled officers. "Good afternoon, gentlemen," he said with polite firmness—a tone that left no room for familiarity. "I am Legion Commander Waistwain." He reached into his vest and withdrew a sealed letter. "By authority of the General Superior, I am assuming command of the forces assembled here." He unfolded the letter slowly. "Would anyone care to inspect the order?"

The tone in his voice made it clear that doing so would be unwise.

Silence.

Steven nodded, as though satisfied. "Good. Let it be noted that I have formally assumed command on this, the seventh day of Earda." He tucked the letter away. "Now then, I'd like to inspect the camp. Please inform me of any issues your respective cohorts are currently facing."

And so the inspection began—an hours-long walk through the encampment. They passed tents and training fields, field kitchens and latrines, weapons stores and paddocks. Finally, they reached the small hill at the center of camp where Colonel Torvessen's tent stood— larger and more centrally located than any other.

Steven climbed the hill with the group, taking in the tent's position with a critical eye.

"I want to personally thank Colonel Torvessen for assuming interim command during my absence," Steven said evenly. "I trust you'll instruct your men to relocate your tent to your cohort's assigned position, so that mine may be erected here."

The colonel smiled—a smile devoid of warmth. "I will not," he said flatly. "I'm willing to let you play commander, but make no mistake—you don't give us orders."

A tense silence followed.

Steven studied the officers' faces. They were uncertain—perhaps even swaying. Torvessen's defiance hadn't landed as strongly as he'd hoped. Steven nodded slightly, as if coming to a private conclusion.

"You do not challenge the contents of this order?" Steven asked, holding up the letter.

"I do not," the colonel replied, standing tall.

"Then are you telling me, here in front of these command-level officers, that you're willing to disobey the will of the General Superior?"

That question struck its mark. Torvessen's shoulders stiffened. The other officers exchanged wary glances.

"No," Torvessen said, slower now. "That is not what I meant. I will obey any lawfully given order."

"But you just said you would not move your tent," Steven said calmly.

"The position is traditionally reserved for the senior-ranking officer," the colonel replied.

"I see. Did the General Superior give you command of this legion?"

"No, he did not."

"So, it's your contention that, although I am in command, you still outrank me?"

The colonel hesitated. "Yes."

Steven's expression hardened. "An army can have only one commander. I respect your rank and your years of service, Colonel, but rank is not the same as command. The General Superior placed me in charge—not you. So, I'll give you one last choice: have your men remove this tent, or I will have it removed for you. And your cohort will be reassigned—permanently. Make your choice, Colonel. Choose wisely."

Later that evening, Steven reclined in his newly erected command tent on the hill, stretched out on a thick fur laid across the wooden floor. His back was braced against a pile of pillows, a glass of wine in hand. Tenebris sat beside him, her back pressed to his chest, sipping her own.

The colonel, though furious, had moved his tent without further protest.

"He'll be a problem, you know," Tenebris said quietly.

Steven nodded. "I know."

"Any thoughts?" she asked, her tone light.

He smiled. "Several. When the opportunity presents itself, I want it to look like an accident. But it should be painful... slow... and obvious that such ill fortune follows those who displease me."

"Ooooh," she cooed, nestling closer. "I do love a challenge."

"What about the others?" Steven asked.

"We'll see," Tenebris replied. "I have eyes on them already. Some will come around to the new reality without issue. Others will go where the wind pushes them. A few, though... a few will prove difficult, and so—"

He smiled, taking another sip. "I do love it when you flirt with me."

She set her glass down and straddled him, her hands running across his chest. "Tomorrow, you'll hold your first war council. Make them think about the task at hand—duty, honor, service to the Order. Remind them of all the good they're doing for those poor, helpless farmers." As she stripped off her jerkin, she added, "Give them plenty of details about the enemy. Let them know they're fighting myth— and that myth has teeth." She leaned in and nibbled at his neck.

Steven emerged from his tent before sunrise, tired and sore. Bris, true to form, had left sometime during the night. A young private hurried up to him with a steaming cup of coffee.

Steven accepted it with a curt nod. The boy turned to go, but Steven stopped him.

"Keep up the good work," he said, taking a sip. "Though I should warn you—nothing in this world is given. You need to see what you want and do what you must to take it. No one gives you anything. You take it."

The private blinked, unsure how to respond.

Steven looked out over the camp, his mind as blank as his stare. "Send word to the other commanders. Staff meeting at the start of third watch."

Tertia. It's called tertia. If you're going to command, start using the right terms, he reminded himself.

"Yes, sir," the private replied, quickly disappearing.

Steven returned to his tent—still a mess from the night's activities—and sat at the small table, setting the coffee aside. He unrolled a large map of Harding.

It's bigger than I imagined—and wasted on nothing but farmland, he mused. *Why are you so interested in it, Cygnus? You don't make moves without purpose. What am I not seeing?*

He picked up the coffee and leaned back, committing the topography of his homeland to memory.

As the sounds of the camp changed and the sun crept higher, Steven knew second watch was nearing its end. He rolled up the maps, donned his best uniform, and made his way to the war tent.

Inside, the other commanders and their adjutants were already gathered. Tenebris stood near the entrance. Steven met her gaze and gave a small, solemn nod. Much would depend on the next hour—and they both knew it.

A large table dominated the center of the tent, bearing a map of Harding. Small carved tokens marked their current positions: five blue for the cohorts, five red for the support trains.

Everyone, including Colonel Torvessen, snapped to attention as Steven entered. He let his gaze pass over them before offering a faint smile.

"As you were, gentlemen."

The officers relaxed, though none spoke.

Steven looked at them—really looked—and exhaled slowly. "I know I'm not the commander you wanted," he began. "I know many of you have doubts about my abilities—as well you should. I would, in your place."

He paused, letting the silence settle.

"I'm here because of my actions in the north. Not because I'm the greatest strategist, or the most decorated—" His eyes shifted to Major Demitri, whose love of medals was well known. "—or the most senior," he added, glancing at Colonel Torvessen. "I'm not even nobility," he said, turning toward Majors Cantor and Polix. "I'm the son of a tailor. A simple man thrown into a situation the likes of which has not been seen on these shores in over five hundred years."

A murmur passed among the officers. Confused glances were exchanged.

"I'm not going to bore you with legends—you've all heard the old stories. The Dokkalfar. His dark governors, the Alkeir. His monstrous legions. Tales meant to frighten children."

He saw it—their discomfort. Their doubt.

And he pressed forward.

"In the north, I learned it was real—all of it," Steven continued. "I stood at the foot of one of the seals that holds the Dokkalfar locked in his prison. I fought..." He paused, glancing away for effect. "...and nearly died trying to protect it. My enemy was one of the Alkeir, and no mortal man can defeat one of them. I was thrown down and left for dead.

"When I came to, the seal was broken—shattered into a thousand pieces. The enemy was gone, headed south, apparently in search of the next seal."

He looked at each of them in turn. Their faces were a mix of disbelief, skepticism, and curiosity.

He smiled. "I wouldn't believe me either. But I ask for your indulgence—just a little longer."

He nodded to Tenebris, who silently exited the tent.

"His army—at least the one I faced—was made up of two distinct and terrible types of monsters. Yes, monsters. The first were ogres: towering brutes, nearly nine feet tall, as wide as two men, with skin so thick a normal sword barely scratches them. The nomads fought them in threes, on horseback, with spears—only then did the nomads stand a chance. Fortunately, we are not facing ogres.

"No," he said grimly, "we face something worse. More feral. More cunning. They call themselves the Klav—part dog, part man. They wear light armor, wield short swords, but they don't need them. Claws, teeth, speed—they're pack hunters. Ruthless. These are our enemy."

The colonel let out a loud, derisive laugh. "Boy, you should leave the Order and become a minstrel. You've got the flair for it."

A few others chuckled, visibly relaxing.

"I don't know what lies you spun to the General Superior to earn this command," the colonel continued, "but I'm not about to go chasing fairy tales and phantom beasts in the name of some long-dead boogeyman no one's seen in over five centuries."

Laughter rippled through the tent again.

Steven simply nodded and smiled. "I wouldn't expect you to believe me. Not without proof."

Just then, Tenebris returned, carrying something wrapped in cloth. She placed it on the table and stepped back.

Steven gestured toward the colonel. "Please. Do the honors."

Still skeptical, the colonel stepped forward and unwrapped the bundle.

Beneath the cloth lay the corpse of a Klav—snarled lips, yellowed fangs, clawed hands, matted fur, and the stench of rot. The room fell silent. The colonel recoiled, muttering a curse under his breath. The other commanders paled.

"Yes," Steven said quietly. "Myth has become reality. These creatures are loose in Harding, terrorizing farmers and travelers. And we've just received word that Cygnus has closed the routes in and out of the Republic.

"But according to my scouts, he's not directing these things. He's letting them run wild. That's our opportunity. They are vicious, but uncoordinated. We have strategy, training, and discipline. They do not. We can root them out—but it will take effort. We'll need to be thorough, precise, and fast.

"And if we fail—" He let the silence stretch. "—if Harding doesn't bring in a harvest this year... what do you think happens?"

The color drained from the men's faces. Everyone knew Harding was the breadbasket of the kingdoms. If it fell, famine would follow.

Tenebris removed the Klav's corpse from the table.

Steven took a seat and gestured to the map. "Now, I'd like to hear your thoughts. How do we best eliminate this threat?"

The others sat down one by one, their silence replaced with uneasy determination.

He waited, watching each of them in turn. They were struggling with the new reality—he understood that. What they suggested next would tell him a great deal about each of them. It would be a good starting point, letting him know who might need special attention down the road.

Major Cantor, an aging woman with streaks of white running through her otherwise jet-black hair, straightened in her chair and composed herself before speaking.

You can take the noble out of the castle, but not the castle out of the noble, Steven thought. *Born of privilege, probably bought her rank. She'll never respect me.*

Still, he offered her a pleasant smile as she began.

"My lord commander," she said in an even, cold tone, offering him only a curt nod. "This is truly incredible news."

Her steps were deliberate as she approached the table, each word carefully measured. "I think I speak for all of us when I say none of us had heard any reports of such beasts before now." She gestured toward the Klav's corpse, as if it were a curiosity in some nobleman's menagerie.

"But," she added, her voice tinged with ice, "before we begin devising a strategy, don't you think it prudent to share whatever intelligence you've already gathered?"

The tone was almost maternal—cool, disapproving—as if she were rebuking a student who'd spoken out of turn.

Steven looked to Tenebris, who stepped forward and replied with quiet confidence, "Our intel is limited, but we've confirmed they operate in small to medium-sized hunting packs. The packs appear evenly spread across Harding, each with its own territory—though it's hard to define where one ends and another begins."

"Perhaps we should send scouts to gather more detailed intelligence before we commit forces to the field," offered Major Demitri. Short and pudgy, he didn't look like a soldier at first glance— but he had a reputation for ruthless efficiency and a brilliant tactical mind.

Cautious, Steven thought. *More calculating than I expected. He's not to be underestimated.*

Steven's eyes turned to Major Polix. The man was meticulously dressed, his fingernails trimmed with near-obsessive precision. He studied the map, tapping the hilt of his sword with steady fingers.

He's weighing his options, Steven noted. *Not afraid of a fight—but he wants to know what's in it for him.* Steven smiled to himself. *I can work with that.*

He turned to the colonel. "How would you handle this?"

Torvessen looked him over, gauging his tone, then gave a quick glance toward the bundled Klav corpse. With a sigh, he replied, "Assign each cohort a region, starting in the north and working south. Each commander is responsible for clearing their region as we push westward."

Steven nodded—it was the strategy he'd intended, but he had wanted it to come from them.

"I agree. We should also establish clear communication between the cohorts. I want the legion moving—as much as possible—as a single unit. Otherwise, we risk allowing them"—he gestured to the Klav's body—"to slip through and regroup behind us."

Major Demitri nodded. "Very well. I'll coordinate the communications. I've used some effective methods in the past. If each of you sends your scout leaders, I'll train them accordingly."

Major Polix looked up from the map. "I may stop by as well. I don't think we should abandon the idea of advance scouting entirely. Even if we scout while we move, it's worth discussing." He glanced at Demitri. "Let's talk privately and see what we can come up with."

Steven sat back, hiding his smile. The meeting had gone better than he'd dared to hope. A quick glance at Tenebris confirmed she was thinking the same.

AN ASSASSIN'S DIPLOMACY

The fire blazed brightly in the waning dark. The moon had set; the sun yet to rise. The night was quiet and cool. Tenebris sat sipping her coffee, watching the flames dance. She smiled. She loved their chaos—their power, their purifying touch. Fire was pure.

She reached out and turned a long iron poker in the bed of coals, lifting it briefly to examine the glowing tip. It burned a bright, healthy red. She pushed it back into the embers and said, almost conversationally, "Almost ready. It's important to get the heat just right—not too cool, and not too hot. Too cool, and it just doesn't have the same effect. Too hot..." She shrugged. "Well, the body has a way of shutting out pain past a certain threshold. So we aim for just below that point. This way you'll feel it in every fiber of your being. And then—we wait. And when your body's recovered just enough... we'll do it again. And again. And again."

She smiled gently, almost warmly, and turned to look at the man tied up beside her. He was completely naked, gagged, and absolutely terrified. His hair was perfectly trimmed, his nails manicured—even his toenails.

"You're killing too many of them," she said softly. "And that's the problem."

She shifted her seat, tucking one leg beneath her, and studied him with something like fond curiosity. "This can go two ways—and I'm going to let you decide which."

Major Polix's eyes widened in the firelight, sweat streaking down his face.

"I can either torture you to death, which I promise you will take quite some time" she said with a flash of white teeth and no emotion in her eyes, "or I can make you even wealthier than you already are."

He blinked, confused, the fire casting flickering shadows across his face.

"You see, I have a little problem—well, four little problems, actually. You commanders. I'm just not getting the sense that you're fully supporting our Lord Commander Waistwain... or seeing the big picture."

He grunted against the gag.

"I know, I know," she said, waving it off. "You're just doing what you believe is right. But here's the rub—it's not right. It's conflicting with the Lord Commander's objectives. And I really, really need you to get on board."

She pulled the poker out of the coals again, examined it, then moved it just close enough to his groin for him to feel the searing heat radiating from it.

He began to scream through the gag.

She moved the poker away and unfastened the gag.

"I'm sorry," she said sweetly. "I didn't quite catch that."

"Please," he sobbed. "I beg you. Don't do this—I'll do whatever you want, I swear."

She tilted her head, considering. "I'm not sure," she said at last, replacing the gag. She touch the tip of the poker on his inner thing just next to his manhood.

He screamed through the gag, she smiled as she removed it. "I want to believe you. I really do. But I also really like the idea of putting this" she held the glowing poker before his eyes, "in some fun places."

He was breathing heavy, tears starting to weal up in his eyes. She removed the gag again, "I swear, let me go. I will do what ever you and the lord commander wants" he wept.

"Yes, that is what the Lord Commander wants" she seemed conflicted, "I really was hoping you have a bit more backbone so I could play some more."

Tears streamed down Polix's face. "Anything," he whispered. "I swear. Anything."

She sighed, glancing down at the poker. "Cooled down too much," she muttered, pushing it back into the coals. "All right. If you're serious—because I am very serious when I say I'd enjoy torturing you to death."

"I am, I swear I am. Whatever you need." He promised.

She smiled and said "Good, then we have a little test for you. With a nice reward, if you pass."

He nodded quickly. "Anything. I promise."

She leaned forward and said, as if it were nothing at all, "I want you to sneak into Major Cantor's tent tonight... and strangle her with your bare hands."

He blinked. "What? She's one of us! And she's been my mentor."

"No." Tenebris turned the poker over. "She's one of *you*. And she'll never accept the Lord Commander. This tactic wouldn't work on her. Besides, I really want someone to die tonight. It can be you ... or her."

He watched her as she continued playing with the fire.

"All right," he said at last, voice quiet and shaking. "I'll do it."

She didn't look up. "You mentioned a reward?"

Now she smiled. She had him. "Yes. Do this. Follow orders. And after we liberate Harding, you'll be granted land. You'll be the first true noble with property and full rights in Harding."

She saw the flicker of hunger in his eyes and knew she'd won.

She cut the rope binding his hands. "Get dressed."

As he obeyed, she continued, "Most of the camp is still asleep—and so she should be. I'll see to it the patrol is elsewhere while you're about your business. You'll strangle her with your own hands. Break her neck if you can. Then get out of there."

She tossed him a glove. "Leave this on the floor as you exit her tent."

Her voice dropped, calm and cold. "And understand this—I have eyes everywhere. If you betray me, try to run, or fail... you'll wish I had used the poker."

He looked at her questioningly but nodded—then turned and ran off into the night, back toward the distant camp.

Steven sat in his tent, reviewing the latest reports from the cohorts, when Tenebris entered. He smiled, almost unconsciously, at the sight of her.

"What news from the south?" he asked. "How do Polix and Cantor fare?"

She pulled off her riding tunic and collapsed into one of the chairs.

"Long ride?" he added, already pouring her a glass of wine.

She took it with a grateful smile. "Long and dreary," she said, taking a sip. She leaned her head back, eyes closed. "Nice to be back." After a pause, she added, "The south has been dealt with—or rather, the necessary actions have been set in motion to resolve matters. Both north and south."

Steven smiled. "Oh, do tell. What has my little kitten been up to?"

"Polix is ours now. Completely." She opened her eyes and looked at him. "I had him kill Cantor. With his bare hands. He now knows exactly what will happen to him if he steps out of line."

Steven's expression hardened slightly. "Did anyone see him?"

She shook her head. "No. I made sure the path was clear. He also left behind a bit of planted evidence in her tent. I only have one more loose end to deal with. Once the news breaks, have an official investigation launched."

Steven frowned. "Only problem is—no one would believe the results of an investigation run by me."

Tenebris smiled slyly. "Assign Major Demitri to oversee it personally. He doesn't like you, and everyone knows how obsessed he is with propriety and truth."

Steven raised an eyebrow, skeptical.

"Trust me," she said. "He'll do exactly what we want him to."

He chuckled. "I do trust you. I just don't know how you do it."

She stood slowly, a glint in her eye. "You're not supposed to. That's what makes me so special." She stepped closer, her voice low and commanding. "I have to be back on the road before the sun comes up." She reached for the laces of her trousers. "So stop what you're doing..." Her shirt dropped to the floor. "And ravish me."

* * *

Major Demitri sat alone in his tent, finishing his dinner. The Lord Commander's written orders assigning him to investigate the apparent murder of Major Cantor lay open on the table before him.

He glanced up at the sound of the tent flap stirring but saw no one there. Shrugging, he returned to his food—until movement at the edge of his vision made him turn.

Tenebris stood beside him, silent and still, dressed all in black. A dark gaiter covered her face below the eyes.

"Enjoying the meal?" she asked politely.

He stared at her in stunned silence before finding his voice. "You're Waistwain's second, aren't you? What are you doing, sneaking in here unannounced? I should have you thrown in irons. I should—"

She placed a single finger over his lips.

"Now, now, Major... is that any way to speak to your savior?" she whispered.

"What are you talking about?" he hissed, though his voice was now low and tight.

She pointed at the half-finished plate in front of him. "It was poisoned. A very nasty, exotic poison. Rare. Comes only from the jungles south of the Five Kingdoms."

His fork clattered to the plate.

"What? Poison? Are you certain? How do you know? What am I supposed to do?" His voice rose in panic.

"Calm yourself," she said. "The more agitated you get, the faster it works." She withdrew a small vial from a pouch and held it delicately between two fingers. "Fortunately for you, I brought the antidote."

His hand shot out. "Then give it to me—please!"

With a flick of her wrist, the vial vanished back into her cloak.

"Not so fast, Major. First, we need to come to terms. I am about to save your life, after all. That must be worth something to you… no?"

"Of course it is," he growled, trying to keep his voice steady. "Name your terms, woman."

She leaned closer, her breath warm on his face. "Quietly now. The more excited you get, the worse it gets for you."

He narrowed his eyes. "How do you know so much about this poison? How can I even be sure?"

She cut him off with a cold, casual shrug. "Because I'm the one who poisoned you, of course."

Anger filled Demitri's eyes, and with surprising speed for his bulk, he drew a knife and lunged. But Tenebris was faster—before he could rise from his seat, her blade was at his throat.

"Easy now, Major. I wasn't lying about the poison accelerating when you get excited."

"Of course I'm excited—you poisoned me! How did you expect me to react?"

She pulled the vial out again and held it between two fingers. "In here are enough tablets to keep the poison at bay for one month. One each morning—no more, no less. Miss a dose, and you'll be dead by nightfall. And before death takes you, you'll know agony like nothing you've ever imagined."

"Why daily? Why would I need to keep taking it?" he asked.

She gave a mock-pitying shrug. "Did I forget to mention? There's no cure. Once it's in you, it's permanent. The pills only suppress the symptoms and keep it from killing you."

He stared at her in disbelief. "Why? Why would you do this?"

"I have a problem," she replied, smiling faintly. "And I need your help."

"You couldn't have just asked?" he growled.

She tilted her head. "This way's more fun."

She stepped back and folded her arms. "Here's the deal. You're going to investigate the murder of Major Cantor. You'll find that she and Colonel Torvessen had a rather loud argument that night—witnesses will confirm it. You'll find a glove in her tent. It belongs to the Colonel."

Demitri's eyes narrowed. "And then?"

"With a heavy heart," she continued, "you will report your findings to the Lord Commander. And when you do, you'll also discover hidden evidence tying the Colonel to Cygnus. He'll be tried and executed for treason."

"I won't," Demitri said coldly. "Kill me if you must, but I will not betray the Colonel—or the Order. Not just to save myself."

Tenebris nodded, as if expecting that answer. "Admirable. Truly. But you misunderstand the stakes."

Her voice dropped. "Even as we speak, I have agents ready to torture and kill your wife, your children, and your grandchildren will be sold on the open market to either slavers or sex traffickers whoever will pay a higher price. And just to put an end to your name, when they're done, they'll plant evidence proving you were the one in league with Cygnus."

She leaned in. "Am I making myself clear?"

He sat frozen, stunned. A sharp cramp twisted through his gut, and he winced.

"Oooh," she cooed. "It's starting. You've only got minutes left before the hours of agony begin. So... what's your decision?"

He held out his hand, defeated. She placed the vial in it.

"Behave, and you'll get a new one before the month is out. Step out of line, and your days—and your family's—are numbered."

His voice was a whisper. "Why?"

She leaned down and whispered into his ear, "Did you think we didn't know about your little pact with the Colonel? That alone is treason."

With a slam of his fist on the table, he looked up—only to find the tent empty.

She was gone.

*　*　*

Five days had past since her visit with Demitri.

Tenebris stood silently behind Steven, who sat in full dress uniform on a makeshift dais. Before him, kneeling in chains, was Colonel Torvessen. His uniform was torn and filthy, his head bowed. On either side, two guards held spears against his back—one nod from Steven, and it would be over.

To Steven's right stood Major Polix, polished and perfectly coifed. To his left, Major Demitri, as rumpled as ever. Neither dared meet Tenebris's gaze.

Behind them stood the remaining senior staff and soldiers from the colonel's former cohort—those not currently deployed.

Steven rose slowly, his face unreadable. He cast his gaze over the assembly.

"Major Polix," he said in a clear, formal voice, "you claim to have charges you wish to present for judgment in the matter of Major Cantor's death?"

Polix stepped forward. "Yes, Lord Commander," he said, his voice loud and confident. "I wish to present evidence proving that Colonel Torvessen was conspiring not only with the late Major Cantor to undermine your command—but also with the enemy."

A ripple of gasps spread through the assembled soldiers.

Steven nodded. "Present your evidence."

Polix gestured toward three soldiers standing off to the side. "We have witnesses. On the night of Major Cantor's death, they overheard the colonel engaged in a heated argument inside her tent, followed by a loud crash. They observed him leaving moments later, alone and in haste. The next morning, the major's body was discovered—along with this."

He held up a single glove for all to see.

"An argument and a glove do not prove murder," Steven said, his tone neutral but watchful.

"Of course not, Lord Commander," Polix replied with a deferential nod. "The colonel is known for his temper, so no one—not even the witnesses here today—thought anything of the shouting at the time. As for the glove, we found its match in the colonel's tent. But again, that alone proves nothing, since we already know he visited her that night."

"Go on," Steven said evenly.

"Examination of the major's body showed she was strangled," Polix continued. "The marks indicate it was done by someone large and powerful. Most of the cohort was deployed that night. Only a skeleton crew of support staff and guards remained in camp, and no strangers were seen entering or leaving. That gave us a very short list of potential suspects."

He paused, letting the weight of his words settle before continuing. "During a search of the major's belongings, we found a letter hidden in her field book."

"What kind of letter?" Steven asked.

"Orders," Polix replied, his voice firm. "From Colonel Torvessen—orders that directly contradicted your own. He instructed her to hold her men back but to report that she was keeping pace."

Steven's brow furrowed. "Do you know why?"

Polix shook his head. "Not exactly. But based on our positioning at the time, it appears he was attempting to maneuver you into a vulnerable position—one that would expose your flank to the enemy."

"That's serious," Steven said slowly, "but still not definitive proof of murder."

"I agree, Lord Commander," Polix said. "But then yesterday, this came into our possession." He held up a small metal cylinder.

Steven raised an eyebrow. "And what is that?"

"A message case," Polix explained. "It was found on the body of a Klav killed by one of our patrols."

"And what does it say?" Steven asked.

Polix unrolled a parchment from within the cylinder and read aloud:

Cantor taken care of. Her second will be easily controlled. In three days' time, the Lord Commander will be exposed enough for your troops to remove him.

The words hung in the air like smoke. A few officers shifted uncomfortably. Steven's face hardened into stone as he turned his gaze to Colonel Torvessen. The colonel did not respond. He did not flinch. He already knew how this would play out. Tenebris, standing silently behind Steven, allowed a thin smile to spread across her face. It had taken her less than half an hour alone with him for the colonel to understand that this had always been the end of his path—that if he resisted, if he showed even the faintest defiance, he would become her personal toy until he died screaming.

Steven composed himself and turned his gaze to Major Demitri. "Major Demitri," he said, voice level, "has Major Polix presented this evidence to you?"

Demitri's voice, quiet and stripped of all passion, answered, "He has, Lord Commander."

"And have you independently investigated this evidence on the colonel's behalf?"

"I have."

"Do you find the evidence credible?"

"I do," Demitri replied, barely audible.

"And do you find it convincing?"

A long pause. Then, almost a whisper: "I do."

Steven's eyes narrowed. "Do you have any evidence to submit on the colonel's behalf?"

"I have none," Demitri said. He swallowed hard, then added, "But though it shames me, I have a confession to make."

Steven hesitated. That wasn't part of the plan. He cast a glance at Tenebris. Her expression was unreadable, but inwardly she tensed.

What is he playing at?

Demitri stood a little straighter. "The colonel approached me in private and asked me to aid him in his efforts to undermine your command. I regret to say... I was weak. I gave him my support."

"What kind of support?" Steven asked sharply, his voice like a blade. A ripple of delight ran down Tenebris's spine at the edge in his tone.

"Nothing treasonous," Demitri said quickly. "I never disobeyed your orders. I simply passed along routine updates—our current deployments, positions, minor intel. Nothing I thought was harmful at the time..."

Steven nodded slowly, letting the room stew in silence before continuing. "Now that you know he was in league with the enemy… does his request make more sense to you?"

Demitri looked down, ashamed. "Yes," he murmured. "He must have been passing the information along to Cygnus."

Steven turned to address the gathered officers and soldiers. His voice was steady, absolute.

"Let the record show that Colonel Varak Torvessen has conspired with a known enemy of the realm, ordered the murder of a fellow officer, and attempted to sabotage this legion and its mission. I, as Commander of the Legion and by authority granted to me by the General Superior, sentence him to death. Execution will be carried out at dawn."

No one protested.

Tenebris's smile, this time, reached her eyes.

Steven sighed. "I do not pretend to understand why you would willfully disobey an order from your duly appointed commander, Major Demitri. But I also hear nothing that reeks of treason. A mark will go on your record—but nothing more."

Demitri stood stiffly at attention and saluted. "Thank you, Commander."

Steven's gaze shifted to the kneeling figure before him. "Colonel Torvessen," he said, his voice sharp and unyielding, "do you have anything to say in your defense?"

For the first time since the proceedings began, the colonel lifted his head. His eyes flicked briefly to Tenebris—just a glance—before he shook his head and lowered it again.

"That is for the best," Steven said coldly. "Such treason deserves no voice."

He stepped forward, descending the small dais with slow, deliberate steps until he stood beside the condemned officer.

"Colonel Varak Torvessen," he continued, his voice carrying across the field, "for the high crimes of treason, sabotage, and conspiracy with the enemies of the Order, I sentence you to death. The sentence will be carried out immediately."

Tenebris watched closely as Steven drew his longsword.

The two guards flanking the colonel forced him to his knees. He did not struggle. He did not beg. There was a quiet acceptance in his bowed posture.

Steven raised the blade. Time seemed to slow. Tenebris leaned forward ever so slightly, her eyes locked on Steven's face. This was the moment—the true test of what kind of commander he would become.

With a single, clean stroke, Steven severed the colonel's head from his body.

There was no ceremony. No flourish. Just the brutal finality of steel.

As the body slumped forward and the head rolled to a stop, Tenebris caught it—that flicker across Steven's face. A slight smile. Brief. Controlled. But it had been there.

And it thrilled her.

Her heart pounded. *Yes*, she thought. *Yes, this is the man I've been waiting for.*

Steven wiped the blade clean, turned back toward the assembly, and gave a single nod. The guards lifted the remains and began to carry them away.

Behind him, Tenebris stood still, the faintest hint of a smile tugging at her lips—satisfied.

FOXES AND HOUNDS

Steven stood over the table, staring in frustration at the board and pieces laid out before him. In his hand, he held a small carved wooden figure of a fox. With a growl of irritation, he hurled it across the tent just as Tenebris entered. The piece struck her squarely in the chest before falling harmlessly to the floor. She bent down, picked it up, and examined it as she walked over to him.

"Rough day?" she asked innocently.

He gestured to the game board. "It's this stupid game Uso mentioned in his last report. I've been trying for hours to figure out the point of it—or even how you're supposed to win."

She returned the fox to the board and began resetting the pieces.

"Hey, I was in the middle of that," he said, shaking his head. "Not that it matters."

"Why does Uso want you playing a children's game?" she asked, curious.

Steven shrugged. "Who knows why that green-skinned bastard does anything? He claims both his military and the general staff of the Five Kingdoms use this game to teach battle tactics. I just don't see it."

"You've never played before?" she asked, raising her eyebrows.

"I'd never even heard of it before the other day," he admitted.

She sat and motioned for him to take the seat opposite. "It's a game kids play in the south. I've heard rumors that some adults enjoy it too, but I never knew it had military applications. Still," she added thoughtfully, "it makes sense when I think about it."

Steven watched her eyes spark as she analyzed the game's potential. She really was something rare. Dangerous, yes—ruthless, even—but brilliant in her own dark way. He found himself smiling wider at the thought.

"First, you need to understand the strengths and weaknesses of each side," she began, picking up one of the carved hound pieces. "They are not equal. The hounds are strong but slow. Their power comes from numbers and teamwork."

She handed him the hound and picked up a fox figure. "Foxes are fewer, but quick and agile. They have high defense and can use obstacles on the board to their advantage."

"Each side has specialized units that follow their own specific rules, and their objectives are different. The hounds win by killing the fox commander or by capturing or killing at least one of each fox specialty unit. The foxes are mission-focused—they win by moving at least half of their units to the opposite side of the board, or by assassinating the Hound Master."

She handed him the fox. "So first, you must decide—are you the fox or the hound? And remember, foxes always go first."

He stood there, examining the two figures.

"That depends on the situation," he said after a moment.

She smiled. "Exactly. Sometimes you're the fox. Sometimes you're the hound."

She swept the game board aside and unrolled a detailed map of Harding. "Let's make this more realistic. In this campaign, who are you truly fighting? The Klav?"

Steven studied the map and shook his head. "No. They're cattle to be driven. The real fight is with…"

He paused in thought. "Three groups, I think. The Odio—who'll eventually figure out what we're doing. Cygnus—our objectives align for now, but that won't last. And…"

He trailed off.

She studied him. "And the third?"

Steven let out a sigh—deep and genuine. "My best friend. Al. The path I've chosen will bring us into conflict eventually."

Her gaze narrowed. "And what will you do when it does?"

Steven's expression hardened. His voice dropped, low and tight with controlled fury. "I'll end him. Once and for all."

She smiled. "Good. Very good. But for now, let's focus on the Odio. I agree—they'll be our first real challenge. So… fox or hound?"

He looked at the two figures again and handed her the fox. "Fox. We're going first. We're more mobile, and we're operating under their radar. They're slower to respond—but stronger when fully assembled."

She nodded approvingly. "Then place your foxes on the map where your cohorts currently are."

He did so, arranging the fox figures across the regions his forces controlled.

"So now what?" he asked. "Wait for the Odio to make their move?"

She shook her head. "No. The point of the game is to anticipate their response before they even act—so you can counter it when they do. You haven't even started playing yet. Right now, you're just setting the board."

She tapped the map. "In advanced versions of the game, foxes can place obstacles on their side. What obstacles do you have at your disposal?"

He studied the board. "At the moment, the Odio don't realize we're working against them. They believe us to be one of their loyal hounds." He picked up one of the Hunter Hound figures and placed it on the map at their current location. "It hasn't dawned on them yet that we're actually…" He picked up a fox figure, "a war fox." He set it down beside the hound.

"So, my objective for now is to maintain that illusion—to keep them believing I'm a faithful hound while I quietly fortify our position. When they finally understand what we're up to, it'll be too costly for them to stop us."

He studied the map again. "I'm hoping to divide Harding into provincial districts, each with a fortified compound where our commanders can assume control once this phase ends. I'm thinking of asking the locals to begin construction on those compounds as we clear each area. Once they're manned, we can start recruiting from the local population."

He looked up. "Very soon, we'll have a formidable fighting force."

She already knew his plans, but she wanted him to verbalize them within the framework of their strategic exercise.

"We've already cleared two districts," he continued, picking up small wooden towers from the side of the table and placing them behind his lines. "We'll begin construction on these two immediately."

She nodded. "Good. Now, what do you think the Odio will do?"

"They'll start to wonder why they haven't heard from their commanders. I'm sure the colonel had standing orders to report back regularly. So I expect they'll send envoys, spies… eventually assassins," he replied.

She studied the board thoughtfully. "Agreed. What do we know of the Order's forces and defenses in the surrounding regions?"

"Luckily for us, it's minimal," Steven said. "The other nations agreed to protect Harding if any one nation tried to claim it outright, and they've insisted the Odio not establish any chapter houses inside its borders. Most of their presence is to the north of us, and a smaller contingent along the eastern coast—a naval presence, primarily, with very few ground forces."

He gestured to the map. "There are only two major access points into Harding from the north." He indicated them with his finger. "The escarpment runs almost from the ocean westward toward the mountains for several hundred miles. At the moment, Cygnus controls both entry points. But I don't trust him—or his troops—so we need to be ready to defend those gates ourselves if necessary."

She examined the map. "Then the board is set. Fox moves first. Knowing what you know, what do you do?"

Steven sat down, his eyes narrowed as he studied the map. His mind ticked through possible scenarios, one after another, each branching into outcomes and countermeasures.

"We continue as we've begun," he said at last. "We start building the compounds and quietly monitor anyone new in camp—anyone who might be a spy or assassin."

"I'll handle that," Tenebris replied. "My network is already embedded. Anyone new will stand out."

He nodded. "Good. Very good."

She watched him for a moment. "What's bothering you?"

"Two things. Cygnus told us to stop at Whittle. That's two, maybe three weeks away depending on the weather. But if I'm truly going to take Harding, I need the Senate either in my control or dissolved—and they're in Torringburgh." He pointed to the city on the map, then looked up at her. "So, do I keep moving toward Torringburgh and risk alienating Cygnus, or stop at Whittle and focus on fortifying our position?"

She walked around the table and wrapped her arms around his shoulders. "That's a choice only you can make. But whatever you do, keep asking yourself—are you acting as a fox or a hound? And should you be acting as the other?"

Steven stared down at the map, then murmured, "That's the other thing. I wonder how Cygnus and Uso see me. Do they think I'm a fox? Or a hound?"

"There is a third option," she said.

"Oh? Do tell."

"Like the Odio, they may see you as one of *his* foxes," she said with a wicked grin. "They may see you as a war fox—something to be moved at their convenience. Someone not worth fearing." She kissed him lightly on the cheek. "That could work in your favor."

She pulled away, adjusting her cloak. "I need to send out a few messages. I'll be back later." With a wink and a devilish smile, she vanished from the tent.

In the days that followed, Steven threw himself into *Foxes and Hounds*, running endless mental simulations of moves and countermoves. He began to see every decision—every conversation, every military maneuver—as part of a larger game. And he began to ask himself, constantly: *Am I the fox, or the hound?*

As the command camp prepared to move forward to rejoin the front lines, Steven walked toward the stables. The camp was abuzz with activity—tents being broken down, supply wagons loaded, and mess lines cleared. As he neared the edge of camp, he spotted Major Polix walking with purpose in his direction.

The man had proven useful—ambitious, sharp, and now loyal, at least outwardly.

"My Lord Commander," Polix said with a polite bow, "may I walk with you?"

Steven nodded, and the major fell in step beside him.

"What news?" he asked.

Polix handed him four message tubes and a sealed letter. "Reports from the front lines, sir," he said, quietly nodding toward the letter— clearly something not to be spoken of aloud. Steven tucked everything into the saddle pouch slung over his shoulder.

"Anything I should be aware of?" he asked in a low voice.

The major shook his head. "Everything's progressing smoothly. The front-line troops are making solid gains, all in line with standing orders. The towns of Oxenford and Eagle Cliff have begun sourcing materials for the compounds. If it's not out of place, I'd be most pleased to be given Eagle Cliff when the time comes," he added carefully.

Steven gave him a puzzled look. "Really? I thought you'd prefer something closer to the capital."

Polix smiled. "I've always loved the mountains. I understand there's some mining underway there—and I do so love precious metals."

Steven smiled in return. "So long as I get mine, I don't see a problem with letting you have Eagle Cliff."

"Thank you, my lord," the major replied. "It'll take us about two days to catch up to the front. Let me know if you need anything while we're en route."

"Actually," Steven said, tapping the saddle pouch, "I'm going to ride ahead to Whittle and wait for the others to catch up. I have a feeling there's business I'll need to handle."

"Understood, my lord." With a tip of his hat, the major turned and walked back into the camp.

Steven watched him go. *Fox. Definitely a fox,* he thought. *The only thing keeping him in line is greed—and Bris. Whatever she did to him, he still won't meet her eyes. I should ask her sometime.* He smirked at the thought.

By the time he reached the stables, his horse was already saddled. He secured the pouch to the saddle, took the reins, and began leading the mare toward the edge of camp. As he walked, a young soldier sprinted up to him.

"My Lord Commander!" the boy stammered, snapping to attention and offering a crisp salute. "Message from your second, sir."

Steven broke the seal and read the note:

My dearest,

I've just received word that Major Demitri has gone and hung himself. The coward—I wasn't done having my fun yet. There are no signs of foul play. I suspect it was just a matter of morals. Apparently, he had some. I'm heading to his camp now and will travel with them to the next site. I'll make sure the transition is smooth and that his second understands the nature of things.

Love,

B

Steven folded the note and thought for a moment. *Demitri was a hound forced to play the fox. It broke him.* He looked at the messenger. "Thank you. You're dismissed."

The boy saluted again. "Yes, sir!" and hurried off—clearly relieved to be gone.

Steven resumed his walk toward the edge of camp. *I'll need to find another plaything for Bris soon. She needs her little distractions now and again.*

His escort was already waiting for him when he arrived. He mounted up and looked at the men, he knew three of them Mathers, Riff and Will.

"Gentlemen, are we ready for a second trip to Whittle?"

They nodded in silent acknowledgment. *In this situation, these men are foxes,* he mused, *but at a word, they'd become hounds. Mine.*

They rode in silence for a while. Once they were out of sight of the camp, Steven reached into the pouch and pulled out the sealed letter. One glance at the mark told him it was from Uso.

Greetings Skarn-Kor,

We have tracked your progress and are well pleased. I hope you're enjoying the game I sent—useful in so many ways. I write to you on two matters. First, a reminder: Our Master does not wish you to move past Whittle. Not yet. You must find a reason to halt your advance. Let me know if you need a distraction or assistance. Second—and more personal—we've received word of the one you betrayed. It seems he and his forces are nearing the western pass.

I would like to say he will die there, but he appears to be quite formidable. Rumor claims even the ogres fear him. They've given him a name in their tongue: Varkûl-Narn—Soul-Eater.

I want to know if you have any suggestions on how to fight a living legend. Do not send a message. Tell me in person when you arrive. You know where to find me.

Steven folded the letter and slid it back into the pouch. *Varkûl-Narn,* he repeated in his mind. *That... is going to be a problem.*

He stared at the letter in silence. *Soul-Eater—not the worst name for Al and that damn sword of his. But how do you kill a legend?* A pang of doubt twisted in his gut.

He glanced at the others, still focused on the road ahead. *He brought this on himself. He could have stayed in the north with his new family. I didn't tell him to come south and stick his neck on the chopping block.*

He folded the letter slowly. *Damn you, Al. Why do you always make me the one who has to choose?*

Turnabout is fair play, he told himself, biting down an old memory. *I still remember when we snuck into Farmer Gerhan's wine cellar. He didn't lay a hand on you—status has its privileges, I suppose. I took that beating for both of us, and I never said a word.*

His anger simmered. *Al is becoming a myth among the ogres—and Steven knew it wouldn't stop there. His legend would spread, growing like wildfire. The goblins don't seem to revere him yet,* he thought. *Yet.*

He steadied his breathing. Even the thought of Al was enough to unbalance him. *Foxes and Hounds—what are you, Al?*

You're on the offensive, so that makes you a hound. But you're outnumbered and unpredictable—traits of a fox. And then there's that sword... No, not a fox. That sword levels the field. You're a hound—strong, relentless, and focused on your goal: to kill the fox—Cygnus. You're blind to all else.

Steven sat back in his saddle. *Then it's time for the foxes to set a trap.*

He suddenly pulled up his horse. The others slowed.

"Everything okay, sir?"

"Yes," Steven said calmly. "We need to stop for a moment. I need to write a letter—and I'll need one or two of you to ride for Whittle immediately. This must reach Uso as quickly as possible."

He reached into his pack and pulled out a blank sheet of parchment, a small quill, and a bottle of ink. He paused, gathering his thoughts, then swiftly penned his message. He folded the parchment, sealed it with wax, and held it in his hand for a long moment.

There's no going back after this. Do I really want Al dead?

I love him like a brother. But he stands in my way. He overshadows me at every turn, and even without trying, he interferes with everything I've built. His jaw tightened. He handed the sealed letter to Will, and with a silent nod, the two men turned and rode off toward Whittle.

It's done, he thought. *Will I be freer for it?*

"Two days," Mathers said, checking his bearings. "All goes well, they should reach Whittle in two. We'll be there in about four, maybe three if we are lucky and push the horses hard."

"Perfect," Steven replied, his voice flat.

THE PATH TO PERDITION

Upon entering the fog, the world itself seemed to fade. Sounds became muffled, sight dimmed, even the scents of earth and battle grew distant—as if he had stepped out of reality into a shadow of it, blurred just beyond focus.

His anger raged within him, a storm desperate to be unleashed. Yet he forced himself calm—just enough to direct his energy where it would be needed. Sight would be useless here. This would require hearing, speed, and endurance.

He listened. There—off to his right—the cackling of a Klav. Further off, the muttered grunts of goblins. All of it designed to inspire fear. But his heart was empty now, fueled only by a thirst for revenge. He had sent his friends into this fog, and they had died. Now those responsible would pay—or he would. Either way, the scales would be balanced.

He moved toward the sounds, focusing on the nearest one. He heard it sniffing, trying to track his scent.

Al smiled. It was close enough.

With a shift of energy to his feet, he launched forward, driving his sword to the hilt in the creature's chest. Its cackling became a horrific whine. Al locked eyes with it, drawing its life force into himself as the blade fed. He could feel the knife wound beginning to mend. With a flick of his wrist, he pulled the sword free, the blade slicing cleanly out the side.

Enlivened by the energy, Al heightened his senses and moved to the next. Then the next. And the next. By the time the fourth fell, the rest had regrouped and were attempting to surround him.

His body hummed with dreadful power, though he was still far from full. The Klav provided only a trickle—enough for now, but he would need something stronger soon. He set his feet, grasped his sword, cracked his neck, and waited.

It didn't take long. They charged all at once, hoping to overwhelm him by numbers.

They failed.

He was a blur. His sword moved like a living thing, slicing and cutting through the pack. Their whines filled the fog, then faded into silence.

He turned his attention to the goblins. They had held back—probably archers, he thought. No matter. He hardened his skin—he likely didn't need to, but he wasn't familiar with goblin weaponry. Better to play it safe. He strode forward, a specter of death in the mist. The goblins, once laughing, were now silent. He could almost taste their fear.

He heard the snap of a crossbow string before he saw the bolt. He turned just in time—it sailed harmlessly past. Three more followed in quick succession. He dashed forward, shortening the distance. Three bolts struck where he'd just been, but the fourth caught him in the gut. It hit hard enough to nearly double him over. The hardened skin held, but the force impressed him.

Those things really pack a punch, he thought grimly.

He heard the goblins reloading. Clutching his gut, he focused on the one who had fired first and sprinted forward. With luck, he caught the goblin off guard—just as it lifted its head, he was there. One quick swing, and its head—still wearing a confused expression—sailed off into the fog.

He closed the distance to the second goblin. His anger rose with each strike, and when his sword plunged deep into its chest, he let the blade feed. Yes he thought to himself. Unlike the Klav, the goblins carried a greater life essence, his blood raced as the sword nourished him. The other two cried out in surprise. Not expecting Al to close the distance so fast, they loosed their bolts hastily. Both went wide.

Al shoved the goblin off his sword. Their energy while stronger than the Klav's—still wasn't enough for him, but he wanted more.

The remaining two drew swords and moved to flank him—one to the left, one to the right.

Al smiled—a dark, heartless smile. Not born of warmth, but of the cold heat of vengeance.

The one on the right lunged. The other tried to come in low.

Al was ready. He caught the first goblin's wrist, twisted, snapped it, and threw the creature to the ground. With a smooth pivot, he turned, avoiding the second's thrust and burying his blade in its belly.

The goblin's eyes went wide with horror. It weakly clutched at Al's sword arm, most of its strength already gone. It gasped to its comrade, *"Velkrin na... Velvarn sha..."* before unleashing the all-too-familiar scream of those doomed to Al's blade.

Al held the gaze until the light faded from its eyes.

Behind him, he heard a blade drop and the patter of feet—the last goblin fleeing into the fog.

Al pushed the body from his sword, seething. He prepared to give chase—but paused.

Wait. Wait.

He could feel it again—something just beneath the surface. A pressure. A presence. Urging him to abandon reason and give in to the bloodlust.

It felt familiar.

Enough, Heriar, he thought. *I will do this on my own. Go back to whatever pit you hide in. I am not—will not be—your puppet.*

Oh, Al. You wound me. I have always, only ever had your well-being in mind. You stand now on the edge of becoming what you were born to become. I was merely rooting for you, came the voice—soft and serpentine, sliding like a whisper through his mind.

Go back. Leave me to my darkness, Al replied coldly.

As you wish. But remember, darkness is my domain. Call to me... if you require my assistance.

And with that, the presence faded.

Al drew in a deep breath and listened. He could hear goblins and Klav gathering, whispering in a language he didn't recognize. Heriar might want him to charge blindly into death, but Al had no intention of obliging him. He would find the one responsible for the fog and bring justice to all who served them.

What did Gutamino always say? "If the enemy can manipulate your emotions, they've already beaten you."

He centered himself. Breathed in. Breathed out. Drawing the sword's energy inward, he contained it. It was more useful when focused—less a flood, more a forge.

The enemies lay ahead, unseen but heard. This would be butcher's work, yes—but not the work of a brute. A skilled butcher was a craftsman. So too would Al be: a craftsman of death.

The Western Pass will run dark with their blood. The hills will echo with their screams.

With sword in hand, he strode calmly toward the gathering host. The Klav caught his scent almost instantly. The goblins—likely emboldened by their numbers—tightened their ranks. Al estimated twenty of each.

I must become a blur. As flexible as water, as hard as steel. I will be the blade itself.

They attacked all at once, believing they'd caught him off guard. But Al had led them precisely where he wanted them. He emptied himself and gave way to instinct. Goblins and Klav darted and snapped, stabbed and tore. Al twisted, turned, leapt, ducked—his blade a deadly song. Some enemies died too swiftly for the blade to drink, while others screamed as the weapon drew their life force.

He bled. He knew it. But to acknowledge it was to feel it—and that he would not do. He pushed the pain away and moved faster.

Then—mid-battle—he felt a new presence.

He held his breath.

It can't be…

From the fog leapt Talionis. The great wolf's jaws closed on a goblin's throat, severing it in a single, savage snap.

Al froze in the chaos, nearly overwhelmed by emotion. He fought it down, even as his eyes misted.

Talionis, he thought, *you have no idea how happy I am to see you, boy.*

Images filled his mind—Talionis running, never stopping, racing south through wild country. Al understood then: the wolf had sensed his need—emotional, physical, spiritual—and come.

Their eyes met. Unspoken understanding passed between them.

Together, they moved like storm and shadow. The tide of battle turned. Coordination among the goblins and Klav collapsed into panic. Disorganized, they fell in droves. Al and Talionis finished them with brutal precision.

When the last enemy died, Al fell to his knees and hugged the massive wolf, burying his face in the snow-white fur. Talionis leaned into him, resting his head on Al's shoulder. They remained there for a long moment before Al stood and wiped his eyes.

"I missed you, my friend," Al said aloud.

An image appeared in his mind—open plains, wild game, the joy of the hunt. He laughed and scratched behind Talionis' ears.

"I'd love nothing more than to go hunting," he said, his tone shifting, "but first, we deal with these invaders."

Talionis growled low. He understood.

Al reached out with his senses again. The goblins and Klav were still out there, though farther now. In the dense fog, it was impossible to judge distance.

"Come, my friend," Al said. "We hunt the one who makes this fog. Then we'll hunt game."

Talionis' tail wagged in approval.

Al stretched out with all his senses. He wasn't sure what exactly he was searching for—only that it would feel different. The beasts were everywhere, but the concentration to the west was denser. That's where he would go.

He sheathed his blade. Both the sword—and Al himself—hummed with pent-up energy.

It seemed the others didn't know they were in the fog—or if they did, they weren't concerned by it. A quick image from Talionis: Klav, off to the left. Al shook his head silently.

We'll leave them—for now. No sense alerting everyone to our presence until absolutely necessary. I want to find their leader. The one responsible for all of this.

They continued on, moving as silently as possible and avoiding patrols. Al wasn't certain, but he felt like he was heading in the right direction.

I'm sorry, my friend, he projected gently into Talionis' mind. The wolf tilted his head, puzzled. Al smiled.

I should have stayed in the north with you. I shouldn't be pretending to be something I'm not. I'm no commander or hero—I'm just a privileged kid with a fancy sword. Steven probably had the right of it all along. The one time I try to act like a leader, I get my friends killed.

Talionis pushed his head beneath Al's left hand as they walked, a silent gesture of comfort.

I'm alright, boy, Al thought, scratching behind the wolf's ears. *I'm just sad you left your home for me. But I'm so damn glad you're here. I wouldn't have survived that last fight without you.*

Images of Talionis' pack—rushing in to save him from the ogre weeks before—flashed in his mind, and he smiled.

Yes, he thought, *they would be proud of you. You saved me, just like they did.* He felt Talionis' happiness at the thought.

Then came a shift. Subtle—but undeniable. Talionis froze, ears perked. Al stopped, his own senses straining to interpret what they were feeling. It was like a storm of chaos held inside a glass sphere—barely contained.

Together, they reached outward, trying to locate the source.

They veered right. The feeling faded.

They turned left—and it surged back, stronger than before.

They climbed a rise, a natural mound of earth. At the top, Al extended his senses again. The mound wasn't solid—it circled a wide depression in the earth, like a bowl. The bottom was obscured by fog, denser than anywhere else he'd seen.

I can't tell if any goblins or Klav are nearby, Al thought. *This... thing... it's interfering with my senses. What about you?*

Talionis gave a soft whine. He was feeling it too.

Al stared into the pit. *We can't go straight down—no telling how steep it is, or how far. Let's look for an opening near the base.*

Quiet as shadows, they made their way down the side of the mound, following its spiral shape. Al realized they were descending, slowly but steadily, deeper into the dome-shaped depression.

When did they even build this? And why?

The first attack came without warning.

Goblins leapt from hidden alcoves carved into the spiraling path.

Talionis twisted mid-step and avoided the ambush, then charged the nearest goblin, slamming it to the ground. The last thing the creature saw was a maw of white teeth closing around its face.

The second goblin landed on Al's back, knocking him to the ground. The goblin thought it had the advantage—until Al shifted, swept its legs with a powerful kick, and rose in a fluid motion. He caught the goblin with a crushing punch to the skull, enhanced by the energy stored within him. Bone shattered. The creature crumpled, lifeless.

Al looked to Talionis, pulling his sword free. "They know we're here," he whispered.

Talionis' ears flattened. His hackles rose.

They proceeded more cautiously now. It gave the enemy time to prepare, but rushing blindly was worse.

Small ambushes followed—two or three at a time—but none managed to gain the upper hand.

They're trying to delay us, Al thought. *Buying time for whatever waits ahead.*

He stopped, turned to Talionis, and met the wolf's eyes.

You can sit this one out, pal. You've already saved me once today, and we have no idea what that thing ahead can do. You could guard our exit.

Talionis looked annoyed. Images flashed in Al's mind: open fields, elk bounding through grasslands.

Al chuckled. *I did promise we'd go hunting. Alright. But be careful in there.*

They rounded another bend—and froze.

Two ogres stood before them. Larger than any Al had ever seen. Fully armored, clad in dark steel. Each carried a warhammer the size of a man.

Northern ogres had been savage and strong—but these were something else entirely. Disciplined. Ready.

Al shifted his stance and slowly raised his sword.

Talionis growled low, the fur along his spine bristling.

And then—the ogres began to move.

"Varkûl-Narn," said the ogre on the left mockingly, pointing his massive hammer at Al.

"If you're trying to insult me, I'm afraid I don't speak your language," Al replied, channeling energy into his limbs and sword. *These two will fill me right back up. No need to hold back.*

"It means 'Soul-Eater.' It's how our northern brothers speak of you," said the ogre on the right, spitting on the ground. "But you're no *narn.* You're just one of these prissy little farmers. I can tell just by looking at you."

Smarter than the northern ogres, too, Al thought. *Talionis—be ready. Let me take the lead. Attack only when you see an opening.*

The wolf growled an acknowledgment.

"I'm going to tear your little head off and give it to the captain for some extra grog tonight!" shouted the ogre on the left. He charged, faster than expected—but Al was still quicker. He dodged the first swing and slashed at the ogre's midsection as he passed. The sword hummed, slicing deep into the metal—but not quite to flesh.

The ogre looked down at his gashed armor. "You little prick. I just polished this bloody breastplate!" Then, from the corner of his eye, he spotted his companion moving in.

Talionis growled a warning.

Al leapt back again, dodging the second attack. He forced himself to stay calm. They were bigger, stronger—but he was faster, more agile. They could only engage him one at a time.

The great wolf sprang up the side of the spiral wall and disappeared into the mist.

"Aww, did your little puppy run away?" mocked the first ogre. "Don't worry—we'll find him after we finish with you."

"I have to say, you southern brutes talk a lot more than your northern cousins," Al said with a smirk.

"Don't compare us to them! We are the mighty Grul-Karn clan. Armies flee before us. We do not hide in the north. We live to fight. And now, these lands will bleed for—"

His voice cut off. Al had slipped in close during his speech and drove his sword up under the breastplate and into the ogre's gut. The beast howled in pain, trying to bring his hammer down on Al, but the sword had already begun its dreadful work. Al rolled clear, pulling the blade free as he did.

The ogre clutched his stomach, stumbling back. His companion caught him gently and lowered him to the ground.

"Stay with me, brother. I'll be right back," he said, his voice low and deadly. He rose, now gripping both hammers—his and his brother's.

"Time to die, little prick!" he roared, charging at Al, swinging both hammers wildly.

Al dodged and ducked, every instinct alert. A single hit would end him.

Then came a scream from behind. The ogre spun—too late. Talionis had reappeared, his jaws clamped around the other's throat. With one savage twist, the wolf tore it out.

"Mongrel!" the second ogre screamed as he dropped to his knees.

Al surged forward and drove his sword through the back of the ogre's armor. The beast began the horrid, echoing scream the blade demanded as it drained his life away.

When the sword was satisfied, Al placed his boot on the ogre's back and shoved, yanking the blade free. He turned to Talionis, now more red than white with gore.

"Oh, you really are a good boy, aren't you?" he said with a breathless laugh.

They rounded the next bend—and stepped out of the fog.

They had reached the center of the dome.

At the heart of it stood a raised stone pedestal. Atop it rested a glowing orb, pulsing with contained power. Beside it stood a goblin in flowing robes, holding a wooden staff. On either side of him stood six heavily armed goblins.

The robed one smiled. "So. The *Velkrin* has decided to join us," he said, raising one hand in a mocking gesture of welcome.

Al and Talionis stepped forward warily, sure of only one thing:

This fight would be unlike any they had faced before.

EMBRACE OF DARKNESS

Al and Talionis stood at the edge of the fog, the world around them sharpening in an instant. The muted haze that had dulled their senses was gone, replaced by a blinding surge of clarity—too bright, too loud, too sharp. A wave of dizziness swept over Al, threatening to drag him down. He closed his eyes and steadied himself, realizing he had amplified his senses so completely within the fog that the normal world now assaulted him. Gritting his teeth, he forced the energy back, dialing it down—not fully, but just enough to regain focus for the task ahead.

The goblins stood staring at them, waiting. The one with the staff seemed almost amused.

"It certainly took you long enough to get here," he said.

"Sorry to have kept you waiting, but I'm sure a few hours couldn't have inconvenienced you too greatly," Al replied, slowly sidestepping left, keeping his eyes on the goblins while Talionis moved right. The air, though no longer the stifling stillness of the fog, still felt off— stale, bitter. Al took in everything. Six goblins stood motionless, watching. The robed goblin held a wooden staff tipped with a strange gem set in a metal claw. Behind him, the orb crackled with untamed energy. Al's ears buzzed from its pulse.

The goblin smiled. "A few hours?" He seemed delighted with himself. "But where are my manners? I am Veshk-Dazhul. At my lord Cygnus's command, I am here to keep this pass closed to all… except you."

"Oh, and why am I so special, Veshk?" Al asked, still circling.

"I think you misunderstood—*Veshk* is my title. *Dazhul* is my name," he said with a wave. "Special? Why, of course you are. You're of great interest to my master and to the entire High Command. You, after all, shouldn't exist."

Al raised an eyebrow. "That's an odd statement."

"Is it? You are *Alfarbani*—or as near to one as has existed in centuries. But *Alfarbani* aren't born; they're made. And only the Dokkalfar is capable of making them. So you can see why everyone is so curious about you."

"So, you intend to capture me?" Al asked, continuing to maneuver. "You may find that more difficult than you suspect."

"I suspected you'd be arrogant," Dazhul said, frowning slightly. "Your age is prone to it. Give you a pretty sword and a handful of strange powers, and suddenly you think yourself a legend. No, I am not here to capture you. I am here to give you a choice. Come willingly. Cygnus will bring you before the Dokkalfar at his awakening, where you may swear loyalty and be rewarded beyond your wildest dreams."

Al stopped. He and Talionis were in position.

"I really am getting tired of being asked to join the villain's side," Al said. "You want to bring back an ancient darkness that will swallow the world whole. I'm going to stop you—starting with killing your master."

Dazhul shook his head. "You know nothing of history. Yes, the Dokkalfar ruled with power, but the world was at peace. Trade flourished. Races lived together. It was the elves who sowed division, who could not stand to see their first and strongest turn protector of all peoples. The Dokkalfar spared them. He gave himself willingly to imprisonment, trusting in the promise of release after one age. But the elves betrayed him. The dwarves built a prison—eternal and cruel. Living seals—turned to stone—hold him fast. But his faithful have waited, and now his time has come. The old powers are gone. The elves vanished. The dwarves weakened. And humans… well, they love gold and power. They will bend easily."

Now, Al said to Talionis in his mind.

The two leapt toward the nearest goblins—but neither moved. Al strained, but his muscles were frozen. His sword refused to rise. He felt Talionis beside him, snarling, but equally paralyzed.

The goblin with the staff smiled. "You didn't think it would be that easy, did you? That you were the only one with a fancy toy?" he said, brandishing his staff. "You will be brought to my master bound in chains. And if I'm being honest, I prefer it this way."

The three goblins near him moved without a word—two grabbing Al's arms while the third produced a set of shackles.

Al's heart raced. He fought with every ounce of strength against the unseen force pinning him in place. *No,* he realized, *the more I fight, the stronger his grip becomes. If he is a rock, then I will be water.*

He relaxed. Drawing in a deep breath, he reached out—not to resist, but to understand. The power that restrained him felt both foreign and familiar, like a sibling to the energy he had grown used to wielding. It rejected him at first, his body unfamiliar with its rhythm, but he overcame that resistance and, instead of absorbing it, he set it aside—building a reservoir. The more he drew in, the deeper it became.

The goblin with the collar approached. As he reached to clasp it around Al's neck, Al unleashed the stored energy. It felt like trying to push a boat upstream in a flood—one wrong surge and he would capsize. *Focus*, he commanded himself, the veins in his neck bulging. Finally, with a soft pop, the energy restraints shattered.

Al was free.

He headbutted the goblin with the collar, sending him sprawling, then brought his arms forward and slammed the two holding him together. The three goblins crumpled in confusion. Before they could recover, Al's blade flashed, finishing them.

Veshk-Dazhul's face twisted in surprise. He raised his staff, attempting to restore the restraints, but Al was ready. Now he knew how to resist and met the incoming force with equal strength. The goblin's frustration deepened.

"Think you're so clever, don't you?" Veshk-Dazhul hissed. "Fine. I won't deliver you alive to Cygnus. He might prefer it this way anyway. Unlike your pretty sword, I have more tricks up my sleeve."

He turned and touched the remaining three goblins, one by one. Each began to hum with energy, their bodies trembling with power.

"They may not be your equal," he said smugly, "and it's a one-time thing for them—but it's three against one. So there's that."

The supercharged goblins fanned out. A glance toward Talionis showed the wolf still bound, straining uselessly against invisible chains.

Al tightened his grip on his sword.

"Before you die," Veshk-Dazhul continued, "I just want you to know how complete your failure has been. You think you've only been in the fog for a few hours? Time doesn't flow so cleanly in the mist. You've been stumbling around for days. And now the clans—your friends—have gathered at the pass, desperate to find you. My goblin army and the Klav are waiting just inside. It will be a bloodbath. I do hope none of your loved ones are eaten by the Klav."

He smiled—all teeth and malice.

Ryanna! Al screamed inwardly.

Enough. If this was the path to becoming what he was born to be—even if it meant losing himself—then so be it.

He moved—blindingly fast—at the goblin on the right, who barely dodged in time, leaving only a flickering afterimage.

Is that what others see when I do that? Al wondered, but there was no time to reflect.

The goblin countered, slashing for Al's neck. Al ducked, grabbed the creature's ankle, and flipped him. Before Al could land the killing blow, the second goblin slammed into him, driving him backward.

If I hadn't hardened my skin, that hit might've killed me, Al thought grimly.

The three attackers began circling.

He looked to Talionis—and tried something new. *Let me see through your eyes.*

The wolf hesitated, confused, but slowly relaxed. Al felt his mind shift. Now he saw through both their perspectives—dual vision, disorienting but powerful.

No time to think. I hope this works, he whispered.

As he had done for himself, he reached out to the force holding Talionis and pulled it in—then forced it out. The pressure snapped like a rope cut mid-tension. The wolf was free.

Al withdrew back to his own senses just in time to dodge another strike.

He smiled at the nearest goblin, who was preparing to lunge. The goblin never saw it coming—Talionis lunged in from the side, jaws closing around the creature's throat and dragging him to the ground. Al heard the sickening snap of bone as the goblin's neck broke.

The remaining two, now more wary, had to divide their focus—two enemies, not one.

A glance at Veshk-Dazhul showed the robed goblin still smiling. He seemed to be enjoying the show.

What is wrong with him? Why isn't he aiding them?

The four remaining combatants entered a deadly, measured dance. Al studied the goblins.

They're skilled—probably have years more experience than I do. They're nearly as fast, maybe even stronger.

He examined their weapons and armor.

A flicker of shared intent from Talionis signaled readiness.

Al focused on the nearest goblin and began feeding his blade. It began to hum, the hilt growing warm in his hand—but not unbearably so. He stopped channeling and planted his feet.

The goblin mirrored him, bracing for the strike, confident it would be blocked.

Al made no feint, no elaborate maneuver—just a clean, sideways slash at the goblin's midsection.

The goblin sneered at the simplicity of it—until the blade passed straight through his weapon, his armor, and stopped just short of his heart. Al let the sword drink deeply, the goblin raising his voice in the all-too-familiar death-song the blade demanded.

The third goblin, distracted by the scream, made the fatal mistake of turning his head. Talionis pounced, jaws clamping down on the back of his neck and snapping it violently. The goblin crumpled beside his comrade.

Al and Talionis turned to Veshk-Dazhul, whose smile had only widened.

"Oh, that was well done," he said with mock admiration. "I do see why they're so interested in you. I'm sure they'll learn what they need from your corpse."

"It's over," Al said, voice low and cold. "End the fog. Tell me where Cygnus is, and I'll let you walk out of here."

He and Talionis began circling the goblin from opposite sides.

"Over? My, aren't we delusional," Veshk-Dazhul chuckled. "You think my power is like yours. It isn't. And now… you'll learn why."

He turned slowly, tracking both Al and the wolf. "You may be fast and strong—but you're predictable. And that will be your undoing."

Al and Talionis attacked simultaneously, leaping at the goblin from opposite sides.

A burst of raw energy exploded from Veshk-Dazhul, blasting both of them back. Talionis landed in a crumpled heap, letting out a sharp whine. Al, though bruised and rattled, landed on his feet, clutching his sword.

Damn it, he cursed himself. *You okay?* he reached out mentally.

The answer chilled him. Talionis was hurt—bones broken. The connection was still there, but faint. A knot tightened in Al's stomach.

Stay down. Don't move. I'll finish this clown, and then I'll patch you up.

Veshk-Dazhul's smile turned to false concern. "Oh no... your little puppy seems to have stumbled. I hope he's alright."

Then, with dark delight, he raised his staff and pointed it at Talionis.

"No!" Al shouted—but too late.

A bolt of lightning erupted from the staff, slamming into the wolf and hurling him across the dome. Talionis hit the ground in a heap—and did not move.

Al reached out—but there was no answer. The bond was silent.

It was as if something inside him had been cut away.

He turned toward Veshk-Dazhul. Blood pounded in his ears.

"Yes. There you are," the goblin said softly, almost reverently. "Now I see the monster they fear. You think you've lost everything. But you haven't. Not yet. Soon, that little redhead you care so much about will enter the fog—and the Klav will feast on her flesh."

He smirked. "Keep that thought with you when you close your eyes for good."

Al stopped listening.

Stopped hearing.

Stopped caring.

He stepped outside himself, watching from above as the figure in the dome—his figure—stood motionless for a heartbeat. Then, with a primal scream, Al launched himself at Veshk-Dazhul, sword clashing against staff.

The goblin was as fast and strong as Al. His staff blocked the sword again and again. Each time he had an opening, Veshk-Dazhul unleashed bursts of energy—but Al deflected them with his blade, pushing forward, relentless and silent.

The battle raged—neither side gaining ground, neither yielding an inch.

This can't be it. I have to have more than this, Al thought.

Another bolt screamed from Veshk-Dazhul's staff, and as it did, Al caught a flicker—the orb behind him dimmed, just slightly.

Coincidence? he wondered. *Only one way to find out.*

He pressed the goblin harder. Every time the staff flared, the orb pulsed and dimmed in response.

They're connected. If I can't break the staff, maybe I can shatter the orb.

No! Heriar's voice roared in his head.

I thought I told you to go away, Al snapped back.

Destroying the orb will break the fog—but releasing that much power will kill you as well.

Al sneered. *When did you start caring about my well-being?*

To be honest—I don't. But I have a vested interest in your mission. If you die, it may be centuries before another rises. Do not destroy the orb.

Al forced Heriar from his mind.

That settles it, he thought. *If that orb is the source of his power—and breaking it will lift the fog and save the clans—then my life will have been well spent.*

He turned his gaze toward the orb.

Veshk-Dazhul's smile vanished. Panic overtook his expression. He unleashed bolt after bolt, trying to stop Al from reaching it. Al blocked each one, step by agonizing step, moving toward the pedestal.

"Don't be a fool, boy!" the goblin screamed. "You'll kill all of us!"

It was Al's turn to smile—serene, unwavering. "I have lived a good life. I met the love of my life—whom you would see dead. My truest companion—" he glanced at Talionis's lifeless form "—whom you did kill."

He took another step. "If by my life I can save her... and avenge him... then I will gladly lay it down."

Each stride brought him closer. With every blocked bolt, he let go—of the rage, of the grief. He forgave his parents for exiling him. He forgave Steven for betraying him. He even released the faces of those he'd slain in battle. The weight in his chest lifted with every memory he laid to rest.

At last, he stood before the orb.

Veshk-Dazhul ceased his attacks. His voice trembled. "Enough. You can go. I will call off the Klav. The goblins. None will harm the clans. Just leave. You may all return to Jasper... please."

Al looked at him—truly looked—and smiled. It was warm, even kind.

"I'm sorry, Veshk-Dazhul. I can't forgive what you've done... but I will not carry the hatred anymore." He turned to the orb, motioning to the devastation around them. "This has to end. And if this is as far as I go—then so be it."

He raised his sword, channeling everything he had left into the blade—every drop of energy, every memory, every ounce of love and pain—and brought it down with a cry upon the heart of the orb.

Veshk-Dazhul screamed.

Time held its breath. Then the orb shattered—white light exploded outward, and silence broke beneath the chorus of every soul the sword had ever consumed. Al watched as not only the orb, but his sword itself, cracked... then shattered.

A storm of energy erupted, a thousand bolts ripping through his body.

He flew backward through the air.

Then darkness. Cold, absolute. He landed beside Talionis.

His breath came in shallow gasps. The ground beneath him trembled. The pedestal was gone—reduced to a crater. Veshk-Dazhul's body lay in ruin nearby, torn apart. The staff was dust.

Al's vision narrowed to a pinprick.

I'm sorry, Ryanna... he thought as the darkness claimed him.

DEATH AND RENEWAL

Al opened his eyes and blinked. He was staring up at an ornate vaulted ceiling, light streaming in.

"Where am I?" he asked aloud, to no one in particular.

"In my house, young one," came a kind, resonant voice. It was firm as a foundation but carried a musical lilt that put him at ease.

Al sat up, looking around—and then at himself. He was dressed in a long white robe… and nothing else. He blinked, confused. *The fight. The explosion.* He remembered now.

"What troubles you?" the voice asked gently.

"I was in a fight. There was an explosion." He quickly ran his hands over his chest—no wounds. "I should be dead," he said.

"You are," the voice replied.

Al turned toward the source. The light was too bright—he squinted, and it dimmed slightly.

A passing cloud? he wondered.

When his eyes adjusted, he saw an old man dressed in a white robe, barefoot, sitting on a raised dais. A massive white wolf lay beside him, its head resting in the man's lap. The old man stroked its fur with quiet reverence.

"He's been waiting for you," the old man said.

The wolf looked at Al, tail thumping softly, but made no move to rise.

Still seated, Al glanced around the building. Light filled the space. Stained glass windows depicted scenes he didn't recognize. Every inch of the wooden structure was intricately carved. Rows of long benches stretched from front to back.

"I know this place," he said in wonder.

The old man nodded. "You've come here several times."

"Never like this. The building I see… it's falling apart. Crumbling, covered in dust and cobwebs."

"That's how your time sees it," the man replied, sadness in his voice. "Those few who can still find it, that is."

"What is this place?" Al asked. "And how can I meet others here while we're alive?"

The old man looked around, as if seeing the space through time. "This building is older than the land. It was here before it—and it will remain long after. It exists in all times and all places. Those few—very few—who can tap into their spiritual nature may enter. But the living can only see it as their time sees it. In its height of glory… or its ruin. Now that you've crossed to the other side, you see it as it truly is."

Al's brow furrowed. "You said I'm dead. Then how can I be here? How is Talionis here?"

The old man smiled, and the warmth of it filled Al's heart. He could sit forever in the calm of that expression.

"You've been taught that life is fleeting. That once the body dies, you cease to exist. But that's only half true. You are both material and spiritual. Your mortal life is merely the smallest part of your journey— but a vital part. When you shed the coil of mortality… you come here."

"You said this is your house," Al said.

"I did."

"Then… who are you?"

The old man let out a long sigh. "That's not an easy question to answer. Once, no answer would've been needed. But the world has wandered so far from the path, any answer I give will only raise more questions." He smiled gently. "Let's just say I'm a gatekeeper, of sorts. All who die pass through these doors. But not all who do… enter the Garden. Some walk away. Others are turned away."

Al's voice was quiet. "And which are we?"

The old man nodded. "Now that is a good question. The answer depends on you—as it does for most. Though they rarely understand the choice."

Al waited.

"Normally," the old man continued, "we would review your life. Everyone holds onto attachments—grief, guilt, anger, unfinished business. Those who can let go… may enter the Garden. Those who can't—or won't—leave."

Al looked at Talionis, who remained content and still. He had never seen the wolf so at peace. He trusted this man absolutely.

"So… I need to choose?" Al asked.

The old man's eyes twinkled. "May I tell you a story?"

Al nodded. The old man motioned for him to sit on the floor in front of the dais, and Al obeyed without hesitation.

"What do you know about the elves?" the old man asked.

"They're supposed to be the oldest, wisest, and longest-lived of all creatures," Al replied.

"No, on all accounts," the old man said, shaking his head. "Humans are the oldest race of intelligent beings, and there have been millions of other species before them—and there will be millions more after. Elves are, or rather were, human. Humans who unlocked a secret they were never meant to find. A former disciple of my master showed another some of these hidden truths. With that knowledge, he discovered a way to 'improve' the human condition—granting near immortality. And so, the first elf was created. His followers came quickly after."

"The Dokkalfar—the goblin said he was the first elf," Al said quietly.

"Yes. Though he went by another name. He held a high position among my master's followers. Many flocked to his new vision, abandoning the true path. He was led astray by another—older, darker. You know of whom I speak. He has whispered to you from time to time, just as he did to the Dokkalfar long ago."

"Heriar," Al said.

The old man nodded. "You did what the Dokkalfar could not. You rejected him. You also turned away from the darkness that nearly overwhelmed you. And in the end, you faced death with no hatred or malice in your heart. That gave me hope—it made me proud to witness such a moment in this day and age."

The old man looked down, thoughtful. "The two of them—Herair and the Dokkalfar—have set events in motion that can end in only a few ways, most of which are not pleasant. But... they also, unexpectedly, gave rise to you. A fortunate accident, if you will."

He smiled warmly at Al. "So I am going to give you an additional choice. You can face judgment, and I have no doubt that both you and mighty Talionis will be welcomed into my master's Garden to lay down your burdens. You've earned that peace. There is no shame in choosing it."

He leaned forward, eyes alight. "Or... I can return you to the world, and try and put an end to the Dokkalfar and his followers before they make more of a mess than they already have."

Al hesitated. "I'm no hero. No leader of men. I'm not sure I can send anyone else to die... or ever pick up that cursed blade again."

The old man smiled again. "You have a kind and gentle heart. That's why I'm giving you this chance. Heroes don't exist in the moment—no one knows they're a hero while they're living it. That's for others to decide later. As for leaders? They're not born. They're not trained. True leaders are followed because people believe in them—in their values, in their courage. People aren't following a farm boy, Al. They're following the man who gave his life to save theirs."

He paused. "I'm not sending you back to be a hero or a leader. I'm sending you back to be your most authentic self. And if others choose to follow, then show them the way."

"As for the sword," he added, "it is destroyed—and I will not restore it. It was an abomination, created for the sole purpose of addicting its wielder to feed upon death."

"But without it, I won't be strong enough to face what's coming," Al said.

The old man shook his head. "That sword was never your true strength. But fear not—I will make it so you can draw energy from the world itself. All living things will feed your strength—not through harm, but through harmony. The world around you is full of life, it will sustain you if you but silence you mind and allow it to."

He raised a hand. "And I will also give you three gifts to help you on your journey. First, you will be able to release the energy you gather in various forms. I'll let you figure that part out for yourself." He smirked.

"Second, you can use the energy to heal others. Similar to how you are able to heal yourself. To do this, you must empty your heart of hatred and embrace all that is good and pure. Then place a hand on their forehead and a hand over their wound and let the energy flow from you through their head and out through the wound. You will know when you have done all you can. And remember, not all wounds can or should be healed."

"And the third?" Al asked.

The old man's eyes twinkled. "I don't want to ruin the surprise entirely. But you have a cousin—someone who shares your trait."

Al blinked. "Cousin?" He'd never heard of any cousins on either side of his family.

"Like you, her power can be awakened. Your third gift—if you both survive—will be the ability to pass on these gifts I've given you.

And if the two of you build families of your own, these gifts will pass down to future generations.”

Al turned to Talionis. “Can my friend come as well?” he asked.

“Only if he wishes to,” the old man replied, glancing down at the wolf. “Otherwise, he is welcome to join his pack in the Garden.”

“The choice is yours, buddy,” Al said softly. “I won’t hold it against you if you want to stay. I’d be lying if I said I didn’t want you to come with me, but I know that comes from a very selfish place in my heart.”

Talionis looked at Al, then at the old man. The old man gave a gentle nod, and without hesitation, Talionis turned and ran into the light.

Al’s heart sank. He nodded slowly. “I can’t blame him. He lost everything so young.” Tears welled in his eyes as he turned to the old man. “I’m ready,” he said.

“You may be,” the old man replied gently, “but your companion isn’t. He didn’t choose to stay—only to meet with the clan while he was here.”

“Seriously? I didn’t know that was an option. Is Glyn here?” Al asked, startled.

“He is. But it’s not an option for you. Talionis’ heart is pure—as most animals’ are. They pass more easily between realms. Humans have a harder time. Even now, you’ve seen things you won’t be able to explain. You’ll try, but your mind will struggle to capture them in word or song. They will live vivid within you but defy expression. That is as it should be.”

Al considered this. “When I go back… what am I to do? End the reign of the Dokkalfar? Stop Herair?”

“Only the Dokkalfar,” the old man said. “Herair is beyond you. He is but the servant of another. Their reckoning will come—by one who was, and who is yet to be. And no sword will he wield. The very foundations of creation will tremble at his approach. But that is not for an age upon an age upon an age hence.”

Al looked down at his hands. “I will try. But I fear the people I love will die because of my choices.”

“To die is part of the journey—all living things must face it. But fear not. If they die, I will be here, waiting to welcome them.”

Al turned back to the old man. Only now did he realize he had never truly seen his face. Even now, his eyes could not rise high enough to behold it clearly.

"Thank you. For everything," Al said simply.

The old man smiled, and warmth filled the space. "I believe in you Al. It is why I sent you that vision on your eighteenth birthday. It why I allowed your blood to awaken. I sensed in you a pure heart willing to do the right because it is right and just to do so. We will meet again, young Albert. And when we do, you will walk in the Garden."

Suddenly, Talionis was by his side once more.

"Awake now, children," the old man said, his voice echoing like morning sunlight through ancient trees, "for a new day is dawning."

Al gasped as breath filled his lungs. The scent of fire, burnt flesh, and blood assaulted his senses. His entire body ached.

Footsteps moved around him. He heard a woman weeping. He opened his eyes.

All around him stood the clans. Ryanna knelt at his side, her face pressed against his chest. With great effort, Al raised his right hand and rested it on her head.

"It's okay, my love," he whispered. "I'm okay."

Ryanna leapt back, stunned, her face a mask of shock and disbelief. "What madness is this?" she cried, grabbing her spear.

The others standing near him stumbled back, eyes wide with awe and fear.

Al smiled gently and laughed. Slowly, painfully, he sat up and reached over to shake Talionis, who lay motionless beside him. "Come on, you big baby," he said with a grin. "There's much yet to do."

The massive wolf stirred, lifted his head, and growled softly. The clansmen stepped farther back in wonder.

"Relax," Al said calmly. "It's me."

The wolf growled again.

"Us," Al corrected—and Talionis snorted in agreement.

Ryanna's expression shifted from disbelief to pure emotion. She threw herself at him, wrapping her arms around him tightly.

"I thought I had lost you," she whispered.

He held her just as tightly. "You nearly did. But my mission isn't done. I've been given a second chance."

"Second chance? By whom?" asked Rogan.

Al opened his mouth to speak—but the words caught in his throat. He sighed.

"I'm afraid that is not a tale I can tell. What I will say is this: not all who fall are truly lost to us. They go somewhere—somewhere beautiful and peaceful. And if we're lucky, we may see them again. But I'll say no more, for it's a truth that is not mine to speak."

He stood. All around him, the clans echoed his movements, murmuring in confusion and reverence, trying to interpret his words.

Ryanna held his arm protectively. "Careful, my love. You were gravely injured."

Al pulled off his shirt and turned to show his unmarred skin. "I am unharmed."

Gasps rose among the warriors.

"What of the others?" he asked, scanning the ruined dome around them.

"Just before we entered the fog, we heard a mighty explosion, and then the fog quickly began to melt away," said Rogan. "Once it cleared, we found our quarry waiting—ready to pounce—but with the fog gone, they turned and fled. So the clans gave chase. Ryanna insisted the explosion had to be you, and that we should hurry and find where it came from. When we arrived… it was a horrible scene."

He looked around grimly. "Where is your blade?" he asked.

"Gone," Al replied, the word bitter on his tongue. "Destroyed in the blast." He sneered, as if the taste of bile had risen in his throat. "And good riddance. It was a device of the enemy—never meant to give us true victory."

Rogan looked thoughtful for a moment, his gaze distant. "Tainted though it was, it was still our best chance at defeating the enemy. Without it, what chance do we have against the rising darkness?"

Al met his eyes, calm and resolute. "Though my sword is gone, I have not lost my power. Fear not. When the time comes, we will be ready. And do not underestimate yourselves—or your clans. There is strength in them that the enemy will come to fear."

He turned, scanning the southern horizon. "Come," he said, his voice quiet but commanding. "We must ride south. My heart tells me that trouble lies ahead."

A PUZZLE AND A CLUE

Tyr stood gazing over the vast open space that would become his new shop. At the moment, it was little more than a large, empty building with high vaulted ceilings and tall windows lining the upper front half. A two-story section was attached at the rear.

"Well, you sure have a lot of room," ventured Gillian, sounding a little unsure.

Tyr smiled. "It's perfect."

Gillian gave him a doubtful look. "If you say so."

"I'll set the forges up here near the front, by the bay doors," Tyr said, gesturing enthusiastically. "Workbenches and grinders down the center, and over here we'll store raw stock and tools." He pointed to various areas as they walked deeper into the cavernous space, finally stopping at the wall separating the main shop from the two-story section. Large interior windows looked out from both floors onto the workspace. "First floor will be offices. Second floor, my residence." He turned to Gillian, beaming. "Like I said—perfect."

Gillian scratched his chin, still trying to see it. "Okay… but I don't see any of that stuff."

"Not yet," Tyr said, nodding. "First, I need to go through Gutamino's documents and figure out exactly what's needed. Then I can lay out the shop properly and start getting everything built."

"Well now, this is perfect," came a voice from the front of the building.

Tyr and Gillian turned to see Master Cowin and Lady Krystal entering.

Tyr smiled like a child receiving a long-awaited gift. "My thoughts exactly."

Krystal embraced him warmly. "I'm so happy for you," she said aloud. Then, with her head near his, she whispered, "And for us."

Tyr hugged her a little tighter in reply.

"No kiss for me?" Cowin laughed. "But I did bring you a gift." He held up a bottle. "It's the best red I could get my hands on—from the hills of Montemajore. I recommend pairing it with lamb or beef."

"Thank you. All of you." Tyr's grin widened. "I still can't believe how much my fortune has changed since arriving here. I've been truly blessed." He looked around the space again. "I'm not much of a cook, but let me run into the city for supplies. I'll cook dinner tonight, and we'll open this wine to celebrate."

Krystal took the bottle from him with a smirk. "I'm a decent cook—I'll supervise. Gillian, you can help carry groceries. Master Cowin, I'm sure your shop needs tending. Shall we say dinner at the evening bell?"

Cowin bowed slightly. "It will be my honor. I know a delightful little bakery—I'll bring dessert."

Krystal curtsied. "Splendid," she said. The group laughed as they made their plans.

The following afternoon, Tyr stood inside the shop, sketching a layout in his notepad and compiling a list of equipment and supplies. He planned to head into the city the next day to begin outfitting the space.

"Hard at work, I see," came a gentle voice from behind him.

He turned to see Gutamino standing in the bay doors, Gillian beside him.

Tyr smiled. "I'd be ashamed of myself if I didn't get the shop running as quickly as possible." He set the notepad aside and gave a respectful bow. "Thank you again for this opportunity."

Gutamino nodded. "I suspected that would be your attitude, so I made sure to arrive before you got too far along. I have a surprise for you. In fact, it's the main reason I chose you," he said, a wry smile spreading across his olive-toned face.

Tyr glanced between Gutamino and Gillian, puzzled. Outside, he could hear the clatter of wagons approaching over the cobblestones.

Gutamino motioned for him to investigate.

Tyr stepped through the bay doors and watched as three large wagons pulled up. The first carried something massive, though it was hidden beneath a heavy tarp. The second was packed with tools and crates. The third carried a team of riggers and their equipment.

"What is it?" Tyr asked.

"A forge," Gutamino said. "But let's go inside before we talk more. First—where do you want it installed?"

Tyr was confused. Whatever was beneath the tarp appeared far too large for a standard forge. But Gutamino was essentially his patron, and if this was the forge he was expected to use, then so be it—it would be given a prime location. He quickly directed the riggers where to place it and how it should be oriented.

Then Gutamino, Gillian, and Tyr retreated into the office. Sparse though it was, it had a table and a few chairs. Once inside, Gutamino gave Gillian a glance, and the boy nodded, stepping outside to keep watch in case the crew wandered too close.

Tyr waited, intrigued. Gutamino's tone was serious, and his manner deliberate.

"Do you know why I chose you?" Gutamino asked.

"Not really, no," Tyr answered honestly.

"You're a very good smith—but not the best. You're highly talented—but so are many others in this city. You're loyal to neither me nor money, so I can never be certain you'll do what I ask—not an ideal candidate, some would say." He said it all matter-of-factly, with no malice.

Tyr nodded. Nothing Gutamino said was untrue. "Then why did you choose me?"

A distant, thoughtful look passed over Gutamino's face. "What do you know of your lineage?"

Tyr furrowed his brow but answered, "My parents came from western Harding before I was born. I'm not exactly sure from where."

"And your grandparents?"

Tyr shook his head. "Never met them. My parents only mentioned them in passing, and never to us kids. I always assumed it was a sore subject and didn't press. All I know is that my father's father was a smith, and my mother's father worked as a guard."

Gutamino's shoulders sagged slightly, and his voice softened. "I'm sorry. Truly. Where I'm from, lineage means everything. I can trace mine back nearly a thousand years. In my country, it's an entire industry."

Tyr tilted his head. "What does that have to do with why you picked me?"

Gutamino raised a hand, motioning him to wait. "Before I answer that, one more question: What do you know of the dwarves?"

Tyr blinked. "Dwarves?" He looked more confused than ever. "Very little, honestly. Before I left Harding, I'd have told you they were myths—like goblins or ogres." He chuckled slightly.

"And now?" Gutamino pressed. "What do you believe now?"

Tyr shrugged. "If the stories you've told me about Al are true, then ogres at least must exist. So I suppose it's possible the others do too. Including dwarves."

"They do," Gutamino said. "At least the ogres and goblins still walk the world. The dwarves... did exist. But no one's seen them since the last great war nearly five centuries ago. Any who try to enter their old strongholds meet gruesome ends."

He paused, then leaned in, lowering his voice. "But while many dwarves opposed the Dokkalfar, some remained neutral. A few even traded with him. 'Loyal' might be too strong a word—but they had dealings."

Gutamino stood and moved to the window overlooking the shop floor. The first wagon had been rolled into place, and the crew was beginning to assemble the rigging equipment to unload the massive cargo.

"What I've brought you is one of their forges—an artifact that remained in the Dokkalfar's possession for centuries. One of the legendary dwarven forges."

Tyr stood as well, moving beside him. The tarp still concealed the object. "You want me to use a dwarven forge? Is that even possible?"

"No," Gutamino said bluntly. "At least, no one's been able to for the last five hundred years. The dwarves weren't fond of anyone else using their things."

"Then what am I supposed to do with it?"

"I want you to figure out how to make it work."

Tyr turned to face him fully. "With all due respect, if no one's been able to use it in five centuries, why do you think I can?"

A small smile played on Gutamino's lips. "Because I believe you have an unfair advantage."

Tyr raised an eyebrow. "And what's that?"

Gutamino returned to his chair and motioned for Tyr to do the same. "I've gathered all the research ever compiled since the dwarves vanished. It's in five tomes—also in the wagon. You have access to the Academy of Learning here in the city. And—" he paused, locking eyes with Tyr, "—because I don't believe the dwarves are gone. I believe they are still among us. Few. Scattered. But here."

Tyr stared. "So... you've found one? Is he going to help me?"

Gutamino smiled again. "In a manner of speaking, yes."

Tyr blinked. "Seriously? Where is he?"

Gutamino leaned forward, his tone gentle. "He's you."

Tyr shook his head. "Please. I've been teased my whole life—every short blacksmith has—about being a dwarf. I didn't expect it from you, though," he said grimly.

"You misunderstand me. I'm not teasing, nor joking," Gutamino said, his tone firm. "I've done my research—ever since Albert first mentioned you back in Morcaster—and I'm convinced that you, and both of your parents, are dwarves."

Tyr's expression remained unconvinced, so Gutamino continued.

"Yes, you're short—but not that short. Just enough to stand out. That's exactly how the dwarves were described by those who actually knew them. And remember, I've traveled with Cygnus, who is far older than the last war and has firsthand knowledge of the dwarves. You're also significantly broader than the average person—even for a blacksmith. You're built differently. Dwarves were known for their strength, endurance, and craftsmanship—all qualities you possess. And you said your parents came from western Harding. If my geography is correct, Harding is bounded to the west and south by major mountain ranges, both of which once held dwarven kingdoms."

"I thought dwarves lived for centuries," Tyr said. "My parents aren't that old."

"Do you know how old they are?" Gutamino asked. "Have they ever told you? Even if they aren't yet ancient, that doesn't mean they won't live for centuries."

Tyr's face was a tangle of disbelief, curiosity, and unease. Gutamino patted his hands gently.

"I believe you are. I could be wrong—but I believe it. And I believe that's why you may be able to get this forge working."

"And if you're wrong?" Tyr asked.

Gutamino shrugged. "Then it remains cold. It was always a long shot. And if nothing else, we'll still have a very skilled blacksmith capable of making some truly exquisite blades."

He leaned forward slightly. "All I'm asking is that you keep an open mind. Try to figure it out. And one more thing—please don't tell anyone about this unless they must know to help you."

Tyr nodded. "Understood."

"Good. Then we'll leave you to oversee the installation. The books I mentioned are in the wagon with the rigging crew."

Gutamino turned to leave, then paused, pulling out a folded parchment and handing it to Tyr.

"What's this?" Tyr asked.

"A letter of credit," Gutamino said. "Present it when you go into the city to buy what you need for the shop. The merchants will bill me directly."

Tyr nodded his thanks as Gutamino departed. Gillian gave an exaggerated look of wide-eyed shock but said nothing—only grinning and waving before following Gutamino out.

Tyr walked back into the shop, where the riggers were busy lashing pulley systems to the overhead beams. He made his way to the other wagon, found the five thick tomes Gutamino had spoken of, and carried them back to his office.

The rest of the day was spent helping the rigging crew install the forge in its chosen place. When they were finally gone, he examined the thing more closely. It was massive—larger than any forge he had ever seen—and clearly not designed for wood or coal. There were ports inside, which he assumed were where the flames emerged, and a series of levers and knobs whose purpose eluded him.

He pulled out his notebook and began a scaled sketch of the forge, annotating it with questions and first impressions beside each component.

By the time he finished, the sky outside had dimmed. He gathered the books and climbed the stairs to his new living space, which he had divided into three sections: a kitchen-dining area, a sitting area, and a modest sleeping corner. He placed the books on the kitchen table and brewed himself a cup of coffee. Looking around, he took stock. It was bare. He had some fruit and stale bread.

It'll do for now, he thought. *I'll walk down to the docks later and find something decent to eat.*

He sat with his small meal and coffee, opened the first book, and began to read. As the sunlight faded, he lit a candle, occasionally referencing his earlier sketch, making notes as questions were answered—and more questions took their place.

He was still reading when the first golden light of dawn began to filter through the high windows. It wasn't until the rich scent of fresh-baked bread filled his nostrils—warm, buttery, and impossible to ignore—that he finally looked up.

Krystal stood before him, smiling softly, holding a covered basket.

He blinked. "What time is it?" he asked groggily.

She shook her head with a small smile. "Oh my," she said with a playful lilt. "You really do throw yourself into your work, don't you?" She placed the basket on the desk in front of him and began unpacking it. First came a small cloth, which she laid out neatly, followed by a loaf of fresh bread, some cheese, dried meats, and fruit. Then she moved to the hearth and placed a kettle of water on to boil for tea.

Returning to the desk, she sat down across from him. "Eat something," she said firmly.

Tyr rubbed a hand through the thick hair on his chin and nodded. "I can't believe I stayed up all night," he muttered, breaking off a piece of the warm bread.

"I can," Krystal said. "My grandfather told me about the forge, and I knew—you'd be drawn to it like a moth to a flame." Her voice was sweet, touched with admiration.

He looked at her through bleary eyes and smiled. "I'm glad you came. Yesterday was... one for the books," he said, chewing another bite.

She glanced around the room, noting the untouched corner of stale bread and dried fruit from the night before. "Did you even eat last night?"

"Not really, no," he admitted.

"Oh my. What are we going to do with you?" she teased, removing the kettle from the fire and setting it aside. Then, with a gleam in her eye, she added, "Come."

"Where?" he asked, blinking away the fog of exhaustion and information overload.

"You're taking me to breakfast," she said, rising and brushing off her hands. "That little tavern you keep talking about. Introduce me to your friends—let them meet the woman who's stolen their smith."

He caught her hand, holding it gently. "Krystal... there's something else. I don't know if it's true. I don't want to believe it—not fully. But I can't ignore the possibility anymore."

She tilted her head, her gaze steady. "Go on."

"Gutamino thinks I'm... a dwarf," he said finally, almost embarrassed by how absurd it sounded aloud.

To his surprise, Krystal didn't flinch. Instead, she smiled and let out a soft, delighted giggle.

"Oh, my dear Tyr. I think you may be, too."

He blinked. "Why? What makes you say that?"

She stepped closer, slipped her arms around him, and rested her head against his chest. "Because you're too good to be just a man," she whispered. "Too noble. Too grounded. Too stubborn. Too kind. There are no humans like you—not really. If you are something more... well, that explains how you won me over so completely."

Rising on her toes, she kissed him quickly, then tugged him toward the door. "Now come on. I want bacon. And I want to see if this tavern lives up to your bragging."

The next two weeks passed in a whirlwind of activity. The shop buzzed with crews setting up machines, benches, and equipment. Deliveries of raw stock and supplies began arriving, and through it all, Tyr spent his evenings buried in the ancient tomes, sketching and refining diagrams of the forge, puzzling over its mechanisms.

Krystal remained by his side, helping him every step of the way—from managing the workers to translating dusty notes. She read alongside him, questioned his ideas, and offered new ones. They made a formidable team.

Late one night, they sat together at the workbench, each nursing a mug of ale. The forge loomed in the background, silent and inert.

"What next?" she asked quietly.

Tyr exhaled slowly. "Nothing we're doing is having any effect. The books are just fragments of guesswork from others who tried and failed. We're repeating their steps." He stared at the forge, its metal surface glinting dully in the lamplight. "I think we need a new perspective."

She looked intrigued. "What are you thinking?"

"The city has an academy of learning. I'd been meaning to go back and discuss the whole dwarf thing with one of the scholars I met. Now may be as good a time as any."

She brightened. "That's an excellent idea. Let's go tomorrow."

His face hardened for a moment in thought, then softened. She'd seen him do this before—when something weighed on his mind.

"Is everything alright?" she asked gently.

He smiled. "Sorry. Yes, everything is fine. I'll come by tomorrow morning, if that's alright?"

"Are you sure? I know you're not fond of the estate. I don't mind coming here."

"No," he said, his tone softening further. "In fact, it's late. Please allow me the honor of walking you home."

She blushed. "My, aren't we gallant tonight? The palace grounds are quite safe, but I'll never turn down such an excellent escort."

They held hands and talked quietly as they walked slowly back to the estate. When they arrived, Lord Dadius was just returning, dressed in full military regalia. He smiled warmly upon seeing his granddaughter—and even when he turned his gaze to Tyr.

"How go the efforts to light the forge?" he asked.

"Not well, unfortunately," Tyr admitted. "But we"—he nodded toward Krystal—"have an idea we're going to look into tomorrow."

Lord Dadius was about to respond but paused when he saw the expression on Tyr's face.

"My dear," he said to Krystal, "might I have a private word with your blacksmith?"

She raised an eyebrow and gave her grandfather a warning look. "You better play nice."

"You have my word," he replied, chuckling.

Once she was inside, Dadius turned to Tyr. "You wanted to ask me something," he said evenly.

Tyr blinked in surprise. "How did you know?"

"Boy," Dadius said with a knowing smile, "I am far older than you can imagine, and I've seen that look in many a young man's eye. Say what you've come to say."

Tyr nodded and took a breath. "I've grown very fond of Krystal, sir. Truth be told, I've fallen deeply in love with her. I would like your permission to court her."

He turned a bright shade of red but held the older man's gaze.

Lord Dadius studied him with a long, appraising look. "What you ask is not so simple," he said at last. "Though I do give you credit for coming to me first. Most today no longer hold to the old ways—I'm glad you do. Especially since Lady Krystal is bound by name and blood, and the choice of her spouse is not entirely her own."

Tyr said nothing, but his eyes showed he understood.

"I'll be honest," Dadius continued. "I've just returned from a private dinner with Duchess Emrite and Count Logan. They've proposed a diplomatic union between Lady Blackthorne and the count's youngest son, Jahn. I believe the two of you are... acquainted?"

Tyr's face fell. "I see," he said quietly. "I don't suppose Krystal—Lady Blackthorne—has any say in the matter?"

"Not officially," Dadius said. "But I am not a harsh man. I love my granddaughter dearly, and I will allow her voice to be heard. Though in the end, the decision will be mine."

He studied Tyr again, as if weighing unseen scales. "I will say this—you may court her. Win her heart if you can. And if you can solve the riddle of the forge—truly solve it, one way or another—then you will have my blessing. If she chooses you in return."

Tyr nodded solemnly. "Then I will redouble my efforts to crack this nut."

He hesitated. "And... what will that do to your efforts here in York?"

Dadius raised an eyebrow and grinned. "You're a good man, Tyr. I've known that since we first met on the road to Jaspar. But tell me honestly—do you truly care if my plans, or those of my master, are hindered?"

Tyr held his gaze. "I don't know your plans. Not really. But if I had to trust my gut... I'd probably say no. I wouldn't be upset."

Lord Dadius laughed—a rich, deep laugh. He clapped Tyr on the back. "Trust your gut, then. It seems to be leading you in the right direction."

BLOOD THAT BURNS

Early the next day, Tyr and Krystal walked down the main avenue, stopping occasionally at various carts hawking their wares as they made their way toward the Academy of Knowledge. At the main gate sat three young students—two males and a female—all in their late teens by the look of them, wearing the long robes of the academics. Unlike the masters, however, their robes were unadorned, marking their status as initiates.

"Good morning," said the girl cheerfully, as the boys stopped their chatter. "How can we assist you today?"

Tyr smiled. "I would like to speak with Preceptor Winslow."

She made a note in a large ledger before her. "And you are?"

Krystal stepped forward, her tone composed but regal. "This is the Royal Blacksmith, Tyr Ranfel, and I am Lady Krystal Blackthorne."

The three students straightened at once. The girl quickly jotted down the names, her previous confidence replaced by a more reserved deference. "Is Preceptor Winslow expecting you?"

Krystal responded—not unkindly, but with a tone that brooked no argument. "The Master Blacksmith is here on palace business."

"Of course. We will take you to him at once," the girl replied, nodding to one of the boys. "Lyle, please escort them."

The young man stood promptly. "This way, please."

He led them into the compound, past long rows of brick buildings and well-manicured gardens. Small groups of students and professors could be seen sitting in circles on the lawns, deep in discussion. Eventually, they arrived at a modest single-story building. Inside was a single large room, cluttered with desks, books, and parchments. A staircase led downward from the far wall. At one of the desks sat the elderly man Tyr had spoken with all those months ago.

"Preceptor Winslow," Tyr said in his naturally booming voice, "I'm sorry to bother you."

"I'll take my leave," Lyle whispered, slipping back out the door.

Winslow looked up from the tome he had been studying. "Ah, the boy who shouldn't has returned," he said with a hint of amusement.

Krystal and Tyr walked to his desk. Tyr unshouldered the pouch he had been carrying and placed it in front of him. Winslow raised an eyebrow and opened it, pulling out the first tome and flipping through its pages. His curiosity deepened as he removed the second and third volumes.

Looking from Tyr to Krystal, he asked, "Where did you get these? And why bring them to me?"

"May I speak plainly?" Tyr asked.

"I would prefer it," Winslow replied, gesturing for them to sit.

Tyr launched into a full account—explaining the dwarven forge, his repeated but fruitless attempts to activate it, the discovery of the hidden chamber, and the theory, held by some, that he might be of dwarven descent.

When he finished, Winslow sat quietly, processing the tale.

"And what exactly would you like me to do?" he asked at last.

"We're at a loss," Tyr said. "I was hoping you might know something that could help me get past the roadblock we've hit."

Winslow eyed the tomes. "Perhaps. But all knowledge has a cost."

Krystal narrowed her eyes slightly. Tyr knew that look—she was now listening very carefully, ready to spot any trickery or deceit.

"What price?" Tyr asked.

Winslow gestured around the room, then broadly toward the rest of the compound. "All of this—this academy—exists because it doggedly pursues knowledge. We have a long-standing tradition: we do not give it away freely."

"Surely, you make exceptions for the Crown," Krystal said evenly.

Winslow nodded. "Of course. But this isn't a request from the Crown, is it? If it were, we would have been summoned formally. This"—he nodded toward the tomes—"is something else."

Tyr leaned forward slightly. "What's your price?"

Winslow rested his hands on the three volumes. "These," he said simply. "They are ancient—firsthand accounts from men across the ages trying to unlock the secrets of a dwarven artifact. Their value to the academy is immeasurable."

"They're not mine to give," Tyr said, rising from his chair and calmly repacking the books into the pouch.

Krystal spoke gently. "Surely there must be another way?"

The old man ran his hand over his face. "You put me in a difficult position," he said. "On the one hand, I have an obligation to the Academy. But on the other... I'm very intrigued by the prospect of seeing an ancient dwarven artifact come to life." He thought for a moment. "I'll make you a deal. I'll tell you what I suspect—right now. No research, no investigation of the artifact, just my gut instinct. If I'm right, and the forge comes to life, you grant me two things. First, the ability to inspect the newly lit forge. Second, the right to examine you—and I mean everything: measurements, history, genealogy, the whole thing."

"Me? Why?" Tyr asked, confused.

"That's my price. Grant me those two things, and I'll tell you what I think. And remember—you only have to pay if what I say works."

Tyr looked to Krystal. She gave a small shrug. She didn't see anything wrong with the request.

Tyr sat back down. "Okay. Deal."

Preceptor Winslow stood and began pacing, like a professor preparing to lecture.

"Dwarves," he began. "At their height, the dwarves had seven great kingdoms—three here in Tirra, and four across the sea in Jotunheimr. At that time, they created machines that could reshape entire nations, and armor and weapons without equal, even to this day. The dwarves guarded their secrets closely. The other races became jealous and envious, desperate to learn how the dwarves wrought such marvels. As a result, the dwarves began locking themselves away, and one by one, the great kingdoms vanished from the world. Any who tried to enter their strongholds met only death."

"By the time of the last great war, only two kingdoms still had any, though limited, contact with the outside world. Ailthain Árdgeal—the Gem of the Northern Lights—was here in Tirra, to the west of Morcaster. Interesting side note: it's said the Altin River was made by them to increase trade. That's why the river runs nearly a thousand miles in more or less a straight line." Seeing their surprised expressions, he smiled. "The other was in Jotunheimr, in the southeast. *Dubhathrán Fældfyr* is what the dwarves from Ailthain Árdgeal called it—'Forges of Darkness.' It's believed they assisted the Dokkalfar in his fight against the free peoples."

Tyr looked puzzled. "Morcaster is in Jaspar. That's the second time I have heard of Tirra, but I don't know where it is?"

Winslow chuckled. "Ah, my friend. I've spent so long among these books, I forget that most people don't know these things." He walked to a stack of parchments, rifled through them, and pulled out a large map, which he laid flat on the table.

"This is a map of Tirra—or most of it," he said, pointing near the top. "From the frozen wastelands of the north, down to the desert of Tuarfel south of the Five Kingdoms, and from the vast Shalmarin Ocean in the east to the mighty mountains of the Ashek Range in the west."

Both Tyr and Krystal stared in awe.

"That's... that's something to see," Tyr said quietly. "I've seen navigational charts and coastal maps, but nothing like this."

"So Tirra is all of this?" Krystal asked.

Winslow nodded. "Exactly. That's the name we give to the western lands. Jotunheimr refers to the lands across the Shalmarin." He gestured to the unmarked eastern edge of the map.

Tyr was fascinated and his eyes scanned the map, "Where is Zamoya?" he asked curiously.

Winslow laughed, "Boy, you never heard of Tirra but you have heard of Zamoya?"

Tyr shrugged sheepishly, "One of the people who was at the boarding house said she was from a place called Zamoya" he said as way of explanation.

Winslow nodded, "I don't have any good maps of that land, we know very little about it, and its people are rarely seen here. Count yourself lucky to have met one – most people here never will. But Zamoya would be down here" he said indicating off the bottom left of the map.

Tyr nodded, "Thank you" he said simply.

"Anyway," he continued, "I digress. The kingdoms. At the end of the last war, the final two dwarven kingdoms sealed themselves away, and haven't been seen since." He looked meaningfully at Tyr. "Or... that's what most people believe. Some speculate that the dwarves didn't vanish at all—but instead left their ancient homes and now live quietly among us."

"Do you believe that?" Tyr asked.

The old man smiled. "I'm beginning to think it has some merit."

"How does this help us ignite the forge?" Krystal asked.

Winslow grew serious again. "The dwarves vanished. All entrances to their cities were blocked or destroyed. The few artifacts that remain are completely unusable—by design. The dwarves never wanted anyone but their own kind to wield their secrets."

"So, you're saying the forge can't be lit?" Tyr asked.

"No. I'm saying it will only light for a dwarf." He paused, then added, "You said you discovered a panel—one that, when accessed, revealed an opening with a handle inside?"

"Yes, but it doesn't move or turn, no matter what I do," Tyr replied.

"If I'm right, it's not supposed to. The dwarves would have found a way to safeguard any artifact of theirs that left their kingdoms. I believe this is a lock—one that must be opened for the forge to ignite."

"How do we unlock it?" Krystal asked.

"With blood," he said.

The two of them stared at him in shock.

"My guess is, you need to reach in and grip the handle firmly. One of those dials or levers you mentioned will probably activate a mechanism that pricks your hand—tests the blood. If it's dwarven, it should light the forge."

"And if I'm unlucky?" Tyr asked.

"Based on what we've seen of those who've tried to enter their kingdoms? It will probably kill you. Though it might only take your hand."

Tyr said nothing. His face was unreadable. Krystal knew he was weighing every possibility.

"Is there anything else you can share with us?" she asked.

The old man shook his head. "Sadly, no. I've studied what little there is on the dwarves, but aside from language fragments and old tales, there's almost nothing documented."

Tyr nodded and rose, shaking the old scholar's hand. "Thank you. I do believe you're right." He looked at Krystal. "Now we have a decision to make."

As the two turned to leave, the old man added, "For what it's worth—I think, if anyone fits the old descriptions of a dwarf, it's you, my friend."

They began the walk back to the palace grounds in silence.

"What are you thinking, my dear?" Krystal asked softly.

They walked a bit further before he answered.

"I'm trying to decide if it's worth the risk," he said quietly.

"If you ask me, I would say it's not," she replied. "You're already a master smith in your own right. Even if you got the forge working, who's to say you'd be able to recreate the weapons of old? There might be special metals or processes lost to time. So why risk losing an arm— or your life—for something that might not be useful in the end?"

"I agree," he said. "And if it were just about me, that would be the end of it."

"Then who else is it about?" she asked, frowning. "You don't need to prove anything to me."

He gave her a solemn look. "Last night, I spoke with your grandfather—"

She stopped. "What did he say to you?" Her voice sharpened with concern.

"No, no—he didn't threaten me," Tyr assured her. "I asked him for permission to court you." He took her hands and looked into her eyes.

She smiled, soft and radiant. "Oh, Tyr… don't you know? You've already won my heart."

He smiled in return, but his voice was careful. "I didn't want to presume. But he told me he'd just returned from the Duchess's estate. Count Logan is trying to arrange a marriage between you and Jahn."

Her face flushed with fury, then fell as tears welled in her eyes. Tyr pulled her into a hug.

"I'm sorry, Tyr. Truly. I would choose you—but some things are out of my control," she said, her voice muffled in his shoulder.

"That's why I'm struggling," he said gently. "Your grandfather told me that if I could solve the riddle of the forge—one way or another—he'd consider your wishes. If there's even a chance… even if it costs me an arm… I feel I have to try."

She wiped her tears on his shirt and looked up. "My heart is torn. This is an unfair choice they're thrusting on you. Do me a favor—say nothing, and do nothing, until I've had a chance to speak with my grandfather. Let me try to convince him."

He nodded. "I'll wait."

They walked the rest of the way in silence, each lost in thought.

Later that afternoon, Tyr entered the smithy alone. The sun hung low, casting golden rays through the high windows. The shop was immaculate—clean, organized, complete. The forges lined one wall. Benches, drills, lathes, and racks of stock stood ready.

And in the center, the ancient forge loomed.

It was the heart of the shop. But it was cold. Lifeless. And the air around it somehow felt... still.

Tyr climbed onto one of the steel benches and sat, staring at the forge. He imagined the future—a shop alive with hammers and laughter, students learning, steel ringing, the air thick with heat and the scent of burning coal. He could almost feel it.

Sliding down from the bench, he crossed to the nearest modern forge and, almost without thinking, lit it. As the fire bloomed and the heat rose, he reached for a bar of cold stock and set it in the flame.

The warmth washed over him.

I swear I breathe easier when I'm at the forge, Tyr thought.

He flipped the steel over. He didn't know what he was making. It didn't matter. He just needed to work. The hammer rose and fell, echoing through the shop—alone, but alive—late into the night.

Tyr woke early, and after cleaning the already-clean shop, made himself a simple breakfast of hot porridge, bacon, some fresh fruit, and a little stale bread. The sun was just beginning to rise as he finished his meal.

The sound of the shop door opening rang sharp and clear through the quiet space. Tyr walked to the second-floor landing and saw Gutamino, Lord Dadius, and Krystal entering. He hurriedly grabbed a clean shirt and went down to meet them.

"My apologies," he said as he approached. "I wasn't expecting anyone so early. I can put some coffee on, if you'd like."

"No need for that, Master Blacksmith," said Lord Dadius, glancing around the shop. "I must say, you've used your time well. I look forward to seeing this shop in full swing."

"As do I, my lord," Tyr replied, offering Krystal a smile—but she didn't meet his gaze.

Gutamino walked over to the ancient forge. "I hear you have news for us," he said softly—less a question than a statement.

Tyr glanced again at Krystal, who still would not look at him. "We went to the Academy of Learning yesterday and met with Preceptor Winslow to discuss the problem."

"And?" asked Gutamino.

"He said knowledge has a price, and the price he asked for wasn't mine to pay."

Lord Dadius and Gutamino exchanged a look. "What was the price?" Dadius asked.

"The three tomes you lent me. They weren't mine to give away. I told him I would need to check with you first."

Gutamino stepped closer. They were roughly the same height, though Tyr was nearly twice as broad. To the casual eye, Tyr might have appeared the more dangerous, but there was something in Gutamino's bearing—a coiled presence—that marked him as someone not to be underestimated.

"So he didn't help you at all?" he asked, his voice barely above a whisper.

He knows. Either Krystal told him, or he has spies. Either way, he knows everything, Tyr thought. *And I've never been good at lying.*

"I didn't say that," Tyr answered, crossing his arms and meeting his gaze. "I said he wanted payment to throw the full weight of the Academy at our problem. But he did give me his opinion—just his opinion, mind you."

Both Gutamino and Lord Dadius seemed to relax. Gutamino stepped back.

"And what did he say?" Lord Dadius asked.

In response, Tyr walked over to the forge, threw a few levers, and turned a couple of dials. A panel slid open, revealing an interior compartment.

The two nobles leaned in, intrigued.

"Haven't seen that before," Lord Dadius murmured. "Is this how we start it?"

"No. At least not directly. I found this earlier this week but couldn't figure out what to do with it. There's a handle inside that won't move or turn. According to the preceptor, it's a dwarven failsafe—something to ensure that only another dwarf could operate the forge."

"How do we test that?" asked Gutamino.

Tyr sighed. "I need to put my hand in, grip the handle, and then activate one of these levers or dials. It's supposed to prick my hand— test the blood. If I'm a dwarf, the forge should ignite. If not..."

"If not what?" Lord Dadius pressed.

Tyr looked from one man to the other. *They already know the answer—they're waiting for me to say it out loud.*

"If I'm not a dwarf, it might cut off my arm... or kill me."

They both regarded him silently, letting the weight of the choice settle.

"I've solved the mystery," Tyr said, "but I'm not sure I want to risk death or dismemberment for something that—even if it works— might not give you what you're looking for."

Through all of this, Krystal had remained silent, her head bowed. But the movement of her shoulders told Tyr she was crying.

What did they say to her? His blood began to boil.

Lord Dadius stepped forward. "It is a lot to ask of someone, Tyr. Trust me when I say that both Gutamino and I have been asked to take similar risks from time to time. We are intimately familiar with the struggle that must be raging inside you now. Neither of us would compel you to do this."

He paused, glanced at Krystal, then looked back at Tyr.

"We need this forge lit, if it can be. We need to know. I know the risk is high, so I offer you a reward just as great. Do this—and no matter the outcome—I will give you my granddaughter's hand. If not, I will understand. But I will be forced to make the politically expedient choice and grant her hand to young Lord Jahn."

He let the words hang in the air. "Not something anyone in this room wants."

"And what do you say to this, my dear?" Lord Dadius asked Krystal directly.

She raised her head, tears streaming silently down her face, but said nothing. The look in her eyes said everything—she wanted Tyr, but she feared for his life.

"And if I die?" Tyr asked, turning back to Dadius. "What happens to her then?"

A wry smile crossed the old lord's face, and he nodded. "Agreed. If you die, she will be permitted to choose her own path in life."

Tyr nodded. Then, without hesitation, he walked over to the forge. Without allowing himself time to think, he thrust his right hand into the opening, gripped the handle, and with his left, pressed the one button he had never seen serve a purpose.

At once, a metal collar snapped around his wrist, followed by a sharp prick in the palm of his hand.

The others stepped back as the ancient forge, silent for centuries, began to hum.

It was reading his blood.

Suddenly, another needle jabbed into his forearm. He felt something cold surge into him, spreading through his veins. His vision blurred. He heard distant voices—an unknown tongue rising in volume. He heard the clang of hammers, the ring of picks, cries of joy and sorrow, laughter and screams. His knees buckled, but he didn't fall.

The cacophony grew—until, suddenly, the words began to make sense. The voices became chants. Songs. Stories. Runes he'd never seen flashed before his eyes—patterns, elegant and intricate, forming and folding inward, channeling energy from the world itself. Knowledge poured into him. And just as quickly, it was gone.

The collar released. He staggered backward.

With a mighty roar, the forge came to life.

Orange light flooded the shop. Pipes shuddered. Gears ground into motion. Flames ignited with a low rumble that seemed to resonate in Tyr's chest. The forge—ancient and forgotten—was alive again.

"Well done, Tyr. Very well done indeed," Gutamino whispered in quiet awe.

Lord Dadius's expression was unreadable. He studied Tyr for a long moment, as if seeing him truly for the first time. Then he gave a single approving nod.

"Come see me tomorrow, Tyr. We have things to discuss."

Gutamino looked him over. "Get some rest. I don't know what happened to you, but it's obvious something profound has. Krystal—see to it that he eats, and rests. I'll send Gillian by. He can run into the city if you need anything."

With that, he turned and followed Lord Dadius out of the shop.

Krystal ran to Tyr and embraced him tightly. "I'm so sorry," she whispered. "He forbade me from speaking. I was afraid for you."

He pulled her close. "It's all right," he said gently. "We can be together now. And I'll make it my duty to never see you cry again. You're too strong, too smart, and too brave for tears."

She looked up at him and smiled through the last of them. "From now on, they'll only be tears of joy, my love."

CRAFTING LEGENDS

Tyr woke in a daze. He didn't remember lying down. He closed his eyes and tried to focus—he remembered the forge, sticking his hand in, and then the sudden onrush of events: knowledge, language, memories of those long gone. Krystal had led him to the kitchen, and he had tried to eat, but the visions kept flashing back, each threatening to overtake him.

That's all I remember, he thought, opening his eyes again. The room was dimly lit. The sun was probably just cresting the horizon outside. As he sat up, he started in surprise—Krystal was in the bed next to him. He hurried out as quietly and quickly as he could, fumbling around in the half-light, trying to dress without waking her.

"You're cute, you know," came Krystal's sleepy voice. "But you don't need to be so quiet."

She sat up, and Tyr quickly looked away—she was wearing a nightgown.

He heard her get out of bed and come up behind him, wrapping him in a big hug and planting a kiss on his cheek. "You need to take it easy," she cautioned.

"I'll let you get dressed," he stammered, and quickly left the room, his face a bright shade of crimson. He could feel her smirking behind him.

He had the coffee perking and some bacon sizzling in a skillet when she came down into the kitchen, a mischievous look in her eyes.

"I thought you liked me," she said in a mock-wounded tone.

"Of course I do. More than like. You're everything to me," he said simply.

"You have a funny way of showing it. You hardly looked at me this morning."

He cast his eyes downward, embarrassed and confused. "We haven't taken any vows. It wouldn't be proper." He paused, then added, "The last thing I remember was sitting in here with you after that damn forge pricked me. I must have blacked out. If I did or said anything yesterday that was offensive, I am most heartily sorry."

Her expression softened, and she came over and hugged him again. "Oh, my dearest Tyr, I'm sorry—I was just having a bit of fun with you."

She guided him back to his seat. "First, you lit the forge three days ago. You've been drifting in and out of consciousness ever since," she said, pouring two cups of coffee and bringing them to the table. Sitting beside him, she set one down in front of him.

"Three days?" he asked, stunned.

Her face grew serious. "You had us all concerned. You seemed to be in some kind of fever dream. The palace physicians could only advise we keep you comfortable and hope it passed."

He smiled weakly. "I guess you drew the short straw?"

"I volunteered," she said simply. "You had just been granted permission to marry me. Did you think I'd let you go so easily?"

The word startled him. "Marry?" he echoed, as though trying it on for the first time.

She gave him an amused look. "What did you think my grandfather was giving you permission for?"

His smile broadened into a grin. "It's just... the first time I've heard it out loud."

The smell of bacon beginning to burn caught both their attention. He moved to get up, but she placed a firm hand on his shoulder.

"Stay. It's your first day out of bed. I'll make us breakfast. You can tell me what happened when you put your hand into that forge."

She glanced toward the workshop. "The damn thing is still alive. No flame, but it's definitely awake—waiting for you, I think."

He ran his fingers through his beard. "It's hard to put into words. I think it's starting to come back to me, though when I try to remember, it's still a jumble—images, voices, fragments. It felt like I was surrounded by hundreds—maybe thousands—of people, each trying to teach me everything about themselves... all at once."

She eyed him curiously. "And now?"

"They're still there. I can feel them... but in the background. And if I pull on one of them, it begins again."

She looked thoughtful. "Preceptor Winslow came by yesterday. At first, he was more interested in the forge. But when we told him what happened to you, he speculated that when the machine tested your blood and recognized you as a dwarf, it either awakened something deep inside you—or imparted something new into you."

Tyr took a sip of coffee. "I'm a dwarf?" he said, half to himself.

She nodded. "Apparently so," she replied, removing the bacon and setting it aside as she cracked a few eggs into the pan.

"We need our own chickens," she murmured.

He smiled at the comment, then turned serious. "Are you okay with that? I mean… I'm not human." He paused. "I'll have to write my folks. No telling how they'll react."

She came over and sat on his lap.

"I don't know what a dwarf is. I only know what you are—the man that I love. And that is all I need."

After breakfast, Krystal headed back to the estate to check in. Tyr put on his work clothes and headed out to the forge. He approached it like a man might approach an untamed horse. As he drew closer, he could feel—more than hear—a low hum emanating from it. He opened the panel, reached in, grabbed the handle, and pushed the button, expecting another prick. Instead, the machine simply roared to life, as if it knew him now and no longer needed to verify his identity.

As he stood gazing at the strange forge, he felt the memories stirring at the edge of his mind, voices rising softly, nudging for attention. He grabbed a piece of cold stock, then looked again at the forge, took a breath, and opened himself to the voices within—and quickly lost himself in the work.

He had no idea how much time had passed when he heard Gutamino enter the shop with Gillian.

Gutamino nodded in greeting. "I'm glad to see you back among the living—we were worried," he said simply, though Tyr could detect no hint of falsehood.

Tyr nodded his thanks.

"I see you've not only lit the forge but figured out how to operate it," Gutamino said, a note of admiration in his voice. "What's that you're working on?" he asked, gesturing to the piece in Tyr's hand.

Tyr looked down and frowned. "I'm not really sure," he admitted, clearly confused. "I just started working and wasn't really paying attention."

Gillian grinned. "That's sort of how I go through most of my day."

Gutamino, ignoring the remark, leaned in to examine the piece. "Exquisite," he whispered. "If it's just a throwaway piece, might I have it?"

Tyr shrugged. "As far as I'm concerned, all of this is yours—you can have anything you like. Let me just finish polishing it and I'll bring it over."

"No need. I'll send Gillian back shortly with some drawings. They are said to be sketches of weapons left by the dwarves. No one's ever been able to decipher them—but I'm starting to believe you will." He paused. "I'll also send over some rare metal. Use it only on approved projects. But you may set aside enough for four or five personal pieces—call it a bonus."

Tyr set the piece down. "Where are my manners? Could I offer you some tea?" he asked, recalling that Gutamino never drank coffee.

Gutamino shook his head. "No need. I just stopped by to confirm you were up—and working. I'll get those drawings and the stock to you. We'll talk again soon."

He turned to leave. "Come along, my boy—we have much to do."

Gillian gave Tyr a mock-exasperated look, smiled, gave a small wave, and followed after Gutamino.

Before the shop door had fully closed, Tyr was already back at work. It didn't take long to finish the piece. When he was done, he held it up and examined it. It appeared to be an intricate spiral of twisted metal, folding in on itself and back out again. He blinked. It looked delicate, almost fragile—but he knew it was strong. Very strong.

How did I get the metal drawn out that fine? He glanced back at the forge and saw several tools scattered around where he had been working—tools he didn't recognize, tools he knew instinctively had come from within the forge itself.

He rubbed his face. *Am I losing my mind?* But no—there it was again, that subtle stir in the back of his mind, a presence behind his thoughts. Something in his blood had awakened, and with it, the knowledge of his ancestors had come alive within him.

About an hour later, Gillian returned with an armful of rolled-up drawings. He walked to the nearest table and laid them out.

"Here you go—courtesy of Lord Gutamino," he said with a grin. "Just a heads-up—a wagon with the stock should be here in a couple of hours. It's coming from the docks, so it'll take a bit."

Tyr handed him a pint of ale. The day was already hot, and he had tapped a small cask from the Drunken Donkey. Gillian's grin widened as he accepted it.

Tyr unrolled the top drawing. At first, it looked like a chaotic mess of lines and figures scrawled over one another. He felt the presence stir within him again, and this time, instead of surrendering to it, he said in his mind, *One at a time. I want to learn. Teach me.*

A single presence responded—stronger than the others. Tyr opened his mind to it.

As he looked at the drawing, the symbols began to shift and reform before his eyes—then snapped back into chaos. Again and again, they shifted, and Tyr realized it was trying to teach him. So he stopped focusing on the image and instead focused on what was happening inside his mind.

The pattern repeated again and again until, at last, he found himself doing it. His mind adjusted, and when he refocused his eyes, the drawing resolved—readable, clear, legible.

Gillian had been watching silently, refilling his pint and returning just as Tyr nodded, his expression changing.

"Anything?" Gillian asked. "Or just a jumbled mess like it is to me?"

"I can read it," Tyr said, flipping through the rest. "I can read all of them. Do me a favor—go fetch my pad and pencil from the office."

Setting down his ale, Gillian hopped off the table and hurried away.

When he returned, Tyr quickly jotted down notes for each drawing, detailing what they were for. When he was done, he handed the page to Gillian.

"Take this to Gutamino. Let him know this is what these are."

Gillian looked at the page and frowned. "Tyr... this makes no sense. It looks just like the drawings."

Tyr glanced down, and everything still made sense to him—until he realized what Gillian meant. He unfocused his eyes and watched the writing shift into illegibility.

Hm. That's interesting, he murmured. "Give me a moment." He rewrote the list, this time intentionally shaping the letters to be legible to others, and handed the page back. "Here. And you owe me for that second pint you thought I didn't notice you swiped."

Gillian gave a mocking formal bow and laughed as he left.

Tyr turned his attention back to the forge. Like the drawings, this time he insisted the memories teach him, not just show him. The day flew by. The stock arrived and was carefully stacked. Tyr pored over the designs, tested new tools, and let his instincts—no, his heritage— guide him. The voices whispered patiently, urging him to learn the language of his people. He obeyed, feeling each word as though he'd always known it.

Throughout the day, he had flashes—visions—of grand subterranean halls lit by golden lamps, of feasts in forgotten languages, of craftsmanship that defied time. As the sun dipped low and bathed the streets in warm amber, he poured the last pint from his now-empty cask and stepped outside, taking a seat in the cool breeze that rolled in off the ocean.

What did Winslow call it? he thought. *The Shalmarin?*

Muírskeld, his ancestors whispered. He smiled.

As the golden day faded into red and the shadows stretched, he heard soft footfalls approaching. His heart lifted at once.

"I was hoping you'd stop by. May I take you to dinner, my love?" he asked, rising as she drew near.

"Oh my," Krystal teased, eyes twinkling. "Aren't you the forward one. Spend one night with a man and he thinks he can take you to dinner whenever he wants."

Tyr blinked, caught off guard. But she spoke again before he could respond.

"I'd love to go to dinner. And I know just the place." She pulled him close, then wrinkled her nose, spun him around, and gave him a push toward the shop.

"But first," she said, "you need a bath and some clean clothes."

That night, over dinner, Tyr told her everything that had been stirring in his mind since she'd left that morning—how he believed his ancestors were instructing him, or perhaps that he was going mad.

She chose to believe the former.

As they stepped out of the tavern into the night air, they found Lord Jahn waiting for them, flanked by four hired hands.

Krystal's expression turned to ice. "What is the meaning of this?"

"Spurning me at a ball is one thing," Jahn sneered. "But throwing me over for a common craftsman? Our houses were to be joined—an intelligent political union. And instead, you're running around with this—this trash from the country."

Tyr could see Krystal's anger rising. Jahn was about to get an earful—but he kept going.

"I am not without mercy," he said, puffing up his chest. "Break it off with this peasant. Tell your grandfather you've reconsidered and wish to be joined to me after all. Do that... and I'll let him live."

"How dare you threaten anyone," Krystal said, her voice cool, calm—too calm. Tyr watched as the four thugs stepped to either side, starting to circle. He felt his ancestors stir. They were... eager.

"Jahn," Tyr said evenly, "walk away."

"That's Lord Jahn to you, peasant. I should have you flogged for your insolence." He clenched his fists, his face reddening. "Enough! I gave you a chance. Kill the blacksmith. Take the girl back to my father's estate."

Krystal's eyes narrowed. Before Tyr could respond, everything exploded into motion.

All four thugs rushed him—thankfully leaving Krystal alone. Jahn turned to leave, but Krystal sprang like a lioness, drawing a knife from somewhere beneath her cloak.

Tyr didn't think. He moved, letting ancestral instincts take over.

The first thug came in fast, knife raised—but Tyr leveled him with a single punch to the skull. As he fell, Tyr grabbed the second by the collar and hurled him into the third, sending both sprawling. The fourth was already on him, knife flashing. Tyr barely dodged the blade and countered with a crushing blow to the back of the man's head. The thug collapsed like a sack of grain.

The two who'd been thrown to the ground scrambled to their feet—took one look at Tyr—and fled into the night.

Tyr turned to Jahn and Krystal.

Jahn was on his knees, whimpering, with Krystal holding a blade to his throat.

"I swear, I swear—please let me live!" Jahn whimpered. Krystal withdrew the knife, and with one final glare at Tyr, Jahn scrambled to his feet and ran off down the street.

"You really know how to show a girl a good time," she said with a laugh.

Tyr smiled—she hadn't been afraid in the least. "I think I'll walk you home tonight," he said.

She wrapped her arms around his and laid her head on his shoulder. "What did you say to him?"

She just grinned. "I merely explained how I felt about him—and what would happen if anything ever happened to you. I think he understood."

The walk back to the estate was quiet. If it hadn't been for Jahn's ambush, the night would've been perfect. After Tyr kissed her goodnight and the door closed behind her, he turned to leave.

"Master Ranfel," came a voice behind him.

Tyr turned to see one of the butlers standing on the landing.

"Master Ranfel, Lord Dadius would like a word with you," the man said. Though phrased as an invitation, it was clear from his tone that it was anything but optional.

Tyr nodded. "Of course." *Is this more of Jahn's mischief?* he wondered.

The butler led him to a quiet sitting room where Lord Dadius lounged in his night robes, two drinks beside him and the note Tyr had sent to Gutamino in his hands. He dismissed the butler with a nod and motioned to a chair across from him.

"Lord Dadius," Tyr said as he sat.

The old man smiled. "You're almost family, Tyr. Just call me Dadius." He set the note down and handed Tyr one of the drinks. When Tyr took it, Dadius raised his own glass.

"To Krystal."

Tyr raised his glass and echoed, "To Krystal." They both drank. Tyr winced—the whiskey burned going down, but it was smoother and stronger than any he'd tasted.

"What do you know of me, Tyr?" Dadius asked.

Tyr thought for a moment. "Very little, actually. I know you, Gutamino, and Cygnus serve the ancient enemy. Why you would do such a thing is beyond me."

"Doesn't that make me your enemy, then?" Dadius asked calmly.

"Maybe. But you've done nothing to harm me or anyone I care about. In fact, quite the opposite—you've helped both Al and me when we needed it. You may yet be an enemy, but I'd need proof before I'd accept it."

"Fairly said," Dadius replied. "It's time you learned a few truths about me. You are on the verge of doing something not seen in these lands for over five centuries, and I want you to know what you're doing—and why."

"I'd appreciate that," Tyr said carefully.

"You also need to know something about Krystal before you marry her. I love her too dearly to let you wed without knowing... and the knowing may change everything."

Tyr looked confused—and angry—but before he could speak, Dadius raised a finger.

"Please. Indulge me a few minutes, and all will be explained."

He took another sip of his drink, then spoke—gazing into the hearth rather than at Tyr.

"I am Lord Dadius of the Blackthorne, Lord Commander of the Dokkalfar's forces, first of the Alfarbani... and kinslayer."

Tyr froze.

"I should explain," Dadius continued. "I was born Darius Czarnorn almost fifteen hundred years ago. I have been—and still am—a loyal servant of the Dokkalfar. I am the first, and strongest, of the Alfarbani ever created. I assumed command of his armies almost immediately. I have waged war on every known continent. And I, along with the Alkeir Cygnus—who is even older than I—am actively working to break the seals that bind our master."

He paused to drink.

"Five hundred years ago, the Dokkalfar sought to sever an unnatural bond he had made with a darker power. No normal method could do it. So, with the help of the dwarves and the Odio, we devised a plan. The Dokkalfar would submit to capture and imprisonment. He ordered his armies to disband. The dwarves took six Odio volunteers and created a prison of living stone to contain him.

"We—his commanders—believed the seals would degrade with time. But they didn't. We were betrayed. The dwarves went into hiding, and the Odio scattered the seals. So we waited. We searched.

And when we found them, we acted. Every time we locate a seal we have destroyed it."

He stopped, lost in thought.

"You said... kinslayer?" Tyr asked, his voice barely above a whisper.

Dadius nodded solemnly. "I did. The Dokkalfar's final command to me before his imprisonment was to kill all Alfarbani created after me. Even he didn't fully trust us. He feared what we might become in his absence. And so... I obeyed. I slaughtered them. My comrades. My brothers."

Tyr sat still for a long moment, then asked, "Why are you telling me this?"

Dadius looked directly at him, the firelight catching the years in his eyes.

"Because you're going to marry Krystal—and Krystal is my granddaughter. Just like Al is my grandson. And just like Al, she has the potential to unlock her Alfarbani heritage."

Tyr's mind raced. *Dadius is Al's grandfather?* Then—"Wait, you were planning on marrying them to each other?"

Dadius cut him off. "Yes. That was the original plan—before Al somehow managed to unlock his blood, which changed everything. But it had been my hope that, since I could sense the blood within both of them—the first two descendants in whom I ever noticed it— their union might produce a true Alfarbani."

"And you want me to make weapons for the Dokkalfar?" Tyr asked, his voice thick with disgust.

"No," Dadius replied simply. "You are but one smith. And I only have a limited amount of dwarven stock. Not nearly enough to forge weapons for an army—but enough to make a few special gifts for nobles here in the West."

"These won't be sent to him?" Tyr asked, still suspicious.

"They will not." Dadius picked up the notes Tyr had sent to Gutamino. "I've jotted down which of these I'd like you to make, and how many of each. And I have a special request."

Tyr glanced over the list. Dadius had only selected three of the seven items—and the simplest among them. He raised an eyebrow. "A request?"

"Albert has passed through a darkness I cannot see," Dadius said, his voice low and serious. "And from what I've read, he's come out of it as something... new. He has many battles ahead—including, potentially, Cygnus. And if he dares, even the Dokkalfar. But the sword I sent him is shattered and lost, yet somehow he still draws power without it." He shook his head, puzzled. "Regardless, Al is going to need a weapon unlike any other. I'm asking you to make it."

Al, what have you been up to? Tyr thought. "How will I get it to him?"

"If he wins the coming battle," Dadius said with quiet certainty, "I think he'll be here before too much longer."

Tyr opened his mouth to reply when the door creaked open and the butler stepped inside.

"My apologies, my Lord," the butler said with a small bow. "But your presence is requested."

"Of course." Dadius finished his drink and stood. "We'll speak again. In the meantime, consider my words."

With that, he turned and exited the study, leaving Tyr alone in the flickering light.

Tyr raised his glass in a silent toast to no one, drained it, and left the estate—his thoughts heavy with destiny and the forge yet to come.

RETURN TO WHITTLE

Steven, Mathers, and Riff arrived at the gates of Whittle around mid-morning. As before, the gates were closed, but this time the guards seemed to be expecting them. As they approached, the large gate swung open.

Once inside, a guard stepped forward. "Welcome back, sir. The magistrate has been eagerly awaiting your return."

Steven gave him a forced smile. "Then I will head there directly."

The guard nodded, clearly relieved. Once they were out of earshot, Steven said to his men, "Head to The Plow and Lantern. Get us a room and let them know we'll be staying a while—they should open us a tab. If you see Uso or one of his men, let them know we're back, though I'd be surprised if he didn't already know."

Mathers nodded, and he and Riff peeled off toward the residential district.

Steven dismounted in front of the Magister's building. *Fox or hound?* he asked himself. *Fpx. Definitely a Fox. Though in this case, the fox thinks he's the hound.*

He steadied himself. *Never let them get under your skin,* Tenebris had taught him. *The moment you do, they win.*

Steven made his way to the Magister's office and waited while the attendant announced him. When he was admitted, he found both Magister Cooper and Commander Wallace of the local militia already seated. Steven put on his broadest smile.

"Gentlemen. As promised—I have returned."

The commander eyed him. "I thought you said you'd return at the head of a legion?"

"Do you want me to march them through the streets, or let them continue hunting down and killing the enemy?" Steven replied, injecting just enough sarcasm to make his point, though he continued to smile. "I have a legion, Commander. I rode ahead to prepare for their arrival. We're going to establish a forward post here—from the Northern Pass to the southern mountains—securing everything behind us before continuing west."

The commander and Magister exchanged a look. Then the commander nodded solemnly. "Then you have my apologies. I admit I was skeptical... feared the worst."

"I, for one, never doubted you," said Magister Cooper. "You have our undying thanks. The people will rejoice that trade can resume."

Steven raised a hand. "Not so fast. I've cleared the land from the eastern border to Whittle—but everything west of here is still under invasion. The Northern Pass remains unsecured. My legion is behind me, making their way forward."

The Magister's smile faltered.

"However," Steven continued smoothly, "once the pass is secured, I do believe limited trade can resume. But it must be regulated. I'll station troops to hold the pass, but only traders with proper permits should be allowed to enter or exit. Otherwise, we risk enemy infiltration."

"And who will issue these permits?" the commander asked, tone wary.

"I think that's best left to the Magister and his militia," Steven said innocently. "As is the collection of any associated taxes or fees."

The commander and the Magister exchanged a knowing look— and the foxes had taken the bait.

"Yes, yes," said the Magister. "It is only right that we do our part in securing the homeland."

Steven gave them a brief rundown of the battles to the east, embellishing just enough to keep them captivated. When he finished, he added, "There's one more matter. The Order has begun constructing fortified compounds across Harding to ensure lasting security. I intend to do the same outside Whittle. I'll be seizing the land of a known traitor for its construction. We'll need laborers—able-bodied men who will be compensated. And Whittle will benefit greatly from its presence... if you know what I mean."

"What do you need from us?" asked the Magister eagerly.

"Nothing yet. First, I need to finish clearing out the enemy. Once that's done, I'll send my adjutant to your offices with the details. You can handle it from there."

He turned to the commander. "Commander, if it's all right with you, I may have one of my men stop by to discuss the possible expansion of the local militia—under your command, of course."

"Expansion?" the commander echoed, confused.

"Of course. The Order can only do so much, and given the new reality in which we find ourselves, I would think an expanded militia—with increased authority—might be something to consider."

Steven watched as Wallace's eyes glazed with imagination. After a moment, the commander nodded. "Yes, of course. We'll be happy to assist in any way we can."

Steven smiled. "Excellent." *Shame you probably won't live long once we're done.* "I look forward to seeing it grow." He shook both men's hands. "If you'll excuse me—it's been a long, brutal road, and I could use a hot meal and a cold ale."

It wasn't long before Steven found his way to The Plow and Lantern, where Mathers and Riff were already seated.

Mathers slid a pint across the table. "How did it go?"

Steven took a long drink before answering. "Good. Very good. I'll need you to pay Commander Wallace a visit."

Mathers raised an eyebrow, intrigued.

Steven smirked. "Not like that. Not yet, at any rate. I've got an idea—and I think he might be key to achieving it. I'll give you the details once I figure them out myself."

Mathers leaned back in his chair, disappointed. "Shame," was all he said.

The next morning, Steven ate breakfast alone in the common room. As he finished a slice of bread, a robed figure slid into the seat across from him. He looked up, ready to chastise whoever dared interrupt him—until he saw the familiar sunken eyes.

Steven sighed. "Uso."

"I expected to see you last night," Steven said, returning to his porridge.

"I was otherwise detained," Uso replied, pausing as the server placed a hot cup of coffee before him. "We don't have coffee in the East. I'm going to miss it when I return home."

Steven said nothing. *East? So, unlike the ogres, he did come with Cygnus.*

"The Master is pleased with your progress," Uso said, pushing a leather bag across the table.

Steven picked it up—hefted it. Heavy. *Cygnus doesn't pay cheap.* He tucked it away. "Any news worth knowing?"

Uso leaned back, lowered his hood, and sipped his coffee. "It seems your friend is… formidable. The Master sent one of his Seers to capture, delay, or kill him at the western pass. It appears your friend was not amused. There's nothing left of the Seer or his forces."

"Seer?" Steven asked.

Uso set his cup down. "A commander—like me—who, also like me, has been gifted with certain…" He searched for the right word. "Tools. Think of your friend's sword—like that, but not a weapon. Each artifact has different abilities."

"So he was powerful?" Steven asked.

Uso nodded. "Very. He had a full regiment—ogres, goblins, Klav. And now?" He spread his hands. "Gone. Like they never existed."

Steven rolled his eyes and pushed the empty bowl away. "Obviously your scouts are exaggerating. I don't doubt Al and his forces beat this 'Seer' and his goons—but that's battlefield luck, nothing more."

Uso shook his head. "No. My scouts watched. Al sent a small group in first—they were quickly killed. Then Al entered alone. Before his reinforcements arrived, the fog lifted, and the Seer's entire force was gone. He did it alone."

He took another sip of coffee.

"His forces are now gathering at the western pass. Soon they'll march on Torringburgh. After that… it becomes difficult to see."

"See?" Steven asked with a smirk. "Do you claim to be a Seer as well?"

Uso gave a dry chuckle. "You speak of what you do not understand. Yes, I hold the rank of Seer—but no, it doesn't mean I can predict the future, fool. It simply means I, too, possess an artifact of the Old Empire."

He composed himself and continued. "Did you not receive the game I sent you?"

"*Foxes and Hounds*. Yes, I did. And thank you—it's proved… useful."

"Good. So you are learning from it, as I had hoped," Uso said, satisfied. "Keep at it. See everything through that lens. If you do, you'll begin to anticipate your opponent's next move with some certainty. Your friend behaves like a fox—though at times he feints as if he's a hound. That makes his movements difficult to predict. In this instance, fox or hound, his next logical move is toward the capital. After that… it depends. We must wait for him to make the next move."

"He's a fox," Steven replied. "And my hounds will close in and put an end to him once and for all."

Uso gave him a measured look. "Don't tie yourself too tightly to one side or the other in the game. There are times when you must be brutal like the hounds, and times when you must be clever like the fox. Your friend knows this—perhaps not consciously, but he knows."

Steven let out a dismissive huff. "If Al is heading to the capital, then I need to head there as well. If he turns east, it could unravel all our plans."

Uso rubbed his chin in thought. "I'll confer with the Master. In the meantime, keep your troops local and let them rest. It will go a long way toward maintaining their trust in you." He glanced around the tavern. "The morning crowd is coming in. Best I make myself scarce. I'll be here most nights if you need to find me."

He drained his cup, placed a few coins on the table, and pulled his hood low as he slipped out of the tavern.

Once alone, Steven opened the letter from Cygnus:

Commander Waistwain,

I have been observing your progress with increasing satisfaction. Your efficiency speaks well of you—though I suspect much of it is owed to the remarkable woman at your side. She is a rare find. Dangerous, yes—but useful. Keep her close, but never forget what she is. Even a gilded serpent bears fangs.

The fortifications rising across Harding in the name of the Odio are a welcome development. Though they wear another banner for now, we both know who will inherit their strength when the dust settles. Maintain the illusion; let them believe it is theirs. In time, all foundations laid in order shall serve my design.

Ensure that Uso remains informed of each site's progress. He will begin seeding the garrisons with forces loyal to our greater cause—quietly, efficiently.

As for your old friend—if fortune favors us, he is already in chains or ash. If not, we may need a more decisive stroke. Should you conceive of any method by which to neutralize him—political, martial, or otherwise—send it through Uso. I am open to innovation.

Hold your position at Whittle. Rest your troops. Prepare the ground. Instructions will follow.

—Lord Trigon

Steven folded the letter and tucked it away.

How many spies does he have in my camp? Who can I trust?

Just then, Mathers and Riff slid into the booth beside him.

"You're up early," Mathers said, motioning for the barmaid. "I figured after a real bed you'd sleep till dinner."

Steven forced a smile. "Couldn't sleep."

"You learn something?" Mathers asked quietly, glancing around.

Steven shook his head. "No." He ran a hand over his face, then smirked. "Don't mind me. We're playing a dangerous game in a big town full of factions. I just don't know who I can trust. Yet."

Mathers nodded knowingly. "Aye. The game is dangerous and dark." He grinned. "But seriously—would either of us want it any other way?"

Steven returned the grin. "No. Probably not."

His eyes drifted around the tavern, remembering the good times he, Al, and Tyr had shared here. *That's the real problem*, he thought. *I'm not sure I trust myself to stay the course. These memories—they threaten to swallow me whole.*

He looked at Mathers and the ever-quiet Riff. "Keep a low profile. You've got the day to yourselves. I'm going for a walk—to clear my head."

Outside, the skies were overcast. Steven glanced upward, shrugged, and pulled his cloak tighter. He wasn't planning to go far, and if it started to pour, there were enough shops he could duck into for something hot while he waited out the rain.

He had just started walking—nowhere in particular—wandering down streets, side streets, and more side streets, lost in thought. A sudden flash of lightning and an immediate crack of thunder snapped him back to reality. The sky unleashed a torrent of rain.

Looking around, Steven realized he had no idea where he was— somewhere in the merchant district, he guessed. He spotted a small shop with its door open and quickly ducked inside.

Shaking the rain from his cloak, he looked around. The interior was dimly lit by a few small lanterns hanging from the ceiling, casting long shadows across shelves that formed narrow aisles from front to back. The shelves were crammed with herbs, jars, and odd contraptions he couldn't immediately identify.

"Ah, a customer come in from the rain," came an elderly woman's voice from somewhere within. "What might you be looking for?"

Steven felt like a child caught somewhere he wasn't supposed to be. "Nothing. I'm sorry—I just came in to avoid the rain," he replied quickly. As if in answer, another flash of lightning followed by a thunderclap rattled the small building.

The old woman smiled warmly. "It's going to blow for a bit. Come in, then. Have a seat. I haven't seen you before—humor an old woman and sit for a spell."

He glanced back at the door. The rain was now coming down in sheets. With a resigned sigh, he slipped off his drenched cloak and made his way toward the back of the shop.

The woman was already pouring two cups of tea and had arranged a few scones and some jam on a small table. She gestured for him to sit and help himself while she brought over the steaming mugs.

Once seated across from her, she took a good, long look at him. "Do you know who I am?" she asked.

Steven shook his head. "No. Should I?"

She grinned. "Better than you know yourself, I think."

Steven leaned back slightly, raising an eyebrow. Dunking a scone into his tea, he said lightly, "You're mad, aren't you?"

She laughed. "Many have said so—and other things not quite so kind," she added with a shrug. Then her voice grew softer, more thoughtful. "I see a darkness in you. You walk a dangerous path… but you walk it willingly, with eyes wide open. That's what's interesting."

The smile froze on Steven's face. Another rumble of thunder echoed outside.

"I'm sure I don't know what you're talking about," he said evenly, though his mind was racing. *Who is she? What does she know? Or is she just a madwoman playing at games?*

"How would you know me?" he asked.

She smiled again, calmly spreading jelly on a scone. "Nothing mystical, if that's what you're thinking."

"Then how else could you know me?" he asked, a touch of sarcasm in his voice.

"By your arrogance, of course," she replied without hesitation.

His eyes narrowed. That struck a nerve.

"Everyone's heard the story of the tailor who betrayed his friend to join the Odio," she said.

Steven's hand tightened into a fist. His mind raced with a thousand possible responses.

"Relax, young Steven. I'm not here to judge," she said gently. "All things happen for a reason. And don't worry—while everyone around here knows the story, few are clever enough to connect it to you. Most are just grateful that you're bringing them hope."

Steven's tension eased slightly. That made sense. Nothing ever happened around here—any news would be passed around like gossip. He hadn't expected to be the subject of any of it.

Outside, the rain continued to pound the streets in a steady roar.

"While we wait," the woman said, "would you like me to read you?"

He gave her a skeptical look. "Read me?"

"It won't hurt, and it'll cost you nothing."

"Then why bother?"

"I'm old. It's raining. And I'm bored. Do I need a better reason?"

Steven exhaled a dry laugh. "Do what you will. As soon as the rain lets up, I'll be gone anyway."

She reached across the table and took his hands in hers, closing her eyes. A sudden gust of wind blew through the doorway, slamming the door shut with a heavy thud and briefly dimming the lanterns.

Then her grip tightened.

She opened her eyes—sharp and luminous—and in a voice that cut through the room with unsettling clarity, she said:

"The wind carries ash, Commander, and I smell burnt souls on your breath.

You walk with iron in your heart... but shadow clings to your heels.

You don't know what you are, do you? Fox or hound? Predator or prey?

That's the trouble with games like these—we all think we know our role... until the board shifts beneath our feet.

Three times the thread of your fate will fray—three plays before the match ends. Not tests of strength, but of self.

The first will come wrapped in silk and screams. A move of silence. One command, and the prey is taken.

You will tell yourself you were the hound—doing what must be done. But if that is true, the scent you follow is blood. And it will be your own.

The second will be blood and fire on cold stone. The fox will run—cornered, outnumbered, but clever still.

A war not yours will find you. And in that moment, you will choose: join the chase, or break the game.

One path leads to ruin. The other—to something far more dangerous: redemption.

The third will burn. The board will collapse. The pieces will lie shattered, and only one move will remain.

You may win the war… or lose the game to save the fox. But only one of you will walk away.

These are not choices of victory, Steven of Southold. They are choices of becoming.

You are not lost—yet. But the road you ride is steep, and the horses of the dead ride close behind."

Her grip weakened, and she released his hands, slumping back in her chair—physically and mentally spent.

Steven pulled his hands back slowly, his expression dark and unreadable. Her words had cut deep—far deeper than he expected. He stood in silence, uncertain of what to do or say.

"You should go, young master," she said softly, her voice barely above a whisper. "The storm has passed."

Without a word, Steven turned and made his way toward the front of the shop. He opened the door.

The rain had stopped. The clouds had broken, and sunlight spilled across the wet cobblestones. He turned back, ready to make a sarcastic remark—

But the building was empty.

Completely empty.

No shelves. No lanterns. No old woman. Just dust, silence, and shadows.

Steven backed out slowly, his heart pounding, and hurried through the quiet streets toward the tavern.

HOMECOMING

Steven stayed close to the inn for the next few days, waiting until word came that his cohort was approaching. As soon as he received it, he wasted no time riding out to meet them. He told Mathers and Riff to remain in town—Mathers had been making steady progress ingratiating himself with Commander Wallace, and quiet, observant Riff was often overlooked but noticed everything that went on around him.

He arrived as the campsite was being pitched, left his mount with one of the privates, and made his way through the growing bustle in search of Tenebris. He found her sitting off to one side, watching the camp come together. The moment she saw him, a wide grin spread across her face—one that matched his own.

He wanted to embrace her, but a public show of affection would raise eyebrows. Instead, he sat beside her and placed a hand over hers. "Anything interesting on your way here?" he asked.

She gripped his fingers warmly but shook her head. "No, just more of the same. Our troops hardly engage anymore. They know now to give a little chase, then let the enemy go."

"You look bored," he said with a chuckle.

She shrugged. "Life in the field. I find my fun where I can, but with you in the city and no one stepping out of line, it's been a dull ride."

"I'm here now. I've got a room at an inn in town—if you'd like to stay there tonight."

She gave him a mischievous, sidelong glance. "Oh, the things we could get up to," she cooed, tightening her grip on his hand.

"Good. I prefer a bed to a camp roll," he said, rising. "Let me tend to a few mundane matters, and then we can head into town."

He paused and pulled a small pouch of coins from his belt, handing it to her.

"What's this?" she asked.

"A thank-you from Cygnus. I figured you earned at least half of it."

She weighed the pouch in her hand, smiled, and tucked it away. "Sweet."

He turned to go when she quietly said, "Steven."

He stopped and leaned in. "What is it, my dear?" he whispered.

"I want to hurt someone. Anyone. Really hurt them." She hesitated. "Is that wrong? Is there something wrong with me?"

It was the first time he had seen her vulnerable. He took both her hands in his.

"Look at me," he said gently. When she met his gaze, he continued, "There is nothing wrong with you. In my eyes, you are perfection itself. Each of us has a calling. Ours is to usher in change—painful, violent, and always resisted. Your gifts, even if they run red with innocent blood, are necessary to bring that change to this ungrateful land."

Her wicked smile returned, the moment of vulnerability gone—revealed for the ruse it had been. "This is why I find you so irresistible. You always know just what to say to a girl."

A few days later, his strange encounter with the old woman had faded to the back of his mind, dismissed as an overactive imagination. He rode west with Tenebris, Mathers, Riff, and fifty soldiers from his cohort, headed for Southold.

The knots in his stomach began tightening as they turned the final bend in the road. The village was close now. Reports had said it had been hit several times by the Klav—mostly the outlying farms.

As the village came into view, the knots twisted into something darker. He forced the grimace from his face. The villagers stood on their porches, watching. Waiting. No cheers. No fanfare for a returning son.

Steven stopped his horse in the center of the village and scanned the familiar faces. He knew them all. His eyes lingered on his parents, then Tyr's, then finally on Al's mother and three of his siblings. Al's father and Marie were nowhere to be seen.

Plastering a smile on his face, he called out in a loud, clear voice: "Southold. You know me. I am one of your own—born and raised. I have heard of Harding's plight and have led a legion of the finest soldiers in the Odio Magisterium. We have freed the lands to the east and are now clearing this region and its surrounds."

No one responded. They only stared.

The knots turned to bile. Rage threatened to bubble up. He glanced at Tenebris—and steadied himself.

"I would speak with the village elders," he said. This time, his tone made it clear: it was not a request.

He and Tenebris dismounted and walked toward a small group of elderly farmers—elders he'd known since childhood.

He paused as he passed Tyr's parents. "I heard what happened in Morcaster. You have my deepest condolences," he said quietly.

The two exchanged glances, and then Tyr's mother replied, "You haven't heard? No, how should you. Tyr is alive and well. He left before the incident and is down in York, finishing his time as a journeyman."

Steven paused. *Alive? How did he escape Morcaster's fate?* Was it luck—or was he involved, along with Al? He smiled. "This is wonderful news. No, I had not heard it before now. Please send my regards when next you speak with him."

He turned and walked past the elders toward the small building used for formal village meetings. The elders remained standing in the street. He stopped and turned to them—dropping all pretense.

"This is not a request. You will meet with me, or there will be new elders," he said.

At his words, the fifty soldiers accompanying him drew their swords in unison. The villagers scattered, retreating into homes and shops in fear.

The chief elder—Wiggins, Steven recalled—raised a hand. "Alright, young Waistwain. Alright. We will hear you."

Once inside, Steven didn't sit. "I can see the village has no love for me. I don't care. I've walked this path with open eyes. And you're lucky that I did—otherwise this land would still be crawling with beasts."

The elders said nothing, only listened.

"Fine. This is what I need from Southold: I need every homestead fortified. Anyone who can hold a tool or weapon should be securing their property. Any homestead not fortified will be treated as enemy-held and burned. The beasts love to hide in abandoned homes. We'll be sweeping the area in the coming days. Keep everyone out of our way and off the roads."

The elders exchanged hushed words until Wiggins spoke up. "Not everyone can defend their homes," he said.

"It's not negotiable," Steven replied flatly. "If they can't, their homes will burn—and they'll rebuild. That's the cost of safety."

He turned to leave—today's meeting had been for show, nothing more.

"Before I go," he added, "I saw Mrs. Ornfel and some of her children, but I didn't see her Pavil or Marie?"

Elder Wiggins's face darkened. "Marie was one of the first killed. Pavil led a group of villagers out to hunt them down and kill them. They never returned. A few days later, a search party went out—found only body parts and bloodied cloth."

Steven nodded. "Understood. Leave the beasts to me. We'll see this threat dealt with. You'll be able to return to something resembling your former lives soon."

He and Tenebris exited the elder house. Outside the village, their soldiers had established a small field camp.

That evening, alone together in their tent, Steven turned to Tenebris with a wicked gleam in his eyes.

She noticed immediately. "What?" she asked, curiosity piqued.

"You said you've been bored lately," he said.

She sat up, suddenly attentive. "Oh, so very bored," she cooed.

He nodded. "I have a mission for you. Tomorrow, when we leave, I'll escort you to the Ornfel farm—Al's family homestead. His mother and siblings, along with some ranch hands, will be going there to fortify the place."

He looked her dead in the eyes.

"I want them all dead. His mother, his siblings. All of them."

She cuddled close, inhaling the scent of his hair, her breath hot against his cheek. "Can I do it myself?" she whispered.

"No," he said. "Not his family. The Klav will kill them. I'll make sure a pack is waiting for you—along with a few goblin drivers. But everyone else there? They're yours. Do what you like. Just leave enough of the family for them to be identified."

Her voice dropped to a sensual whisper. "So… I can do anything I want with them, short of killing them?"

He nodded. "Consider it my gift to you. A little fun during these long days in the field."

She pushed him back and began undressing him. No more words were needed.

Two days later, Steven walked the town walls, looking west over the fields—toward Southold.

Tenebris had slipped out the night before.

Uso had promised that a pack of Klav and a few goblin handlers would be waiting for her near the Ornfel farmstead.

I'm sorry, Al. But you deserve this.

My own parents didn't cheer my return. Why is that, Al? Because of you. You—exiled as a traitor, wanted by the Odio for murder—and still, they and the village choose you over me. Well, damn you. You killed my parents' love for me. So now, the forces at play will take those you love from you.

This won't make us even, Al. Far from it. And what of Tyr? Is he in on this too? I'll spare his parents—for now. There's still a chance you played him for the fool, just like you played me. If not, then in time, we'll find a suitable reward for them as well.

"Morning, Commander," came a gruff but kindly voice.

Steven looked up to see Commander Wallace standing behind him. He gave a small nod in acknowledgment.

"Any sign of the enemy?" Wallace asked.

"No," Steven replied. "We've pushed them westward. Today, my forces are moving north to retake the pass. After that, we'll begin sweeping past the outlying villages in the coming days."

Wallace nodded his approval. "Good news indeed," he said, his voice growing serious. "And none too soon. The harvest's going to be thin this year, but thankfully, the beasts left most of the crops alone. We should have enough for ourselves, and still send out some shipments."

Steven's gaze turned cold. "Remember—no one travels to the pass without a permit. Anyone caught crossing will be imprisoned. Their goods will be confiscated."

The commander nodded again. "We've already established a department to issue the permits and collect the fees," he said, lowering his voice. "Confiscated goods have markets too."

Steven gave him a knowing look. "Then I trust you'll make sure they find their way to the right places. Just ensure the Order gets its fair share."

Wallace bowed slightly in agreement and continued his patrol along the wall. Steven turned and made his way back to the Plow and

Lantern. He found Mathers and Riff in a side room the inn had given them, to use as a makeshift office.

Mathers rolled his eyes as Steven entered. "I have many talents. Okay, maybe not many—but the few I have, I'm very good at." He gestured toward the papers on the table. "Paperwork isn't one of them."

Steven chuckled. "Understood. Send a runner to Major Polix. Have him send over one of his scribes—someone discreet."

Mathers let out a theatrical sigh of relief. "Thank you, sir."

"I have another job for you anyway," Steven added.

Both Mathers and Riff paused what they were doing and looked up.

"You remember where the Ornfel farm is?"

"Yes, sir."

"Good. I want you both to ride to Southold in the morning. Gather a group of villagers—tell them you're going to burn any unmanned farmsteads and that you want locals with you. That way, if someone doesn't answer to a stranger, maybe they will to a neighbor. Make sure you get to the Ornfel farm tomorrow. But don't go there first—hit at least two others first to make it believable."

Mathers and Riff nodded.

"How many men should we take?" Mathers asked.

Steven shrugged. "Enough to look official."

Mathers stood. "We'll leave at first light. I'll only take a handful of men—and all mounted. We'll be able move fast."

"You should find me here when you return," Steven said. Then his voice dropped. "And Mathers—make sure that farm is burned to the ground. Understood?"

"Yes, sir."

That night, Steven sat alone in the common room, nursing an ale. Uso was off talking with one of his contacts. A handful of soldiers drifted in and out as the evening wore on.

Tonight ends it, Steven thought. *Al's ties to Harding—burned away, just like that farm will be.*

His fingers twitched.

Why do you force my hand, Al? Why?

He took a long sip, leaned back in his chair, and closed his eyes.

Then a voice—clear as a bell, but soft as a whisper—spoke in his mind.

"So… you chose the leash. The hunt begins, and the first blood is yours."

A chill crept down his spine, despite the warmth of the tavern.

For just a moment, he smelled smoke—sweet, like blossoms burned in spring—and heard the sound of a woman's soul breaking, one scream at a time, as everything she loved was devoured before her eyes.

His eyes shot open, and he looked around, half-expecting to see Talia standing beside him. But he was alone at the table, while the common room pulsed with laughter and song. He took another sip of ale, but in his mouth it tasted like smoke and blood. He glanced down—just for a moment, the contents appeared thick and crimson. He blinked. It was amber once more, the familiar hue of ale. He took another cautious sip. This time, it tasted only of honey and barley.

He exhaled deeply.

So. It's done, he thought.

He called the barmaid over and handed her two silver coins. "Bring me something stronger," he said, "and make sure I end up in my room tonight."

In the blink of an eye, the coins vanished into her pocket, and she gave him a wink.

He woke with a pounding headache, Tenebris curled beside him. She must have returned sometime in the dead of night—or very early that morning. Groggy, he got up, dressed, and was about to head down for coffee when he heard her voice, low and drowsy:

"Bring me a cup when you come back, my love."

He smiled. She always found a way to make him smile.

"Of course, my dear."

"And bacon. Lots of bacon," she added.

Twenty minutes later, he returned with a tray—coffee, eggs, sausages, toasted bread with jam, and more bacon than one person could reasonably eat. He set it down at the small table, and the two of them dug in without ceremony.

"Any problems last night?" he asked between bites.

She set down her fork, her eyes glowing with twisted satisfaction. "Steven, it was glorious." She closed her eyes, savoring the memory. "May I tell it?"

He shrugged, still chewing.

"I had to be careful," she began, her voice lilting with cruel delight. "The youngest two were only five or six—probably couldn't take too much pain—but oh, how they screamed. As did his brother. If I thought he'd have survived the process I would have skinned him alive, in front of the mother... but alas, he was too young and frail. Still, the screams—oh, Steven, their screams were like nightingales to my ears."

She sighed dreamily, then continued.

"The mother... she broke. I did nothing more to her than make her watch. That was enough. Nothing I could've done to her would compare to the pain of watching her children writhe, slowly losing hope. She begged me to kill her. Begged. But I said no. No—she would live long enough to see them torn apart. The Klav feasted while she screamed. Faces left intact, as you requested."

Tenebris took his hand, smiling with radiant, monstrous joy. "Then, finally, I let them tear her to shreds. It was perfect. If only you could've been there."

...and the first blood is yours, whispered the memory.

My hand was forced, Steven thought. *What was done is horrible—but justified.*

"So," she asked, her tone returning to normal, "what's next?"

He smiled faintly. "I take it your boredom is... sated?"

Her grin was wide, her eyes gleaming. "Oh yes. I can't do that too often—I might lose myself entirely." She chuckled, but then her tone turned serious. "Thank you for humoring me. I know what I've done. I must take joy in it—not because I want to, but because it's what I'm called to do. If I don't... if I let kindness grow in me, I might hesitate. And that hesitation could get one or both of us killed. So I must kill the kindness in me first. There's room for only one love in my heart— and it's you."

Steven nodded. "I understand. I walk a similar path—different means, same end. And what I do, I do so we can achieve our goals. Because I, too, only have room for one love."

They shared a rare, quiet moment. No schemes. No blood. Just a mutual, dangerous affection.

Then Steven added, "As for what's next—we wait. The northern pass should be under our control soon. Mathers will come across the remains of the Ornfel family later today. He'll report back tomorrow. The day after, we return to Southold."

He looked out the window toward the horizon.

"We'll tell them we hunted down and slaughtered every last beast. And in honor of the Ornfels, we'll raise a fortified compound on the ashes of their farm—to protect the village and the town."

THE JOURNEY WEST

Steven and Tenebris sat leisurely in the Magister's office with both Cooper and Wallace. They laughed, shared stories, and played the part of affable guests. But if the magister and commander had been paying closer attention, they might have noticed that neither Steven nor Tenebris showed even a flicker of true mirth. It was all a performance—to keep their hosts at ease while they bided their time.

"I am pleased to say that the permit office is open and already quite busy," said the magister excitedly.

"No pushback on the permit fees?" Steven asked, watching the two men carefully, weighing their usefulness.

Cooper shrugged. "Minor complaints, but nothing of concern. Most folks are just happy the trade routes are opening again, even in a limited capacity. They're more than willing to pay to keep them that way," he added with a grin.

Wallace lowered his voice and leaned in slightly. "It would be a shame if—every so often—a random attack happened along the route. If it did, the magister could levy a tax to fund additional militia patrols to serve as caravan guards between Whittle and the pass."

Steven eyed him for a moment. *It didn't take more than a nudge and a little coin in his pocket to put him on the board,* he thought. *Greed.* He caught Tenebris's glance—she was thinking the same. *This land is ripe for conquest. The non-farmers are tired of being the lowest rung. I can work with this.*

He smiled at Wallace. "An interesting idea. Of course, it would require the cooperation of the beasts," he said innocently.

Wallace smiled broadly. "I have the utmost faith in the Lord Commander."

Steven nodded with a sly grin. Keeping the people too afraid to travel without an escort could prove very useful going forward.

A knock interrupted the conversation. A minor functionary opened the heavy oak door and bowed slightly. "My apologies, Magister, but Lieutenant Mathers has just arrived from Southold with urgent news."

The magister nodded and waved him in.

Mathers entered and waited for the door to close behind him. He glanced at Cooper and Wallace, then at Steven, who gave a subtle tilt of the head. Mathers nodded slightly, understanding the cue.

"What news?" Tenebris asked.

"Sad news, I'm afraid," Mathers said solemnly. "We checked the farmsteads held by the locals. Three of them had already fallen by the time our forces arrived. They were unable to hold out against the beasts."

Steven nodded, his expression appropriately grave. Both Cooper and Wallace looked genuinely disturbed.

"Any survivors?" Tenebris asked.

"No, ma'am," Mathers replied. "The beasts were brutal and efficient. The locals who accompanied us were able to identify most of the dead. We burned the remains—along with the buildings—to prevent the beasts from using them for shelter."

Steven's voice tightened. "Do you know which farmsteads they were?"

"Caddleback, Ornfel, and Wickerman," Mathers said.

"Ornfel?" Steven turned to Tenebris. "That's my dear friend Al's family homestead." His voice caught. "You said none survived?"

"No, sir," Mathers said softly.

Steven turned away from the others, as if to compose himself. "I… I can't let their deaths be in vain." He took a breath, then spoke without turning. "Magister Cooper, with the family gone, I assume the land reverts to Whittle's control?"

"It does, Commander," Cooper said, his voice tinged with sympathy. "And you have my deepest condolences regarding your friend's family."

Steven lifted a hand to stop him, as if the pain were too fresh to hear condolences. After a moment, still facing away, he said, "Then that settles it. I had been undecided about where to build the compound. Now I know. We'll build it on that land. Not just a compound, but the Chapter House of the Order in Harding."

"I think that's only fitting," said the magister.

"But what about your friend Al?" Wallace asked. "Wouldn't possession fall to him?"

Steven turned back around, his expression composed but mournful. "Unfortunately, Albert was exiled from Harding for capital crimes. I may not believe him capable of such things, but the law has passed judgment. He cannot own land—nor can he return without risk of arrest or execution."

He returned to his seat and caught Tenebris's eye, offering her a smile and a wink.

"There is one more thing, sir," said Mathers.

"By all means," Steven replied.

"Both here in town and when speaking with the locals, there's growing concern that there may be traitors among them. They've started to question why some farms are hit repeatedly while others remain untouched."

Steven adopted a look of careful consideration. "Interesting. The enemy within—always a real threat, and one that's nearly impossible for any outside force to uncover on its own." He glanced at Tenebris. "Any thoughts?"

She scrunched her face in feigned contemplation, then let her eyes settle meaningfully on Wallace. "What if—and this is just a suggestion—Commander Wallace were to form a special unit? One made up of loyal citizens. They could observe their neighbors quietly, report any suspicious activity, all without raising alarm."

She leaned in slightly. "I have some experience with these kinds of operations. It might be wise to implement such a network in all towns and villages. That is, of course, if the commander is willing to take on a new, secret title—Spymaster for Whittle. Only a few would ever know. You'd be compensated by the Order, naturally."

Wallace looked skeptical at first, but the mention of additional coin seemed to win him over. "I'll do whatever I can to be of service," he offered with a nod.

Steven smiled. "Excellent. Tenebris will bring you up to speed."

When Steven and Tenebris returned to the inn, the barmaid caught Steven's eye and subtly nodded toward a cloaked figure sitting alone in the common room.

Uso, Steven thought.

With a glance at Tenebris—who gave a slight nod—he moved to join the covert goblin.

Steven sat across from him. "How is it no one's pulled your hood back? You spend an awful lot of time in here."

Uso shrugged. "I'm careful. A few have seen me—the barmaid, the innkeeper—but a little coin buys silence."

"A useful truth," Steven said dryly, reflecting on how quickly local officials could be bought.

They waited as the barmaid brought a pint and a bowl of steaming stew to Uso and returned shortly with the same for Steven.

"A messenger rode in hard this morning," Uso said. "It appears your friend is finally making his move."

Steven took a sip of ale and let the stew cool. "Do we know where he's heading?"

Uso shook his head. "Not yet. Doesn't matter. The master wants you to take your forces west and ensure he doesn't escape east."

Steven blew on a spoonful of stew and muttered, "If I hadn't been stalled here, I'd almost be there by now."

"You shouldn't question him so openly. That said, your time here's been… productive."

Steven finished chewing and drained the rest of his ale in one go. "Fine. I'll issue the orders. We'll ride out tomorrow morning. But it'll take days for the main legion to catch up, even at double time. Maybe a week to reach Torringburgh."

He did some rough math in his head. "If I send the cavalry ahead, they could be there in half that time."

Uso nodded. "Sounds right. Leave a few trusted men behind to watch things while you're gone."

Steven stood. "I had the same thought."

That evening, Steven sat in his tent with Tenebris and four couriers. He handed each of them a sealed order.

"Get these to the other commanders immediately. There's no time for delay. You're to tell them to avoid engaging any enemy forces along the way. Cavalry is to ride ahead to the rendezvous point. Infantry is to move at double time. The specific orders are in each letter. Understood?"

The couriers nodded silently.

"Good. Dismissed."

They saluted and exited quickly.

Tenebris, already half-undressed, slowly approached him with a sultry grin, beginning to remove her shirt. "I thought you promised me a real night's reward," she purred.

Steven smirked and reached for her—just as the tent flap flew open.

Captain Tuttle barged in. Tenebris hissed in fury and quickly covered herself.

Steven, with barely contained rage, turned on the intruder. "Captain, you'd better have a very good reason for barging into my tent unannounced in the middle of the night," he said through clenched teeth.

"Settle down, boy," Tuttle replied coldly. "I got you into this Order, unless you've already forgotten. I'm here on the orders of the General Superior himself. He wants to know what you've been up to—why he hasn't heard anything from you or the other commanders since this campaign began. And if I don't like your answer, I'm to assume command and send you back to the Chapter House in chains."

If Tuttle thought this would unnerve Steven, he failed to read the man.

A slow smile crept across Steven's face, his voice calm and unbothered. "Oh? He did, did he?"

He turned and walked to his large chair, sitting down in a relaxed sprawl. Behind Tuttle, Tenebris dropped the shirt she'd been using to cover herself and, without a word, strode past the confused captain toward the entrance. Just as Tuttle began to turn his focus back to Steven, he felt the cold kiss of a razor-sharp blade at his throat.

Steven's voice was quiet and cool. "Here's how this is going to work, Tuttle. My second is going to explain a few things to you. And once you understand—how long that takes is up to you—I'll give you a new mission. Do you understand?"

"How—?" Tuttle began loudly, but the blade pressed tighter, and a thin line of blood trickled down his neck. He lowered his voice. "I don't know what game you think you're playing, but there's no way—"

Tenebris struck him hard at the base of the skull. The world spun, and Tuttle crumpled to the ground.

He awoke hours later. Naked, gagged, and hogtied, his limbs ached and his skin stung. Tenebris stood near the fire, slowly rotating an iron rod glowing orange at its tip. His eyes went wide with terror.

Steven raised a glass and smiled. "Ah, you're awake. Good. I've always wanted to see my second truly in her element."

By morning, Tuttle—hollow-eyed and weeping silently—was released. Still trembling, he was handed back his clothes. Steven applauded Tenebris and kissed her deeply.

"That was incredible. You are a master of your art."

She cooed and blushed with pride.

Steven turned back to the captain with a hard stare. "Now tell me your orders."

Tuttle's voice shook. "I… I am to return to the Chapter House and assassinate the General Superior undetected… and then await further instructions."

"Dismissed, Captain," Steven said coolly. "But before you go— kneel before my second, kiss her feet, and thank her for her… instruction."

Tuttle's eyes filled with tears again as he dropped to his knees, obeyed, and staggered out of the tent moments later.

As the cavalry assembled later that morning, Mathers and Riff rode up and saluted.

"You called?" Mathers asked, waiting for orders.

Steven nodded as he mounted his horse. "Yes. I want the two of you to pick twenty or thirty trustworthy infantry to stay behind under your command. Keep everything we've set in motion moving forward."

He handed Mathers a sealed letter. "These are instructions from Tenebris regarding the special unit formation we discussed."

Mathers tucked the letter away and nodded. "Understood, sir. Anything else?"

Steven shook his head. "Just keep an eye on Uso. Don't be obvious—he's an ally, but I don't trust him."

Mathers smirked. "Got it."

"We should be back within the month," Steven added. "This shouldn't take long."

They rode hard, stopping only long enough to feed and water the horses and themselves. After three days, they crested a low ridge. The towers of Torringburgh lay just beyond the next day's ride.

"We camp here," Steven ordered.

One of his officers spoke up. "Commander, we still have a few hours of daylight—should we press on?"

Steven shook his head. "And we will. Some of us. If Dis-Ornfel left when predicted and took the eastern road, we'd have seen him by now—or overtaken him. That means he's either north or south of us, and I want to know which before we move further."

The officer nodded. "Understood. I'll send out scouts at once."

Steven dismounted and walked over to Tenebris, who was stretching after the long ride.

"I could use a bath," she said wearily. She sniffed at him and wrinkled her nose. "And so could you."

He gave a tired smile and nodded, though his eyes continued to scan the distant hills.

She wrapped an arm around his waist. "What's troubling you?"

"He's close now," Steven said in a distant voice. "The fox is on the move. I've sent out the tracker hounds. He'll be flushed out soon enough."

"What will you do when we find him?" Tenebris asked, watching his face closely.

He looked at her, eyes distant. "I'm not sure. A choice has been laid before me. I know what I must do—I just don't know if I'll be strong enough when I come face-to-face with my old friend."

"You have a will of steel," she said firmly. "Doubts are normal. I have them all the time. But I've learned to stamp them down, to find pleasure in the pain of others. It's petty, it's cheap—but it's my lot in life. I play the hand I was dealt. And if I must play it, then I'll wring what joy I can from it. The others suffer—but so do I. They stand to lose. I've already lost everything. So I save my pity. They don't deserve it."

"I know," he said softly. "And though I still consider him a friend... I can't forgive him for creating the man I've become."

She hugged him a little tighter. "Then I should thank him," she whispered. "Because I love the man you are."

Steven continued to scan the horizon.

The fox is on the run... and the hounds are closing in.

A woman's voice—soft as breath, distant yet piercing—echoed somewhere in the depths of his mind: *Two threads left—how will you choose?*

As if summoned by the question, he heard it: the clash of battle, horns blaring, drums pounding, men screaming as they died. A sharp pressure bloomed behind his sternum—like something unseen pulling away from his heart. The air thickened, heavy and dry. For a moment, every color around him seemed muted, washed in the pale gray of ash.

He tried to ignore it—the whisper, the chill, the dimming of the world—but it clung to him like smoke to a funeral shroud.

Then came a sharper voice, near and real: "Steven."

Tenebris.

It snapped him back.

He blinked, looked around. The sounds were gone. The sky was bright. The camp bustled in quiet readiness.

But inside, there was no peace. No screaming wind, no spectral voice—but a silence too loud to ignore… and that same lingering pressure in his chest, like a judgment unspoken.

He told himself it was strategy. That mercy had no place in war.

But part of him—the part that still remembered what mercy felt like—had stopped believing him.

ALFARBANI AWAKENED

Al patted the old mare on her neck. "You smell it, don't you? The land of your birth. I smell it too," he said. The mare seemed to walk more easily than she had since they'd first left his little village.

Ryanna rode up alongside him. "Are you alright?" she asked softly, so only he could hear.

He looked at her and smiled—the pale white skin of her face framed by the deep, rich red of her hair, and set like two emeralds were the deepest green eyes he had ever known. He smiled again, a smile born deep in his heart. "I love you," he said simply.

She blushed—no easy feat for someone seldom caught off guard. "You should die more often," she teased.

"Once is more than enough for now, thank you," he replied light-heartedly. "But I mean it. And I know I haven't said it as often as I should. Since I left my home, my life has been one big, scary mystery—with dark revelations about what I am, who I'm hunting, what he's trying to do—fighting monsters of myth and legend. But through it all, the one truly good thing that has happened to me, the one thing that would make me do it all again, is meeting you."

She nudged her horse closer and took his hand. "Al, you are the bravest and most skilled warrior I have ever met. And you are also the kindest—not given to the blood rage as many warriors are. You make me see things in ways I never imagined, and I would not give that up, or any moment with you, for any amount of glory in battle."

"Tonight, when we camp, I would like to approach your father for permission for us to stand before the elders and receive their blessing," he said.

"It is not needed, Al. We have already given ourselves to each other. The blessing is a tradition of the clans; they do not hold you to that," she said, curiosity behind her words.

He nodded. "I know. I also know it is a major event in the clans—an acknowledgment of the couple as a family. The clans have made an exception for me, but I know it would mean a lot to you, your father, and the elders if we submitted ourselves to their judgment and blessing."

"You would do this for me?" she asked.

He looked into those deep green pools. "I would do anything for you."

She smiled and tightened her grip on his hand. Then her mind seemed to rush away, and she released him. "I have much to do," she said in near panic. "I must find my spear-sisters." She looked back and turned with a broad grin on her face. "I will see you at my father's tent tonight," and rode off into the caravan.

The mare nickered, almost as if telling him it was about time. He smiled and patted her neck again. Leaning forward, he whispered in her ear, "I agree, little lady. I agree."

That night, Al walked through the camp to Rogan's tent. The clansmen greeted him as he passed, but he detected a subtle change in them. It seemed he had moved from valued fighter and reluctant leader in their eyes to something more akin to a myth walking among them. He frowned. It made him sad—that subtle shift he could feel, that created a gap between him and them, a gap he wished wasn't there. He hoped in time, as they realized he was the same man he had always been, things would return to normal. But deep down, he knew that was unlikely.

When he came to Rogan's tent, his mind let go of the depressing thoughts of separation and instead leapt to happier ones—of union and belonging. A young female warrior stood outside the tent. She waved for him to approach and, opening the tent flap, gestured for him to enter. He smiled his thanks to her as he did so.

The tent was brightly lit by a central fire. Rogan sat on the far side from the entrance, perched on a large stack of pillows and furs. Standing next to him, dressed in her warrior garb and holding a large spear, was Ryanna—her flaming hair tied back, her face unreadable and stern. She stood tall, strong, proud, and unmovable. Six women of the Spears sat in front of Rogan three on his right and three on his left, facing each other, their spears lying beside them. As Al entered, their heads turned to face him and they reached for their spears—but otherwise made no move.

Al dropped his smile. This was a ceremony, and he cursed himself for a fool for not asking how it was meant to proceed. He stepped forward, and the two women closest to him—on his right and left— jumped to their feet, spears leveled at his chest.

Rogan, still seated, spoke in a clear, commanding voice. "You come before me with fire in your eyes—and ask for what is not easily given." He gestured toward Ryanna. "This is no simple woman. She is a proven warrior, a leader of spear-sisters, her mind honed through trial and bloodshed. You would take her from that role—diminish our strength to raise your own. So I ask: Can you stand in battle when she cannot? Will you suffer the blows meant for her? Will you be the shield in her absence, and the sword in her silence?"

Al looked at the women holding their spears toward him, then back to Rogan. "I would never take her from her appointed task, nor deprive her of the joy of battle. She is no prize to be claimed, nor burden to be protected. She is a warrior—and I would stand by her side, not in front of her. With my sword, I will strike down any who threaten her or the clan she loves. And with my shield, I will guard them both—until I fall, or the danger passes."

Rogan and Ryanna shared a small smile. Al knew these were not the formal words of the ceremony, but they seemed to suffice. The two women sat down, placing their spears beside them with tips facing away.

He stepped forward, and the next two women rose and leveled their spears. Again, Rogan spoke. "Ryanna is more than a warrior. She is one of a rare few who may rise to sit among the Elders. She is the voice of generations yet unborn, the keeper of story and tradition. She will guide those who come after—and carry the legacy of the clans into the years beyond us. Can you walk beside her not only in battle, but also in belief? Can you set aside your pride, and let her voice be the one that leads when the time demands it?"

Al thought for a moment, weighing what was really being asked. "I know the wisdom and truth of her words. I see the time she takes to train those in her charge, the way she honors the clan and you by her words and deeds. I would never deprive the clan of such a leader. She would have—as she already does—my complete trust and faith in her judgment. And when her voice must rise, I will quiet my own, because I trust her as I trust my sword arm."

The two women sat and lowered their spears. Al stepped forward again. He glanced at Ryanna—she was stunning. The next two spears stood. He turned his eyes back to Rogan as he spoke once more.

"You ask for my daughter—not only in love, but in loyalty. You would make her your future, and she would carry your name. But she is also of my blood—flesh of my flesh—and those who carry that line will carry more than just your legacy. Will they be taught the stories of Rogan? Will they honor the line that shaped her? Will they speak the names of their mother's clan with pride?"

Al looked at Ryanna again. Children. He hadn't truly considered it before—but now the thought was real, tangible... and somehow right.

First Cygnus, he thought. *Then we build.*

He turned back to Rogan.

"I am an exile. An outcast. A creature born of war and shadow. I have no name fit to offer—only myself. And yet, I ask for this gift in full humility. If we are blessed with children, they will be raised with the clan, taught your words, trained in your customs, and strengthened by your stories. They will speak your name with pride—not just as their mother's father, but as a man whose strength and wisdom helped shape who they are."

The final two warriors lowered their spears and bowed their heads. Rogan stepped forward and took Al's left hand and Ryanna's right, placing them together. He stood, looking at both of them.

"Ryanna, I have found this man worthy to fight beside you, to support you in your choices, and to father your children. What say you?"

She looked deeply into Al's eyes, and with a broad smile replied, "As a warrior, I acknowledge his prowess in combat is unequaled among any in the clans. As a potential Elder, I say that I have found him knowledgeable, kind, and charitable. He is respectful of the clan and its ways. As a woman,"—her voice softened—"he has won my heart many times over."

Rogan, with tears in his steely face, said, "Then with my whole heart, I give you my blessing to stand before the elders."

That night, after Ryanna had fallen asleep, Al quietly left the tent. As he walked through the camp toward its edge, he was joined by Talionis, moving silent as a ghost. Al ran his hand through the thick fur on the wolf's neck.

"Not tired either? I'm going for a walk, if you'd like to join me." A vision of rabbits popped into his head.

Al chuckled. "If you can find any, you're more than welcome to go get them."

Once clear of the campfires, Al breathed deeply, taking in the scents of the grasslands. He looked south. Soon they would be entering the farmlands. *I'll have to send envoys to let the people know we're coming. I don't need angry villagers thinking we're the enemy.*

He looked at Talionis. "I can't believe we're not tired," he continued, speaking mostly to himself. "It's been a crazy day. I mean—we both died. By rights, we should be exhausted."

Talionis ignored him, nose to the ground, sniffing the air. He looked up at Al, who nodded. "Go ahead," Al said, and the wolf bounded off in search of prey.

The old man said I can gather energy from nature, Al thought. He had learned how to do that with Gutamino, but back then, it had only been a trickle—and it took days to store anything significant. Even then, there had been limits.

He shrugged. *Only one way to find out.*

He sat down in the grassy field and opened his mind to the world.

The result was immediate and overwhelming—like unplugging a dam. Energy surged into him in a rush. Sights, sounds, emotions—all flooded his senses. He gasped and immediately shut himself off from it.

Breathing heavily, he muttered, "That's... different."

Already, he could feel the power coursing through him. It was more than what the sword had ever granted him, even after two kills. *Do I need more than this? Morning's still far off. I'm not tired. Talionis is hunting. I guess it's better to find my limit now—when I don't need it—than later, when I do.*

He took a deep breath and centered himself. This time, he opened himself to the world gently—just a crack, allowing only a trickle of energy. He could feel the ground itself feeding him. He opened the gate a little further. The flow strengthened. He could hear animals all around—some sleeping, some hunting, some merely stirring.

He felt Talionis following a scent: a boar, several hours old. Al focused on that trail and opened the gate wider. Faint voices echoed at the edges of his awareness. Were they real or imagined? One seemed familiar. He followed it.

The world blurred, and suddenly he was looking down on a familiar tavern—one he hadn't seen in a long time. On a chair, smoking a pipe, sat Old Joe. Then, just as quickly, he was back in the field.

Real or imagined? he wondered. His body bristled with energy. He held as much now—if not more—than he ever had with the sword. And he knew he was nowhere near his limit.

Better not push my luck on the first try. Let's see how long the energy lasts—and what I can do with it. The old man said I could heal as well as harm.

He reached out with his mind to Talionis, letting the wolf know he was heading back. But Talionis should enjoy his hunt.

Back at camp, Al made his way quietly to the recovery tent, where the wounded lay. Some had taken serious blows while hunting goblins and Klav.

He entered the dark tent. He needed no light—darkness shone as bright as day to him now. He approached the most grievously injured man: a sword wound to the gut. They had made him as comfortable as possible, but no one expected him to live more than a day or two.

Al placed one hand on the man's head and the other over the wound. Closing his eyes, he drew on the energy surging through him, channeling it through the man's body in from the hand on his head and out through the hand on the wound. He willed the damage to be repaired.

The man screamed awake, rousing others. Guards rushed in—but seeing Al, they hesitated. More people gathered outside. Al continued the flow of energy. When he sensed the damage was fully healed, he stopped. The man was sweating, but his eyes were clear. He no longer screamed.

A healer approached cautiously and examined him. Her jaw dropped.

"What? What is it?" asked one of the guards.

She turned to Al, eyes wide with awe and fear. "He's healed," she stammered.

Rogan and Ryanna arrived, concern in their eyes.

"I wasn't sure if it would work," Al said quietly. "So I didn't want to raise anyone's hopes. I also don't fully understand how I did it—so I'll need to practice, starting with those most in need."

He leaned against Ryanna. She looked at him worriedly, but he smiled.

"I'm alright. I drew in a large amount of energy earlier, and this took most of it. I'll need rest—and time to recharge—before I can do more."

Rogan looked over the remaining wounded. "No one else is near death. Let the others heal naturally. Save this gift for when it is most needed."

Al nodded. "I will trust your counsel on this."

"Come. It's still several hours until daybreak," she said, looking at the gathered people. "Everyone needs their sleep. We have a long road ahead tomorrow, and the enemy could strike at any time."

Back at their tent, Al lay down beside her and watched as she drifted back to sleep. *Even after all of that, I'm not tired.* He quieted his mind and figured that if sleep was going to elude him, then at least he could meditate.

He found himself back in the old building—broken and run down, as he had always seen it, except for when the old man was there. He sat on one of the dusty benches and watched as Talionis joined him.

"Learned a new trick, I see," he said to the wolf with a grin. They sat in silence, enjoying the calm as Talionis curled up at his feet.

When Al opened his eyes, dawn was beginning to creep over the horizon. Ryanna stirred, so he rose and got dressed. He dug through his belongings and pulled out the sword Tyr had given him when they fled Harding together. Tyr had said his father made it. It was a beautiful weapon with perfect balance. Al strapped it on and headed out, allowing Ryanna to wake in her own time.

A young boy ran up to him. "Sorry to bother you, but the elders would like a word."

Al nodded. *To be expected. I'm surprised it took them this long.*

He made his way calmly through the encampment. People were just beginning to rouse and start the day. When he reached the central tent, the flap was already open, so he poked his head inside. Chief Elder Fenwick stood chatting with Corvus and Wilna. Upon seeing him, Fenwick waved him in.

Al bowed as he approached.

"You have been a busy little warrior, haven't you?" Fenwick laughed.

Al paused. Fenwick spoke lightly, but Al sensed unease behind the words. The other two elders, too, wore expressions of uncertainty. *They do not know what to make of me,* he thought sadly.

Al nodded. "I don't ask for forgiveness. In my fight with the goblins, much of who I was died—and something new took its place. Whether that is for better or worse, I cannot yet say. But where there was doubt, there is now certainty. Where there was fear, there is acceptance. And where there was hatred, there is now understanding."

The elders looked at each other, trying to make sense of his words.

"We don't understand," said Wilna.

Al replied, "I know. It's not something I can explain in words. Hopefully, through my actions, you'll understand. Hopefully, so will I." He paused, his eyes going distant. "There is darkness ahead. I must try to push it back. I have been given"—he hesitated, searching for the word—"certain gifts, that, if used properly, may allow us to triumph. But I cannot do this alone. I need all of you by my side. Alone, I am a sputtering candle in a howling storm, doomed to be extinguished. But together, I can be the dawn that chases the night away."

"How did you heal a dying man?" Martin asked.

Al met his gaze. "The same way I burned dozens of Klav in a fireball on the path up to the Citadel."

"Your sword was destroyed," Martin said.

Al nodded. "Yes. And my heart sings with joy that it was. The sword left death and chaos in its wake. Like a beast, it fed upon those it killed. Now, without it, I am nourished like the mighty oak—by the world itself. And while death and decay are part of that world, so too are birth and renewal." He looked down at his hands. "It is the same power—but the vessel that wields it is not. These hands can now heal as well as harm."

"We follow you because we believe your cause is just. Do you still seek to keep the Dokkalfar from escaping?"

"I do," he replied.

"And if we fail?" asked Fenwick.

"Then I will face the Dokkalfar on a distant battlefield. At the end, either light or darkness will rule the day," Al said, his voice distant.

The three shared a quiet look and nodded—some unspoken agreement.

"Very well, Al. We follow you still. May you always take the day," Fenwick said.

TORRINGBURGH

The clans had moved steadily south toward Torringburgh, keeping their most vulnerable in the center of the caravan, flanked by mounted warriors at both the front and rear. Progress was slow, but Al didn't want to risk Klav or goblins harassing them along the way.

On the fifteenth day, Tyfin and Rogan rode up to join Al and Ryanna at the front of the line. Al watched them approach—Rogan tall and stern, his presence commanding, and Tyfin, smaller in stature and less physically imposing. Rogan had spent his life in the unforgiving northern tundra, forged by combat and hardship, while Tyfin had grown up behind the walls of a fortified town, where the closest thing to battle had been a tavern brawl. Still, Al trusted them both. They were good men, strong leaders, and indispensable in their own ways.

The Rogan, a warrior's warrior, bore a title earned only once per generation—bestowed through combat and proven leadership. He was Al's tactical expert. Tyfin, on the other hand, was a master of logistics. Years of managing trade with the southern lands had taught him how to keep a mobile army supplied—knowledge that kept the clans fed and moving.

As they rode alongside, Tyfin glanced around. "I thought there'd be more," he said. "People. Houses. Farms."

Al smiled. "We've been traveling through farmland since we left the pass. We passed two towns," he added, gesturing eastward. "The farms here are enormous—mostly wheat. You could walk a day or two and still be on the same holding. The buildings are spread out, but usually within a day's walk of a town. There are smaller villages scattered in between."

Rogan remained expressionless. "I'm more concerned by the lack of enemy activity," he said.

"Maybe they retreated ahead of us. We are a large force," Tyfin offered.

Rogan nodded slowly. "Maybe. But that could mean they're flanking us—or worse, following behind."

He turned to Al. "I'd like to send out patrols to look for signs of them."

Al hesitated. The last time he'd sent scouts, Glyn and his team had never returned. Still, Rogan was right—they needed information. "Alright," Al agreed quietly.

"We should also name a replacement for Glyn," Rogan added. "Without a lead scout, we're traveling blind."

Al turned to Ryanna. "You and Tyfin spent the most time with Glyn and his scouts. Work together to identify the top candidates. Give your recommendations to the Rogan, and he can select the one best suited to lead."

"How much farther to Torringburgh, do you think?" Tyfin asked.

"Well, it's just over a hundred-fifty miles south of the pass. We're covering ten maybe fifteen miles a day—on a good day," Al said.

"That can't be helped," Ryanna added. "Not with the wagons and herds."

Al nodded. "True. But with luck, we'll reach the city tomorrow or the next day. Rogan, if your patrols head south, keep an eye out for road markers. Harding posts signs at crossroads and major routes."

Rogan gave a firm nod.

That night, as Al sat by the fire, Ryanna joined him. She slipped her arm around his and rested her head on his shoulder.

"What's troubling you, my love?" she asked softly.

Al stared into the flames for a long moment. "I'm not sure. Just a sense of unease."

"About what?"

He glanced at her and smiled. "I've been learning to draw power from the world around me. With your help," he added with a wink. "I think I'll be able to fight as I did before—if I can keep reinforcing the blade mid-combat. But unlike the old sword, I'm not sure how I'll draw in energy during a fight."

She gave him a quizzical look, so he continued, "The Alfarbani blade was designed to feed both itself and its wielder during combat. That allowed its bearer to use energy freely without fear of depletion. But the only way I currently know to gather natural energy is through meditation. In battle, that won't be an option. I'll need to be far more restrained—or I could exhaust myself and be left defenseless."

She nodded thoughtfully. "I suppose the sword had its uses."

Al shook his head. "The cost was too high." He sighed and glanced into the distance. "That's not what's bothering me, though."

His voice grew quieter. "Since I began drawing from nature itself, I can feel that something is… wrong. Something is out of balance."

Ryanna considered his words. "Any idea what or where this wrongness might be?"

He shook his head. "No. And I'm not even certain I'm right. It could just be nerves. There's so much I still don't understand."

She pulled him closer, and he smiled, placing a soft kiss on her forehead. "Don't worry. I know what I need to do, and when the time comes, I won't hesitate. Right now, I'm just trying to understand my new limits—and this sense that something in the world isn't as it should be."

A boy, one of the young runners the elders used to deliver messages, approached the fire and stopped a respectful distance away. "My apologies for the interruption," he said.

Ryanna sat up. "No bother. What word from the council?"

"From the Rogan, First Spear," the boy corrected politely. *First Spear* was the formal title given to Ryanna when command of the clan spears had passed to her. "He suggests we return to the main road tomorrow."

Al and Ryanna exchanged a look, then Al nodded. "Tell him the message is received."

The boy nodded smartly and darted off into the darkening camp.

"What should we expect from the elders of this land?" Ryanna asked.

"I'm not sure," Al admitted. "The senate is composed of landowners from all across Harding. I'd hoped Cygnus just passed through here on his way to the Southern Kingdoms, but considering what he did at the pass, I fear he left forces behind. Especially since we haven't seen a single worker in the fields."

Ryanna leaned back against him. "A marauding horde of monsters is a pretty good reason to stay home."

He chuckled. "Maybe. But I'm not sure my pa would've agreed." They both laughed softly.

Al's expression sobered. "Honestly, I don't know how they'll receive me. I'm an exile. By law, I should be arrested."

She sat up slightly, her eyes narrowing. "They wouldn't dare."

"I doubt it," he said with a grin. "Not with a sizable force at my back. More likely, they'll let us pass without incident. They should be grateful the western pass has been reopened."

At Rogan's suggestion, they rejoined the main trade road. By the second day, the city of Torringburgh was in sight. Al, Ryanna, Tyfin, Rogan, and Talionis stood together at the edge of camp, gazing toward the distant walls.

"What can you see, Al?" Rogan asked.

Al adjusted his vision, narrowing his eyes. "I think you overestimate my eyesight," he replied with a grin. "But from what I can tell, the gate is closed, and I don't see anyone moving between the city and here."

"Thoughts?" Rogan asked.

"Leave the main force here," Tyfin suggested. "Take a small group—fewer than ten—to the city. Be at the gate before sunrise. I'm sure they've already seen us, so an envoy won't come as a surprise."

"Take Ryanna and Tyfin," Rogan added. "I'll stay behind with the wolf."

Talionis gave a low growl of protest.

"Sorry, boy," Rogan said with a smirk. "You and I tend to leave a strong impression."

In the end, it was decided that Al and Ryanna would meet with the Senate. Tyfin would bring a runner to request permission to visit the markets and secure supplies for the caravan. If granted, the runner would return with drivers and wagons.

The next morning found the four of them on horseback, waiting in front of the gates for the first light of day.

Once the sun crested the horizon, they didn't have to wait long.

"Hail, travelers," came a voice from the ramparts. "What brings you to Torringburgh in such dark times?"

"I am Albert Dis-Ornfel of Southold. I would speak with the Senate, if they will hear me," Al called up clearly.

"An exile? Why have you come—do you bring more woe upon these lands?" came the skeptical reply.

"No. I come in peace, and with an offer of help. I would not have crossed the pass if the need were not great," he shouted.

"The pass? The western pass is open?"

"It is now. We cleared the pass and slew those who held it—ten days past."

There was murmuring on the battlements. Al didn't need to focus to know what they were saying.

"You may enter. Follow the guard to the Senate Building, and they will hear you."

"I thank you. One more boon I ask: this is my supply master, Tyfin of the northern Talpan Clan. Might he meet with your merchants? We are in need of resupply."

"Coin—and even more so, barter—is welcome in these dark times. We will assign another to guide him to the merchant district."

"You have my thanks," Al said as the city gates began to swing open.

Ryanna, Tyfin, and the boy looked around in awe at the crowded streets and towering buildings—none had ever seen a city before. Al smiled. He had really only seen one himself: Morcaster. In many ways, Torringburgh was similar. Like Morcaster, it was divided into unique districts, each with its own architecture and rhythm. But unlike Morcaster, it seemed to be filled mostly with farmers and craftsmen. Absent were the wealthy merchants and decadent nobles—and he hoped the darker elements, like the ones that had shaped Gillian's childhood, were also nowhere to be found.

Al and Ryanna headed straight to the Senate Chambers and were quickly ushered in. The room was mostly full—it seemed they had indeed been expecting a delegation, just as Tyfin had said.

Al looked around. The building was beautiful. From the outside, it appeared imposing—solid stone and austere—but inside, it was warm. Dark-stained wood gleamed under the lamplight, carved with intricate patterns, many of them honoring the harvest. The Senate chamber itself was arranged in a large semi-circle with five rising tiers. Al knew from his studies that there was a seat for every town in Harding. He scanned the crowd, wondering if the representative from Whittle was among them.

In front of the senators was a wide, low section for petitioners to stand while addressing the chamber. Beyond that, slightly elevated, were rows of benches for the public to observe.

A young page in formal attire motioned for Al and Ryanna to enter the speaking area. They did so and waited as the senators took their seats. The chatter slowly died down. At last, the senator seated dead center on the lowest tier rapped a gavel against the desk.

When silence fell, the page stepped forward and, in a clear, high voice, announced, "By the authority of the High Republic of Harding, this session is called to order. The Right Honorable Senator Kirth presiding. Let those who wish to be heard stand forth to be recognized." He bowed and stepped aside.

An older senator, dressed in white with a large gold medallion resting against his chest, set the gavel down and turned his attention to them. He picked up a slip of paper and, placing a pair of spectacles on his nose, read aloud: "Albert Dis-Ornfel of Southbend?"

"Yes, sir," Al replied in a strong, clear voice.

The senator removed his glasses and folded his hands before him. "We are told you've opened the Western Pass?"

"We have. The goblins and Klav who held it have either fled or been killed."

The chamber erupted into low chatter. Al focused his hearing—many senators seemed stunned. They hadn't known who or what their enemy was.

Senator Kirth rapped the gavel again. "My apologies," he said, directing his attention back to Al. "But did you say goblins and Klav?"

"I did. And I understand your confusion. Like most of you, I knew nothing of such creatures beyond the bedtime stories told to me as a child. It was only when I found myself heading toward the frozen tundra of the northern plains that I ran afoul of them. Since then, my life has been filled with myth made real," Al said evenly.

The chamber erupted into renewed chatter.

"Why should we believe an exile?" shouted a senator in long blue and green robes. Al noticed for the first time that the senators were grouped by robe color—blue and green on the right, gold and white in the center, and black and red on the left. The senator who had spoken now stood, his voice ringing with skepticism. "What proof does he bring? For all we know, it could have been his own forces holding the pass!"

More murmurs followed—some in support, others in opposition.

"Nonsense!" barked a senator in gold and white. "We've all heard the reports of dog-like creatures attacking in packs. Do you truly believe this is unrelated?"

Another round of shouting followed.

"Silence!" Senator Kirth thundered, slamming the gavel against the table. "This is a serious matter. Let us try—at least once—to hear it out without descending into a tavern brawl." He lowered his voice, trying to steady the mood in the chamber.

Turning back to Al and Ryanna, he continued, "I would like to dismiss your story as madness, but as each of you knows, we have been beset by foul beasts for which we have no name. So if 'goblin' and 'Klav' suffice, let them stand. But I must ask—why have these creatures come south? Were they fleeing from you? Did you push them into our lands?"

Al shook his head. "No. I claim no victory over them—at least not in the north. Their army is strong, and I fear it is growing stronger. These goblins were not with them when I first encountered the Klav. They must have joined as the horde moved south. I had believed they were heading for the Five Kingdoms. I had hoped they would pass through Harding as quickly as they passed through Jaspar. But something has changed."

Quiet murmurs rippled through the chamber again. Al noted that the senators still only conferred with others wearing the same colored robes.

"What connection is there between the frozen north and the Five Kingdoms?" asked a senator robed in black and red.

"What are these creatures after?" another added. "Surely you have some idea—or why else would you pursue them?"

Al hesitated. Ryanna gave him a subtle nudge.

"This may be harder to believe than goblins and Klav," Al admitted. "What do you know of the old stories—of the Dokkalfar?"

He began to recount his journey, from his exile to the fateful battle with the Alkeir.

"An Alkeir?" interrupted the same blue and green-robed senator from before, now nearly shouting. "You? You faced an Alkeir?"

He scoffed and spread his arms dramatically. "No one stands before an Alkeir and lives to tell the tale. I think we've heard enough of these fairy tales. If this is the best he offers, I'm inclined to believe he brought the beasts here himself."

"That is not true!" Ryanna shouted, her voice ringing clear over the noise. "This man, who was wrongfully accused, robbed of his name, and exiled by this very land—not only faced an Alkeir, he killed one. And now he returns to the land that cast him out—to save it."

Silence fell.

"Impossible," the senator muttered—not with anger, but with disbelief. "No human can kill an Alkeir. It's not possible."

Al bowed his head slightly. "I am not human," he said softly.

His words cut through the chamber like a blade. All noise ceased.

He focused inward, drawing the energy gently into his palm. Holding out his right hand, he concentrated. For a moment, nothing happened—and then a small flame sprang to life above his palm. The senators gasped. Several chairs scraped against the floor as men stood or backed away. He clenched his fist, and the flame vanished.

"I am not human," he repeated. "Though I was raised as one— and believed, with all my heart, that I was. If I had not been exiled, I likely would have lived and died never knowing the truth. But during my travels, in order to survive, a deeper part of me awoke. Through pain and loss, I discovered that I am an Alfarbani."

He let the silence linger, then continued.

"I did fight and kill an Alkeir. But there was a second. The battle that felled the first nearly claimed me as well. I was too wounded to challenge the second. He did not believe I would survive the night. And before my eyes—he destroyed the seal. Then he took my friend… to torment and kill him later."

It took several strikes of the gavel before order returned.

Senator Kirth leaned forward, setting the gavel down with care. "You've given us much to consider," he said slowly. "But let us set aside the tales for now. Tell us—what is it that you seek from us?"

"I was going to just ask for permission to pass through the land. I had no idea that Harding had fallen under attack. So while I still ask for permission to pursue my foe, I offer you my assistance. I have a sizable force—we can try to clear the land for you."

"I am sure he left these forces here to slow me down, but I cannot and will not leave Harding defenseless."

The old senator looked around and then back at his colleagues. "Let us recess briefly to weigh your words."

Al and Ryanna were left alone in the Senate assembly chamber. Time dragged on—an hour, then two. Just as they began to wonder if they had been forgotten, the senators came shuffling back in and took their seats.

The old man banged his gavel and called the assembly to order. "Forgive our delay, but we looked into your exile. It seems it may have been unduly hasty, and for that, you have our sincerest apologies. But even if it wasn't, your offer to help free this land of the forces that have been a blight on our very existence these many months would have been more than enough reason to lift your banishment and restore your name to you. Therefore, it is with great—"

"Please," Al interrupted, "I beg of you, hold your pardon. I go to an uncertain doom, and as such, a pardon—while greatly uplifting— would do me little good. I would ask another favor, if I may be so bold?"

The senator nodded for him to continue.

"I have brought all of the northern nomadic clans with me. It is this army that I will use to cleanse Harding and, hopefully, stop the Alkeir. They have left their homeland to free yours—and to prevent an even greater darkness. I know the lands to the west are sparsely inhabited. I would ask that the clans be allowed to use this land for their cattle. And should Harding ever find herself in need, the clans will come to her aid."

The old man looked around the chamber at the other senators. "This should be agreeable. We could use the increase in trade, and having a strong western force would be most welcome. Send us the elders of the clans, and we can work out the details. Is there anything else we can assist you with?"

Al looked at Ryanna, who said, "Only where these beasts are most abundant, so we may begin our hunt."

The senator smiled in approval.

Al and the clans broke into units that spread across the land, hunting down the enemy wherever they could be found. In the fourth week of their efforts to root out and destroy the klav and goblins, Al received word that the Senate wished to speak with him.

When Al, Ryanna, and Rogan arrived at the Senate, a young page led them past the assembly chamber to a large exterior garden at the center of the building. Senator Kirth stood waiting.

"Greetings, mighty warriors. Harding has finally begun to breathe easier, thanks to your efforts. Please—walk with me," he said.

The four of them strolled through the garden.

"I thought it would be easier meeting this way than dealing with the politics of the full assembly. I've received word that the Odio have not been idle—they've successfully rid the lands from the east all the way to Whittle. While this is indeed joyful news, as you are well aware, the Odio always attach a price to anything they do." He shrugged. "That is a problem for another day. Today, I have news of your quarry."

"With the roads open again, and with the assistance of your commander Rogan, we've been sending out scouts in all directions to find word of the enemy. Two days ago, we received word that the enemy appears to be gathering his forces at the Southern Pass. By all accounts, it is a sizable force—and the road from the pass leads directly to Torringburgh. We beg you to gather your army and push back this enemy. If this is the quarry and the fight you were looking for, it gathers now in the south. Besides, on a more personal note, Torringburgh would be unable to repel this enemy. If you do not face it, we will be overrun."

"We can offer some help. We have not been idle while you were away. Our citizens—mainly farmers and craftsmen—have been showing up and volunteering in droves. They want to fight with you to protect their land."

"How many strong?" Rogan asked.

"As of this morning, close to three thousand," Kirth replied.

Al's mind raced. Three thousand—but all untrained and probably poorly armed. I can't afford to be picky. Three thousand... I will find a use for them. And if I can't, Rogan or Ryanna most assuredly will.

Al bowed slightly. "Have them assemble south of the city in the morning. It will take a couple of days to recall my forces, and then we will march to the pass. Now, if you'll excuse me, there is much to be done."

Al, Ryanna, and Rogan turned and left. As soon as they were clear of the building, Rogan spoke.

"Three thousand untrained soldiers isn't a gift," he said.

"I know," Al replied. "But it's not a burden either. There must be something they can do—if nothing else, it will free up our trained warriors."

The three walked in silence for a few paces, each considering the situation.

"Send them to the Western Pass," Rogan suggested. "It's seen no action since we broke through. Recall the forces we have stationed there—or at least most of them."

Al nodded. "Yes. And anywhere else we can leave a small number of trained fighters. Pair them with these recruits. What else?"

Rogan continued, "Put them in the rear during battle. Their only job will be to hold the line. If any of the enemy breaks through, they're to swarm and overwhelm them. That way, their numbers work to their advantage, and we minimize their risk of being killed."

Al gave his approval with a sharp nod. "Good. It's the start of a working plan. Let's keep refining it. In the meantime, send out riders and recall the forces. It's a week's ride to the Southern Pass—the sooner we begin, the better."

He turned to Rogan. "Find Tyfin and have him get the support wagons moving immediately. We'll overtake them within a day or two, depending on when we're able to march."

With that, the three of them headed back to camp.

A HUSH IN THE FIELDS...

It was three days before Al and the spears began riding south. They moved ahead of the foot soldiers but never more than a few hours' distance. Rogan was concerned about splitting the forces too much in case the enemy launched a surprise attack.

On their second day, a rider approached as they were setting up camp. It was one of the scouts. Al met the man as he rode in.

"What news?" he asked, sensing the urgency in the scout's demeanor.

"Sir," the scout said sharply, "a large force has been spotted to the east. When they saw us, a few rode out under a flag of truce. They claim they are with the Odio Magisterium and wish to parley with you."

"How far away are they?" Rogan asked.

"A couple of hours' ride. They've camped for the night but said if you wish to meet, they will await you on the field."

Rogan shrugged. "Better to talk than fight a needless battle."

Al nodded. "Agreed. Senator Kirth mentioned they had freed eastern Harding."

"He also didn't sound like he trusted their motives," Ryanna added.

"Might want to post a few additional sentries tonight," Al said. "Talionis and I will take a loop around the camp now and then, just to make sure we have no unexpected guests."

Rogan shook his head. "The extra sentries should do the trick. Besides, you need your sleep."

Ryanna scoffed. "Sleep? I don't think he does that anymore."

Al looked a little bashful. "I sleep. It's just that ever since the events at the pass, my body doesn't seem to need as much rest."

Rogan nodded. "You do what you feel you must. I won't pretend to understand what happened at the pass. But from where I stand, I see only positive changes. So I won't complain if your bedroll remains cold."

"Speak for yourself," Ryanna said wryly.

Al looked at her, trying to determine if she was being serious or teasing. Rogan laughed.

"I'm not stepping into that hornet's nest. I'll let you two sort it out. I'll be ready to ride by first light."

Al waited until Ryanna had fallen asleep, then quietly made his way out into the night, where Talionis quickly joined him. Scratching the giant wolf's ears, Al gave him a look. Talionis was likely full-grown now, his head reaching Al's chest—broad of shoulder and utterly imposing. Al was so accustomed to him that he barely noticed how intimidating the wolf's presence could be.

"Let's go see what we can find," he said.

An image of a deer popped into his mind, and Al laughed. "Work first. But if we see nothing suspicious and you catch a scent, then yes, you can go hunt."

The wolf's tail wagged happily.

As they walked, Al attempted to reach out with energy, but without a target, it was scattered and frayed, revealing nothing. He looked at his hand. That ball of fire was something—but he wasn't sure how useful it would be in a fight.

"Maybe I could start the cooking fire afterward," he joked to himself.

I wonder if I can throw it? He stopped and concentrated. The ball came easier this time.

The more I do it, the easier it becomes. I'll have to remember to practice anything useful I figure out.

He looked at the burning sphere in his hand. He could feel its heat, though his palm remained unscathed. Scanning the fields for a target and finding none, he hesitated.

Maybe throwing flame into a wheat field isn't the smartest use of my time.

He looked up and shrugged. Gathering his energy, he imagined a spring beneath his hand and compressed it just under the ball of flame. He moved his arm upward toward the sky and released the imaginary spring.

The ball of flame shot into the air, and to his surprise, it remained alight even after leaving his hand. With a thought, he ended the concentration, and the flame blinked out of existence.

The night remained calm; no one approached. Al sat in the field, sensing Talionis on the hunt, and smiled.

What can I do? he asked himself. *I have my normal abilities—a skin tough enough to stop arrows and most blades, speed, strength, enhanced vision and*

The night sky was mostly clear, but a few clouds were beginning to gather. The only two abilities Al had truly mastered were healing—which quickly drained his energy reserves—and the fire orb, which, while entertaining, had limited utility in battle. He had to maintain concentration to hold its shape and flame; otherwise, it would simply unravel and extinguish itself.

He thought for a bit. Healing was straightforward. He could use that after battles as needed, focusing first on the gravely wounded, then recharging before continuing. As for the fire orb, it had no immediate battlefield use.

His mind wandered: memories of his homeland, his friends, Morcaster, and the frozen north. When he looked around again, dawn was beginning to creep over the horizon. As he rose, he noticed Talionis had returned sometime during the night and now lay beside him, clearly well-fed and resting. His hunt had been successful.

By the time Al returned to camp, Rogan and Ryanna were already waiting, his mare saddled and ready.

"Would you like me to round up an escort?" Rogan asked.

Al shook his head. "No. The Odio are annoying, but little more. If they have more than a handful waiting, we can just withdraw."

The three of them, joined by Talionis, rode to the location the scout had mentioned—a low hill surrounded by grasslands. From the top, they would be able to spot an enemy coming from a mile away. As they approached, they saw three figures on horseback waiting.

Al focused his gaze. The woman had a stern demeanor and a scar across her face; he sensed her wounds ran deeper than skin. The man on the left radiated nobility—his attire and bearing screamed entitlement. Al turned his attention to the figure in the middle, head bowed.

His heart skipped a beat.

"I'll be damned," he muttered.

"Something wrong?" Rogan asked quickly, scanning the area.

"Wrong or very right. The one in the center is Steven," Al said, still not believing it.

"The one Cygnus killed?" Ryanna asked, confused.

"He took him. I assumed he killed him. He must have escaped somehow," Al said, trying to make sense of it.

"Or was let go," Ryanna added.

"Or believed he escaped but was permitted to," Rogan said. "We're dealing with the Alkeir. Anything is possible."

Ryanna hesitated. "I don't trust him, Al. I know he's your friend, but people change. We may not want to believe it, but they do. The man who rode with us to the Citadel—he wasn't a friend to you or the clans."

Al sat silently for a moment and sighed. "This changes nothing. We're here to hear what they have to say. Let's see what my friend can tell us about what happened after the fall of the Citadel."

The three rode on until they were just a horse's length away from the Odio delegation. Steven and Al stared at each other.

"Steven," Al began. "I thought Cygnus had killed you."

Steven smiled—all teeth, no warmth. "I'm not so easy to put down. But never mind me. Look at you, bringing your friends all the way south. A little late, perhaps, but I suppose you get points for effort."

Al laughed and rode forward until he was side by side with Steven. Steven's companions looked ready to strike, but he halted them with a simple gesture. Al embraced him.

"You can bluster all you like, my friend. I am too overjoyed to care. I thought I had lost you and had vowed to make Cygnus pay for it."

Steven looked confused, even conflicted, but returned the embrace. "I've missed you too, old friend."

Al guided his mare back in line with Rogan and Ryanna.

"It seems fate has brought us together again. My scouts say you have a force moving south."

Al nodded. "Yes. We've cleared this area and reopened the Western Pass. But we've received word that the enemy is gathering at the Southern Pass. We're heading there now to strike first. With our combined strength, we should be able to rout them."

Steven said nothing.

"What?" Al asked.

"It is a solid plan. But these are not strictly my forces—they were given to me with a single task in mind. I will have to consult with the other commanders," Steven said, glancing at the woman beside him. Something unspoken passed between them. "We will do our best to convince them. There is a hill near where the enemy is gathering—it's where my scout hides to keep tabs on them. I will bring my forces there if I can. If you see me on the hill, wave your vexel and we will engage."

Seeing the blank look on Al's face, he added, "Wave a red flag for me to advance."

Al sensed the woman beside Steven begin to reach for something beneath her robes, but a low growl from Talionis—and the sudden fear in her eyes—stopped her. The wolf's hackles were raised.

"Any news of my family? I heard you liberated Whittle," Al asked hopefully.

Steven's face turned somber, and he looked away briefly. "I'm sorry, Al. We arrived too late. The house was overrun by the Klav. There were no survivors."

Al's heart sank. "I see," he said softly. Then he looked Steven in the eye. "I'm glad you arrived when you did. I'm sure many more would have died if you hadn't. Please, do what you can to convince your commanders. Harding needs their help."

Without another word, Al turned his mare around and rode back to camp in silence. Neither Ryanna nor Rogan spoke—they knew his heart was breaking.

That night, in the quiet of their tent, he lay with his face buried against Ryanna's chest and wept quietly. In the distance, as if feeling his friend's pain, Talionis howled mournfully.

Two more days passed. The camp was set up for the final time. The battlefield lay ahead. With his vision, Al could see the enemy's campfires already glowing. Tomorrow, they would clash.

The battle plans were finalized—Al had little input, deferring to the clan chiefs and elders. He walked through the camp, sensing the tension. From fire to fire, he moved, listening to bravado, fear, and hope. He knew Ryanna and Rogan were doing the same.

Later, when silence settled over the camp, he walked out alone toward the battlefield. The field—once a farmer's potato patch— seemed to hold its breath.

He sat, quieting his mind and reaching out. Behind him, his people rested fitfully. Ahead, the enemy felt the same blend of fear and anticipation. They were not evil—not the average soldier, at least—they too had loved ones somewhere.

He slipped into the old building. No flickering lights greeted him this time—only a few dim candles. In the back, shrouded in darkness, stood the near-skeletal figure of Cygnus.

"I wondered if you would come," Cygnus said.

Al smiled and sat. "It hasn't been that long. After the way you left last time, I thought you didn't want to see me anymore."

Cygnus grinned—genuine, but grotesque. "I'll admit, Albert, you've grown. If you still had your sword, even I would hesitate to cross you. How did you survive? And apparently unscathed, no less. Come, enlighten me with the tale—it must have been glorious."

"You seem to know much already. I didn't think any of your minions escaped," Al replied.

Cygnus scoffed. "I do not need the feeble-minded to relay information to me. As long as the orb existed, I could witness the battle myself. I saw your wolf take a mortal blow. I saw your blade shatter and its fragments tear into you. Yet here you stand. So tell me—how did you survive?"

Al ran his hand over one of the wooden benches and glanced at the stone steps where the old man had once sat. "I'm afraid you wouldn't be capable of understanding what happened. But survive I did. And I'm coming for you."

Cygnus sneered. "Boy, I have seen the years pass more than a thousand times. There is nothing beyond my comprehension. And come for me? You were no match for me even with that sword. Without it, you're nothing. Come, and your death will be waiting."

"You keep mentioning the sword. That blade was cursed. Like you, I knew the hunger it brought—the need to feed. I'm well rid of it. But just because I no longer gorge on the dead and dying doesn't make me weak," Al said. "I don't need chaos to sustain me. You say my power is diminished—I say it's magnified. That sword was an anchor. Now I sail freely."

"Nice imagery. But every ship needs an anchor. Without one, you're liable to crash on the rocks—or drift into oblivion. That blade didn't just weigh you down—it focused your energy. It was also your sails, gathering and harnessing power. You've seen what I can do. I bend the weather. I craft artifacts that mimic that power and grant it to others. You destroyed one of them." Cygnus shook his head, disapproving. "In time, you might have learned such arts. But without the blade, you're just an anomaly."

"Why have you come?" Al asked.

"Curiosity. Nothing more. I suppose I must make the offer one last time—Lord Dadius would be cross if I didn't: join us. But we both know that won't happen. We're destined to meet again in battle. And you will die—by my hands."

"You're not here," Al said flatly. He closed his eyes and reached out with his mind. "No—you're many miles to the east. You won't be on the battlefield tomorrow."

Cygnus blinked in surprise, unsure how Al had sensed his location. He forced a smile. "Sadly, no. I'm about my master's business. But if you survive, we'll meet again—and settle this once and for all."

Al's face went blank. A truth rose from deep within him, and his voice carried the weight of it.

"No. My death is not yours to claim—and yours is not mine to grant. But know this: you will fall—not in battle, but at the height of your glory—by the hand of one you call ally."

Cygnus' grin vanished. "Nonsense. You will die screaming beneath my hands. I will tear your—"

Al raised a hand, cutting him off mid-sentence.

"Enough. This is not your house, and you are no longer welcome here. Do not return."

With a wave of his hand, Cygnus vanished from the old building, a look of astonishment and rage on his face.

How in the world did I do that? Al wondered.

He blinked and found himself back in the field. The night wore on. He centered himself again and this time reached out and thought of Ryanna. At once, he was watching her quietly sharpening her spear. She was among her warriors and would remain there until the battle was done. It was their way. He watched her. Of all the things he had encountered—good and bad—she was the one gem he held fast to, the one hope his heart still trusted. As if sensing his attention, she looked around, searching for him.

He threw his mind further afield. Dadius had told him Tyr was alive and working in York, and—of all things—courting his granddaughter. Al watched as the fields and farms of Harding gave way to the great southern mountains, then eastward until they reached the vast ocean and a mighty walled city. Buildings flew past until he arrived at a large smithy. One ancient, strange-looking forge burned as bright as the sun. Even in this form, Al could feel its heat. The clear, sharp ring of hammer on metal pierced the silence, rhythmically beating out its song.

There, shirtless and sweating at his labors, was Tyr. He had grown—not taller, but broader. He now sported a full beard and worked with an intensity Al had never seen in him before. Standing beside him was a beautiful blonde, her hair tied back, wearing a leather smock and assisting Tyr in his work.

If that is Dadius' granddaughter, I can see why Tyr has fallen for her, Al thought with a smile.

He looked at what Tyr was forging—it seemed to be a mighty blade. Al could feel the power being beaten into it. This was no ordinary weapon.

You have truly grown, my friend.

He breathed himself back to the field again and this time thought of Steven. He quickly flew the distance between the two camps.

He has come, Al thought with a smile.

But when he tried to look in on him, he saw only outlines—shadows within shadows—and could make out nothing. That troubled him.

What game do you play, Steven? Eventually, you need to grow up and choose your path, he thought ruefully.

He returned to himself and meditated, drawing in as much energy as he dared for the coming battle. In the distance, a cock crowed, calling the sun to rise. Al opened his eyes and looked out upon the hushed fields.

May the blood you drink today not be spilt in vain.

THEY RODE OUT WITH FIRE IN THEIR HEARTS

The twilight breathed cool across the grass. A new day was beginning—and not just any day. *Lursel,* Al thought to himself. The summer solstice. A festival of light and labor in Harding—one of the few still widely observed.

No festival this year. Last year, I was in Morcaster working for Gutamino. So… two years. It feels like a lifetime ago, he thought, the memory tinged with quiet sorrow.

Al sat still, sword sheathed beside him, as the camp behind him stirred. The world was waking—he heard it all. He breathed in the predawn air and listened: the wind, low and long, snaked its way through the open field in front of him. Behind him came the distant cracks of canvas as tent flaps were tugged free. He heard the footfalls on hardened dirt, the muffled grunts as the warriors donned their worn leather armor.

Slow snorts came from the horses, stamping and shuffling as saddles were thrown onto their backs. Al closed his eyes and breathed deep: oil, iron, wool, sweat, fear. The men knew this might be their last morning, but none gave in to it.

Al opened his eyes and looked to the east. On the low hill, there was still no sign of Steven or his forces. He turned to the south. Far across the potato fields, the enemy was waking as well. Though he didn't understand their tongue, the sounds and emotions echoed those of his own camp.

He stood and walked over to the infantry. He had refused to take his mare into battle. *Besides, I'm a better fighter on the ground than I ever was on horseback,* he had told himself. He joined a small unit of front-line foot soldiers—drawn from the best of the volunteers and as many of the clans as could be spared. The nomads were a mobile army, almost exclusively mounted, but there were enough—roughly two hundred— to form two units: one of archers and the other of foot soldiers.

"Takeshi!" came the cheer from a small group of foot soldiers. Al smiled. They were from the Talpan clan—most of this unit was, since they rode the least among the clans.

Al greeted them as he entered the ranks, among civilian volunteers and northern clansmen alike.

"What are our orders?" asked a young man Al didn't know. He could sense the fear of uncertainty in him. Al put a hand on the man's shoulder and reassured him with a smile and a firm grip.

"We are to wait until the cavalry signals us. They'll ride out and test the enemy's line—looking for weaknesses and traps. Once they assess the situation, the bannerman will wave a blue flag and point to where we should engage. At my command, we'll run into the fray and remind them that this is not their land—and they are not welcome."

The others nodded, drawing some reassurance from Al's confidence. Looking at their faces, he wished he were a better speaker. He wished he had the words to inspire them. They looked like they needed something.

"I'm no great general," he said aloud, "and I don't pretend to be a man of stirring speeches. I'm a simple man. But it's the simple man who tills the field, who harvests the crops, who forges the blade, who raises the family. It's the simple man who protects his home.

"And I believe that we—simple men—can do great things. We can push this army of invaders back to the dark corners they crawled out from. I won't promise you victory. Some of us will die. But I *can* promise you this: I'll be with you. Shoulder to shoulder. I will fight, I will bleed—and if it's my time, I will die fighting to free this land from the darkness that stands before us."

A cheer rose from the unit. Al could feel it—just a little—the fear giving way to fire.

Then Talionis approached. The great wolf met Al's gaze, calm and waiting. Al knelt, took the beast's head in both hands, and looked into his eyes.

"Go with her," Al whispered. "Stay with Ryanna. Keep her safe."

He paused, pressing his forehead to Talionis's. "And keep yourself safe too. I don't want to lose either of you."

Talionis licked his face once, slow and deliberate, then turned and ran—not as a beast fleeing battle, but as a guardian obeying command. Al watched him disappear between the tents, toward Ryanna and her spears.

Al turned his eyes back toward the battlefield. Fires were being lit along the enemy's flanks. If all went as planned, more were being lit behind their lines—a distraction. Rogan had said, *With luck, the enemy will think we're flanking them.* Al hoped he was right.

Horns sounded all around him—loud and clear. He could feel the sound in his chest. As one, the cavalry rode forth.

Almost as if in response, drums—deep and resonant—began a rhythmic beat from across the field. With his vision, Al could see the goblins marching out in tight formation, shield to shield.

He watched as the cavalry rode out to meet the goblins, slowly at first but gaining speed until they reached a full gallop. As soon as the riders got within range, the goblin archers—stationed behind the shield wall—let loose a volley. Most of the arrows fell short, but a few found their marks.

Once the arrows were loosed, the cavalry split. Ryanna and her spears veered toward the western portion of the shield wall. Brevton of the Jinto clan led his riders to the east. In the center, riding hard and true, was Rogan—charging ahead of the main cavalry force directly at the goblin line.

Again and again, the goblins fired. Al watched as both horses and riders fell. The clan archers held back—still out of range. At a signal from Kylindo, they split into two units, repositioning on either flank to gain a better angle.

The two forces clashed—rider against shield. Spears thrust forward—most deflected, some striking true with the horrible wail of pierced flesh. The cavalry wheeled away as arrows continued to rain.

As the flanking cavalry came around again, Klav erupted from trenches hidden in the field—dug by the goblins in advance of the battle. Terror gripped the horses, but Ryanna and Brevton rallied their warriors and cut down any Klav that stood in their way.

Now within range, the clan archers began firing, targeting the lightly armored Klav. The cavalry regrouped and charged again, each unit pressing hard against the goblin line.

One of Rogan's bannermen waved a blue flag—the signal Al had been waiting for. The banner pointed west.

With a scream, Al led the foot soldiers into the fray, charging the southern flank.

He hardened his skin, sharpened his blade, and hurled himself into the battle. He moved with lethal grace, slipping into the warrior's trance. Time slowed. He dodged, countered, and struck in a seamless dance. Where his sword passed, screams followed, and bodies dropped. To the watching warriors, he was less man than myth—a dancer clad in red-shadowed death.

As he fought, he began to hear whispers rising from the goblins: "*Kelvakor.*" The name spread like contagion—fear rooted in legend. They began to fall back, unwilling to face him. Al pressed into their ranks, exploiting every gap.

His men picked up the word and began shouting it as a rallying cry.

Despite the chaos, Al tracked the broader battle. Rogan and the main cavalry attacked the center shield wall. Ryanna and her spears targeted the southern line. Al glimpsed Talionis tearing through enemies with primal fury. The screams of the dying followed him.

Assessing his unit, Al found they were faring well—some injured but luckily none had died. They had mainly faced Klav while Ryanna struck at the goblin line. He saw her forces break through and drive toward the archers behind the shields. The southern line erupted in motion.

Al and his foot soldiers pressed hard to keep the goblin shield wall from turning on Ryanna.

The goblins faltered as Al's blade shredded their defenses. Their line began to buckle—besieged from front and rear.

Then came a sound Al knew too well—a mighty roar. Several ogres surged toward Ryanna's position. He saw her rally her spears, tighten their ranks, and bring down the lead ogre through sheer coordination. But with six more charging, her unit was forced to retreat to the front and regroup.

The battle dragged on from early morning into late afternoon. The field ebbed and flowed—neither side gaining nor holding an advantage.

Then, as suddenly as it had begun, horns and drums sounded. Both sides withdrew from the blood-soaked field.

Al stood still, listening. For a moment, there was only silence— no blades, no horns. Just the crackle of fire and the wind whispering over the dead.

He turned to withdraw, but Rogan rode up to him.

"Hold, Al. You and I still have business to attend to."

Al, drenched in blood but uninjured, looked up at Rogan, puzzled.

Rogan pointed with his chin. Al turned as Rogan dismounted, watching as two goblins approached. Al noted that these goblins had not engaged in the fight. The one on Al's left wore highly polished and ornate plate armor with an elaborate helm.

The goblin removed his helmet. "I am Major Drarthknol," he began, his voice clear and calm. "Our general wishes to know if you will honor the ritual of battlefield courtesy—so each side may collect their dead and wounded."

Al studied him. The goblin's bearing was dignified, even regal. His tone lacked mockery. He was not what Al had expected—not at all.

He glanced at Rogan, who gave a slow, silent nod.

"Of course," Al said simply.

The major nodded his thanks and, redonning his helmet, the two turned and walked back to their lines.

What are you up to? Al pondered. *Why give us the chance to collect our dead and dying?*

He looked at Rogan. "It seems not all goblins are the same. Why would they offer us the chance to collect our dead? To be honest, I'm surprised they even care to collect theirs. Do you think it's a trap?"

Rogan shrugged. "It is common courtesy among the clans, but we are all brothers. I didn't expect it in this situation—or with this enemy." He looked thoughtful. "It seems we have more in common than I thought. And if this is an example of their officers, they may present more of a challenge than we expected."

Al and Rogan walked back to the camp.

"No clear winner," Rogan said, "but we gave as good as we got." He patted his horse's neck.

Al was silent. *We didn't win, nor did we lose—so what was the point?* he wondered.

He heard shouting from the camp. Looking up, he focused his vision. The soldiers were pointing to the east. Al turned to see what was causing the stir—and smiled.

There, atop the eastern hill, a lone rider held a high banner. The camp stirred. Al narrowed his eyes. Black and white. A symbol of the Odio. His heart skipped. Steven had come.

He nudged Rogan and pointed to the hill.

Rogan's brows furrowed. "Interesting. We'll need to adjust our battle plans tonight. I'll gather the clan and squad leaders. Be at the command tent after supper."

As soon as they entered the camp, Rogan began shouting orders for all able-bodied soldiers to head out to the battlefield and recover the fallen—and, if luck was with them, any survivors. Al quickly checked with his unit. Thankfully, he had lost none to the battle, though several were badly wounded.

That night, Al and Ryanna sat together in the command tent as new plans were drawn up, relying heavily upon the Odio to help break the line. The thought of the extra force lightened the otherwise somber mood within the tent.

"Not a win, not a loss. So—a tie," Rogan said. "What worked?" he asked those assembled.

"From my vantage point with the archers, I'd say Brevton's and Ryanna's flanking maneuvers were able to successfully pressure the goblins on both sides."

"And forced them to reveal the Klav earlier than they expected, I imagine. They were probably supposed to come at us from behind and cause chaos," added Brevton.

Murmured agreement ran through the tent.

"Don't forget your archers. Splitting them and allowing them to adjust helped us control—or at least limit—battlefield movement."

"Good job breaking through the line, Ryanna. Though those damn ogres limited how much damage you could do, it showed them we can break their line when we need to."

"Let's not forget Al," Rogan said, looking him in the eye. "He won't say it himself, but my men said the goblins fell back in fear of him and gave him a new name in their tongue: *Kelvakor.*"

"Any idea what it means?" asked Brevton.

"No, but I think I saw them carrying a few wounded goblins back to camp. We could ask them. Which brings up another question—are we taking prisoners?" he asked.

The tent fell quiet.

"We will not kill the wounded or the captured," Al said. "I don't believe they will either, though I'm not sure. But an enemy that honors battlefield courtesy—I imagine they'd be open to prisoner exchanges. Also—do not take any of their wounded from the field. Captured in the fight is one thing. Let them reclaim their wounded, and we will reclaim ours."

"As for what didn't go as planned—well, that's easy to see. We underestimated their discipline. We thought their line would break, but it didn't. We—and by that, I mean me—didn't capitalize on Ryanna's breakthrough. It's something we should have anticipated and planned for. And their damn archers were more effective than we expected." He paused. "And we still have an unknown number of ogres to deal with. Unlike the ones back home, these are heavily armored and will require more than three warriors to take down."

At that point, they began strategizing a revised plan for the next day. Al stood quietly in the back, letting Ryanna and the others lead. This was not his strong suit—he was more of a one-at-a-time fighter.

The hours ticked by, but eventually, the new plans were drawn up. Al was about to leave with Ryanna when a soldier entered and handed Kylindo a slip of paper. Rogan, guessing its content, spoke. "Tell us. What is the butcher's bill?"

Kylindo passed the sheet to Rogan. "One hundred thirty dead. At least two hundred wounded. About half of those should be able to fight tomorrow."

Rogan shook his head. "No—hold them back. With luck, and the additional Odio forces, we won't need them." He paused. "Have them gear up just in case. I fear this enemy is more clever than we anticipated."

Ryanna kissed Al and headed back to her spears. Al, not needing sleep, went to check on the wounded. Several large tents had been set up for the most seriously injured. Al gathered natural energy and went from bed to bed, doing what he could without draining himself completely, stopping only to recharge as needed. By the time he was done, everyone was at least stabilized, and a few were well enough to return to duty.

He then visited the tent where the captives were held. Guards posted all around let him pass without challenge. Fifteen goblin soldiers sat chained together, looking forlorn. Upon seeing him, their eyes filled with fear.

"Kelvakor," one of them whispered.

Al ignored the name for the moment. Four of the goblins were wounded and lay groaning. Al stepped toward the nearest; the others shrank back. Gathering his energy, he touched the goblin and let the healing flow. The goblin's wounds closed, and his breathing steadied. The others watched in awe—and greater fear. Al healed each of the wounded in turn.

When he had finished, he turned to leave. One of them whispered in awe, "Zhar'malok."

Al stopped. "What does that mean? And what does *Kelvakor* mean as well?"

The goblins exchanged uncertain glances.

"You have nothing to fear," Al said. "You will not be harmed while in our care."

Still, they hesitated. Finally, one spoke. "The mercy that burns. You heal us to mock us. To show us you are in command. That is *Zhar'malok*."

"I heal you because you are hurt and it is within my power to help. Interpret that however you wish. And *Kelvakor*?"

"That means the burning silence. Your blade cuts through armor and shield like fire through paper. And it makes no sound in the cutting. You are truly terrifying."

Al left, unsure if he had done any good—but feeling better for having tried.

He returned to his spot outside the camp. Talionis was already waiting. Al ran up and hugged the great wolf.

"I'm so happy to see you," he said.

Images from the battle flashed into his mind—kill after kill— Talionis excited to share his deeds.

Eventually, the wolf settled and curled up beside him. Al looked east, toward where the Odio banner still flew.

"Don't betray us, Cutter. We're all counting on you. Now is the time to let your true light shine through," he said aloud.

Talionis huffed. He had no faith in Steven.

Al closed his eyes. He may not need sleep, but he did need to center himself—and gather as much energy as he dared.

THEY BLED IN SILENCE BENEATH BROKEN SKIES

When morning arrived, Al and Talionis headed to the staging area. Al looked up, clouds were beginning to roll in. *A storm in* brewing, Al thought to himself. With a thought shared between them to remain safe Talionis headed off to find Ryanna. Al greeting his unit, all of them seemed to be in good spirits, yesterday had been brutal, but they had survived, today they hoped to gain the advantage.

"What's the word, *Kelvakor*?" asked one of the men with a smile.

Al returned the smile. "Same as yesterday. We support the cavalry. Wait for the blue flag. With luck, we'll be joined by the Odio at some point. Know your target—the last thing we need is to kill a friendly."

At the mention of the Odio, all eyes turned to the hill. The banner still flew, and three riders on horseback sat waiting for the signal.

"So much for this season's crops, I guess," Al said quietly, looking out over the once-untouched potato fields, now trampled under hoof and foot, soaked red with blood. *This was a family's livelihood,* he thought sadly. *If they are still alive,* he reminded himself. *There will be no livelihood for anyone if the enemy isn't dealt with.*

Across the fields, the drums began to beat and, as if in answer, horns sounded behind him. He watched as the goblins began their slow march forward—and the long line of cavalry began their charge. Slowly, then faster and faster, until they reached a full gallop. Al felt the ground vibrating beneath his feet as the horses pounded across the field. The goblin shield line tightened, bracing for the inevitable clash. Arrows filled the sky. At the last moment, the cavalry swung wide and bore down from the west, meeting the shields with a thunderous crash. The wall buckled but didn't break. The cavalry came about and struck again—and again—all while contending with the constant hail of arrows.

Al watched the battle rage, waiting for the signal. This part—the part where he wasn't in the midst of it—was the hardest. He tried to detach himself, to watch the battle objectively, but it was difficult. His eyes always searched for Ryanna or Talionis. He could sense the wolf—sense his excitement, his thrill in the kill. Through it all, Talionis stayed close to Ryanna, always with an eye on her.

As he watched the ebb and flow of the battle, he sensed it before he saw it—the subtle shift in the lines. The shield wall was beginning to buckle, and the goblins began pulling forces from the eastern flank toward the center to reinforce it. That was the moment Rogan had been waiting for. The blue banner flew, then dipped to the east.

"That's our sign!" yelled Al as he charged headfirst into the weakened eastern flank. As soon as they engaged, the bannerman began waving the red flag to call the Odio forward. Again and again, he gave the signal. Al risked a quick glance—the three mounted figures still stood atop the hill. The one in the center held the banner of the Odio.

Al focused his sight on the hill. He saw Steven, with the woman and the noble from before. Almost as if he sensed Al watching, Steven threw the banner to the ground. The three of them turned their horses and slowly retreated down the hill—away from the battle.

The Odio would not be joining.

A sword thrust at Al failed to pierce his hardened skin, but it snapped him back to the moment. Furious, Al reacted—too close to draw his blade, he backhanded the goblin without restraint. He felt the neck snap, the jaw break, as the body crumpled lifeless to the ground.

He forced himself to calm. *Emotion in battle will get me killed. Steven has chosen his path. It doesn't change mine.*

From his vantage point on the hill, Steven sat horseback with Tenebris and Major Polix on either side. He watched the infantry charge. Even from this distance, he could see Al—fast and terrifying, the one the goblins fell back from.

"There's the signal," said Polix as the red banner was waved.

Steven said nothing. He kept watching Al, that blur of death on the field. He noticed Al watching him. *Him and that damn sight of his. Fine—you see me, I see you. And here is what I think of you.* He held up the banner—and dropped it to the ground.

"Come. We're done here," he said, and turned his horse. The three withdrew from the hill, leaving the battle behind.

As they rode, a voice as clear as a bell echoed in Steven's mind:

So the fox runs alone. You saw the game and chose the board. You watched the match and turned from the fire. You were never the hound, Steven… and now you are not even the hunter. One move left. One piece to play. But if you wait too long… the fire will consume even that.

Steven hardened his face—but rode on all the same.

Al quickly rallied his unit. With no support coming, their best option was to wedge themselves between the eastern flank and the center to prevent Rogan and Brevton's units from being surrounded. As the shield wall began to crack, the fighting became brutal—man-to-man. Like the day before, goblins tried to skirt around Al, but he adapted—using speed and agility to close gaps and confront them head-on.

A sudden cheer erupted from the cavalry. Al looked up and saw that both Rogan's and Ryanna's units had broken through—Rogan at the center, Ryanna on the west. The goblin archers were fleeing, and their forces were shifting, now threatened from three sides.

But just as momentum seemed to shift in their favor, chaos erupted.

Klav sprang from freshly dug pits behind the lines, harassing the cavalry that had broken through. As the goblin archers retreated, a division of heavily armored ogres charged onto the battlefield. Riders and horses stumbled into hidden gullies, falling helplessly. It had all been a trap.

Talionis fought fiercely, but Al could sense the wolf tiring. Through their bond, he felt Ryanna keeping her spears tight and organized—splitting into smaller units to tackle the ogres, while others engaged the Klav. The goblins were, for the moment, forgotten.

Get her out of there! Al thought desperately, knowing full well she wouldn't abandon her warriors. And Talionis would never abandon her. Al and his men now risked being encircled. He poured more power into his sword, enhancing his speed and strength. Any advantage mattered.

Then came a cry of despair from Rogan's position. Al turned quickly and spotted the chief in single combat with a massive ogre. Rogan's forces had been cut off. He managed to land a spear thrust beneath the ogre's armor, but the beast retaliated with a crushing blow from a massive warhammer, hurling Rogan from his horse. Rogan crumpled, unmoving.

Al's heart dropped. They had been outplayed.

Ryanna's scream of anguish echoed across the battlefield as she watched her father fall. Before she could react, goblins swarmed her, dragging her from her horse and stabbing at her. Al focused his hearing—he heard the blades strike, heard her cry out in pain. He felt Talionis launch into the fray, but more goblins overwhelmed the wolf as well.

Now it was Al's turn to rage. He prepared to surge forward, but one of his men called out, "Go, Takeshi! Go save your woman—we'll hold here!"

Al gritted his teeth. He gauged the distance. Then he froze. He turned back to his men—fighting, dying. *I can't leave them now, they'll be slaughtered.* He looked towards where Ryanna had fallen, *I'm sorry my love, stay alive, I will come for you.* Behind him, a cavalry horse screamed as its leg snapped in a rut, throwing its rider into the Klav's waiting blades.

This battle is lost.

He caught the bannerman's eye and motioned for him to sound the retreat. *The enemy has taken this day. All I can do now is save who I can.*

Horns sounded. The push became a desperate withdrawal. The goblins, bloodied and tired, gave only minimal pursuit. Al paused halfway between the battlefield and the forward camp. He could still sense Talionis—alive—and through him, Ryanna. Captured.

After both sides had withdrawn, Major Drarthknol and his aide walked calmly through the field of the dead toward Al. Again, neither had taken part in the battle.

The major saluted as he approached. "Your army fought well today. If the Odio had engaged, I dare say you might have won the day—if not the war," he said candidly.

"You don't seem surprised by their betrayal," Al said, watching the goblin carefully. "From what I saw, you paid them little heed."

"To be honest, they caused quite a stir among us last night, but then word came that they had already sworn allegiance to Cygnus." Seeing the look on Al's face, he smiled. "Sorry, but I can't tell if the fact that they are sworn to Cygnus—or that I'm admitting it— surprises you more."

"Both," admitted Al.

"As to the first, their commander has been working with Cygnus for some time now. Maybe 'working with' is too strong a term. Let's say he's not openly working against Cygnus's interests. So while he is not exactly an ally, he is also not an enemy. As for the second, I see no need to hide the fact. You saw for yourself—he turned from the battle."

Al said nothing, so the major continued. "I hear you've been given the name *Kelvakor* by the foot soldiers." The major nodded with approval. "I admit, I am impressed and honored to fight against one such as you. If we do lose this battle, there will be no shame in it—we will have died fighting a true warrior." He saluted Al again. "Will the courtesy be honored tonight?" he asked.

"That depends," Al said coldly. "You have taken two whom I hold most dear—a red-haired woman and a large white timber wolf. I want your word as an officer and a gentleman that they will not be harmed."

The major thought for a moment and nodded. "Indeed. I do not know the woman, but any we've taken captive—if they are injured—are being tended to." He looked at Al, his expression hardening. "May I assume ours are as well?"

"They are," Al replied.

The major didn't seem convinced. "I don't mean to doubt you, but our experience in these lands has shown your kind to be rather brutal with captives. So let me be clear: if you mistreat our soldiers in your care, you best hope you win. Otherwise, no mercy will be shown to any of you."

Al nodded his understanding. "I am being honest. And if you doubt me, then know this: those we hold captive gave me a new name when I used my abilities to heal them."

"And what name is that?" the major asked.

"*Zhar'malok*," Al replied.

The major looked surprised—and perhaps a little fearful. "Indeed?" He seemed genuinely shaken. "I do believe you. As for the wolf, I will send word to the general. It is a magnificent creature. I believe he intended to keep it for himself, but I will let him know its value to you. And should you win this battle, we can discuss it further. In either case, I assure you—no harm will befall him, and he will not be mistreated."

Al nodded—it was the best he could hope for at the moment. "I appreciate your honesty. So let me return the favor. You and your forces have not truly seen what I am capable of. I want there to be no misunderstanding—tomorrow will be the last day of this battle, and it will not end in your favor. Tell your general unless he wishes to see what the *Kelvakor* is truly capable of, he should surrender before we engage."

The major seemed more intrigued than annoyed. "I will relay your message. But I would prepare for battle all the same," he replied with a faint smile. "As you may have noticed, all goblins love a good fight."

Al strode back to camp, his mind a blur. He motioned for the units to go collect the dead and the dying. He stood at the edge of camp waiting. He knew Talionis was alive and chained behind enemy lines, but otherwise unharmed. He was anxious—wanting to break free, to get to Ryanna.

Easy, boy. Save your energy. She is all right for the moment. I need you to be strong and to be patient. The fight will come—but for now, rest, he said in the wolf's mind.

He felt Talionis relax and lie down. And he watched the enemy.

Soon the dead and dying were brought into camp. A loud commotion caught Al's attention—they had found Rogan. And he was still alive. Barely.

Al rushed to him. Rogan was gravely injured; the blow had nearly crushed his chest. He was unconscious and likely bleeding internally. Al closed his eyes and pushed everything he had into the wounded chief. When he was nearly drained, he attempted something new: to tap into the source while healing—something he had never dared before.

The sensation was strange. It wasn't the vast, overwhelming floodgate he accessed through meditation, but rather a steady current—consistent and strong. The key was regulation: matching the energy he pushed out to what he drew in. Slowly, very slowly, he felt Rogan's body begin to mend.

One hour passed. Then a second. Then a third. Finally, Al stepped back, exhausted.

"It's done," he said. "The rest is up to him."

He paused, breathing hard. "Give me a moment to catch my breath, then take me to the next."

Kylindo handed him a small bowl of stew. "Not yet. No one else is in danger of dying. You need to rest—and we need you in the war tent."

Al wanted to refuse, but the stew smelled good, and he was drained. So he nodded and followed Kylindo to the tent.

Inside were the unit leaders, acting commanders, and clan elders. All eyes turned to him. He faced Brevton.

"You're the most senior. I acknowledge you as acting commander."

Brevton shook his head. "No one is going to take that position, Al—except you. You're the most skilled warrior among us. All the clans acknowledge this."

"I'm no general. I'm barely a unit leader. And even then, I've only been following the plans you already laid out," he protested.

"Our tactics lost us this battle," Brevton replied. "We all agree—we will follow where you lead, to victory or defeat."

Al was about to argue but stopped. Time was slipping away, and they couldn't afford to waste it. He closed his eyes. *Could I modify what I learned from Gutamino to fit a larger force?* If he treated each unit like an individual, set them against other units like counters on a board...

"I learned something while healing Rogan," Al said. "How to prevent my energy from depleting. That might give us—just possibly—the opening we need."

Everyone leaned in, listening.

"I'm going to unleash the power inside me. I don't know exactly what I'll be able to do, or how effective it will be. But I'm fairly certain it will cause enough of a disruption that they'll have to focus on me first. When they do, I need the rest of you to act in smaller, flexible units. Right now, we're playing their game. Tomorrow, they'll be forced to play ours."

He looked around the tent. "No horns tomorrow. When their drums sound, we'll answer with silence. You will be the stillness before the storm. I'll walk out alone to meet their shield wall. No one engages until I unleash everything I have. When they reel from it, you'll charge forward in groups no larger than twenty. And I want you to be like water—move fluidly. Don't follow their expectations. Let the battlefield dictate your rhythm. Use misdirection. Strike at the moment they least expect it."

The others nodded, some murmuring approval. Soon they dove into the finer details. Al took his leave and returned to the wounded—tending friend and foe alike—before going back to the field to meditate before battle.

THEY RETURNED WITH ASHES IN THEIR HANDS

Al gathered more energy than ever before. He could still take in more, but time was short. As he had done while healing Rogan, he kept the flow open in the background. He did not move to the others today. Today, he would walk alone.

He waited—hardened his skin, enhanced his reflexes, dipped into the warrior's mind. Today, they would see what he had become. Even he didn't know what that would be.

Drums sounded from across the battlefield, answered only by silence.

They beat louder.

He heard the goblin shield wall advancing, their chanting and taunts echoing across the field. Still, nothing from the clans.

Drawing a deep breath, Al strode forward alone. He could sense confusion building in the enemy lines.

The drums beat faster.

Still, his forces held.

As he approached, the goblins loosed a volley of arrows. With a measured exhale, his body ignited in radiant flame. Arrows that touched the aura turned to ash. He could feel the enemy's anxiety growing, hear their heartbeats quicken. His pace remained steady, deliberate.

At a command, three armored ogres burst from the line, massive hammers swinging.

The first screamed in agony at the aura's touch.

Then Al became a blur—his sword tearing through armor, muscle, and bone. In an instant, the goliath lay dismembered and burning behind him.

The other two hesitated.

One swung his hammer, careful to stay outside the aura. He grinned as the blow fell—until Al caught the weapon mid-swing with his left hand. Al smiled at the ogre's shocked expression.

Panic overtook the creature. It dropped the hammer and turned to flee, but Al was faster. One clean stroke cut the ogre in two. Without stopping, he completed the motion and took the third's head.

He stood still, composed himself, and drew a steady breath. Then, without a word, he resumed his walk toward the goblins.

He was close now. The arrows had stopped. Panic rippled through the klav, hidden behind the lines. The goblins held formation, but uncertainty clouded their ranks. Even the ogres faltered.

I draw my strength from nature itself, Al thought. *Let's see if I can return some of that back to it.*

He knelt, struck the earth with his hand, and pushed energy downward. It exceeded what he was taking in, but he didn't expend it all. He forced the energy beneath the enemy line, then drove it upward.

A low groan rumbled beneath the goblins. Confused, they glanced about as the ground trembled. Hairline cracks split open beneath their feet.

Then the ground erupted.

A surge of energy burst upward in a deafening blast. Goblins were shredded where they stood, their bodies hurled apart, gore splattering the survivors.

Silence followed—brief, unnatural. Both sides stood stunned, struggling to comprehend the devastation.

Al stared at the smoldering crater—fifty feet wide, jagged and raw. The shield wall was obliterated. He leveled his gaze across the field. He could smell their fear.

Then chaos.

The cavalry charged from behind. The goblins broke—some fled, others tried to rally and swarm Al in desperation. The klav, panicked, erupted from their trenches with howls and whines, attacking anything nearby—even each other. Ogres turned and fled south, trampling their own.

A flash of lightning split the sky. Thunder rolled across the valley as rain poured in sheets. But around Al, droplets hissed and evaporated into steam upon touching the aura. The goblins recoiled. Even nature, it seemed, dared not touch him.

As the goblin horde closed in, Al expanded the glowing sphere around him, pouring more energy into it. As the light encompassed the enemy, they burst into flame, screaming and thrashing. When they retreated or fell, he pulled the aura back in and focused on gathering energy once more.

The enemy gave him wide berth now; none dared approach. Instead, they turned on the cavalry running them down. But they could form no line. As soon as they thought they'd pinned a unit down, it dissolved, only to be replaced by another coming from a new direction—while the first reformed and struck elsewhere.

As the battle devolved into chaos, Al turned his gaze to the tent on the hill behind the lines. He could feel Talionis there. He knew Ryanna was too. He began his slow walk again, the enemy shrinking away as he passed.

He saw the major standing beside a larger goblin—the general, he assumed. Both waited patiently. Al sensed neither fear nor anger from them.

As he got closer, two robed figures stepped forward, taking position in front of the officers. Each carried a staff. Al could sense the energy in them—similar to his own, but different. Like the seer he had once fought. No doubt they were the same kind.

He stopped. His energy was nearly restored. The two descended the hill toward him.

The last time I fought one, I died. I won't get lucky twice. I need to be careful.

They flanked him, taking positions to either side. Al stood calmly, pulling in more energy. *Their attack will come when I least expect it.*

The two exchanged glances. Whatever they were planing would happen soon.

Without warning, both moved as one. Lightning leapt from their staves. Al was fast—but not fast enough to dodge. The bolts struck his protective aura. He felt it begin to crack as they poured more power into the attack.

No time to create a feedback loop.

Instead, he summoned two fire orbs, one in each hand, and hurled them.

They hadn't expected that. Forced to counter, they dropped their attack and raised shields of their own. The orbs struck, fizzling against the barriers. The seers eyed Al warily. This would not be as simple as they had hoped.

I have to destroy the staves. It may kill me, but if I don't, I'll run out of energy before they do.

Even as he considered his options, the seers changed tactics. They cast arcs overhead that formed an electric cage around him. He tried the fire orb again—it fizzled on contact. The cage was shrinking, tightening. They meant to crush or fry him.

Fire is useless. Water would be deadly—to me. What about earth?

Al focused. Instead of touching the ground, he visualized his intent and pushed energy into the soil beneath the seer to his right.

The ground shifted. The seer fell backward, breaking the cage.

Seizing the moment, Al surged forward and drove his sword through the fallen seer. He kicked the staff away and turned to face the second—sword in hand.

Now the odds are better. I can counter his energy. He can probably counter mine. Let's see who fights better.

Al closed the distance. Like the first, this seer matched his speed and strength—but not his skill. Soon, the seer was sweating and retreating. When an opening presented itself, Al took it, removing the seer's head with a single strike.

He sheathed his sword and continued toward the officers. As he approached, the major stepped forward, drawing his blade. Al reached for his own, but the general stopped the major with a hand on his shoulder.

The major stepped back and sheathed his weapon. The general drew his own sword—then knelt, offering the hilt to Al.

"We stand defeated," he said. His voice was elegant, refined, resonant with the experience of many battles.

Al, still radiating with light, looked down on him.

"The prisoners?"

"Alive and well," the general replied, eyes cast downward.

"The wounded?" Al's voice was firm, unyielding.

"Those who could be saved have been," came the general's measured response.

"My wolf?" Al already sensed Talionis nearby, but he wanted to hear it aloud.

"Tethered, but unharmed," the general confirmed.

Al released the shield around him, and the glow faded. He could feel the collective exhale from the goblin officers.

"Signal your troops to lay down their weapons," he said. "Anyone who does so will not be harmed. Any who continue to fight will be shown no mercy."

He took the sword from the general, who then stood and stepped back.

With a nod from the general, the major gave the command. Al heard the fading clamor of combat as word spread and weapons were lowered.

He looked back at the officers. "Where is Cygnus?"

The general straightened. "Gone before the first day."

"Where to?"

The general sighed, weariness catching in his throat. "We are truly beaten. You have earned the right to know. He returned to York. Said his task here was finished. I believe he'll head east as soon as he's able. And after witnessing your strength today, I can't blame him."

Al narrowed his gaze. "Where did the ogres retreat to?"

The general let out a sharp laugh. "That's the question, isn't it? Not only did the southern ogres bolt, but the northern ones we held in reserve vanished as well. My guess? They're halfway back to the Wastes already."

"What becomes of your forces now?" Al asked.

The general met his gaze without hesitation. "I don't know. We brought death and destruction to this land. And though you have every reason to hate us—I sense you do not."

Al nodded slowly. "If I have my way, the Klav will be hunted to extinction. I've found no honor in them. As for you and your soldiers—that's not for me to decide. That judgment belongs to those you've wronged."

The general gave a solemn nod. "Fair. And we'll face that judgment with heads held high." He hesitated. "But might I ask one boon—for myself and my officers?"

Al arched a brow.

"I would request parole. Restricted to an area you designate, but with free movement within it. That way we can maintain order among our troops."

Al considered. "I'm inclined to agree. But that, too, falls to the elders. I'll support your request when we meet with them."

Just then, Brevton rode up with a contingent of fifty horse. Al looked up.

"Have some of your men release the prisoners and bring the wounded to camp," Al said. "The rest are to remain with the goblins. Ensure order is kept."

He turned back to the general. "Break camp. Move your forces east of ours. Keep them in line. Tonight, you and your officers will dine with us—and we'll meet with the elders."

The general and the major saluted.

Al turned and strode toward Talionis, who was close. It didn't take long to find him.

The wolf leapt to his feet as Al approached, and Al dropped to his knees, throwing his arms around him.

"You have no idea how happy I am to see you," Al said. Then, rising, he snapped the chains holding Talionis with his bare hands. "Now let's go find Ryanna."

As if on cue, Talionis bolted toward a tent at the edge of the encampment—the one where the wounded had been taken. He pushed the flap aside with his nose and disappeared inside.

Al followed.

The interior reminded him of the field hospital they'd used before—rows of cots, each holding a patient, bandaged and carefully tended. Each prisoner was chained to their cot but otherwise appeared well cared for. The room buzzed to life at Al's entrance. Wounded or not, cheers and calls rose from the captives.

But his eyes were only for one.

There, lying still but awake, was Ryanna—red hair tousled, bright green eyes locked on him. Talionis sat loyally beside her cot, tail wagging once.

Al approached cautiously, uncertain how bad her wounds truly were.

She smiled. "About time you showed up," she said weakly.

Her torso was wrapped in bloodstained bandages—stab wounds, bruises, signs of a brutal struggle before they'd taken her prisoner. He knelt beside her and took her hand.

"I'm sorry," he said. "I was... unavoidably delayed."

He placed his left hand gently on her forehead, his right on her abdomen. Closing his eyes, he channeled his power through her, guiding energy into broken flesh, shattered bone, and torn muscle. Her breathing eased.

"I love you," she whispered.

Then, finally safe, Ryanna slipped into sleep.

Al turned as his soldiers entered the tent with the goblin major. The major's eyes were wide with disbelief.

"Let me tend to the most severely wounded before you take them," Al said. He looked at Talionis. *Go with Ryanna. Stay by her side until they get her back to camp. I'll be here for a while.*

As they removed Ryanna and the other lightly wounded, the wolf padded alongside them—silent, alert, and intimidating. Any goblin foolish enough to test them would be met by the fury of a very protective timber wolf.

Al moved from patient to patient, mending the worst injuries, resting as needed to recharge his strength. When he finished and the last of the wounded were carried out, the major stepped forward and bowed.

"I do not know what you are," he said. "I will not even pretend to understand. But you are something new. Something different. I'm guessing you healed my troops the same way?"

"Those who needed it," Al replied simply.

The major nodded, thoughtful. "Then the title they gave you makes sense—though I fear it falls far short of the truth. You have the hands of a healer, the heart of a warrior, and the power of something even greater within you."

He saluted. "It was truly an honor to meet you."

Al returned the salute as best he could—awkwardly, but sincerely. The slight smirk on the major's face told him he had done it wrong, but it seemed to be appreciated all the same.

That night ran long.

The goblins were disarmed, and their camp reestablished on the east side of the field. Riders kept watch, but the enemy showed no signs of renewed aggression. The ferocity of earlier days had left them; they now sat quietly among their tents.

The council of elders and clan chieftains met late into the evening to debate the fate of the prisoners. Even Rogan insisted on being carried in to attend.

By the time the meeting concluded, only one decision had been reached: the goblin officers would be granted parole. Any violation would result in immediate execution.

Al left the council early and returned to Ryanna. She was resting in their tent, with Talionis curled protectively at her feet. Al sat beside her, offering quiet comfort as the night wore on.

In the soft light of dawn, her eyes opened. He lay down next to her, brushing a hand through her hair.

"I'm sorry," he said gently.

She blinked, puzzled. "For what?"

"When you fell… I wanted to run to you. But if I had, my unit would've been overrun. If I had lost you…" His voice faltered.

She touched his cheek. "Oh, Al. You did what you had to do. I wouldn't have been happy if those men had died so I could live. I'm a warrior—like you, like them. We all know the risks. We fight because it's needed, not because we want to."

She smiled softly. "So let's speak no more of it. You chose correctly."

Then she shifted, stretching with a groan. "Now, more importantly—what is there to eat? I'm starving."

He sat up, chuckling. "That might be my fault too."

"Oh?" She raised an eyebrow.

"I think the rapid healing burns through your body's energy stores. Side effect, maybe."

She rolled over with a groan. "Good. Then as punishment, go fetch me something to eat."

He stood and bowed with exaggerated grace. "At once, milady," he said with a grin.

That afternoon, Al sat beside Ryanna and Talionis near Rogan's tent. The older warrior was still unable to walk unaided, propped up by pillows and stubborn pride.

"I heard a rumor you're planning to leave us," Rogan said, eyeing Al sharply.

"Cygnus left for York four days ago," Al answered. "If I travel light and hard, I can close the gap. With luck, he'll linger in York long enough for me to catch up."

Rogan frowned. "And then what? From the sound of things, he's already done what he came to do."

"That may be," Al said, "but as far as I know, the Dokkalfar isn't free yet. And even if he is—if all I can do is deny him one of his Alkeir—then at least I will have done something."

"York isn't some little outpost, Al," Rogan warned. "I've been speaking with the volunteers. It's a huge, stone-fortified capital with a large standing army. They may not take kindly to you strolling in and killing someone."

Al nodded. "I know. But I still need to try."

"How many will you take with you?"

"Only Ryanna and Talionis."

Rogan looked ready to object, but Al raised a hand to stop him.

"You need your forces here. The Odio has joined with Cygnus— that means eastern Harding is occupied. Your work isn't finished. These are just men now—no monsters, no seers with strange powers. I trust you to do what needs to be done."

He hesitated, then added, "If possible, try not to kill Steven. But if he forces your hand... then so be it."

Ryanna placed her hand on Al's shoulder, grounding him.

"I'll try," Rogan said quietly. "Even if I do take him alive, I'm not sure he'd thank you for the mercy."

Al nodded. "I know. I'm beginning to believe his betrayal runs deeper—and started longer ago—than I ever imagined. But I can't shake the feeling that he still has some part to play."

He paused, the weight of too many memories heavy on his face.

"But then," he said with a sad smile, "I've been wrong about him many, many times."

EPILOGUE

Al, Ryanna, and Talionis stood along the side of the road. In the distance, the tall white walls of the city of York loomed. Al knelt before the great wolf and took his head in his hands.

"You know the plan," he said. "Stay close to the city, but out of sight. We'll find a way to get you in safely—or we'll come back out to you. First, we need to see if our prey is within."

The giant wolf let out a huff—part annoyance, part understanding. With a final look at Al and Ryanna, he bounded off the road and disappeared into the thick forest.

Al and Ryanna mounted up and rode toward the gates. The white walls grew larger with every stride.

"I never imagined such a thing," Ryanna gasped. "I thought the Citadel was impressive."

"The Citadel *was* impressive," Al said. "This is just on a different level."

The wall stretched north and south as far as they could see. The gates stood open, a steady stream of people and wagons passing through under the watchful eyes of armed guards. More guards patrolled the wall above, alert and focused.

These aren't bored town watch, Al thought. *These men are trained and ready.*

He and Ryanna fell into line, slowly approaching the gate.

"Where do we begin?" Ryanna asked.

Al shook his head. "Not sure. If he's anything like Gutamino, he'll be in the wealthier districts. We'll need to find those first."

As they reached the front of the line, a guard stepped forward. "Names and reason for entry?" he asked in a brisk, professional tone.

Before Al could answer, a familiar voice chimed in. "No need for that."

A young noble stepped forward confidently. "They're here on official business. I'm to escort them to the palace immediately."

The guard looked the young man over, then glanced at Al and Ryanna. After a brief pause, he nodded. "Very well. But you'll need to walk your horses through the city. No riding—except for carriages."

Al and Ryanna dismounted. Al eyed the young noble—something about him was familiar.

"Gillian?" he said, realization dawning.

The boy grinned broadly. "Took you long enough, big brother." He gave Al a quick hug. "I've been waiting forever for you to show up."

He turned to Ryanna with a mischievous smile. "And who's the lady?"

Al took Ryanna's hand. "Gillian, allow me to introduce you to Ryanna, First of the Spears, of the Hugga Clan. Ryanna, this is—"

Gillian cut him off with a flourishing bow and took Ryanna's hand, kissing it gallantly. "I am Gillian—street waif of Morcaster, foundling of Albert, and apprentice to the great Gutamino."

Al laughed. "He's as quick with his hands as he is with his tongue too—so keep a hand on your coin purse."

He looked Gillian over. "I'm very happy to see you. And it seems you're doing remarkably well for yourself."

Gillian struck a pose, arms wide. "Oh, these old things?" he said, mocking his fine attire. "Please."

Al's expression turned serious. "Since you're here to meet us, I assume you know why I've come."

"I do," Gillian said. "And I've been instructed to bring you to Gutamino as soon as you arrived."

"Then lead on," Al said. "And while we walk, tell me everything that's happened since we last saw each other."

By the time they reached the estate where Gutamino was staying, Al and Gillian had caught up. Gillian had handed off their horses to a palace squire at the gates.

"Before we go in," Al said, "I heard Tyr is in the city—and working for Gutamino?"

Gillian nodded. "I'll take you to the smithy after this. They're expecting you."

He led them through the estate's elegant halls to a large, richly appointed office. Al was struck by how much it resembled the one he'd stayed in back in Morcaster.

As they entered, Gutamino rose to greet them. Graceful as ever— like a cat, and just as deadly, Al thought. He quietly readied himself to pull energy if needed.

Gutamino bowed. "Mr. Dis-Ornfel," he said smoothly. "It lightens my heart to see you again. And the lovely Ryanna." He bowed once more. "Truly, I am honored today. Please, come in. Sit. I've prepared tea, if you'd like."

Gutamino led them to a small sitting area. No one sat.

"What did you do to Morcaster?" Al asked bluntly.

Gutamino's face took on a pensive, hesitant look, as if he were deciding how to answer. He sat down and poured himself a glass of tea, gesturing for them to do the same. Neither Al nor Ryanna moved.

Gutamino sighed. "I did what I was ordered to do, Al. It may be hard for you to understand, but I have a master to answer to—and he has one as well."

"That's it? You killed an entire city—men, women, children— over a hundred thousand lives… because you were told to?" Al asked, his voice tight with mounting anger.

Gutamino, apparently unfazed, simply said, "Yes. I know it's not the answer you want, but it is the truth."

"Why? What was to be gained?"

"Confusion. Cygnus was beginning to move his forces into Harding. He needed the North to be distracted. Morcaster gave him that distraction."

Al clenched his fists, struggling to contain his rage. Gutamino watched him with quiet approval.

"I see you've learned your lessons well," he said. "And from what I hear, you've taken them to unbelievable heights. When you left, you were far below me in skill. Now, on your return, I am as an unarmed child before an armored knight. If you're here to kill me, there's nothing I could do to stop you."

Al glared at him. "I *should* kill you. It would be justice for Morcaster alone." He glanced at Ryanna. "But your life and your crimes are not mine to judge. Your master's life, however… Where is he hiding?"

Gutamino smiled and took a sip of tea. "That is how I know I cannot stand against you. You've grown powerful enough that even the Alkeir flee before your wrath. He's gone—sailed away yesterday on the evening tide. Back to the East. Back to his master."

"If he's gone, why are you still here?"

"I have my orders, and there is still work to be done. Diplomatic work, so to speak. I am his envoy here in York."

Al turned to leave.

"Are you sure you wouldn't like some tea?" Gutamino called after him.

"Don't let our paths cross again, Gutamino. My mercy has its limits," Al said without stopping.

Gillian followed them out and quickly led them to the smithy.

The shop was huge, clean, and well-lit. Al marveled at the strange forge—the same one he had seen in his vision. As they entered, a deep, resonant voice boomed across the room.

"Hayseed!"

Al turned just in time to see Tyr barreling toward him. He hesitated, unsure what to do, and then Tyr grabbed him in a vice-like hug that nearly knocked the wind out of him.

"I feared the worst when I heard about Morcaster. I didn't know you'd survived until I met Gutamino."

Catching his breath, Al clapped Tyr on the shoulder. "Same. I only learned you were alive a short while ago—thanks to Dadius."

Tyr looked confused. "When did you run into him? I hadn't realized he'd left the city."

Al smiled. "We have much to catch up on." He glanced past Tyr and noticed the blonde woman following him. He raised an eyebrow. "A lot, indeed."

Tyr blushed. "Please, allow me to introduce the Lady Krystal Blackthorne, granddaughter of Lord Dadius."

Al's smile froze. *That's right, he said he was his granddaughter She seems innocent enough, and Tyr obviously trusts and loves her… but can I trust her?* He bowed slightly. "A pleasure to meet you," he said.

Krystal curtsied gracefully. "And you as well."

"Allow me to introduce Ryanna of the Hugga Clan, First Spear of the Northern Clans."

Tyr bowed low, apparently practiced in courtly manners. Krystal curtsied again. Ryanna nodded in return, unfamiliar with southern formalities but respectful.

Tyr smiled. "Please, I've been dying to catch up. I've prepared a meal for us."

"Wait—one thing. Is there any way to get an animal in here unseen?" Al asked.

"What kind of animal?" Tyr replied, confused.

"A really, really large timber wolf," Al said, grinning.

Tyr's eyes widened. "Why in the world would I want to do that?"

"Because," Al said, "he's a dear friend who's saved my life more times than I can count."

Gillian said, "I can get him here unseen, but is he going to let me approach him? I don't feel like being eaten."

"I'll let him know you're a friend. And thank you, Gillian." Gillian looked like he wanted to ask how Al would let the wolf know—given that he wasn't going with him—but finally just shook his head and chalked it up to more weird Al stuff.

The four of them sat down and began to eat, trading stories of their travels and travails. At one point, Tyr stood and said, "Al, I have to formally apologize for stealing your woman."

Al and Ryanna exchanged confused looks, while Tyr and Krystal both smirked.

"Al," Tyr continued, "let me introduce you to your former fiancée." He gestured to Krystal.

Al blinked. "Seriously? How in the world did...?" He trailed off, baffled.

Tyr laughed. "Exactly how we felt when we figured it out."

Al raised his glass. "To the happy couple. Love will always find a way."

The four of them drank to that, and laughter filled the room well into the night.

As they sat nursing their ales, Al said, "I have something to tell you." He looked at Tyr. "Turns out I'm not human. I'm an Alfarbani."

Tyr shrugged. "I always knew you were a little strange," he said with a smile. Then, slapping Al on the shoulder, he added, "But guess what? Turns out I'm not human either. Apparently, I'm a dwarf."

Al stared at him. "Seriously?"

Tyr nodded. "Yup."

Al took a sip of ale. "Wonder what Steven is."

Without missing a beat, Tyr replied, "Just an asshole."

Krystal and Ryanna exchanged glances as Al and Tyr continued catching up.

"You love him, don't you?" Krystal asked softly.

Ryanna looked at Al and nodded. "With all my heart." She turned to Krystal. "And you love Tyr, I see."

"Yes. He's like no one I've ever met—kind, strong, talented, brave, and tender. All in the right measures," Krystal said, her eyes on him.

Ryanna nodded. "I'm happy for you. Such a man is hard to find—and a worthy catch. May I ask you something?"

"Of course," Krystal replied.

"You're a warrior, but you dress like a princess. Why?"

Krystal hesitated, caught off guard. But after a moment, she relaxed. "You have very sharp eyes. No one here has seen me as anything other than a helpless little girl—except Tyr. He's always treated me as an equal."

"And Al," Ryanna added simply. "He sized you up the moment he saw you. But why hide it? You should be proud to be a warrior."

Krystal sighed. "Life at court is not so simple. My grandfather is Lord Dadius, a powerful warlord. He insisted I be trained by the best—just in case the day ever comes when I need to defend myself or someone I love."

Ryanna nodded. "Those are good reasons. I won't pretend to understand the ways of southerners, but I can respect your ways all the same. Your secret is safe with me."

"Does he know?" Krystal asked.

Ryanna froze, her expression startled. "I barely know myself. How do you?"

Her right hand brushed instinctively over her belly.

Krystal shrugged. "Call it a gift, I…sense things and occasionally see things that other don't. Do not fear, I will say nothing. That happy news is yours and yours alone to share."

"There's one more thing," Tyr said, pulling a folded letter from his vest and handing it to Al. "A parting letter—from Lord Dadius."

Albert,

I must write this in haste. Your unexpected victory has changed the timeline—well done. I've been ordered to return east for the Dokkalfar's awakening. The last of the seals has broken, and now he begins to stir. I tell you this because I am not your enemy. I've been playing a dangerous game for more than five hundred years… and I'm still playing it.

I am the last of the created Alfarbani—and the first. It was I who slew the others at my master's command. I am also the only one who was not made sterile. For centuries, I tried to create more of my kind. I failed—until you.

Yes, you. You are my grandson, and the only one who has ever fully awakened the Alfarbani blood.

I've guided you where I could, when I could. And I have watched your progress with pride in my heart. You've surpassed all those who came before. Even Cygnus fears you now.

I tell you this because I believe only you can stop the Dokkalfar from ascending. But don't rush after us. His army is vast, and it will grow as he awakens. You'll need allies. Cygnus believes I was forging ties with the Five Kingdoms for the Dokkalfar—but I wasn't. I made them for you.

Gather their armies. Call the clans. You'll need every sword if this fight is to be won. And one more thing—your cousin, Krystal. I believe her gift may manifest as well. If it does, guide her. Train her. She may be the future, if we fail.

If we meet again, it will likely be on opposite sides of the battlefield. Once my master returns, I will be compelled to serve. You will have to kill me. Do not hesitate. I won't be able to show you any mercy.

Good hunting,

—Lord Dadius

Al lowered the letter and looked at Tyr. "Have you read this?" he asked.

Tyr shook his head. "Not mine to read."

Al handed it to him. The others looked on curiously. His eyes lingered on Krystal, weighing something in his mind.

"What?" she finally said.

"Damn. To be fair, some of this—the part about Krystal—he told us already," Tyr muttered as he finished the letter and passed it back. He handed it to Ryanna and Krystal.

At that moment, the shop door opened and Gillian entered—with Talionis at his side. The wolf stood as tall as the boy. Both Krystal and Tyr instinctively stepped back.

"It's okay. He's a dear friend," Al said, resting his forehead against the wolf's.

"What do we do now?" Ryanna asked.

"Wait—wait, I almost forgot," Tyr interrupted, hurrying to the office. "I heard your blade was shattered." He returned carrying a large bastard sword in an ornate, gilded sheath and handed it to Al.

"What's this?" Al asked in wonder.

"One of the finest dwarven weapons I've ever made," Tyr replied. "I had a general idea from Lord Dadius of what you needed. It should hold up to whatever you push into it."

Al glanced sharply at Tyr. "It doesn't…"

"No," Tyr cut him off. "No, it does not draw power from those it bites. I wouldn't know how to make it do that—nor would I want to. But unlike the other blades I've made for Gutamino, I did forge ancient dwarven runes into this one. I think I know what they're supposed to do, but to be honest, I'm walking blind with most of it. I also worked them into the sheath. Time will tell what—if anything—they do."

He drew the blade. It sang as it left the sheath. In Al's mind, he heard a familiar woman's voice echo: *Solaisgair.*

"I hear you," Al whispered. "Your name is *Solaisgair.*"

"That's Dwarvish for Bringer of Light. It's a fitting and worthy name" replied Tyr hearing Al name the sword.

He pushed energy into the blade. It leapt to life, burning with a brilliant blue flame. The others stepped back, awestruck.

With a thought, Al extinguished the flame, sheathed the weapon, and hugged Tyr.

Then he turned to Gillian. "Any chance you can get us an audience with the king?"